Also by Howard W. Lewis

The Daedalus Rimes Saga

Daedalus Rimes I
Essence

Daedalus Rimes II
Afterdeath

Daedalus Rimes III
The First Galactic War

Daedalus Rimes - AFTERDEATH

af·ter·death \ˈaf-tər-,deth\ n **1**: an existence after life **2**: a later period following one's death

Book-2 of the Daedalus Rimes Saga

A Novel by
Howard W. Lewis

DAEDALUS RIMES - AFTERDEATH

PRINTING HISTORY
AuthorHouse / February, 2010; Daedalus Rimes - Afterdeath

Visit our website at
www.authorhwlewis.com

ISBN: 978-0-9887504-3-2 (e)
ISBN: 978-0-9887504-4-9 (s)
ISBN: 978-0-9887504-5-6 (h)

For my family, friends, editor and illustrator whose support and encouragement has helped me through the long process of bringing the Daedalus Rimes Saga to life.

Excerpts from the interrogation of Ruth Tuman

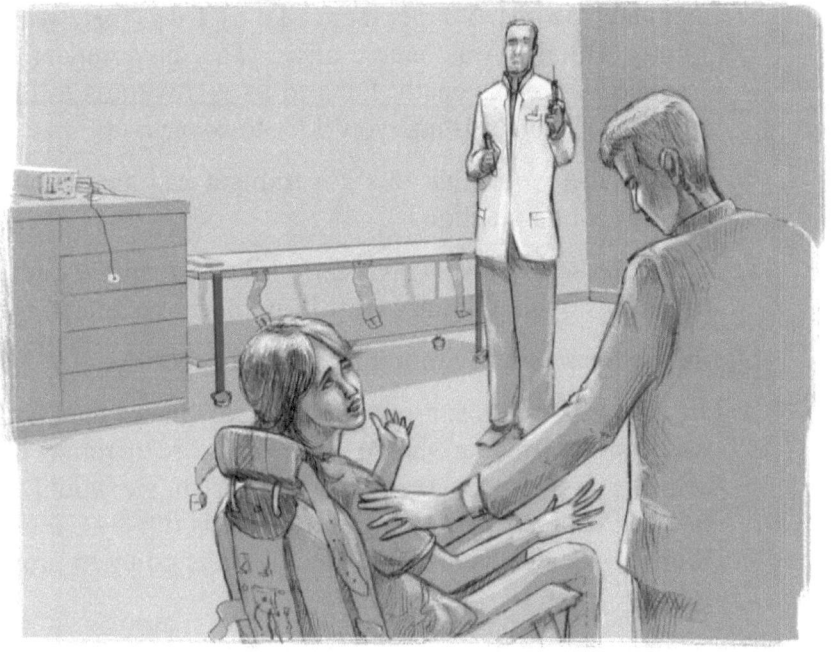

Q: When you say "abducted," do you mean "taken by force"?

A: Yes, I think I've made that pretty clear. Paralyzed and taken, I think that would be considered force. Are we going to go through this again? Am I a prisoner?

Q: Just answer the questions. How many people were taken?

A: Eleven. Twelve counting me.

Q: Only four were returned. Tell me again what happened to the others.

A: I told you, seven were returned. The others don't want to come back.

Q: Three of the seven returned were dead, two of them at the hands of your friends, the Korlah. Why would the others want to stay?

A: They don't trust the government.

Q: Why?

A: Because of the evidence. Proof that the government lets them take people. You let them take us. I was there when Jimmy Bourke was eaten alive. The government is responsible for his death. Each of us is a witness to that atrocity. The others think you'll try to cover it up.

Q: What makes you think this government had anything to do with your abduction?

A: After we escaped, we were nearly killed by military craft trying to stop us. Military craft from this government.

Q: Military spacecraft? From this government?

A: Oh, please. Don't insult my intelligence! One of the pilots was captured. Teela should have left him to rot in his cell. If it weren't for Teela and the Korlah, we would all be dead. Someone in this government is dirty—Captain Ramsey is evidence of that—and Teela is going to prove it.

Q: Tell me about Teela.

A: What do you want to know?

Q: One of your companions told us an interesting story about how she thinks Teela learned English. Why don't you tell me how this alien creature learned English in such a short period of time?

A: Teela's put her life on the line for us since the day we met. She wants to help her people, and she wants to help our planet survive.

Q: How did she learn our language!

A: I don't care! I genuinely believe she wants to help, and that's all I really care about.

Q: From what you and the others have told us, Dade Rimes was badly injured, but he was nowhere near death. Tell me how he died.

A: I don't know how he died. They took him and that was the last time I saw him alive.

Q: Did you see what they brought back? They skinned his face and hands, split him open and dissected him. This was the man who saved your life and the lives of the others, and you don't care how he died?

A: Of course I care, damn it! Jesus, I think about it all the time. I tell myself he would have wanted it. I mean, if that's what it took to save us, to help Bill, to get us home, he would have said, "Hell yeah, me first!"

Q: Are you implying that he volunteered to die?

A: Dade was a good man! He would have done whatever it took to get us home.

Q: Do you believe Teela took Dade's mind? His memories?

A: I don't know. Maybe.

Q: What makes you say that?

A: I could hear him.

Q: Hear him? How?

A: Bill was the first to notice, maybe because he was blind. The way she talked, things she would say. Dade had a way of saying things. When Teela got pissed off, she sounded just like him.

Q: Didn't that concern you?

A: Yeah, I guess.

Q: The ability to manipulate a person's thoughts or take their memories is alarming. Wouldn't you agree?

A: Yeah, sure, I guess.

Q: We think your mind may have been manipulated. We have reason to believe portions of your memory have been removed or altered. Do you believe that's possible?

A: I don't know. Possible, maybe, but I don't think . . . my mind has been affected.

Q: What is your mission? What is it that the Korlah want you to do?

A: For Christ's sake, I don't have a mission. How many times do I have to tell you that?

Q: Then tell me about Rebecca. What is her mission?

A: Who?

Q: Rebecca. What is her mission?

A: I don't know a Rebecca.

Q: It was you who gave me Rebecca's name. Of the eleven people you were with, you named Rebecca as one of them. Would you like me to play the recording again?

A: No, damn it! I told you, I don't remember.

Q: And you don't find that strange?

A: Of course it's strange. Everything about this is strange! — What the hell is that?

Q: Something to help you relax.

1 - Demand

"Anywhere would be safer than this planet."

The words hung in Julie's mind as she watched the sun rise through the clouds. She contemplated the strange morning visit as the morning dew vanished and the dull gray of dawn became vibrant morning. The world had never seemed so beautiful or fragile than in the hour since her husband's death had been confirmed. She was aware that her heart and mind were askew.

He's not dead, Julie thought. She smiled and stood up. He wants my help, but he's too proud to ask for it.

The visitor's psychic projections had stunned her, but half an hour of sunrise on her front step brought her back to herself. She slipped her jacket off and went back into the house, to the thin, rectangular device the visitor had left on her kitchen table. She opened the lid and spoke to the darkened screen.

"Hello." Multi-colored specks twinkled faintly. After a long pause, she tried again.

"Hello, do you hear me?"

Other than the flitting lights, there was no response. Frustration and panic surged.

"You have to talk to me!" she shouted. "Do you hear me, God damn it? You said you would talk to me." The screen lit up so brightly that she squinted and leaned back.

Hello, Julie. The words were thoughts directed into her mind.

"Who is this?" Julie demanded. The woman's voice was distinctly human but unfamiliar.

Souls must be allowed to go free. Rejoice in the good that Daedalus accomplished in his afterdeath. Allow him closure. Without it, his tortured existence cannot end.

"That was Dade, wasn't it? He was in Teela's body, but it was him. He was here. Why are you talking to me? Where is he? He said I could talk to him," Julie cried.

I cannot allow that, Julie. For this world to survive, his soul must depart. I cannot allow you or anyone else to interfere with that.

The words were imparted with intense feelings of fear and loathing. A cold knot formed in Julie's gut and made her shiver. She pushed her chair back from the table and reached out to close the device.

"No!" Julie yanked her hand back. "I don't know who you are, and I don't care. I know Dade, and I know he has something more to tell me. Now you get him, or explain why I can't talk to him."

As you wish, the woman's voice replied. Remember, Julie: what is shall remain, and cannot be changed.

A long pause followed. Julie listened to her own rapid breathing. Just as she started to demand a response, the voice continued.

As you know, after she received your husband's essence, Teela became obsessed with saving everyone. In doing so, she neglected to save herself. By the time she left the campaign vessel she was dying; the essence of your husband was killing her. The words entered Julie's mind and the kitchen dimmed. She and the device seemed to move towards each other, but rather than collide, they merged, and as the memories flowed into her, she felt like she was falling.

Howard Lewis

2 - Unity

Like a guest in the home of a stranger, Daedalus felt out of place within the body he shared. The clarity of the sensations both familiar and foreign combined to create a disquieting sense of tactile disorientation. Repeatedly examining the hands attached to arms he controlled, yet he knew were not his, he found two opposing thumbs and claws that he knew he should be able to extend; yet his mind was unable to locate the muscles that controlled them. His vision both near and extremely distant was exceptionally clear, and even though the images he perceived lacked even a hint of color, his perception was enhanced with a thermal aura that added a surreal dimensional glow. He moved the tip of his tongue slowly through the inside of his mouth and examined the canine fangs that extended slightly out of the lipless opening. To touch, feel and explore these physical elements allowed him to confirm that which he already knew.

Daedalus was certain that he was awake and that this was no dream. Although he could recall the activities and events that had occurred since his transfer into Teela's mind, the memories seemed unreal and dream-like. He would have liked to confer with Teela, but her presence was unavailable. His body, or as he realized mid-thought, her body, the body he now controlled ached from bruises, burns, and lack of rest. While her mind rested, his mind continued to drive the body, pushing it beyond the limits of physical exhaustion.

At the insistence of both Shawaugh and Dooaugh, he finally ate some biscuits and drank some water, but refused the rat-like braddle they also offered. The biscuits had a savory, almost nut-like flavor. Once chewed and mixed with the water from a ration flask that Shawaugh made certain remained full, they proved to be quite appetizing. Eating and drinking to the point of discomfort, he began to feel an overwhelming sense of lethargy. Barely able to keep his eyes open, he had a sudden realization that to sleep would mean releasing the grasp he had on this body. Frightened at the prospect of returning to the dream-like coexistence, likening it to death, he fought the lethargy by walking the narrow corridors of the assault pod.

Hoping to make conversation with Beth, Daedalus returned to the cargo vessel where he had left her after the departure from the Campaign vessel. This vessel was of the same design and dimensions as the one the Kahshinki used during the collection of the humans, except the rows of gurneys had been replaced with large, deeply padded chairs. The area behind the control consoles where the Kahshinki had fed on Jimmy was filled with a set of six additional control stations and panels, three on each side facing each other and divided by the consoles that were sloped like drafting tables. Unlike the control consoles at the forward end of the vessel, these were unmanned, de-energized, and dark.

In the front row of the passenger section, on the deeply cushioned chair closest to the far wall, Beth lay on her back, one arm across the chair next to hers and the other arm hooked over her face, snoring loudly. Gently lifting her arm, Daedalus sat down in the chair next to her and held her hand in his. He examined the familiar human hand, discovering that he could see the thermal differences which appeared as gradients formed by the blood pulsing through the veins in her wrist. With an instinctive action, not born of his memories, he tilted his head and brushed the tips of his crown tendrils on Beth's skin, both smelling and tasting her scent, a scent he recognized from a memory somewhere deep within the mind he shared with Teela. Watching the rhythmic pulsing of her blood, reassuring and hypnotic, his eyelids slowly grew too heavy to hold open, and finally closed. As the brief transition into sleep occurred, Daedalus was no longer able to resist the numbing paralysis sweeping him away from his control over Teela's body.

"Bring forward your first memory and follow it to me," a distant voice in the darkness called.

"What?" Daedalus asked. He had heard the question quite clearly, but the meaning of it eluded comprehension and he hoped for an explanation.

The voice repeated the question, again and again. Like an echo, before the first faded, the next would begin. He would have closed his eyes to concentrate, but they were already closed. With a chill induced by dreadful thoughts, a feeling of unease flowed up his spine causing Teela's unconscious body to shudder.

I remember my death. Daedalus thought, recalling the last moments before transfer. However, the memories that followed were vague and confusing. The voice in the dark recesses of his mind continued, calling for his attention.

I am the light, I am the path, and I am the receptacle for new life. Bring forward your first memory and follow it to me, the voice cried, this time much closer, insistent, desperate and demanding.

Yes, I remember, Daedalus thought, recalling how his memories had flowed, the clarity of the recollection and the detail of the sensations. Suddenly, he could smell damp pavement, hear the wheels of his tricycle rattling over the uneven sidewalk. The black and white colorless curtain lifted and he found he was looking over the blue-tinted chrome handlebars of his bright red tricycle on a street dappled with green, yellow, and white light filtered through the branches overhead. The flow of memories progressed more slowly than the torrent experienced during transfer. He relived his life in intricate sensory detail. But it was not just his life, along with his recollections were memories and perceptions that belonged to Teela.

At first, their memories were like oil and water, separate and distinct. Slowly they began to mix, joining together like finely woven fabric.

Teela woke up with a cramp in her side. Dooaugh helped her sit up as Teela massaged the area.

"You must eat," Dooaugh said handing her a biscuit and flask of water as Shawaugh turned the lights in the transport up. The thought of eating made Teela nauseous.

"I'm not hungry," Teela said with a yawn.

"Eat!" Shawaugh demanded with a scowl.

With a sigh, Teela took the offered biscuit and ate it. When she finished it, Dooaugh handed her another. She ate biscuits and braddle until she thought she was going to burst. Sternly refusing when she could eat no more she was relieved to see Beth rise through the portal and provide her with an excuse to stop.

"Hello Beth," Teela called out.

"Hey kiddo! Glad you finally decided to wake up," Beth said. "We were starting to get worried about you."

As she looked at Beth, memories of the events preceding their departure flooded Teela's mind. Teela dropped her eyes to the floor and tried to swallow the lump that had formed in her throat.

"Beth?" she said with a shaky voice, looking up. "I'm … sorry … about Crystal," she sobbed weakly and then burst into tears.

Beth knelt, facing her.

"I told you, it was my fault, not yours. Get a grip," she said.

Teela continued to cry, her sobs bordered on wails. With a move both subtle and swift, Beth's right hand moved up and across, slapping Teela sharply across the face.

Teela's head snapped to one side as both Dooaugh and Shawaugh leapt to their feet. Beth moved back and crossed her arms. Teela looked at her with an expression torn between shock and anger. Dooaugh and Shawaugh stood on either side of Beth poised to defend Teela.

"Stop sniveling, it's disgusting. Okay, Crystal's dead, I'm sorry, you're sorry, now get over it. While you've been sleeping, I've been looking around. We have some serious problems. And, by the way, you've been sleeping for about two and half days, you need to eat and you need to drink or you're gonna get sicker than you already are, dumb shit. And by the way, you look like hell." Beth growled.

"What have you seen? What's wrong?" Teela asked, wiping the tears off her face with the back of her hand.

"Once you're done taking your rations, we'll go for a walk and talk!" Beth said.

Rising to her feet and ignoring Dooaugh and Shawaugh, Beth walked to the end of the aisle and took a seat in the last chair. Reclining, she appeared as if she was going to go to sleep.

Having consumed all that she could, Teela pushed past Shawaugh and unabashedly relieved herself at the nearest waste disposal unit. Teela took significantly longer than most Korlah to cleanse her hands in the static field of the disposal unit. Then she withdrew a small towel no larger than a handkerchief and used it to systematically wipe down her body. Periodically she placed the towel into the static field and then shook out the dust before continuing. When she was finished, she folded the towel neatly and slipped it back into one of the pockets hidden in the seam of her tunic.

With an air of confidence that contrasted wildly from the sobbing despair of a few minutes previous, Teela donned her vest, boots, and belt. As soon as the swords were attached to the rings of her belt, she placed her hands on the curve of her hips and faced Beth.

"Quit pretending to sleep. I am ready for that walk you mentioned."

Beth stood and walked over to the food containers that contained Teela's rations.

"You're not done eating," she said dryly noting the single braddle and container of water that remained.

"I ate all that I can, I'll finish it after my walk!" Teela spat, not wanting to repeat the argument she had with Shawaugh and Dooaugh, who insisted she eat everything now.

"And if more rations are distributed during our walk?" Beth asked.

"I'll eat it! Now, can we go?" Teela cried.

"You betcha, by golly. Glad to see Dade's back in the driver's seat," Beth said, smiling broadly as she headed for the portal.

"You know, I think that old geezer can read minds," Beth called out as she drifted through the portal.

"Her name is Dooaugh. Reading minds is only one of her many talents," Teela answered, stepping into the opening over Beth.

"What? What do you mean?" Beth asked.

Upon contact with the floor of the corridor, Teela took off at a brisk pace, her arms crossed in front with her hands on the hilts of her swords. Beth had to double step to close the gap between them.

"What's the hurry? I've been waiting days for you to wake up. I have questions … concerns. You think maybe you could…"

Teela stopped abruptly and turned to face Beth.

"What! What is it now? What have I done to deserve the 'wrath of Beth' this time?" Teela asked, her eyes flashing with pent up anger.

Completely taken off guard Beth stepped back.

"Nothing … no wrath. I told you I was sorry that I've been such a bitch. What do you want, blood? Oh, wait a minute, I think I already gave about all I have," she said, the defensive sarcasm back in her voice. "Listen … Dade … I'm trying real hard to be a team player here. The last thing I want is to piss anybody else off. There's a pretty stout military presence on this vessel and I was wondering if this is a peace mission or what?

"It's a peace mission first, and 'or what' second," Teela replied tersely.

"If you're trying to inspire me to collaborate with you on this, you may be taking the wrong approach," Beth said evenly.

"I haven't lied to you yet. Withheld information maybe, but never lied. You know those little rodents we eat?"

"Yeah, had a few while you were sleeping."

"We keep them contained in large vaults. We dump in our garbage, waste, and the ground-up remains of our dead. Beetles and worms eat the organic debris, and the braddle eat the beetles and worms."

"A little more info than I needed. And your point is?" Beth asked.

"I recently got a little more info than I needed!" Teela cried as she closed the distance between them. "We are nothing more than braddle, chickens or pigs. The Kahshinki are not expanding their empire or even randomly pillaging hapless planetary systems. They are farmers, or more appropriately ranchers, returning to planets that they have stocked with their favorite foods, harvesting and gathering the crops as they ripen. It's no coincidence that our two species are so much alike, you see, we come from the same genetic stock." Teela put her head down and swallowed hard, fighting the despair that woke her from the fitful nightmare of sleep.

"Jesus Dade, who fed you this line of bullshit?" Beth asked, her voice lacking conviction.

Teela looked up, meeting Beth's eyes. Focusing her thoughts, she imparted the feeling of defeat and overwhelming hopelessness that now plagued her. Beth staggered back a step and choked back an involuntary sob.

Daedalus Rimes died on a table with Teela 10127. His thoughts and hers combined to create me, but rest assured I am neither. Feel me … feel who and what I am, Teela said, imparting both words and emotions telepathically.

"Fuck!" Beth cried, breaking eye contact with Teela and turning away. "Stop it! Don't do that! That really fucking creeps me out." She rubbed her eyes, trying to erase the images that had accompanied the stream of condensed thoughts.

"Those are my thoughts and feelings Beth. That's what I'm thinking about, it's who I am, and what I am struggling with. I'm not trying to deceive you. You need to realize that Daedalus is gone and it is only his memories that remain."

"Cut the bullshit. It's more than memories. I talked to Dade and he wasn't gone. Jesus Christ!" Beth cried, shaking her head and shoulders to clear the residual feelings from her mind. "If that's really what you're thinking about, what's keeping you from putting a gun in your mouth and blowing both your fucking brains out?"

A smirk akin to a sad smile twisted Teela's face. "I tried to blow my brains out once, it didn't work out. Both Dade and I should have died a long time ago, but we didn't. Now that we are together, we have come to realize that our lives only have importance because others depend on us, they have faith in us even if we do not," Teela's voice waivered, becoming little more than a whisper. "We're already dead, this is no longer about what we want."

"Cut that shit out. You're not dead, and you're not alone. I'm sorry my attitude sucks, that's just me. But try to see it from my point of view. You want me to believe you, while at the same time you keep secrets. Tell me how you ... no, I want Dade to tell me how he would react if he were in my shoes."

"Let's walk," Teela said, taking Beth by the hand as she would one of her Birth Section sisters.

Over the next several hours, they walked up one corridor, around the circumference and down another, covering each narrow corridor and passage repeatedly while Teela told Beth everything she knew, describing transfer, explaining the details of the Korlah Mission, Shyron's past, and the disturbing discoveries that Afron and Gremensh made in the map room which revealed the intent and purpose of the Kahshinki harvest.

3 - Awakening

Ruth stood at the window staring out into the star saturated void of space beyond. She remained there long after the others, tired or bored, returned to their seats. She hoped she would get to see the smaller vessels again, the ones that looked like the stereotypical flying saucers. But those that departed shortly after they dropped out of the black lightless space disappeared and had not yet returned. The pilots of their vessel had left shortly after Captain Ramsey's assault, and in their place, two armed guards now stood watch at the front control area. Since the guards were stationed, Ruth had seen them replaced at least four times now, and suspected that they had been changed several times while she slept. Food had been distributed six times, but the meager ration of one biscuit and the little bag of water failed to abate the nagging hunger that was interfering with her ability to think.

How long has it been since our departure? Ruth thought. *Three days, maybe four?* She wondered how long it would take before the others began thinking Captain Ramsey's idea of taking over wasn't so bad after all. Thinking was what she did best, or at least that was what she had always told herself. She could figure out a plan of attack for almost any technical problem. 'Observe, analyze, evaluate, and the course of action will inevitably be revealed as self-evident.' Unfortunately, the course of action she had trained to take was related to problems associated with electrical engineering, and even though she did not honestly believe that they should take any action against the Korlah, she knew that if they needed to, she would be at a loss for how to proceed.

For the first time since their departure, she wished Beth were there. Beth would know how to deal with Captain Ramsey. They had stripped the Captain down to his briefs and locked him in the storage room alongside the one where the remains of Jimmy Bourke lay frozen. Ann said she had read somewhere that taking a person's clothes away would make them feel vulnerable and less likely to commit an aggressive act. Marsha and Catherine had gleefully stripped the unconscious pilot at the mere mention of the idea before roughly shoving him into the tiny storage room.

"What are you smiling about?" Marsha asked as she approached, having observed Ruth's face reflected in the window.

"Oh, I was just thinking about when you and Cathy stripped Captain Ramsey," Ruth answered, turning to face Marsha.

"Yeah, that was fun," Marsha said with a smile that quickly faded. "Hey, listen, I don't care how long it takes to get home, but the others are saying that it didn't take this long last time. They're getting worried, it doesn't look like we're going anywhere and they think the time between food distributions is getting longer." Marsha looked out the window to avoid the frown that now creased Ruth's face.

"That's what they're saying, is it?" Ruth asked

"Look! A ship is coming!" Marsha cried.

Ruth turned back to the window. The object approaching from an angle below the lip of the window required that she move around Marsha to look out and down at it.

"It's not flying straight," Marsha commented, noting the craft's conspicuously eccentric wobble, which translated into a rolling and curving path as the craft approached.

"It's coming awfully fast," Ruth said with concern. "It's gonna hit!" She grabbed Marsha by the waist and dragged her away from the window.

The approaching ship swung in an upward curve, its bottom stopping a few feet away. The wobble caused the edge of its bottom to rhythmically approach to less than a foot from the window. After a few seconds, the ship slowly moved away toward the aft end of the assault pod.

"Damn that was close," Ruth said as she expelled the breath she had been holding.

Running back to the window, they watched the wobbling craft move away. Its normally satin black finish was mottled with white blotches surrounded by web-like gray streaks etched into the smooth surface. A few moments after it disappeared out of their field of view, a sharp jarring thump reverberated through the ship as it docked.

"There were marks like that on our ship," Ruth said.

"Whatdaya mean, our ship?" Marsha asked, still straining to see the craft now out of view.

"When we first arrived on the big ship, the one we came in on, it was all shot up like that one."

"You think it was attacked by Captain Ramsey's buddies?"

"I don't know. Maybe, but I hope not."

"What's going on over there?" Marsha asked, noticing the rest of their group looking out the other side of the craft. The group included Rebecca, who had not said a word nor left her seat except to use the bathroom since their departure.

Joining them, Ruth could see an assault pod like theirs slowly approaching with an escort of several disc-shaped craft. Turning to assume a position alongside theirs, one of the beetle-shaped cargo ships separated from the main cigar-shaped assault pod and rotated so that its underside faced their ship. With slow precision, it approached and docked one vessel over from where they were. A barely perceptible shudder was felt when this craft, much larger than the damaged disc, docked.

"Teela is here! She has come to take us home!" Rebecca cried.

"Becca, you should sit down sweetheart," Ann said, believing this to be another of Rebecca's delusional outbursts. Although a Korlah doctor had treated her broken collarbone, Rebecca had remained withdrawn and silent until now.

"We must first pass through the gates of hell. Once our guardian angels have dispatched the demons guarding them Teela *will* take us home," Rebecca exclaimed, tears welling up in her eyes.

"She could be right. It could be Teela and the others. We've probably just been waiting here for them," Ruth said, her statement as much hopeful anticipation as logical summation.

The women formed a ring around the portal in the floor that the Korlah had kept sealed since the incident with Captain Ramsey.

"Where are they? How come they're not here yet?" Tiffany called from the seating area where she had taken refuge just behind the divide.

"It's only been a few minutes, sweetheart," Ann said. "They might have some sort of protocol that they have to go through, something that could take awhile. We just need to be patient."

Staring at the floor, Ruth silently prayed Teela had returned, not knowing how she would deal with the panic and questions that would follow if she had not. Just as she was about to offer an alternate explanation for the arrival of the other vessel, the polymorphic material of the portal melted away into the adjacent floor material as it opened.

Beth rose up through the portal opening; her graying hair was neatly combed back and tied into a short ponytail. She wore a black Warrior's smock cinched at the waist with a belt tilted slightly to one side by the weight of a sword that hung at her hip. Clearing the opening in the floor, she stepped forward, the women who had tightly encircled the opening moved back to permit her entry.

"Beth! We are so glad to see you," Ruth cried, moving in and giving the solemn woman a hug. Ruth glanced down through the opening and saw no one else below. "Where are the others?"

"Teela will be here in a few minutes. Bill decided to stay and teach the Korlah English," Beth said flatly, avoiding eye contact with Ruth.

"Are you kidding me?" Ruth asked skeptically while others in the group just snickered.

"No, really. He has a girlfriend that wants to marry him or whatever it is that they do. He said he's going to teach them English," Beth repeated, still avoiding eye contact like a child caught in a lie.

"Where's Crystal?" Marsha asked.

Beth's voice choked off from the deep regret of what she would have to say. She wiped her sweating palms on her hips as she tried in vain to regain the composure she dreaded she would lose in front of these women. Raising her head, her eyes red and rimmed with tears, she took in a shuddering breath and scanned the group.

"She's dead," Beth choked out from quivering lips.

"No! Oh no!" Marsha screamed, bursting into tears. Catherine grabbed her and the pair began to cry in unison.

"God, I thought they said she was going to be alright?" Ruth asked as she put a comforting arm around Beth's shoulders.

"Crystal died defending the honor of the human Race," Teela said, stepping away from the portal in the floor. The women, distracted by Beth's entrance had not noticed Teela until she spoke. They turned their attention from Beth, and waited for further explanation.

Dooaugh rose through the opening next and stepped to the side. She placed her back against a wall in a defensive posture borne of concern over the close proximity of the aliens that were crowding the area.

"The Korlah of my vessel are divided," Teela said. "There are those who believe that the human species is our enemy and should be destroyed, or at the very least, left for the Kahshinki to harvest, and there are those of us who hope we can form an alliance with humans and defeat the Kahshinki once and for all. The leader of those who opposed the alliance ordered you killed. I had the vessel you are on depart to protect you, but before I could get to Beth and Crystal, our enemies cornered them. They could not escape. To buy time, Beth challenged them to an honor fight. No fabricated weapons are permitted in such fights, I must clarify 'fabricated', because we Korlah are equipped with deadly weapons that are permitted in fights of extreme honor. These are fights to the death." Pausing, Teela bared her fangs and extended her razor sharp claws in a menacing display to emphasize her point.

"The Korlah oath 'By fang or by claw' is an iteration of the honor fight; it is how we once settled all of our serious disputes. Fang and claw fights were outlawed centuries ago and are only fought clandestinely, and only then in cases of extreme circumstance. In such a fight against a Korlah it should be easy to see that a human would be at a disadvantage. Beth and Crystal faced champions of this sport. The fact that they were victorious brought great honor to the human species in the eyes of Korlah warriors. The fight was bloody and short. In the end, Crystal and one Korlah lay dead. With the other Korlah in a coma, only Beth remained standing to claim honor before she nearly bled to death.

"News of the fight spread quickly through the ship. Humans immediately became a species of exceptional honor. Those Korlah who speak of this are saying that humans have no fear of injury or death, and instead of fang or claw, they fight with lethal brute force. After the fight, support for the forces challenging the alliance collapsed. I believe that if this fight had not been fought,

18

and if Beth and Crystal were not the victors, I would not be here now to take you home.

"Where is the human pilot? I need his help," Teela asked.

"Good luck. He's locked up in a storage room for trying to hijack our ship," Ruth replied. She then brought Teela up to date with a detailed description of Captain Ramsey's failed mutiny.

"This is not good," Teela said. "I need him to communicate with the forces blocking our approach to Earth. If he doesn't cooperate, the human pilots manning those ships are going to die. I hoped when he heard the story of your abduction he would reconsider his loyalties," Teela said, her shoulders dropping in a physical response to her disappointment.

"He said even if we somehow get back, the government would make us all disappear. I think he's afraid they're going to make him disappear as well," Ann said.

"We have a plan to enlighten him," Ruth said, "but we needed some muscle. We were waiting until Beth and Bill got back, but I'm sure Beth will provide all the muscle we need."

"I have a few ideas of my own," Teela said, gazing thoughtfully in the direction of the storage room. "The Commander of this mission is waiting to see me, I can't keep her waiting. Work out the details of your plan and I will be back shortly to assist you."

Excusing herself, Teela was about to leave until she noticed Rebecca and Dooaugh standing apart from the others facing each other as though engaged in conversation, but not speaking.

"Dooaugh! Let's go," she called in Korlah.

Dooaugh turned toward Teela and as she did, Rebecca reached out and took her by the hands.

"Can't she stay? We were having such a nice chat," Rebecca said, smiling pleasantly for the first time that Teela could recall.

"This one ... this Rebecca hears my words as I hear hers. She hears the Gods as I do. We were meant to find each other, as you were meant to become Shawlmon," Dooaugh exclaimed passionately, the wild look of a zealot having returned to her ebony eyes.

19

"You two can talk later. I need you with me, especially now," Teela pleaded, masking her true fears with the genuine concerns at hand, in hopes that Dooaugh would not see through the ruse.

"Yes, of course you do," Dooaugh said slowly while making an apologetic palm display. Turning, she and Rebecca embraced, touching foreheads in a display of affection common between Korlah. Teela was surprised by the ease and comfort with which Rebecca performed the unfamiliar act.

Teela and Dooaugh proceeded to the command center of the assault pod to meet with Director Challmara, Mission Commander. Upon entering the ring-like area that encircled the forward end of the large assault pod, the odor of feces assailed her crown tendrils and reminded her of the unpleasant tasks associated with cleaning up after the young shells in the birthing section. Looking around, she expected to find a damaged waste reclamation unit. In the command chair in the center of the control ring, Challmara sat partially reclined and leaning to one side. Teela thought she was asleep at first, until she could see Challmara was watching her approach. The source of the odor became evident as Teela neared her friend.

"What has happened?" Teela exclaimed, taking Challmara's hand and kneeling next to the chair.

"I was damaged during our departure. Our biotech was able to repair the damage to the bones and muscles of my back, but the part of me that provides control of my legs and other functions is damaged beyond repair," Challmara explained patiently, using terms she knew the uneducated birthing unit would understand.

"Why has no one cleaned you? Why have you been left like this?" Teela asked, appalled that Challmara had sat for days in her own excrement. "Get some towels and some water," Teela called to Dooaugh, who had already moved off anticipating her request.

"Do not waste water on me. I no longer have utility for this mission," Challmara said weakly.

"You certainly do!" Teela cried. "Such injuries are not terminal. I will send you back to the Campaign Vessel at the first opportunity and they will repair you or you will transfer."

"You despise transfer. If I take the mind of a child, you will despise me. I would rather cease," Challmara said.

"This is not about you, and this is not about me. The needs of the mission far outweigh my disdain for transfer. You are far more valuable to the mission than a child. So, if it becomes necessary, I give you my blood oath that I will not despise you," Teela said as she lifted Challmara from the chair and lay her down on the floor.

"What are you doing? I can clean myself," Challmara protested, guessing Teela's intent. "Don't, please Teela," she pleaded, embarrassed by the lack of privacy in the close quarters of the control room.

With a sweep of her eyes and a telepathic command, Teela demanded privacy. She knew that Challmara undoubtedly refused assistance, but that did not allay her disappointment in the failure of those present to assist their director in her damaged state. The technicians and pilots immediately turned their attention away from Challmara and Teela, several making apologetic gestures as they did.

Dooaugh returned with a bundle of towels, but before she could explain why she had no water, Teela received a mental vision of a young warrior refusing to give Dooaugh a ration of water without authorization. She snapped her head to the direction aft, her angry thoughts shooting through the bulkheads like a bullet and slamming into the young warrior's mind.

"Don't be concerned about the water, it will be delivered," Teela said reaching for the towels. "Thank you, Dooaugh."

Dooaugh handed the towels to Teela as she knelt down alongside her.

"Contrary to the belief of warriors and pilots, birthing units can work and listen at the same time," Teela announced after a few moments.

When Challmara did not speak, Teela continued.

"You can give me your report unless you would rather wait until I am done."

Running into the control room from a nearby corridor, a young warrior slid to a stop, dropping one of the bags of water she held cradled in her arms. Hesitating as though she could not decide whether to stop and try to pick it up, she saw Dooaugh and made her decision. She ran to Dooaugh and dumped the water containers in front of her. Following a rapid apologetic gesture, she ran back and picked up the dropped container, quickly delivering it as she had the others. Wiping away a thin stream of blood flowing out her ear canal, the warrior made one last palm display before bolting from the room.

"She would have released the water with proper authorization," Dooaugh said with an air of concern. "Your projection was ... unnecessarily powerful. Too powerful, I believe you may have damaged her."

Dooaugh's comment was nothing more than an observation; Teela however, perceived it as an accusation.

"It was an accident. I don't even know how I did it," she said defensively. "Get me a clean uniform for the Commander," Teela ordered.

The dramatic shift in personality was not lost on either Dooaugh or Challmara. Dooaugh bowed respectfully before leaving at a pace that demonstrated obedience yet was sufficiently relaxed to indicate she was not fearful of reprisal.

"You have changed. What has become of the gentle Teela I remember?" Challmara asked placing a hand on Teela's knee.

Teela looked up from her ministrations to meet Challmara's eyes. Challmara looked away immediately, a feeling of dread filling her mind at the brief moment of contact.

"The Teela you remember has ceased. I am someone new, someone different. You will always be a part of my existence, and I hope that I have not changed so much that I cannot continue to be a part of yours," Teela said, watching as Challmara squirmed under her gaze.

The room remained uncomfortably silent while Teela finished cleaning and dressing Challmara. After returning with the uniform, Dooaugh moved off without comment and busied herself, monitoring the displays at the various control stations. Challmara's face remained pinched in an expression of embarrassment and shame throughout Teela's activities. Challmara's silent dismay became most evident when Teela affixed a makeshift diaper of towels before replacing her uniform. When she was finished, Teela lifted Challmara and gently placed her in the Command chair. She cleaned her hands meticulously in the static field of a nearby waste reclamation unit, then picked up the three remaining bags of water. Opening one, she handed it to Challmara, who reluctantly accepted it. Setting one of the remaining two bags in Challmara's lap, Teela then opened the last, which she consumed in a single gulp, literally pouring the contents down her throat.

"Drink your ration, Commander," Teela demanded, the moment she finished consuming hers.

Challmara drank her water, not as Teela had, but in several large sips intended to give the valuable ration the respect it deserved. The behavior was not lost on Teela.

"Water is the least of our concerns," Teela said. "I have brought sufficient rations to augment this vessel for the remainder of our mission. We are going to a planet covered with water. If we want, we will be able to bathe in it, even swim in it. I will not permit the most valuable member of this mission to cease for lack of a substance as insignificant as this will soon be," Teela declared in a lecturing manner tinged with dominance that Challmara had never seen her use before.

After a long pause, once Challmara realized that Teela, the Assistant to the Potentate, had finished speaking and was waiting for acknowledgement, Challmara replied, "Yes, Your Eminence."

Unable to stand, as she should have when being addressed by a Superior, Challmara straightened in her chair to the maximum extent that her disability would allow. Staring forward, her gaze respectfully below that of Teela, she waited patiently for her next command.

"How long must I wait for your report?" Teela demanded, once she could see Challmara growing uncomfortable with the long silence.

Too shocked to be angry, Challmara gripped the arms of her Command chair and swallowed deeply to regain control of her emotions.

"I have developed a new weapons system based on the pulse-blade as demonstrated by you in the battle with Afron's forces at the Health Section bulkhead. The new system provides both defensive and offensive capabilities. It will absorb all pulse and particle energy within collection range. The energy can either be stored or discharged at a level slightly below that received, due to inherent losses in the energy transfer. The stored energy can be amplified and discharged at a significantly higher energy level than that received. The first two actions require no energy, the last does. However, it only requires the energy equivalent to one tenth of a full-power tight-focus pulse. With the new system installed, the enemy will continue to recharge our power cells while depleting theirs."

"How long will it be until we have a functional prototype? Teela asked.

"The new systems have already been installed on this assault pod and all of its heavy fighters. I have ordered the systems, which were assembled during your transit, installed on the assault pod that brought you. Unfortunately, I have insufficient materials on hand to outfit the four additional fighters. But I'm not concerned. There are other modifications that will give us a significant advantage in battle." Challmara said, pausing to enjoy the look of anticipation on Teela's face.

"What modifications?" Teela finally asked.

"Our analysis of the enemy craft turned up some interesting innovations and new technology. First, the control system has been modified from the dual panel arrangement to a pair of articulated handles and pedals that control the ship's movements. Control sensors have been incorporated into the handles that control weapons and communication functions. This arrangement provides the pilot with control over both movement and weapons firing and frees the sub pilot to concentrate on targeting and communications. I project that this will improve the efficiency of control and weapons functions by more than 40 percent.

"The communications system, although based on archaic technology, is a revolutionary concept that we have modified into a superior method for relaying information audibly rather than visually. The enemy system takes sound, converts it into pulses that it then encrypts and transmits in a photon pulse. Then the pulse is decrypted and recombined into energy pulses that reproduce the sound. This permits communication without requiring the participants to share visual time with weapons and control displays. I have calculated that this by itself will add an additional 20 percent efficiency during battle evolutions. The weakness of this system is that it becomes inoperative during both transition, and hyper-light speeds. I have modified the projection system so that during transition and hyper-light, the signals are fed into the balance moderator of the respective ship's plasma drive. This creates an equivalent rhythm in the plasma wave that can be received simultaneously by all vessels within ten light cycles. This means that if they attempt battle at anything above sub-light, we will have a tremendous advantage."

"The encryption the humans are using, can we break the code. Will we be able to intercept their communications?" Teela asked.

"The coding that the humans have incorporated into their communications system was designed to circumvent the Kahshinki communication interface. The Kahshinki have apparently discovered it and have added a ciphering organ into the flux suppression array. This transmits the cipher code on a plasma wave, allowing us to monitor their communications and even interrupt them with overriding signals.

"As expected, the Kahshinki do not trust their new allies. The weapons system pulse integrator is the standard sealed type of Kahshinki fabrication. To our benefit, the humans have apparently not yet discovered how to replicate this form of biotechnology. My technicians have successfully dissected the integrator and identified the signal that inverts the weapon's pulse. This and all other known destruct signals are currently being programmed into all our weapons defense systems. We failed to determine the exact signal that disables the engines before biological decay of the captured component. However, based on the data we were able to recover, we have narrowed the possible sequences down to only a few million combinations. We are currently developing a program that will systematically generate signals within the predicted range at a rate of 20,000 combinations per bit. When a positive result is obtained, the vessel that achieves it will automatically emit a communication pulse that will inform and reprogram all of our other vessels with the correct disable code. The implementation of the destruct and disable systems are projected to be complete on all independent weapons systems within the next two shifts."

"If you can figure this out, is it not possible that the humans could also? In which case, we must not count on this as an advantage.

"Even without the ability to disable their engines and weapons, we still will maintain a significant advantage. The vessel the human was piloting is not of standard Kahshinki fabrication. It is constructed mostly of materials and fabrication technology that is grossly inferior to anything I have ever seen. Even during the periods of accelerated Campaign construction activities, we have never produced anything that approaches this level of inadequacy. The shield plating is one tenth what it should be. Each pulse cannon is only capable of a focused pulse, and is of such an anemic energy signature it will take a minimum of five direct hits to penetrate the standard armor of our light fighters.

"What surprised me the most was the power cell; it has less than half the capacity of a standard cell. This means that the human pilots who were chasing your human friends were well beyond their range and nearly out of power when our forces engaged them. They had to know they were sacrificing their existence to pursue that transport, yet they continued. Even though they only faced apprentice pilots on their first patrol, it is a great tribute to their piloting skills that they survived as long as they did and were actually able to destroy several of our craft. But they will not face training craft this time. They will face the greatest pilots and the most sophisticated craft and weaponry in the history of Campaign. I guarantee this will be a rout of the enemy's forces that will surpass any victory we have ever achieved."

Teela stood motionless, staring at the viewing window. Long moments passed and Challmara began to fidget nervously, unsure why Teela had made no comment.

"You are a genius," Teela said looking from the window to Challmara. "How could you think that your utility was lost? This mission would be lost without you."

Teela nervously wrung her hands together as she walked back to face Challmara, who read Teela's body language as being counter to the vocalized praise.

"Everything you have done exceeds any expectations I could have imagined, and will surely benefit the success of this mission. However, this mission will fail without an alliance with the humans. It will be incredibly difficult for me to negotiate an alliance if we annihilate their defensive forces. I want it understood that we are not to attack human forces unless absolutely necessary to prevent the loss of Korlah existence. If our shields are as superior as you claim, we should be able to safely implement a directive that requires avoiding and evading their weapons fire without endangering the existence of our pilots. Let's use this opportunity to learn as much as we can of their offensive tactics while developing our defensive strategies."

"But there will never be such an opportunity. If we reveal our capabilities, and the humans are permitted to survive, they will utilize the information to compensate for their weaknesses. We must annihilate all opposing forces during the first wave," Challmara exclaimed, unable to comprehend Teela's logic.

"If I succeed in obtaining an alliance, these highly skilled human pilots, that you are so anxious to destroy, will be working with us to defeat the Kahshinki."

"We will not be facing just the humans," Challmara countered, "I sent a scout craft to probe their defenses; it discovered a number of bases under construction within an envelope of planetary debris. Only one has been completed and appears to be operational. It is of an extremely unusual design, half is set up in the traditional configuration of a defensive Kahshinki outpost, and the other half is ... well ... different. I believe the unusual construction materials and techniques are consistent with those found during the analysis of the human fighter craft. The scout that obtained this information was at first attacked by vessels matching the capabilities of the captured human fighter.

"Unconcerned by the low power pulses that were being used against it, the scout completed its study of the base and was preparing to depart when it was attacked by Kahshinki craft with full weapons capability. If it had not been stripped of pulse weaponry and equipped with dual power cells and an auxiliary jump coil, it would not have been able to out-jump and lose the pursuing Kahshinki craft. As a result of damage to their atmospheric control system, the sub pilot ceased while in transit, and the lead pilot's respiratory system is so badly damaged our biotech does not believe repair is possible.

"I am certain this base has both human and Kahshinki forces on it. We must destroy their craft and capture this base or we will have no chance of protecting the approach of our Campaign Vessel." Challmara crossed her arms as she finished speaking in an attempt to convey her unwavering belief in the importance of her argument. Lacking control of her lower back muscles she began to lean over, forcing her to abandon the body language she was accustomed to using and hold herself upright.

Teela sensed Challmara's frustration and humility. She fought to overcome the emotions that would affect her ability to make decisions necessary to accomplish the mission goal.

"I am not a military strategist, and I recognize that as one of many weaknesses," Teela said, pausing to straighten her robe and fasten the top clasp on her vest before continuing. "I must rely on your judgment Challmara if this mission is to succeed," she said. "What I need, Commander is to reach the leadership of the planet, while at the same time minimizing the appearance of being an invading force. Once there, I will need the time left before the arrival of the Campaign Vessel to obtain and maintain an alliance." Briefly pausing, Teela consciously forced her tightly clenched fists to relax. When she continued, the stiffness of her body and speech aptly reflected the formality of the directive she was issuing.

"Formulate a plan that will minimize the loss of human life while achieving whatever military goals you feel necessary to ensure the safety of our Campaign Vessel and the human planet.

28

During the execution of this plan, I will consider the loss of human or Korlah life, in any unbalanced proportion to be a failure on your part. Once you have developed a plan, send it to me for approval."

"Yes, Your Eminence," Challmara replied, her response a trained reflexive action when receiving a formal command.

Distressed over the impact Teela's directive had on the plans and activities already in motion, Challmara lamented her injury, and the possibility that she would be unable to accomplish the task in her debilitated condition. Teela who had remained standing alongside the chair tilted her head, hearing Challmara's thoughts as clearly as if they were spoken words. Putting her hand on Challmara's, Teela leaned close, concentrating in order to telepathically impart feelings of confidence and reassurance as Shyron had once done to her.

Challmara, I have always admired your confidence and strength of character. There is no one that I would trust more with me on this mission than you, she said. Removing her hand from Challmara's, Teela bowed respectfully and left the control room.

Soft murmuring voices, like whispers in the distance, acted to mute the natural thrumming sound in the assault pod. Teela realized the whispers were the thoughts of those around her, and like spoken sounds, they would rise and fall in volume when she turned her head. Stopping in the opening of the access hatch that separated the Control Room from the adjacent corridor, Teela closed her eyes and moved her head slowly to scan the room she was about to leave in an effort to focus on the haunting sounds. The thermally sensitive pits of her hisnah produced ghost-like images. The heads of these images always gave off a more defined signal than the bodies, and it was from those bright spots that the voices were emanating.

Not voices! I'm hearing thoughts. Teela noted, correcting herself, not wanting to fall victim to Dooaugh's delusion that spoken words and thoughts were the same. Alarmed by some of what she heard, she focused on one particularly disturbing source.

"*Not attacking. Stupid. Stupid.*" Sounding like an angry voice, Teela heard the thought clearly. "*New system is untested. Shawlmon a Birther. Cleaning filthy stinking mess, no honor. Why wasn't stupid damaged Commander reclamated? It was her incompetence that caused the damage. It was my skill that saved this vessel. I should have been promoted. I should be Commander! Shawlmon is more concerned with the beasts than honor.*"

Teela found that she could focus on the source of the thought. Like sound, it came from a direction, providing a path to the source. Teela walked toward the source as she listened, her claws straining against the tough material of her gloves as she clenched her fists in anger. Walking up from behind, she stopped just alongside the assault pod's Senior Pilot. Sensing her presence the pilot turned and looked up into Teela's face.

The rage Teela was straining to control was visibly evident by the fully engorged state of her crown tendrils. The sporadic curling of her upper lip repeatedly exposed her fangs in a fearsome display of hostility.

The pilot recoiled to the full extent possible without abandoning her chair. Taking the pilot by the upper arm, Teela pulled her back and then leaned in close until her face was nearly touching the pilot's.

Do you cherish your existence, Senior Pilot? Teela demanded telepathically.

"Yes ... Yes, Your Eminence," The pilot cried, wincing from the intensity of both the telepathic message and the feelings of hostility that Teela was projecting.

But do you cherish it enough to follow a filthy stinking Birther that is more concerned in obtaining an alliance with the beasts than honor? Teela asked.

"I ... I ... I'm sorry," The pilot cried, her initial shock quickly turning to terror, her crown tendrils blanching white at the realization that Teela had read her thoughts.

Teela released the pilot's arm and tugged at the fingertips of her glove to loosen her claws, which had penetrated the tough fabric.

I have a task for you. If you succeed, you will be the next Commander of this assault pod. If you fail ... well, you will wish for an end to your existence.

The pilot did not have to acknowledge Teela's projected thoughts, Teela could sense that the pilot was horrified, anticipating that Teela was about to assign a task that would assure failure and result in her death.

Until I am able to return Commander Challmara to the Campaign Vessel for repairs, it will be your responsibility to clean and care for her waste disposal needs. You must convince the Director that you want to do it, that it is your honor to do it. While you are performing this task, I want you to imagine what it would be like if you were damaged as she is. I also want you to imagine what it would be like if you were reassigned to the Population Section. Imagine being under the supervision of the lowest ranking birthing unit in the section, and it was your responsibility to drag yourself around by your arms while tending to the waste disposal needs of at least 100 young shells. Imagine doing this for two out of three shifts for the rest of your existence. If you fail, Senior Pilot, you won't need to imagine such an existence.

The pilot stared silently for a moment, unsure if Teela had finished with her. Rubbing her arm, bloodied by Teela's claws, the pilot finally spoke.

"I will not fail, Your Eminence. I am sorry. My thoughts were careless and without honor. My doubts are founded in fear and uncertainty, not yours or the Director's abilities. I give you my honor until I prove to you I am worthy to ask for it back."

"I await your success. Roche Hah! Senior Pilot," Teela said verbally, while giving a clawed salute before turning away and heading for the corridor where Dooaugh stood waiting.

Ignoring the stares of Challmara and the others, Teela headed out of the Control Room without further comment. Dooaugh fell into step behind Teela as they headed back to the transport containing the humans.

"Why don't my thoughts anger you, Shawlmon?" Dooaugh asked, hearing Teela's thoughts of concern about bringing Dooaugh back into contact with Rebecca.

"They do, and stop calling me Shawlmon," Teela snapped. She stopped suddenly, just after passing some technicians transferring equipment from a hover cart up into one of the attached fighters. She turned around and approached a technician that was standing back watching the others move the equipment a piece at a time.

"You are the Senior Engineering Technician," Teela stated, stopping to face the technician she recognized as a longtime friend of Challmara's.

"Yes Teela, I mean … Yes, Your Eminence," the technician responded, bowing awkwardly.

"You are aware of the extent of Director Challmara's damage?" Teela asked.

The technician visibly stiffened. The fact that her crown tendrils barely changed shade was a tribute to the control she had mastered over her emotions. Although the technician was able to mask her physical responses, the emotions she was feeling hit Teela like a wave, washing over and through her. Grief, guilt, and fear saturated her thoughts, emanating from the technician like radiated heat. Feeling as though she could absorb the emotions, like a battery accepts a charge, Teela basked in their intensity, only sensing the basis of the thoughts after the raw surge of feelings had subsided.

"I am not going to ask you to reclamate Challmara," Teela said. "I want to know if you could build a chair with the same ability of a loading platform, one that could be controlled by the person sitting in it, something small and mobile, able to negotiate portals," Teela said.

The technician's emotions reflected immediate and intense relief. The technician shifted her gaze from Teela to the hover cart. The technician's thoughts of design and construction for a chair with a grav-plate and controls flashed into Teela's mind.

"Yes, you want it for Director Challmara, to facilitate her mobility, yes I could. Not a chair though, a chair would limit her access in many parts of the vessel," the technician answered, contemplating the problem as she spoke. Teela saw the design in the technician's mind changing and modifying to an articulated device that could shift from seated to standing position while at the same time floating its occupant into and through both horizontal and vertical access openings. Details of controls, control features, and ergonomics combined into an elaborate design with parts and materials availability.

Teela closed her eyes allowing the images flowing into her mind to congeal into sharp definition. It was as though these were her very own thoughts, and although she had no previous technical training or experience, she immediately understood the detailed purpose and intent of each assembly design and modification that would be necessary. The images vanished as quickly as they appeared, replaced by the image of a face, her face.

"Your Eminence?" the technician asked at the same instant that Teela opened her eyes causing the image to vanish. Teela knew something extraordinary had just occurred. She had been in the technicians mind, used her memories and looked through her eyes. Although she wanted to explore the phenomena further she deferred to the matter at hand.

"Both designs are excellent ideas," Teela said closing her eyes to recall the images. "Build the simpler version at the earliest opportunity and the more sophisticated design with the articulated framework after that. This task cannot detract from you current duties but must be done as soon as possible.

Just then Teela cried out, wincing from a sudden pain in her temples. She pressed her palms to the sides of her head in an effort to contain the sudden pressure that she felt growing within her skull. Not waiting for a customary response from the technician, Teela departed with a cursory salute, continuing down the corridor, weaving from side to side toward the transport access hatch. Her face contorted from the discomfort she was experiencing, she walked past the access before stopping. Along with the headache, a noise, a muttering, whispering buzz grew in intensity until she felt as though her skull would burst.

Disoriented, she leaned against the wall, covering her ears and shaking her head in an effort to stop the noise and pain.

When she closed her eyes, blurred images and fractions of crisp visions flashed through her mind, often overlapped with others, a kaleidoscope of unrelated thoughts that were not hers. Letting out a shrill whimper, Teela slid down the wall into a seated position. Opening her eyes wide, she tried to stop the whirling images, but they continued like a fog that obscured the clarity of her vision.

Dooaugh appeared in the fog, crouched before her. She held her hand in front of Teela's face and said something, but Teela could not understand the words over the cacophony of sounds that permeated her mind. She looked at the hand in an attempt to understand what Dooaugh intended. As she looked, the sounds seemed to lower in volume and intensity. The harder she focused on the hand, the lower the sounds became until she could finally hear Dooaugh's voice.

"Use your dark eye only, concentrate on my hand, and I will teach you what you need to know," Dooaugh said.

Reluctantly, Teela closed her eyes, fearful that the images would return. She discovered that the thermal image of Dooaugh's hand dominated her vision and the more she concentrated, the weaker the images became until they faded completely. Although the images had dissipated, the soft murmuring voices continued, but at a barely perceptible level. Concentrating now to calm the panic that had caused her pulse to race, Teela cautiously reopened her eyes.

"You are hearing the thoughts of others and seeing the elements of their memories. Let me enter and I will help you learn the art of mind talking," Dooaugh lectured.

Teela could feel Dooaugh's mind attempting to press into hers. Realizing that resisting would not facilitate Dooaugh's efforts, she consciously lowered her mental guard and opened her mind to allow entry.

"I spent over two cycles lost as you just were. During that time, I gouged out my own eyes to stop the images, and drove slivers of metal into my ears to stop the voices. But they would only stop when I passed out, returning with my consciousness, and continuing until once again I passed out. I was allowed to continue my existence so that my condition could be studied. The biotechs repaired my eyes repeatedly, but found no need to repair my ears once they realized I could hear without them." Dooaugh shifted to a kneeling position, straddling Teela's legs.

"You have awakened a new set of senses, which you are unable to control. Now you must learn to control them. What I will give you took me many cycles to master. You have a gift unlike any I have ever seen, many times greater than mine. You will not need to sacrifice a portion of your existence as I have to master this gift. With this knowledge come all of the sensory perceptions that accompany the memories and the pain of how they were achieved. Without taking your body, I will give you my existence. All that I know, all that I am, will become yours," Dooaugh said as she pressed her face, or more appropriately, the sensory pits of her hisnah against those of Teela's.

High-pitched screams of terror and pain radiated outward from the vessel dispersing into the void of space beyond. A technician down the hall turned, not sure what had drawn her attention. Seeing the two crouched on the floor, she dismissed the sight as a romantic interlude, not uncommon in areas of minimal privacy, and returned to her business. Teela continued screaming, shrill screams of terror, fear, and agony that could not be heard, and did not require lungs or air, screams of a mind being saturated with experiences few could endure in a lifetime, compressed into a few moments. She made only a soft wheezing sound as her body tensed and her lungs emptied of air.

4 - Collaboration

Captain Ramsey moved as far away from the gurney as the small cell permitted. The acrid smell that he had come to associate with Kahshinki filled the small room. The corpse on the gurney was frozen, but now that it was in a warmer room, the frost on the eyelashes had begun to melt. The water trickled across the milky eyes and dripped in rivulets down the ashen cheeks like tears. Captain Ramsey tried turning away, but kept finding himself drawn back to the dead man's face.

Why had they put this guy in here, who the hell was he anyway? These thoughts and others more gruesome plagued his mind.

Where he had once felt unafraid of the possibility of his death, he was now considering the unpleasant forms it could take.

The more he thought about it, the larger the knot in his stomach grew, until finally the smell and images it produced caused his stomach to rebel, and he vomited in the corner of the cell.

It's the damn food, those tasteless fucking granola bars, he thought, trying to rationalize his anxiety. Unable to get around the gurney, he leaned over it and pounded on the center of the oblong hatch.

"Get this fucking thing out of here, God damn it! Do you hear me? Get it out!" Ramsey shouted at the top of his lungs. Receiving no response, he leaned against the door on the heels of his palms.

What thing are you referring to? Came a voice from the other side of the door, or was it the other side? He looked around for speakers and found none.

Ramsey held his breath to listen.

Did I really hear that? Or am I starting to go nuts, he thought.

"Who's out there?" He shouted.

Who's in there? responded the voice. Again, he looked around. The voice seemed to come from everywhere and yet nowhere.

"Ramsey, Jason, Captain, United States Air Force, 597077767," He answered, backing slowly to the far wall of the cell.

Okay, I've been expecting to be interrogated; I guess this is how it starts, Ramsey thought as he returned to the corner where he had vomited. Looking back down at the pale face frozen in agony, his rising anxiety and the smell of vomit caused him to gag involuntarily. He was about to try to swallow the lump he felt in his throat when the movement of air in the room informed him the door to the cell was opening.

Two Korlah looked in, checking things out. A Korlah female wearing a long, ornate, red and blue robe stood behind them giving directions. One watched him closely while the other moved the gurney to sit diagonally across the cell, trapping him in the corner. The female walked in and stared at him. He wasn't sure, but he believed it was the same Korlah the others claimed had the mind of a human.

Turning to the guards, she said something in their coarse language. The guards did nothing at first, until she repeated it more loudly. With visible reluctance, they closed the door leaving her inside with him.

"Phew!" Teela said waving her hand in front of her face. "Does Korlah food disagree with you, Captain? Or are you ill perhaps?" She asked politely, making an obvious visual examination of the vomit the Captain was standing in with his bare feet.

"Get this thing out of here, it's making me sick to my stomach," Ramsey groaned.

"Thing? I hope you aren't referring to your planetary brother as an impersonal object," Teela replied without emotion. "Oh, I'm sorry, you probably haven't been properly introduced. Jimmy, this is Captain Ramsey. Captain Ramsey, this is Jimmy Bourke. You'll have to forgive Jimmy, he hasn't been very talkative since the Kahshinki had him join them for an in-flight meal. We thought you might want some company, and ... well, Jimmy's been dying for some. In fact, when your repulsive little friends were doing this to him, he was screaming for God and Jesus Christ to join them."

Captain Ramsey swallowed deeply, looked down at his feet, and said nothing in response. After a long pause, Teela continued.

"Standing by and doing nothing when your own kind are being kidnapped and murdered by something as disgusting as the Kahshinki is a pretty pathetic thing for a military officer to do. But to knowingly assist in the perpetration of such acts, this is a concept we Korlah cannot comprehend. Please tell me what motivates your species to turn on one another, and allow or participate in something as horrific and dishonorable as this?"

"Ramsey, Jason, Captain, United States Air Force, 597077767," the Captain answered in a monotone voice, looking down at his feet.

"If you don't like Jimmy's company, I can arrange for you to share a cell with your boneless bug-eyed associates, I'm sure they'd love to see you instead of their next ration of protein cakes. But I won't make that decision; I'll leave it up to the group of humans you attempted to murder."

The Captain looked up, chewed his lower lip, remembering not to open dialog with the enemy, then looked back down at the puddle beneath his feet. Leaning against the wall, he began stirring the drying vomit with the big toe of his right foot. After another long pause of silence, Teela knocked on the door. The guards cautiously opened it, and let her out.

Captain Ramsey cursed under his breath, damning every step he had taken that had brought him to this cell. He wanted to get into space so badly he was willing to do anything to get there. He had never cheated or lied, but there were things worse than lying and cheating. He volunteered for anything and everything. Things no one else would do, bad things, things you would be ashamed to admit; things that were fortunately secret, of which the public would never know. The black ops missions were exciting at first. Eyes Only, Top Secret, all that mysterious, political intrigue bullshit. However, most of the missions involved killing people who didn't know it was coming, and never had a chance to defend themselves. He never had to look his victims in the eyes. He was a high tech, high altitude killer, doing the dirty jobs nobody else wanted, and nobody wanted to talk about. Why did he think space would be any different? His first meetings with the Kahshinki Earth side, gave him a real uneasy feeling. They referred to them as the 'toads' back then, and they looked bad and smelled worse, but they had the most remarkable technology, and the Government wanted as much of it as they could get. Price was no object. So what the hell, they were his ticket into space. He just did what he had to do to make certain he was selected for this operation.

Faster-than-light spacecraft, particle beam weapons, artificial gravity, this was shit he never dreamed he would experience in his lifetime. He heard rumors that some of the earlier pilots had taken trips to Alpha Centauri and back; he was hoping he would get his chance at a deep space mission. But the other stuff, the areas the toads had made off-limits for the pilots, and the stories and rumors he was hearing on station had started to bother him. Nothing had ever bothered him before, nothing, zero, zip.

He prided himself on his ability to put the ugly memories behind him, and to move onto the next job. He was always thinking about the next job. It made forgetting much easier. Until now, that is. All the ugly memories were coming back to haunt him. Every black op, all of the bad things he had ever done were flooding his mind, filling him with guilt. Was this how he was going to die, regretting everything he had ever done, regretting his whole life? He crouched in the corner and put his head between his knees, wishing again, he had not worked so hard to get here.

Teela left the door to Ramsey's cell and approached Ann who was standing with Tiffany in the forward section of the transport. Tiffany smiled slightly then her face returned to its usual blank emotionless stare. Ann shook her head "no" when Teela looked at her. Teela walked over, gave Tiffany a gentle hug, and held her close while she whispered into her ear.

"Jimmy's dead, you know that. He died without being able to fight back, without being able to help you. But even though he's dead, Tiffany, he can still fight for us, for you. He can still help beat these monsters and get you home. But he needs your help. He can't talk, so you are going to have to talk for him." Teela turned Tiffany to face the door to the cell. "Jimmy's in this room, he's with Captain Ramsey. We know that he was helping the monsters that killed Jimmy. You know how awful Jimmy looks, how much they hurt him. Try not to look at him when you go in, but you need to tell this man about Jimmy, about his hopes, his dreams, about how much he loved you. You need to tell this man about the life he has destroyed, so he will stop helping the monsters, and help us instead. Can you do this for us Tiffany?"

Tiffany just stared at the floor without making a sound.

"Ann, you're going to have to do the best you can. I don't believe Captain Ramsey liked his job, or the Kahshinki. I think he believes he was serving his country, just following orders. All we need to do is convince him that he was mistaken," Teela said, as she guided Ann and Tiffany toward the door.

The guards opened the door, and after making sure it was safe, allowed Ann and Tiffany to enter. The instant her eyes focused on the gurney, Tiffany let out a blood-curdling scream that lasted the entire capacity of her lungs. Then, grabbing a breath, she started a second scream. Teela instantly regretted the decision to bring Tiffany into the room. In the middle of the second scream, Tiffany stopped and stood looking down at Jimmy's contorted face. By this time, Captain Ramsey had pressed himself into the corner, no doubt wishing he could disappear into it. He stood there motionless, staring wide-eyed at the screaming woman.

"Jimmy, oh no, no, Jimmy. Oh please God no..." Tiffany whispered.

Dropping to her knees, she reached out and gently brushed a lock of hair off his waxen forehead. Ann knelt alongside her, glaring contemptuously at Captain Ramsey. Over his initial shock, he looked back down at his feet, not wanting to meet Ann's angry eyes.

"Don't cry, Jimmy, I'm here now," Tiffany said, wiping the condensation from Jimmy's cheeks. "You're so cold ... so very cold." She paused and looked up at the man standing in his underwear in the corner. "You helped them do this to my Jimmy? Why would you do that?" Tiffany sobbed. Coughing, she wiped a thin rivulet of snot from her nose with the back of her hand.

"She's talking to you!" Ann hissed. "If you haven't got the guts to answer, the least you could do is have the decency to look into the faces of the people whose lives you've helped destroy."

Looking up to meet Ann's challenge, Ramsey's effort to look cold and unconcerned looked more like an affirmation of his guilt.

"We met at school, Jimmy and I," Tiffany said speaking in a detached dream-like trance. Taking Jimmy's cold and lifeless face in her hands, she gently massaged the contorted muscles around his mouth and eyes.

"We're getting married next June, after Jimmy graduates. He doesn't want to wait, but I said we should. He's going to be a teacher, physical education. He loves kids, you know. Wants to coach football, said he's always wanted to be a coach. I'm sorry I couldn't stop the pain Jimmy. I'm sorry. I'm ...," Tiffany threw her head back and let fly another deep-lung scream of anguish. "Sorry … so sorry," She began sobbing over and over.

When Tiffany began to climb into the gurney Ann grabbed her under the arm and pulled her away. Turning as she pushed Tiffany out the door, she spit, just missing Captain Ramsey, hitting the wall next to him instead.

"Asshole! Mother Fucking Pig!" She shouted as the guards closed the door. "Bad idea! This was a real bad idea!" Ann cried angrily at Teela while holding and partially supporting Tiffany, who was now sobbing hysterically.

"Nothing about any of this is good, but I believe it was necessary," Teela said apologetically. "I am certain she got to him. She and Jimmy stabbed him in the heart, and what's left of any bravado he may have had is bleeding out right now."

"I don't give a damn! It was a bad fucking idea," Ann snapped. With a frown directed at Teela, Ann gently guided Tiffany away from the storage room.

Was it necessary? Would it work? Did it work? God I hope so, Teela thought, as she watched the two women leave. She unconsciously clenched her fists, the claws now beginning to work their way through her gloves stinging her tender palms once again.

From the corner, Captain Ramsey looked at the young man on the gurney. The girl had softened the contortions of his face and partially closed the lids on the milky eyes. Not nearly the frightening specter he was, Jimmy almost looked peaceful. Studying the spit on the wall next to him, Ramsey reached up and wiped it off with his middle and forefinger of his hand. He examined the viscous bubbly mass for a few seconds and then flicked it on the floor.

I wish they would just kill me and get this bullshit over with, Captain Ramsey thought. Sliding back down the wall, he placed his head between his knees and waited for the next round of recrimination he was certain would come.

Beth marched up to the door of Captain Ramsey's cell, stood at attention and saluted Teela.

She's not acting, Teela thought, returning Beth's salute.

Remaining stiffly at attention, Beth waited while the guards opened the door and removed the gurney containing Jimmy. Then she marched forward two paces into the cell, snapped a precision turn on the toe of her boot and resumed her stiff stance facing the corner where Captain Ramsey stood. The guards closed and locked the door as soon as she was inside.

That poor son of a bitch, Teela thought as the door of the cell closed.

Ramsey stood up when the guards opened the door and watched with relief as Jimmy's gurney was pulled out, wondering what would come next. But what came next, he never could have imagined, not in his wildest dreams. A human female, dressed in a black uniform embroidered with the same glyphs used by the aliens, marched in, turned and assumed a military 'parade-rest' stance with the legs apart and hands interlocked behind her back.

"Ten hut!" Beth shouted.

"Who the Fu …," Ramsey started to say, but before he could get any further, Beth closed the distance between them, and had her nose pressed against his.

"Don't open your fucking mouth unless I tell you to, scum bag, or I'll use it to shovel that puke up off the God damn floor!" Beth shouted into the Captain's surprised face while he drew back until he found himself trapped against the wall.

"I don't …," Ramsey started to say as he moved to push her away. However, at the same instant his arms moved up and forward, his legs were swept out from under him, and an instant later, he found himself face down in his own vomit, one arm twisted painfully behind his back, and his testicles in the crushing grip of his assailants other hand.

"Let go!" Ramsey screamed, getting a painful twist of his arm and squeeze on his testicles each time he struggled.

"You will not speak unless I tell you to, and if I have to tell you one more time, you will be known as 'nutless' for the remainder of your short and miserable life. Do you understand me, scum bag!" Beth shouted into his ear at the top of her lungs, while giving his testicles an especially painful twist.

44

"Yes Maa'm," he choked, gagging from the nauseating pain and stench of the vomit his face was being pressed into.

Releasing his testicles and grabbing him by the hair, Beth twisted his head around until her nose was nearly touching Ramsey's puke-covered face.

"I am Sergeant Major Porter. When you speak, it will be when I tell you to. The first word out of your mouth will be Sir, and last words will be 'Sergeant Major Sir'. If you fail to perform this simple task, I will clean that vomit off the floor with your scum-sucking mouth, then I'll kick the shit out of you, and clean that up with your God damn mouth. Do you understand me you low life, worthless sack of shit?

It had been a long time since Captain Ramsey went through basic training, and although the boot camp he remembered was not this rough, he knew the drill.

"Sir, yes Sergeant Major Sir," he moaned hoarsely.

"What? I can't hear you shit head"

"Sir, yes Sergeant Major Sir!" He shouted as loud as he could, hoping it would be loud enough.

"I'm going to let you go now. If you make the fatal mistake of thinking you can take me down, I promise that you will fail, and I further promise that I will carry out each and every one of the threats I made earlier. And when I'm finished, I will have the guards feed your bloody remains to the ugly little fuckers in the next cell."

Releasing Ramsey's hair and arm, Beth stood up and moved the two steps back and resumed a parade-rest stance.

"TEN HUT!" Beth shouted once again.

This time, Captain Ramsey scrambled to his feet and stood at attention, the shooting pains in his testicles making him grimace with the effort. Beth moved to attention, turned, marched to the door, and knocked twice. The guards peered in cautiously and opened the door. Beth stepped aside as the guards slid in two empty food storage containers. Then one guard handed Beth a box and a fist full of log bars, before stepping back out and shutting the door.

"At ease, Captain. Move this box into that corner and then sit on the other box, facing it," Beth ordered.

Moving out of the way, Beth turned and faced the door as he moved the boxes, obviously challenging him to attack her. He guessed her height to be about five feet ten inches, and weight to be over two hundred pounds. By the visible definition of the muscles in her neck and arms, and the apparent lack of fat, it would be a tough fight even with an advantage. Believing Sergeant Major Porter to be true to her word, Ramsey thought better of taking the bait.

Beth turned around to find Ramsey sitting exactly as she had instructed. She set the portable log reader on the box in front of him, lifted the viewing screen, and snapped in the first log bar. She tossed a handful of military dog tags onto the table in front of the Captain as the image of a desolate planet filled the screen.

"All right shit head, it's time for a brief history lesson, and some current events. Pay close attention, there will be a test afterwards," Beth said. She displayed the log of the planet Korlah showing the aftermath of the Kahshinki retaliation, the attack on the Korlah Campaign vessel, the abductions of the humans by the Kahshinki freighter, including some graphic views of the Kahshinki eating Jimmy, and some in-flight views of the space battle between the Korlah and the human piloted Kahshinki fighters. Standing directly behind and over the Captain, Beth shouted the narration, somehow finding a use for every foul word she knew, and she knew plenty. All in all, it was a much more colorful and emotional narration than Teela had provided when she first explained the details of their abduction. The main difference from what Teela had shown back on the Campaign vessel, was the editing of the part where Bill and Dade killed the Kahshinki crew. As far as the Captain knew, they were in the room next to his. When the last log finished, Beth pulled the bar from the reader slot and closed the viewer.

"As a result of your actions and those of Earth's leaders, the Korlah have good reason to toss each and every one of our dumb asses out the nearest air lock and proceed to Earth and nuke it to oblivion. But that's not why they came here, and that's not really what they want to do. They will take their pound of flesh for the unprovoked attack. There's nothing you or anybody can do to dissuade them from that objective.

"I'm sure you didn't get where you are today by obeying international laws and treaties. Governments have historically obeyed only the laws and treaties they want to, finding a reason to break the ones they don't. There may not be a treaty with the Korlah, but we do have laws against murder, kidnapping, assault, the use of chemical weapons, and conspiracy to commit such crimes. The Korlah have the same laws, which is the only fucking reason why you and I are still alive.

"The Korlah Leadership has reluctantly agreed to allow me and the others of our group the opportunity to negotiate the surrender of those responsible for the unprovoked attack of their vessel and the murder of over two and one half million of their citizens. Before they are turned over to the Korlah, it is my personal goal to see those same individuals charged and convicted on Earth for their part in the crimes they have committed against humanity. After that, I hope to negotiate a mutual arms treaty for the defense of Earth and the destruction of the Kahshinki Invasion Force."

Beth paused and waited, hoping the Captain would try to speak so she would have an excuse to inflict more physical punishment. Sitting straight up, looking forward and not moving or speaking, the Captain recognized the bait.

"What do you think of all this, Captain Ramsey?"

"Sir, I believe the Sergeant Major is in over her head, and I believe she will find herself blown to bits if she, or anyone else attempts to approach Earth. Sergeant Major Sir!"

"That's why I bothered to jerk your head out of your ass and showed you what's really going on. With or without your help, we will be going to Earth. With your help, fewer lives will be lost, yours for starters, and the probability for success will be improved. Without your help, you will definitely die, I will probably die, and the future of our planet will be left at the mercy of two titanic superpowers. The Kahshinki will rape the planet, using its natural resources to build more invasion vessels for their Galactic expansion, and the human population will be used to stock their ship's larder for the long trips. They will build and fill ships until they run out of resources. When they finish, they will sterilize the planet, exterminating any survivors.

"If the Korlah can't work out a deal with Earth's leadership, they won't bother to try to conquer Earth, that's not their objective you see. They will bomb the planet with the same weapon that was used to fry their world, just to deprive the Kahshinki of resources.

"With an alliance, the people who are in power now will be removed. You help us and I'll put a good word in for you with the new administration. Time is critical Captain, you need to make a decision, and you need to make it now. What's it going to be?"

"Sir, I cannot and will not do anything to aid a foreign government to raise arms against the forces and government of my country. Sergeant Major Sir."

Beth took a deep breath and let it out with a grunt of disgust. "I spent twenty-three years as a United States Marine. I understand what you're feeling, and I understand the motivation. There was a time in my career that if I were in your place, I would probably say the same thing. Before I left, there were too many military engagements where innocent people and good loyal soldiers died for unjust causes. If you honestly believe what you have done is just; then you deserve to die, and I will enjoy hearing you beg for God's forgiveness. Get up, Captain Ramsey," Beth said, stepping back from where the Captain sat.

Captain Ramsey slowly stood, reluctant to expedite whatever plans this brutal woman intended for him.

"Right face!" Beth shouted, and the Captain pivoted on his toe and heel to the right. "March over to your puke filled corner Captain and stand there facing the corner, do not turn around," Beth instructed.

The Captain did as she told him. The hair on the back of his neck and underarms rose in fear. The lump in his gut began to ache, and he had an overwhelming urge to urinate. *How's she going to do it? Break my neck? A knife maybe, or she's going to beat me to death, whatever it is, she's probably going to enjoy it."* He closed his eyes tightly, listening to her movements behind him and anticipating his death.

Someone knocked on the door. He did not dare turn, certain she was waiting for an excuse to keep the promises she had made earlier. He could hear the shuffling of feet behind him. *They're taking the boxes out*, he concluded from the sounds.

"Please turn around, Captain," Beth said, sounding apologetic.

As the Captain turned, Beth snapped a salute and held it. The boxes had been removed from the room and she was standing in front of a gurney like the one Jimmy had been in, only this one was empty. Six Korlah were lined up across the wall behind the gurney, and two more standing at the door. Ramsey stood there looking, feeling suddenly sick to his stomach. He weakly returned Beth's salute with a puzzled look on his face.

"What … what are they … wh … what are you going to do," Captain Ramsey asked, his mind considering the worst. Clearing his throat, he tried without success to swallow the bitter bile he could taste rising into his throat.

"I'm sorry, Captain. I hoped you would recognize how wrong our Government has been, and how wrong you have been to follow their instructions. I hoped you would make the right choice and help us expose them for the fucking murderers they are. The deal was, if you helped, you lived, and if you didn't help, you would die. My fellow passengers have selected the method of your execution. I won't lie to you, you are to be strapped into this gurney, and you will be moved into the cell with your chosen allies. If they release you, then you will remain housed with them for the duration of this engagement. The others, well, they think your allies are going to eat you, and I would tend to agree with them."

"This isn't right," Ramsey said, his voice weak. "Sergeant, you can't … you shouldn't let them do this to me.

"If it's any consolation, Captain, I voted against this. I was awake when Jimmy died, I wouldn't wish this on anyone. If it were up to me, I'd beat you to death. Jimmy Bourke was a big guy, a body builder. My guess is he outweighed you by more than thirty pounds. He screamed like a girl for the first six hours, and then cried like a baby for the next four before he finally died. My bet is you won't last half that long, but it will probably seem like eternity," Beth said, turning and walking to the door. "Remember Captain, this was your choice, now try to die with some courage and dignity."

The image of the Kahshinki spitting the repulsive black acid-like enzyme onto Jimmy to dissolve his flesh, and then sucking it back up, filled his thoughts as the six guards moved cautiously towards him. His stomach rebelled at his recollection of the Kahshinki feeding on Jimmy, and vomit charged up his throat and spewed out his nose when his tightly clenched mouth refused to open. While he was coughing and choking on his own vomit, the guards forcibly placed him onto the gurney and strapped him down. His resistance was minimal, although he wanted desperately to resist, instead, he found his body and limbs feeling heavy, weak, and unresponsive.

With numb detachment, he studied the gently curving arch of the vessel's roof as he was moved out of the cell. Bluish green light radiating from the material of the ceiling and walls illuminated the area in a soft glow bathing the guards and everything around the gurney in a nightmarish hue. The guards maneuvered him out of the cell with three on each side, like pallbearers carrying a coffin. Waves of uncontrollable shakes flowed up and down Ramsey's arms and legs, the movement causing the gurney bindings to tighten in response. The guards turned the gurney perpendicular to the wall facing the side his head was on, positioning it next to the doorway of the adjacent storage room. Tilting his head back, Ramsey could see the arch of the oval doorway through which they would carry him. The guards stopped and began putting on protective armor, gloves, and masks.

Breathing quick shallow breaths, Ramsey could feel a panic attack coming on. He recognized the symptoms, having felt them before. He had always been able to control the panic associated with taking dangerous risks, but unlike now, he had always had some control over those situations and was able to overcome the fear that caused them.

One of the Korlah guards cautiously cracked open the door to the other room, releasing the putrid stench of the Kahshinki within. The smell rolled out and across the Captain like a dense fog, the nauseating odor engulfed his senses, a vision of Jimmy's contorted face filling his mind.

"No!" Ramsey screamed. "No! Wait ... Sergeant! Please wait, come back ... please wait!" The Captain finished with a sob and another fit of shakes.

Something in the cell moved close to the door. One of the guards shouted and the door slid shut. The face of one of the Korlah, one not wearing protective gear appeared over his, bending over the gurney.

"Sergeant Major Porter has left, apparently uncomfortable with your ... choice. I will relay any final message you have," Teela said politely and sincerely, bowing her head respectfully when she finished.

"I ... I've ... changed my mind," Captain Ramsey said weakly, his voice cracking with each word.

"Is that your message? Will she understand what it means?" Teela asked innocently.

"What! No, you don't understand. Don't put me in there with them! I'll ... I'll help the Sergeant. Please, get Sergeant Porter. Don't put me in there!" Captain Ramsey pleaded.

Teela cocked her head, like she didn't understand, stood up, said something in Korlah to the guards and walked away.

"Wait!" Ramsey screamed after Teela. "I changed my mind. Please wait," he sobbed weakly as the guards resumed their positions around the gurney.

Moving the gurney away from the cell door, the guards proceeded past the rows of chairs and out into the central area of the vessel, approximately to the same area that Jimmy Bourke had been consumed. The journey was too short to provide Captain Ramsey any time to reflect on the reversal of his decision. And although only a short period of time elapsed, his mind raced with the thoughts of what would now be expected of him.

Once Captain Ramsey was around the corner, Teela walked back to the room and entered. She quietly thanked the guard inside for assisting with her ruse while closing the biotronics access cover on a communications device and source of the foul smell.

Captain Ramsey knew that all the pilots believed if they were captured and faced with torture or death, they were not really expected to suffer or die, rather than reveal perceived secrets. The defense program was set up so that each segment was compartmentalized, so that a security breach in any one section would not jeopardize the security of the others. They had probably already changed the manning, sortie schedules, and communication frequencies anyway, so whatever he told them would not matter. Both the Military and the Government would deny everything, even his existence, so it did not really matter what he told them.

The guards moved the gurney to the center of the main room against the rear wall of the control area. They released his bindings and stepped back. Ramsey sat up and surveyed his surroundings. Goose pimples rose in response to the chill from the sweat that covered his body. Teela walked up to the gurney and looked down on him as he nervously looked around.

"Your clothes are there," she said, pointing to his uniform and boots on the floor by the wall. "There is a waste collection device just above your clothes. If you're unfamiliar with its operation, I will show you how to use it. Now get dressed," she ordered.

Beth and the other women stood together near the control stations at the vessel's forward end. The hostile glares they gave him, made him uncomfortable and he shifted his eyes to his flight suit that lay neatly folded by the wall next to his boots. He examined the oval protuberance that looked like a sink, except it hung low on the wall.

Must be a crapper, he thought, examining the translucent bottom. Reaching in, his fingertips passed through what he thought to be a glass bottom. An electrical arc flashed from the surface across his hand. Jerking his hand back, he examined his fingers for damage, finding none, he gratefully proceeded to empty his bladder.

While dressing, he noted that all the rank and mission insignias, with the single exception of an American flag on the chest, had been neatly removed from his jumpsuit. He was lacing up his boots when the floor in the center of the room began to change shape, flowing up in smooth symmetrical columns. When the material stopped flowing, an oval table and six stools stood in the center of the forward chamber.

Beth, Ann, Ruth, Teela, and Shawaugh, sat down at the table, leaving a single stool near Captain Ramsey empty.

"Please sit down, Ramsey," Beth said, directing him to the stool.

"Sir, yes, Sergeant Major Sir," Captain Ramsey shouted.

"From now on, you can call me Beth. I believe you've already met Ruth and Ann. This is Teela and Shawaugh of the Korlah Peace Delegation. I have chosen to dispense with the use of rank in an effort to unify our group. With the help and cooperation of the Korlah, it is our goal to become humanity's ambassadors for a peaceful settlement of the current crisis."

As Beth spoke, Teela translated the conversation for Shawaugh.

"Ramsey, you need to understand, if they believe you are lying, or have any reason to believe you are holding back information, I won't be able to stop them, there will be no second chance. You need to understand, this is the only chance you're going to get."

Ramsey swallowed deeply, nodding his head. "Yeah, I get the picture," he said, almost whispering.

"How many pilots, and how many long-range fighters are stationed at your outpost?" Teela asked.

"We're talking about American lives Sergeant! Friends of mine," Ramsey said looking at Beth, pleading with his eyes.

"I know Jason. I know," Beth said gravely. "Please answer the question, before they consider your response a refusal."

Captain Ramsey looked down at his hands and did what he had not done in a long time; he told the truth.

"Twenty experienced pilots, not counting myself and the other nine that were in my sortie. We had close to 100 fighters when I left. We're supposed to be training their pilots to fly them, but they're a bunch of stupid clones that can't even speak English," Ramsey said without looking up.

"These pilots, are they human clones, or are they Korlah, like me?" Teela asked.

"human, can't be more than twelve- or thirteen-year-old kids, little girls. Shaved heads, tattooed on the face, just like ... you," Ramsey said, looking up at the markings on Teela's face.

"What about the human technology being used?" Teela asked. "The modifications to the instrumentation, controls, weapons and communications systems that have been made to the vessel you were piloting. Were the other fighters, the ones at the base, made by human fabricators to the same specifications as the one you flew?"

"I'm not a technician, all I know is that some of it is ours, and some is theirs. Our people have been working around the clock on new modifications. They dicked up a bunch of the fighters with a new communications system. Fortunately, mine hadn't been outfitted yet. The toads absolutely hated it when we switched to audio from that piece-of-shit signal system they use. I mean, what a dumb-ass system. So the trade off was a software system to translate our audio communications into their light language and vice versa."

Ramsey stopped when Teela held up her hand. Shawaugh had begun speaking to her in Korlah, interrupting what Ramsey was saying. After a short discussion with Shawaugh, Teela spoke.

"We would like to be certain we understand what you said. Did you say that you have developed a communications system that converts Kahshinki into audible English. Is that correct?"

"Yeah, but sometimes it doesn't make sense, in fact it usually sounds like gibberish. Vocabulary problems, I guess. But the computer nerds were working on it when I left."

"Your vessel had mounts on it that looked as though they were designed for mounting additional weapons," Teela said.

"Yeah, another failed modification. They're multi-purpose mounting points for missiles, bombs, or guns, intended primarily for atmospheric flight. Our attempts in space to use the missiles at normal maneuvering speeds, has been ... less than promising.

54

The computer nerds are supposed to be working on a speed lock out, so we can't accidentally fire the weapons at speeds where we could fly into our own ordinance. That system hasn't been installed yet, so after losing a few pilots and fighters during testing, we stopped playing with the stuff. Anyway, it's only good against stationary targets, or vessels with little or no maneuverability. The Earth based program is supposed to be working on that technology, and our group is supposed to be refining high speed tactics, and teaching their dumb-ass pilots how to use them."

"Jason, I get the impression that you don't like the idea of teaching the clones," Beth said.

"It's not just me, none of the pilots like it. The clones, we call them twins, are a bunch of sexless, soulless zombies. The toads monitor the training real close, and that tends to rub the guys wrong, so naturally we find any excuse we can to screw with the program. We're not teachers, we're test pilots. We've been flying ten or more of the new fighters out every six months for the last seven years, lost maybe a dozen or so during training and weapons accidents. The danger of flying new craft is half the fun, test pilots and special op's people know the risks. Hell, we enjoy the risks, but there's something else going on that's not helping the situation. Rocket jockeys are a pretty tight bunch, we keep in touch, ya know? And nobody, none of the new arrivals have seen or heard from any of the guys that were supposed to have rotated back to Earth. My rotation would have been up next month, and I can tell you, my group was getting nervous."

"How many clones have been trained?" Teela asked, trying to refocus the questioning on critical information.

"Two classes of ten each, but I wouldn't call them trained. Truth is, they don't know jack shit. They might know enough maybe to keep from killing themselves on takeoff and landing, but not one of them would stand a chance against a seasoned pilot. The next class was due to graduate a week … well, a week after I left."

"So there are actually forty trained pilots at the outpost, maybe more by now?" Teela asked, pointing out his failure to mention the clones.

"I can't tell you for sure," Ramsey responded. "I think they're shipping their pilots off the rock the same day they graduate, but what's really happening on the toad's side of the base is anybody's guess."

"You taught them English?" Beth asked.

"Not exactly conversational English, but enough to follow instructions and read the instrumentation. We didn't really have time for anything else. Anyhow, the toads chaperoned them like a bunch of mother hens, figured we might try to jump one, I suppose."

"During my time in the Marines," Beth began, "I learned that there is a lot of truth in rumors, more sometimes than there are in official communications. Tell us any scuttlebutt, rumors, or stories you've heard since you arrived on station."

"Man, you have to be kidding. How much time do you have?" Ramsey asked, rubbing his face and stretching in a demonstration of how tired he was beginning to feel. "All we do when we aren't flying is sit around and bullshit with each other. Most of it's really stupid, hell I've made up a few whoppers myself." He finished with a big exaggerated yawn causing Ruth to follow suit.

"Tell us about the ones that aren't really stupid, the ones your gut tells you might be based on fact," Beth pressed.

"You want to hear about rumors? Okay, there is this one story, passed from one group to the next for the last few rotations. It's about a Kahshinki transport with engine problems. The patrol on station at the time picked it up near Earth and brought it back to the outpost. The pilot that towed them into the hangar was there when the Kahshinki opened the hatch. He heard voices and screams calling for help coming from inside, human voices. Story goes that when he reported it to his X.O., they went back for a look-see, and found it being guarded by armed spaghetti heads ... sorry, Korlah," Ramsey apologized looking at Teela and Shawaugh.

"That's all right," Teela responded. "We call them duplicates."

"Yeah, well the duplicates wouldn't let the X.O. look inside, and the Kahshinki played dumb, like they didn't know what he was asking them. By the time the X.O. went to the Commanding Officer and together they made it an issue, the freighter was repaired and on its way. Supposedly, the C.O. and X.O. were both really pissed that the Kahshinki had shined them like that, and canceled all missions, sending a formal complaint up the chain of command. The C.O. ended up getting relieved of his command. Both he and the X.O. were sent back Earth side, and a new, more politically correct C.O. and X.O. were assigned.

"I only heard that story one time, but it made an impression. Nobody mentioned it again until my patrol got the word to retrieve the freighter that landed me here. We were just trying to disable that piece-of-shit bus, until it smoked Captain Reynolds' fighter. After that, the C.O. gave the word to destroy it. If we had all fired when we were ordered to, that freighter would be space dust right now. Several pilots questioned the C.O. about destroying a vessel that may have humans, maybe Americans aboard. They made the mistake of mentioning the story, and the C.O. went ballistic, had a shit-fit right there, saying he was going to court martial the next son of a bitch who mentioned it. That little bickering session bought the pilot of the freighter enough time to start jumping in and out of hyper-light to shake us off. We were running out of juice, but the C.O. ordered us to continue the pursuit. I think the others may have been saving power, can't say for certain. However, the only ones making any hits that day, was the C.O. and his butt boy. The rest of the guys weren't taking shots when they should, and were missing shots they never should have, or would have, if they hadn't believed the story, and now they're dead." Ramsey stopped, scrunched his eyes shut and began massaging his temples in an effort to disguise the act of wiping tears from his eyes.

"Do you wish you had taken your shot when you had the chance?" Beth asked.

"Oh, I did," Ramsey replied, his voice sounding tired. "You see, I was the C.O.'s butt boy, we were the only assholes to score any hits that day."

Beth gave him an understanding nod in response to his admission of guilt.

A long pause followed. When no other questions were asked, Beth looked around and took the initiative to bring the meeting to a close. Teela directed the guards to return Captain Ramsey back to his cramped cell until a decision on how to guard and house him could be determined.

"I think that went well," Beth said with a positive smile after the door to Jason's cell was closed.

"I think he's a sneaky little shit, and I don't believe we should trust a single word he said," Ruth said, placing her palms on the table and leaning forward to emphasize her opposing view.

Teela stood, and then while staring at the center of the table, as if looking at something that was not visible to the others; she began to speak slowly and mechanically as though evaluating each word as she spoke it.

"Nearly everything he said was true, or at least, he believed it was true. He is hiding something about the number of fighters and the new weapons systems. Something that he thinks will give them an advantage."

"Are you gonna trip out again?" Beth asked in a gruff manner. "Ever since you and the old geezer, what's her name? Doodad?

"Dooaugh" Teela corrected.

"Whatever. Since you got back from your walk with her you've been acting real drifty. What happened? Is there something we should know?"

"People have died. More are going to die, human and Korlah. I wish I could stop it, I wish I could find some way around it, but I can't. This is my responsibility, my burden, and I am having difficulty choosing the path we will take. I fear no matter what I do, it will be wrong. I have no choice, but to make a choice...," Teela said, her voice trailing off, becoming barely audible. "I need more sleep," she said, looking up from the center of the table, as if the thought had just occurred to her.

58

Dooaugh took Teela by the arm, led her to the back, and placed her in a chair. Taking the chair next to Teela, she sat down. Teela feigned sleep, wishing her tumultuous thoughts would subside long enough for it to become genuine. Meanwhile Dooaugh drifted off and began softly snoring.

Are you really tired? Daedalus asked Teela after Dooaugh was asleep.

Yes, exhausted. Monitoring Captain Ramsey's mind was tiring. Now let me sleep, Teela answered, with a conscious thought.

Dooaugh is dangerous. What I saw when she was in your mind scared the hell out of me. She really believes you're a god incarnate. When she realizes otherwise, I think she'll try to kill you.

That's why we must rest, our minds must be strong.

I don't feel tired, why don't I feel it?

I don't know. But when I sleep, you need to sleep with me. If you don't rest, we'll get worse.

You know I don't mean to hurt you.

Yes, I know. Go to sleep! Teela replied, her irritation evident in the emotional tenor of her mental voice.

Rebuffed, Daedalus withdrew from Teela's conscious state, and although frightened of slipping back into the stygian hell of nothingness, he was more afraid of causing Teela additional harm. Reluctantly he released his grasp on the conscious level of their combined existence, allowing Teela's body and mind to rest.

5 - Interception

Challmara glided through the assault pod performing her preliminary shift inspections. When she was finished in the forward command section, she stopped at the forward-most bulkhead and gazed out the viewing port. The device on her back made a low humming sound, a constant reminder of her physical disability.

Although the device, not unlike an elongated backpack, had no restraining straps, a feeling of binding across her midsection caused her to tug repeatedly at the hem of her tunic in an effort to alleviate the unpleasant sensation. Not wishing to offend her Lead Technician, she had graciously accepted the device, commenting on its many beneficial qualities while refraining from making any mention of the minor discomfort that was now a nagging irritation.

Placing her palms on the cold panel that served as a window into space, Challmara stared at the bright star in the distance; the Sun of the human planetary system. Shyron had given her free reign to make whatever modifications were needed to gain technological superiority over the enemy. But Teela was now demanding that she withhold using the advantages that would ensure a swift military victory.

The thought that she would have to submit her plans to Teela for approval caused her considerable anxiety. The realization that the little birthing unit she had once wanted to protect and care for was now her Superior arrived with punishing clarity. Teela had refused to recognize the limitations that her damaged condition would create, and instead gave her cold emotionless orders, placing the responsibility for failure of the mission on her. The Teela she knew would never have treated her with such disrespect.

My Teela no longer exists, Challmara thought, removing her hands from the icy surface of the window. *This creature I am forced to obey is not even Korlah anymore.*

She looked over to the lead pilot, who looked back, giving her a respectful nod. Challmara smiled and rubbed her hands together to warm them as she considered how fortunate she was to have such loyal friends. If it had not been for the compassion of her lead pilot and the skill of her Senior Technician, whose assistance helped to restore her confidence, she was certain she would have been completely incapable of meeting Teela's demands and would have suffered unmentionable shame and dishonor.

Challmara had no time to worry about such personal tribulations; the enemy craft were en route and would be arriving shortly. Time would not permit presenting her plans to Teela for approval. The military decisions would be her responsibility, Teela had made that perfectly clear, and under the circumstances, she would have it no other way.

Her decision made, she slapped the viewing screen with her palms and gave the bothersome tunic one last tug, more from nervous tension than discomfort. Crossing her arms at the waist, she turned around by manipulating the controls attached to her left wrist. Supported by the gravitational field of the device, she floated silently across the control room to where Shawaugh and the pilots were patiently waiting her decision.

"Director Shawaugh," she said as she approached. Shawaugh acknowledged Challmara with a slight nod of her head.

"Our scouts have detected only the one molecular disruptor on the human planet. The Kahshinki attempted to mask its radiation signal by locating it underground. That will make this an exceptionally difficult mission and there will be only one opportunity to capture it. You will need the element of surprise, and we can only hope that any Kahshinki stationed with the device are cowards." Challmara wrung her hands nervously, immediately cursing the fact that her comments demonstrated her lack of confidence in Shawaugh's ability to succced.

"My warriors will not fail," Shawaugh declared. "On our return from this mission, any Kahshinki we capture will be returned to Shyron as a gift. During the victory Spectacles, I will take the existence of two Kahshinki at the same time. Like the human warrior that is now Teela, I will do it without fang or claw."

Challmara nodded her head in agreement, acknowledging Shawaugh's statement of confidence. The words, 'the Warrior that is now Teela' rang in her mind. Steeling herself to keep from blanching, Challmara felt suddenly guilty for her angry thoughts. Twisting her hands together, she cleared her mind of the personal thoughts and emotions that plagued her ability to think, and concentrated on the present crisis.

"Proceed with the attack as planned. May the Gods of Korlah give you strength and protect you," she said, surprising Shawaugh with the politically dangerous religious reference.

"Director Challmara, if I fail the planet will burn. If it burns, I will burn with it. But you and Teela will be left to face the dishonor of my failure. What will you do?" Shawaugh asked.

"With or without the humans, Campaign will be fought in this system. We will have ample opportunity to regain any honor lost."

"By fang or by claw, Roche Hah!" Shawaugh replied, growling the farewell while making a clawed salute.

"Roche Hah," Challmara muttered, mechanically returning the salute.

After Shawaugh and the pilots had departed, Challmara returned to her position at the monitor. Once again she pressed her palms against the cold surface for physical reassurance, she stared into the field of stars. Her gaze settled on the one bright star. The thought she had repeatedly struggled with once again returned. She cared deeply for Teela, as she always had. But ever since the last time they had been together in her quarters, she knew it was no longer Teela she longed for. It was the warrior that is now Teela. She looked down at the legs that dangled lifelessly beneath her and lamented silently, believing that any hope of a continued relationship had been damaged along with her utility. And now she had ordered the implementation of plans that Teela had not approved. She knew she would be fortunate if Teela permitted her continued existence until their return, when Shyron and the Council could decide her punishment.

The movement of the fighter and troop carriers as they departed from the assault pod drew her back to the matters at hand. She watched as the light fighters, heavy fighters, and troop carriers performed an intricate alignment of their vessels into two sphere shaped groups, the troop carriers at the center and the heavy fighters around the periphery. Once the two groups had formed, they moved slowly away and suddenly blinked out of sight. Challmara moved back to the command console and activated the alarm.

The Korlah klaxon, a deafening sound, resembled a long drawn out screeching of brakes. The alarm was accompanied with flashing white lights at all monitors and communication panels activated to announce an emergency situation. The nature of the situation then scrolled onto the communication screens.

With the sounding of the alarm, every member of the crew on the base ship, and those on each of the vessels attached to it were required to prepare for battle or respond to an attack as defined by the visual announcement. Window densities were increased to match that of the hull armor, rendering them opaque, weapons were energized and unnecessary power loads secured, and all penetrations between the base ship and attached vessels were closed. All remaining personnel not manning control, defense or damage control stations took positions in chairs or bench-like areas, protected from abrupt motion by the restraining action of the gravity fields the seats generated.

Her heart pounded painfully from the slug of adrenalin the alarm had stimulated as Teela leapt from her chair and charged to the front of the vessel. She scanned the communication panel, read the standard battle preparation announcement and noted immediately that nearly all the fighters and transports were gone and the assault pods had moved into a defensive position placing their relatively undefended aft portions between them.

"Where are the fighters? What is the threat?" Teela demanded of the pilot.

"Director Challmara has ordered the fighters out on missions, Your Eminence. I have not been informed as to the nature of the missions, but I suspect they are intercepting the enemy forces approaching our position," the pilot answered.

"What? Why wasn't I informed?" Teela cried, her voice rising as she realized that her worst fears had materialized.

"Your Eminence," a voice crackled over a speaker mounted to the side of the communications console in a crude manner that indicated function was all that was considered during installation. "I apologize for not waking you, but there was no time. My scouts have reported a large group of enemy fighters performing a systematic sweep of this sector. It won't be long before they locate our position," Challmara announced, as the communication console repeated her message in the traditional array of flashing lights.

"Our fighters must not attack them!" Teela cried.

"I am using our fighters to secure the enemy base while their fighters are here attacking us," Challmara said. My scout identified the humans' communication signal. You will be able to speak with them once they are within range. We will not need fighters to protect us; the new defensive array is fully functional and will be capable of absorbing the pulse energy of one or more combined attacks before a discharge pulse will be required. If you are able to negotiate with them, a defensive pulse will not be required. However, if you are unable to negotiate, I estimate that a single defensive pulse discharged at a projected amplification ratio of ten to one, will result in complete destruction of all attacking craft within a nominal flash span of our vessel."

"I will intercept them with this transport. It will be easier to negotiate," Teela responded breathlessly, the panic she felt tightening her chest and throat.

"No! I will not be able to control the defensive pulse. If you are too close, you will be destroyed with the enemy craft. You must not leave the protection of the Pods," Challmara said.

"Pilot, depart and proceed to intercept the incoming vessels," Teela ordered.

"Teela! Please, you must not leave the protection of the Pod!" Challmara cried, her voice amplified by the speaker.

Do not force me to repeat my order, Teela warned the pilot telepathically, the message delivered with an emotional tone that indicated failure to comply would be taken seriously.

These were confusing times for the warriors and pilots of the mission. The rumors, the gossip, and the events that were unfolding did not reinforce what they had come to believe. Teela was the Assistant to the Potentate, this much they knew and believed to be certain. The belief that Teela was the reincarnation of Shawlmon was not widely accepted, and the rumors that Teela was a mind talker created an atmosphere of fear rather than loyalty. These thoughts and others raced through the pilot's mind as she manipulated the controls of the vessel, which disengaged it from the assault pod. She was silently grateful that Challmara was not present, as it would have been difficult to take Teela's orders over those of her close friend and shell mate.

"You are not betraying your friend," Teela said, placing her hand on the pilot's shoulder.

The pilot's fear and panic when she realized her thoughts had been read caused Teela to pull her hand away as the pilot cringed from the contact. She withdrew her mind as well and apologized for the invasion with a thought.

Without being directed, the pilot entered the commands on her console that caused a command chair to flow up out of the floor like liquid and take shape in the central area of the vessel behind those of the crew. Teela recognized that the pilot had silently acknowledged her authority and took her position on the command dais.

"Challmara, I would like …," Teela started to say, stopping when a heavy fighter on the assault pod lifted off and banked sharply up and assumed a position alongside her Transport.

Your thoughts foretold these events. I will be your escort, and assist with the demonstrations that will be needed. You and I no longer have need of words. Our minds have joined, our eyes, our actions are now entwined. Your words can no longer deny what your mind says.

"Dooaugh!" Teela cried as a visual image of her transport as seen from Dooaugh's perspective flashed into her mind.

A rattle of noise she immediately recognized as the thoughts of those around her rose and ebbed as she struggled to control the flow. Closing her eyes she found she could see through those of Dooaugh, feel her emotions and share her thoughts. But it was more than that, she lifted the hands that belonged to Dooaugh and turned them over slowly, examining the gnarled and scarred knuckles.

I am yours Shawlmon, as you will it, so it shall be," Dooaugh said, the thought coming to Teela, not like a telepathic message, but as though she had thought it herself.

Teela shook her head and opened her eyes, the images vanished. Fearing what she experienced was a hallucination, she scanned the compartment with her mind to verify that Dooaugh was not there.

"Bring me the human pilot!" Teela shouted to the guards assigned to protect the Korlah crew from the humans.

"Proceed to intercept," Teela ordered the Korlah pilot. Her mouth felt dry and she swallowed with effort. She straightened from her slouched posture and mentally tried to dismiss the feeling of uneasiness that overshadowed the confidence she wanted to portray.

As though connected by an invisible force, Teela's transport and Dooaugh's heavy fighter banked as one before they sped off and disappeared among the dots of light that illuminated the darkness of space.

6 - Gauntlet

Drifting among asteroids 250,000 miles from the Kahshinki base, Lahsoon, and the assault group she led, sat and waited patiently for the signal to commence their attack. As she monitored the long range sensors of her heavy fighter, Lahsoon watched with alarm as twenty light fighters lifted off from the Kahshinki base. The group of fighter craft formed into four attack waves of five fighters each, and departed on a heading toward the assault pods. Her instinct was to intercept and attack the fighters, but her orders were explicit: do not attack until directed. Failure to obey would disrupt the timing that Challmara emphasized would be necessary for Mission success, not necessarily her success.

At least they are being predictable, Lahsoon thought, noting the traditional Kahshinki grouping of five fighters in each attack formation. The group of twenty-two vessels she commanded consisted of six heavy fighters, twelve light fighters, and four troop transports. It would be the job of the fighter craft to clear the way so that the transports could stage a ground assault. Grouped into two triangular formations consisting of two light fighters followed by three heavy fighters and then followed by four more light fighters, each of the formations would attack in waves from two directions. The development and use of heavy fighters was solely a Korlah innovation. Slow and cumbersome, the heavy fighters were nothing more than mobile artillery, carrying an arsenal of high-energy pulse cannons and particle weapons that were capable of penetrating even the multi-feet armor of a Campaign vessel.

The Kahshinki weaponry and tactics had not changed in nearly a thousand cycles and twelve campaigns. The Korlah, however, discovered that by changing and improving their tactics and weaponry, their success in battle was nearly a foregone conclusion. Only now, with their pilot and warrior ranks stripped to 4 percent of normal, the superiority of their weapons would provide little advantage if they had no pilots to fly them.

Once the Korlah fighter craft completed the main assault of the base defenses and resistance had been quelled, the troop transports would land and disgorge their cargo of twenty warriors each. Certain to be outnumbered and outgunned, Lahsoon hoped the Kahshinki would have no surprises and that Challmara's new weaponry would function as planned. From an outlaw rebel leader to a Campaign Fighter Group Commander, Lahsoon knew this would be a definitive point in her existence, where she would either live up to Director Challmara's expectations, or prove Director Shawaugh's protests of her appointment to be valid. In an effort to conceal her nervousness from the crew, Lahsoon leaned back in her command chair and crossed her arms and took the opportunity to wipe her perspiration soaked palms onto the sleeves of her tunic.

The attack order from Challmara came as a series of flashing lights on Lahsoon's communications console. With the message only partially decoded, Lahsoon ordered the attack to commence by transmitting the traditional Korlah attack signal, "Roche Hah" on Korlah as well as Kahshinki communication bands.

During the early campaigns, the attack signal was intended to honor the Kahshinki duplicates, clones identical to themselves, whose existence they would be forced to cease. To the Kahshinki, the signal had become a feared precursor to Korlah attacks that would not end until the Kahshinki surrendered or all Korlah attackers had been exterminated. The signal became so feared in fact, that many Kahshinki would flee the battles and leave their troops without leadership during critical stages of the conflicts.

The light fighters darted forward, followed a few moments later by the heavy fighters. At nearly light-speed velocities, and on a collision course with the far side of the asteroid base, the light fighters altered their trajectory at the instant before impact. They made a nearly ninety-degree turn and proceeded over the jagged surface, which they cleared by only a few feet as they continued on toward the side of the base the scout had identified as belonging to the Kahshinki. The heavy fighters, slow and much less agile, arched slowly and into a much higher altitude than the light fighters. The speed differential between the light and heavy fighters opened a gap between the two waves with the light fighters entering the perimeter of the base before the heavy fighters crested the uneven horizon behind them.

Sensing the attack, the Kahshinki automated defense stanchions on the base perimeter energized and pulsed in response. By rocketing outward away from the asteroid's surface, the light fighters dodged the high-energy particle weapons blast, but not before automatically noting the locations of the defensive weapons and feeding that information to the heavy fighters coming behind them. Moving up and away from each other in erratic loops, they successfully dodged the multiple blasts that attempted to track their trajectory. They disappeared in directions different than the one from which they came, drawing fire away from the heavy fighters now cresting the horizon. With the coordinates of all defense stanchions now loaded into their weapons targeting systems, the heavy fighters began destroying the enemy defense weapons the moment they cleared the horizon.

With systematic consistency, the light fighters would dart forward, retreating with orchestrated precision, only to repeat the process as the heavy fighters followed, destroying the numerous defensives of the Kahshinki base with their powerful pulse weaponry. Unable to cope with all the defensive weapons at once, the heavy fighters began taking numerous hits. Although covered with thick energy absorbent and reflective armor that was capable of handling up to five direct hits, the energy of the blasts was now being absorbed by the array of antenna that Challmara's technicians installed. Normally concerned with the depletion rate their high-powered weapons had on their vessel's power cell, the pilots found that the enemy blasts were recharging their power cells as fast as their weapons were depleting them. Feeling impervious, they quit taking evasive actions and assumed stationary positions within the perimeter of the base and were leisurely destroying the defense systems.

When an enemy fighter attempted to launch from the hangar opening, one of the heavy fighters moved into a position blocking the hangar launch bay. Situated directly in front of the base entrance, the Korlah fighter began taking multiple blasts from the heavy pulse artillery that sat recessed and protected deep within the opening. Even though the fighter was discharging its weapons at the maximum rate, it was now unable to dissipate the absorbed energy quickly enough to prevent excessive saturation of the power cell.

The heavy fighter began glowing and emitting lightning-like arcs of energy to the nearby structure and ground. Tilting suddenly, as the escaping energy plasma from the ruptured power cell incinerated the pilot and crew, the fighter arched downward, crashing and exploding as it hit the rocky surface. The energy released by the explosion blasted a crater fifty yards across and thirty feet deep, ejecting rocks and debris in all directions. The force of the explosion hurled the other five Korlah fighters away from the asteroid. Pocked with multiple craters from the blast, the fortified entrance to the Kahshinki base puffed plumes of atmosphere at several locations. Along with the atmosphere, debris and bodies were being expelled as the pressurized atmosphere within the outer sections of the enemy base vented to the vacuum of space.

Taking advantage of the moment, Kahshinki fighters began to pour out from the hangar opening of the now damaged structure, firing blindly into the cloud of debris as they emerged. The balance of the Korlah light fighters had assumed positions over the base in anticipation of just such a launch. Unable to perform a light-speed jump so close to the asteroid, the Kahshinki fighters were forced to run the gauntlet of Korlah fighters as they emerged. Two out of three were destroyed by the synchronized firepower of the Korlah vessels. The first Kahshinki fighters that slipped out immediately began to engage the Korlah fighters disrupting the effectiveness of the gauntlet and facilitating the escape of the others. Of the thirty enemy fighters launched, eleven survived to engage their twelve tormentors.

Waking in great pain, Lahsoon wiped blood from her eyes and felt her head for the source. A deep crease in her forehead and cheekbone marked the spot where her head struck the armrest of her chair. Sharp pains from her neck and shoulders brought her back to full consciousness.

"Report!" she cried weakly, her voice causing a sharp stab of pain in her head.

Using the sleeves of her tunic and palms, Lahsoon worked at clearing the coagulating blood from her eyes. The spiraling stars in the viewing window indicated the craft's stabilizing system was either damaged or off-line. The fact that she and the crew were still in their seats indicated the gravitational drive was still functioning. The weapons technician was lying to one side of her chair, her head cocked at a severe angle back and to the side, mouth and eyes wide open. From the diminishing thermal signature, Lahsoon knew she was dead. The pilot and communications technician were both slumped forward on their consoles, but their thermal signatures were strong. Moving with mechanical stiffness, Lahsoon made her way to the side of the pilot's chair, each step causing sharp pains to her neck and back. Lifting the pilot off the console, she leaned her back into the chair and was relieved when the pilot groaned in protest. Lahsoon initialized the stabilizing system, bringing the spinning to a stop. Turning the ship, she faced it toward the battle that was currently in progress. Lifting the weapons technician from her chair, Lahsoon took her seat and checked the status of the weapons system while closely monitoring the progress of the battle.

It became immediately apparent that the enemy pilots were well trained, flying lightly armored fighters with high-powered weaponry. The lighter craft proved exceptionally nimble, quickly shifting from the role of prey to predator as they began to score numerous direct hits while avoiding the firepower of the Korlah craft. Realizing that the enemy fighters were buying time for the enemy ground forces to prepare for an assault, Lahsoon moved to the communications console and ordered the transports to commence a ground assault on the base.

"Your orders, Commander?" the pilot groaned, straightening up in her chair.

"Move in and provide cover for the transports," Lahsoon snapped, resuming her position at the weapons console.

Controlling seven weapons and three targeting systems, the weapons console was a formidable challenge during combat conditions for even the most well-trained technician. Lahsoon was familiar with the operations of the console, but had neither trained nor drilled in the combat exercises practiced daily by those bred for the occupation. Unable to manipulate the controls quickly enough to target the enemy craft, she abandoned use of the targeting controls and began firing randomly using nothing more than visual alignment of the cannon with the anticipated positions of enemy craft. Diving between the transports and enemy craft, Lahsoon's heavy fighter absorbed the brunt of the enemy assault. Blasts directed from Lahsoon disintegrated first one then another of the enemy fighters. The pilot watched with amazement as her blasts disintegrated a third when the targeting console indicated that there was no target available. Using the hole opened by Lahsoon's fighter, the transports charged into the enemy hangar absorbing the blasts of the proximity cannon within.

"Commander, how are you targeting?" the pilot asked as she positioned the fighter to guard the entrance of the base from any of the enemy fighters that may have attempted to re-enter.

"Visually," Lahsoon grunted as she fired another shot that came so close to an enemy craft that it cartwheeled momentarily from the energy wash.

Stretching to reach the communications console, the pilot switched on the audible communications system.

"Attempt visual targeting, control systems have been compromised, attempt visual targeting!" she said, leaning toward the microphone while adjusting the alignment of the fighter to face the incoming enemy craft.

The battle quickly degraded into a brawl, a dogfight at sub-light speeds quickly spreading out and away from the asteroid. Even though they repeatedly hit the Korlah craft, the Kahshinki did not succeed in destroying any. After suffering five losses, the enemy craft pulled back and formed two groups of three fighters each. Spying one of the disabled heavy fighters, one of the Kahshinki groups broke away and formed a single file column with the intention of performing a strafing run, certain that their combined firepower would penetrate its armor. Firing as they passed, the first two Kahshinki scored direct hits on the tumbling Korlah fighter.

At the instant the third enemy pulse struck, the fighter began shimmering with absorbed energy. With a blinding flash, the energy discharged in an intensive pulse that radiated in an outward sphere of white light and conical shafts of particle energy. Caught within close proximity of the powerful pulse, the four Kahshinki fighters were instantly disintegrated. Expanding outward, the leading wave of concentrated energy passed over one of the other disabled Korlah heavy fighters, and as it did, each fighter pulsed instantaneously. The combined energy of these pulses joined that of the first, and as the subsequent waves of concentrated energy passed over the other Korlah fighters, each in turn pulsed as their weapons defense systems discharged to prevent an overload condition. A chain reaction of weapons pulsing followed, with those at the center pulsing numerous times before their energy had been sufficiently dissipated.

The area where the fighting craft had been boiling with activity became suddenly silent. Debris from shattered craft, the white-hot metal still sparkling, continued to burn as the self-generated oxidizers fed the chemical reactions. With crews slumped unconscious at their controls, the remaining Korlah vessels that had not detonated tumbled through space littered with the debris of the shattered Kahshinki fighters.

Meeting little resistance, the Korlah warriors secured the hangar and were making their way into the main structure when the base was rocked by shock waves from the battle being fought outside. Undeterred by the multiple concussions that threatened to collapse the structure around them, the Korlah warriors systematically moved through the enemy base on a mission to exterminate any and all resistance. The armored suits, developed by the Korlah for such assaults, were nearly impervious to small weapons fire, and the pulse weaponry they carried was nearly as powerful as that of a light fighter. Walking into numerous ambushes, they moved slowly forward, the gravitational grip produced by their suits keeping them from being blasted off the ground. If one fell, two more stepped forward firing their cannon until the enemy and the structures they hid behind were destroyed.

The majority of the Kahshinki resistance force was grouped in the outer levels during the Korlah assault of the base. Most of the enemy forces were killed by the explosive decompression of the outer levels, those that survived were quickly terminated, and the remaining unarmed laborers, technicians, and pilots were captured. As a bonus, the warriors captured a half dozen Kahshinki hiding in the hold of a transport damaged by falling debris.

The Kahshinki, the prized catch of the battle, were quickly bound and placed in one of the Korlah transports for return to the Campaign Vessel. The remaining captives were separated. The laborers and technician clones were led away in groups to be used for repair and cleanup activities. The soldier and pilot clones were separated into two groups, human and Korlah. The Korlah clones, identical genetically to their captors would be saved for spare parts, the human clones had no purpose or utility as far as the Assault Commander was concerned so they were moved into a corner in preparation for termination.

Litnauh had accepted the assignment of Assault Commander at Shyron's request, but it was her friendship with Challmara that convinced her to agree. She trusted Challmara's judgment above all others and was honored to be a member of her mission. Intently aware of the recording device that was part of her armor and the log it was generating to document her actions, Litnauh reconsidered terminating the humans. She was certain the order to preserve the humans was stupid, but violating it would reflect badly on Challmara's leadership.

Marching slowly in front of the human duplicates, Litnauh studied the faces and features of the humans. They were certainly duplicates, differing in age by no more than ten cycles, she recognized three genotypes within the four areas that were being utilized. Technicians and laborers were of the same genotype, tall and lightly muscled compared to the soldiers. Unlike the humans she had seen, the thin, lifeless filaments that grew from the heads of these units were cut short. The pilots were small by comparison, lightly built with filaments on the head so light they could hardly be seen. Only six of the Soldier units had survived the battle. Impressed by the quality of their resistance, the Commander stopped and studied the damaged soldiers closely.

Captured only because they were too severely damaged to continue fighting, they now glared defiantly at their captors from where they sat, or were lying on the debris-littered floor. Dark skinned like the male human she had seen, these units were large boned and heavily muscled, even more so than the human called Beth, and if Beth could defeat Ruwaugh and Apoulauh, then these units were potentially much more dangerous.

Litnauh silently pondered what it would take to provoke the prisoners so that she could exterminate them as allowed by the battle doctrine. Looking around at the other warriors in the area, she quickly amended her thoughts, fearful the rumors that Shawlmon could hear thoughts might be true. Shouting angrily, she ordered the human prisoners moved to the base barracks and confined there until clarifying instructions could be obtained. The prisoners that were Korlah duplicates she ordered moved to the base biorepair facility where they would be utilized for spare parts before reclamation.

Her communications equipment unable to make contact with Challmara, Litnauh moved outside of the structure and attempted contact again. While attempting a third time, the ground in front of her exploded, followed by two more explosions, one of which struck her armor. Dust and debris filled the air in the extremely low gravity of the asteroid. The area around Litnauh, however, quickly cleared as the gravitational effect of the armored suit caused debris to drop to the ground. Taking a defensive stance she aimed her weapon in the direction of the assault, pausing when she realized that it was coming from the adjacent human base. Well out of range of small arms fire and confident that her armor would protect her from this archaic projectile weaponry, she lowered her weapon and turned to face her assailants, waiting patiently as the remainder of the dust in the area dissipated.

In the distance, on the ridge between her and the main structure of the human base, she could see the thermal silhouettes of several faces peering out from the boulders behind which the human soldiers were hiding. Trained in low gravity combat, Litnauh raised her weapon and fired with practiced precision. A cluster of boulders behind the humans exploded, pelting them with debris, some as large as basketballs. She targeted one of the humans as it prepared to fire another rocket-propelled grenade. The pulse blast detonated the grenade before it was fired, killing the human and those nearby when the fragments of shrapnel punctured their pressure suits beyond their capacity to self-seal. Drawn by the explosions, several other warriors emerged from the mouth of the hangar and engaged the assaulting force; the devastating effects of their combined weapons fire turned the ridge of boulders into a gravel-strewn field littered with the organic remains of the human soldiers.

Without knowing what level of sophistication the humans possessed in the form of sensors and detection of approaching light-speed craft, Shawaugh made the conservative assumption that it would be as good as the Korlah systems, which were now believed to be superior to those used by the Kahshinki. Following Challmara's advice, Shawaugh maneuvered her Assault group to the far side of the planetary system's sun. Skirting the sun's corona and using its gravitational field and particle radiation to accelerate, her formation charged the Earth in a momentary burst of hyper-light. Approaching in single file so that even if they were detected, their numbers would not be known, the group did not decelerate until just before entering the outer atmosphere.

Appearing at first as a dot of light in the center of her screen, the glistening planet festooned with wisps of vaporized moisture filled the screen in an instant. Just before entering the atmosphere, the light wave compression drive automatically secured, and the gravitational generator switched from amplification to reflection mode. Shawaugh paused in awe to gape at the water-covered planet so much like Korlah. In her moment of distraction she failed to notice the threat warnings on her console.

The military satellite rotated and launched three high velocity rockets, each tipped with a tactical nuclear warhead, as Shawaugh's group passed. The energy pulse released as the warheads detonated within close proximity of the Korlah craft caused the windows to automatically become opaque, preventing the light energy from causing flash burns to the pilots. The concussion, which would have shattered conventional craft, merely tossed the tight formation into disarray. Within the craft, the crews were protected by the gravitational stasis designed to eliminate the effects inertial energy caused by rapid changes in direction. Uninjured and undamaged, Shawaugh and her attack group were more irritated than surprised by the attack.

"Fighter Eight; identify and destroy source of attack. Clear this sector and hold position," Shawaugh ordered, using the voice communications for the first time since their departure.

"Roche Hah!" the pilot of the eighth and last fighter in the group responded, as she reversed course and vectored her craft to destroy the satellite.

On the ground, deep within a mountain, in a large concrete bunker code-named "Watch Tower," an Air Force Colonel stumbled around his desk, his eyes locked on the largest screen centered on a wall covered with smaller status and monitoring screens. The panel he watched showed eight white dots in relation to earth. Next to each, elevation, speed, and heading displayed a real-time status of the craft being tracked. As he watched, one of the dots reversed course and headed back in the direction it had come. The physics were impossible to conceive, how a craft traveling at mach-4 could reverse course and be traveling in the opposite direction at the same speed in an instant. He had seen this before, but not at these speeds.

"We have an audible!" One of the technicians shouted.

"Let's hear it," the Colonel replied.

Shawaugh's voice, a language comprised of thick consonants with rolling R's sounding much like growls emanated from the area speakers.

"Bogey sierra five just terminated sentry Charlie seven four."

Turning back to his desk, the Colonel picked up a red phone with one hand and flipped open a cover revealing a large black button. Pressing the button, he sat on the corner of the desk and spoke into the phone.

"General, this is Watch Tower. We have a confirmed code-black, Sir.

"Eleven confirmed contacts, Sir.

"Three auto launches; nukes. Precision targeting, direct hits with negative results.

"No, Sir. They're communicating audibly on normal frequencies. Translators are on it, Sir.

"Yes, Sir. Thank you, Sir," the Colonel said before dropping the phone back into its cradle.

"This is not a drill. We are under attack!" he shouted as he stood.

Using the energy signal produced by the Kahshinki weapon as a beacon, Shawaugh altered her course onto a heading directly toward the source. Three heavy fighters led the triangle-shaped formation with three transports at the center, followed and flanked by five light fighters. Once on the heading, which was then verified clear of obstructions, they jumped the distance at near light speed, transiting the 750 miles from the Gulf of Mexico to the sky above Area-51 in less than .004 seconds. Unlike hypersonic travel, speeds approaching light cause the vessels to literally fly through the atmospheric molecules without disrupting them. On the radar screens of the Air Force technicians monitoring the craft, the signals they were tracking disappeared.

However, the computers that now backed up those technicians tracked the craft to their new location and automatically shifted the displays and coordinates in the command bunker.

Looking like a rocky outcropping on the outskirts of the military base, the access to the underground facility that housed the Kahshinki and the planet killer they had constructed was invisible to the naked eye. The road to the construction site had long since been restored to the rocks, sage, and cacti of an undisturbed area of desert. Access was now through a long tunnel from the main buildings under the adjacent runway and desert. Shawaugh had no intention of using the tunnel. Instead, she and the two other heavy fighters took up positions over the rocks where the facility lay ninety feet below ground. The three transports took turns firing specially adjusted beams of high velocity particles at the desert below. The rock and earth immediately vaporized sending a plume of white smoke, ash, and dust that rapidly rose into the desert sky.

In the sky over the base, the five light fighters began responding to a multitude of missiles and projectile weapons that were being directed at them from the main base. As per their directive, they responded first to the threat, then its source, firing only after they had been fired upon, and only at the individual source. Within the first ninety seconds, the five fighters destroyed all of the automated phalanx guns and missile launchers that were directed against them.

Although the pilots of the Korlah fighters could easily destroy the aircraft that were launching on the far side of the base, they instead flew intimidating maneuvers around the fragile atmospheric gliders to demonstrate the futility of any attempt to engage the technologically superior Korlah craft. Positioning themselves directly in front of the aircraft the Korlah taunted the pilots with a choice of turning or slowing to avoid collision. One pilot called their bluff and charged forward at full throttle unloading his arsenal of air-to-air missiles, banking hard at the moment before collision only to lose all power as his craft entered the electromagnetic field that enveloped the Korlah fighter. With the engine no longer producing thrust and its electronic and hydraulic control systems useless, the aircraft designed solely for powered flight stalled, pirouetted on its tail, and plunged toward the earth below. The pilot, like several others faced with equally unsalvageable circumstance, managed to pull the lever that manually initiated the mechanism and rocket beneath his seat, ejecting him from the doomed craft moments before impact. For over a dozen other pilots, lack of altitude, stubborn determination, or the steep rocky hillsides proved to be fatal.

In the four minutes and thirty-seven seconds it took the Korlah transports to vaporize twenty feet of rock, concrete, and steel into the subterranean tunnel below, the base defensives had been neutralized, and twenty-six of the thirty-seven state-of-the-art jet fighters that engaged the Korlah lay burning on the desert floor. The remaining nine jet fighters still flying, their weapons depleted, turned away and retreated.

With access to the subterranean tunnel achieved, the transports then landed in close proximity around the conical crater they burned into the earth. Positioned to form a protective barrier around the opening, the warriors exited the inner side of the transports with practiced precision, floating mobile pulse cannon into the gaps between. The retrieval team, identifiable by their significantly lighter armor, dropped into the crater in groups of five each using armored loading platforms.

Returning to holding positions thousands of feet overhead, the five light fighters monitored their threat panels for additional aerial threats while the heavy fighters hovered a few hundred feet above the transports and provided cover for ground threats. The light fighters to the west identified the incoming craft. Unlike the atmospheric gliders, the incoming vessels were powered by gravitational drive engines and were coming at speeds in excess of mach-4. Although they had been briefed that the humans may employ Kahshinki technology against them, they were also told that Kahshinki fighters would be lightly armored with equally underpowered weapons, and like the fragile atmospheric gliders, they must not destroy them unless forced.

When the Korlah pilots noted that they would be outnumbered six to one by the incoming enemy craft, they took no chances and treated their attackers with cautious respect. Moving to intercept, they formed a defensive line, yet continued making erratic and random directional changes to prevent the enemy craft from obtaining weapons lock.

With functional inertial field suppressors, the Korlah pilots were able to make instantaneous directional changes during the initial moments of interception. Within seconds, each Korlah fighter was directly behind a human fighter with its weapons locked on the inferior craft. The spacecraft the human pilots were flying lacked inertial suppressors resulting in intense gravitational forces as the pilots tried to turn the high-speed craft and lose the enemy they believed were trying to destroy them. Although wearing state-of-the-art flight suits designed for high G's, the speed and maneuverability of the technologically advanced craft far exceeded the frail physiology of the humans attempting to pilot them.

Dodging from behind one human fighter to the next, the Korlah pilots demonstrated the superior maneuverability of their craft. For several minutes, the Korlah successfully evaded the pulse blasts of the human fighters until the taunting antics brought one fighter into a direct point-blank enemy blast. Thinking she had just invited the end of her existence, the Korlah pilot peeled away from the group, amazed to find that not only was her craft undamaged but her power cell had been recharged 20 percent. Informing the others that she had verified the effectiveness of their new defense system, she charged back into the fray with renewed confidence.

The walls inside the crater were glazed with material that moments before had been molten. The radiated heat of the walls illuminated the bottom of the shaft with a dull glow. Unaffected by the scalding heat, the warriors descended into the caldera, their weapons poised as though it were possible for some threat to be waiting below. Although lighter versions of the armor worn by the field warriors above, the suits worn by the retrieval team were in no way light. Composed of a mechanical exoskeleton, the suits provided protection from projectile as well as energy weapons, maintained thermal and atmospheric life support, and amplified body movement to allow motion while increasing or decreasing their gravitational weight as needed.

Hovering inches from the bottom, the warriors stepped off the platforms onto the still malleable surface of the cooling slag. Their boots leaving footprints in the slurry of rock and steel, the warriors proceeded through a jagged opening in the side of the crater that marked the location of a tunnel that would lead them to their objective. The charred walls and floor quickly changed to tile and paint within a few yards of the crater. Steam and smoke flowed past the warriors as they progressed further into the undamaged section of tunnel. Fire suppression spigots in the ceiling, having completed their automatic discharge, now dribbled onto the warriors as they paused to target their portable pulse cannon on an armored door that had automatically slid shut to protect and isolate the chamber beyond from just such an assault.

The third pulse bent the door inward forming a six foot concave blister with a center that was glowing white-hot. The fourth pulse blew the blister inward spattering the Marine contingent beyond with molten steel. Screams preceded a cacophony of weapons fire and explosions as those Marines still able, fired rockets, grenades, and bullets through the white-hot hole in the door.

The quantity of projectiles emerging through the door was so intense that it took three tries before the warriors were able to get a pulse grenade through the opening. The grenade, adjusted to be non-lethal, discharged an energy pulse within the small room that dissipated into the steel lining after passing through the convenient saline medium of the Marines' bodies.

Without further resistance, the Korlah proceeded into the foyer beyond the steel door, which led to a series of hallways and chambers. Following the signal produced by the molecular disintegrator, the warriors blasted through two more reinforced doors before entering the chamber where the weapon was housed. Within the room, lower gravity created by an altered gravitational state indicated that Kahshinki were present. Although capable of handling higher gravity fields, the Kahshinki, with their boneless bodies, were flattened onto the ground and forced to slither about, looking like four legged octopi out of water. Their suits compensating for the near weightless conditions of the room, the warriors charged in.

In the center of the room, a black cylindrical object nine feet long with spherical orbs at either end that sparkled with iridescence sat strapped atop a cradle that was fastened to the floor. The warriors were met with high-energy pulse blasts, which sent them sprawling onto the floor. Those behind them threw in pulse grenades intended to stun the Kahshinki. Following the pulse blasts, the remaining warriors charged in. Two Kahshinki were immobile on the floor, but a third was at the device manipulating controls. The warriors blasted it with their pulse weapons sending it spinning through the air and into the far wall where it slowly slid to the ground in the low gravity.

The iridescence of the orbs on the device began to scintillate with counter-rotating flashes of light, which struck the surfaces of the room and warriors' armor, leaving faint energy burns wherever they touched.

"It's been activated!" one of the warriors screamed.

"Then we must act quickly," the lead warrior responded calmly. "Take the Kahshinki back to transport-three for evacuation, so that as we give our existence, we will do so knowing that their honor will be taken as they cower in Spectacle." Dropping onto her knees, the lead warrior began to examine the cradle the device was resting on.

"Empty transport-two of everyone with the exception of the pilot," the Lead Warrior commanded, rising to her feet. "We will move the device in groups of two. Have the groups stay behind cover until the assigned group ceases. We have less than ten bits. Execute!"

Stepping back from the device, she made an adjustment to her weapon before pointing it at the cradle under the device. Firing a concentrated pencil-sized pulse at the cradle, she cut a slot into the thick stanchion about a quarter of the way through it. Three more pulses and the device leaned over and fell slowly to the floor in the low gravity, the orbs arcing and crackling. Throwing her weapon to the floor the lead warrior turned and watched with satisfaction as the Kahshinki, their heads bagged and tentacles trussed together were dragged from the room. When two warriors moved in to pick up the device, the lead warrior stepped between them.

"You!" she said singling out the warrior in front, a youngster that had only recently been admitted to the warrior ranks. "Stay back a safe distance, destroy our weapons and equipment. Leave nothing for the beasts."

"Roche Hah!" The young warrior grunted deeply, making an awkward single clawed salute in the heavy armor.

Ignoring the energy beams that were rotating more quickly and growing in intensity, the warriors lifted the device and carried it from the room as quickly as their armored suits permitted. Outside the room where gravity was no longer modified, the weight of the device became a significantly greater burden, and their progress slowed. Their armor suits providing augmented strength made their movements look mechanical and robotic as they plodded down the corridor toward the foyer.

For the next team of warriors waiting to assist, the effects of the device became apparent as the first team slowed to a shuffle before stumbling into a wall and falling to the ground as the disassociation of the water molecules in their bodies began causing massive cellular break down of their organs and tissues.

The intensity of the reaction continued to increase. The orbs began sending arcs of static electricity intermingled with the energy beams as the second team stepped over the bodies of the first, and carried the device into the foyer. Traveling no more than fifteen paces, the second team succumbed to the growing effects, collapsing and dropping the device. Realizing the futility of attempting to carry the device by hand, the third team disconnected the mobile cannon from its platform and then loaded the device onto it before they too collapsed. Although significantly easier to move, the proximity required to operate the platform brought the warriors into the intensely lethal field of the device. The length of time, from approach to death was now approximately thirty seconds and growing shorter with each second as the device continued to gather energy. By the time it had been relayed onto the loading platform in the crater, eighteen of the twenty warriors of the retrieval team lay dead or dying along the evacuation path.

Clouds began forming and dissipating in the atmosphere around the device. Flashes of energy resembling lightning sparked between the clouds and the device, sending thunderous sonic booms rolling across the desert. Roiling out of the crater like smoke from a witches brew, the clouds enveloped the teams of warriors around its perimeter.

From behind the protective enclosure on the armored platform, one of the last warriors from the retrieval team initiated the controls that caused the platform to float straight up out of the crater and into the open underbelly of the designated transport hovering above it. The shielding protected the platform operator only long enough for her to initiate the controls for lifting, as it lifted away toward the waiting transport, she tumbled lifeless onto the floor of the crater. Without anyone to slow or stop the rapid ascent into the transport, the loaded platform crashed into the interior roof. Damaged from the impact, the platform and device would have dropped back into the crater if the pilot had not closed the opening in the bottom of the transport at the moment of impact.

The molecular disintegrator was now moments away from a sustained chain reaction that would begin to ignite the planet's complex hydrocarbons and cause an atmospheric burn that would last until all organic material on the surface of the planet was reduced to its basic atomic composition. The pilot had no time for mistakes, no time to question the order she had been given. If she failed, this planet would die ... as hers had. Like many of the warriors that petitioned to participate in the retrieval, she was many cycles beyond her utility. Had it not been for the Kahshinki attack, she would have been reclamated eleven cycles ago at forty and replaced by a younger and more capable unit. Having monitored the progress of her warrior sisters, the pilot beamed with pride at the honor they had demonstrated, and was prepared, if not eager, to join them in the nothingness that marked the end of existence.

At the instant the transport lurched with the arrival of the device, the pilot initiated the automated program that sealed the hold and activated the engines. Closing her eyes and clearing her mind, she leaned her head back, opened her hands in a respectful palm display to the Gods as she embraced the end of her existence. Without the shielding provided by the protective armor worn by warriors, the pilot died within seconds.

Its gravitational drive set to attract the sun and repel the earth, the transport hurtled skyward without a sound, disappearing into the deep blue desert sky in an instant. Achieving maximum velocity within a few seconds, the transport jumped to light speed before detonating in a spectacular flash that doubled the Earth's daytime illumination for a fraction of a second.

In keeping with Korlah military doctrine, the damaged and ceased warriors were left where they fell. With the same efficiency that they demonstrated during deployment, the surviving warriors packed up their gear and climbed into the waiting transports. Rocketing vertically skyward about 50,000 feet, the transports followed the heavy fighters through a cordon cleared of mettlesome projectile weapons by the light fighters. Resuming the triangular formation in which they had arrived, the Korlah vessels jumped to light speed and vanished from the Earth's satellite surveillance network.

7 - Truce

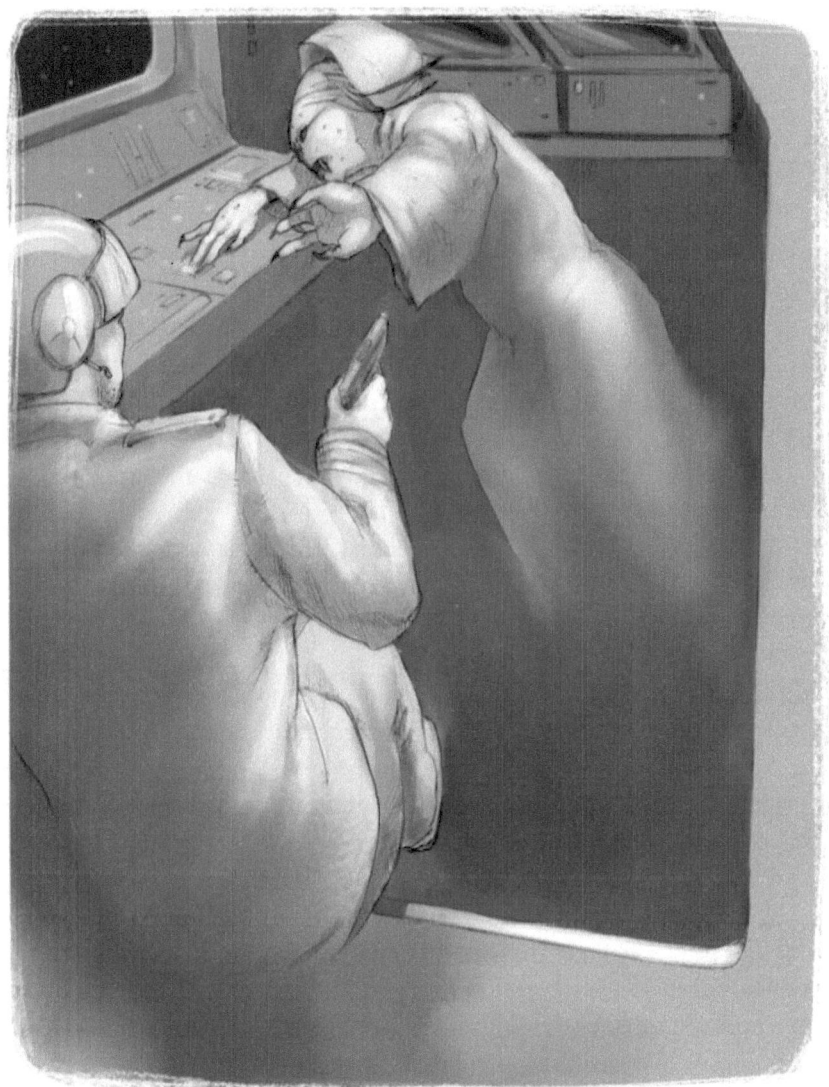

The door to the small storage room that was serving as Captain Ramsey's cell opened without a sound. The silence of the room was immediately inundated with the sounds of talking and the rustle of heavy armor. Looking up from his seat in the corner, Jason found two warriors standing on either side of the door. As he rose to his feet, one of the warriors motioned with a slow swiping motion of her clawed hand for him to come out. Following the wordless instructions, he exited the room.

A soft voice, clear with purposeful enunciation, brought Captain Ramsey's gaze to the side of the entrance where he found Beth standing with her arms crossed firmly at her chest. Her head tilted slightly down and her pale blue eyes peered out from the shadow of her brow. Her blank emotionless face presented an eerie specter in the green glow of the lamp overhead.

"We're going home. If that means over your dead body, I will arrange it. Am I making myself clear?" Beth asked as she uncrossed her arms, anticipating a response that might require their use.

Stopping, Captain Ramsey glared back for a moment before rolling his eyes.

"Good God woman, give it a rest," he drawled, shaking his head slowly before turning and following the guards to the forward end of the transport.

Seeing Captain Ramsey approach with the guards, Teela stood for a moment, and then sat back down, her anxiety apparent in the way one hand nervously massaged the other.

"Captain, we will soon be within communication range of vessels that I believe are manned by your fellow pilots. I want this contact to be peaceful. Will you help us?" she asked.

"Said I would and will, but you're wasting your time. This is what they've been training to do. They won't talk and they won't listen. They'll follow their orders, and I guarantee that they have been ordered to attack and destroy any contacts that can't provide the current encrypted pass code," Captain Ramsey replied, stopping a few feet from Teela's command chair.

Teela slid to the edge of the seat as though she could not decide if she should stand or sit. Looking into Captain Ramsey's face, she looked beyond the eyes both familiar and alien and into the emotions that swirled within his mind.

"I believe you, Captain, but you must try. If you don't I will be forced to kill them," she responded softly, sensing no malice in the Captain's thoughts.

The speaker near the pilot hissed and crackled as a voice bellowed out. The communications technician nearly jumped out of her seat to adjust the volume on the unfamiliar equipment.

"Rambo, Zippy here, got two contacts: stationary, bearing forty seven, mark two two zero."

"Hammer, Skidmark fall back and cover our rear. Zip, you found them, lead us in."

"Thanks, Colonel. Alpha group, take the cargo, Bravo the fighter. On my mark, break and commence attack run."

"Colonel? When? How did that fat little fuck make Colonel?" Captain Ramsey exclaimed. "How do I talk to these guys?" he asked jabbing a finger at the speaker.

"This is the microphone," Teela answered. "Touch the indentation here when you wish to be heard."

Surprised by Captain Ramsey's eagerness to participate, Teela slid back in the command chair and flexed her hands over the ends of the armrests in an effort to relax and counter the intense urge to clench her hands into tight fists. Although she had rehearsed this moment over and over in her mind, and believed that she was thoroughly prepared, she found that she was feeling wholly inadequate. Hoping for a miracle, yet expecting the worst, she notified the guards to be prepared in case Captain Ramsey had to be subdued.

While Teela was speaking with the guards, Captain Ramsey pressed the indentation and spoke into the microphone using a deep husky voice.

"Hey Ram-bone, who'd you blow to make Colonel?"

After a long pause, with no response, Captain Ramsey spoke again, this time using his normal voice.

"Hey fellas, this is Captain 'Hollywood' Ramsey making his first on screen appearance after a long and unapproved leave of absence. Really Ramos, when the hell did you make Colonel?"

After a long pause. Ramsey leaned forward and was about to speak when the speaker crackled to life.

"I made Colonel eight months ago. That was a year after Captain Ramsey and all members of the patrol he was with disappeared. If you are who you say, then you know what I'm going to do next."

"Your Eminence, they are switching to another encrypted frequency," the communications technician announced.

The speaker remained silent, emitting only a slight hiss with an occasional crackle of static.

"Attack enemy. Destroy all enemy. Attack enemy. Destroy all enemy," a computer generated voice announced over the speaker in English.

"They are receiving communications on the Kahshinki translator, Your Eminence," the communications technician explained.

"Can they still hear me?" Ramsey snapped.

Teela conferred with the communications technician for a moment before responding.

"They are now using encrypted code bursts for ship-to-ship communications. My technician informs me that the audible communications you make should still be available to them," Teela answered.

Ramsey jammed his thumb down onto the indentation by the speaker and began shouting.

"Don't be stupid Ramos, we need to talk. The technology the toads gave us is obsolete. Your armor and weapons are inferior. One freighter like the one I'm in destroyed half of our patrol, and that was with a civilian that had never flown anything, sitting at a panel built for a toad. These two vessels have the firepower and armor to chew you up and spit you out. Have the balls to take a minute and listen to what I have to say."

Ramsey lifted his thumb and straightened up, staring into the stars outside the screen before him straining to see the craft he knew were closing on attack vectors.

"Do they hear me?" he asked.

The view screen before them began to fill with fighter craft as they blinked into view slowly spread out around them.

"It would appear as though they have. Keep talking," Teela said calmly, her demeanor masking the anxiety that threatened to choke her voice.

"The toads are eating people. That's right, 'The Story' is true. Only what you don't know is that the enemy they said is coming to get us is really after them, not us. Don't fuck this up Rambo, there are American citizens here with me ... women. The spaghetti heads we've seen are like the cloned humans we call Twins. The toads used them to build a slave army and then used that army to conquer their planet. Sound familiar? Unfortunately for the toads, the spaghetti heads got loose and have been chasing them across the galaxy with the intention of rubbing 'em out. They're called Korlah and they tell me they want to negotiate an alliance. This is a mission of peace and everyone listening is a witness to that." Ramsey paused and swallowed, staring out the viewing window.

"Rambo, this is Hammer, we got multiples coming up fast on our six. I'm counting four five-packs. Looks like the toads don't trust us to do their dirty work," The speaker crackled.

"Well, Ramsey," Colonel Ramos interjected, "I guess our little talk will have to wait until after your new friends demonstrate their military superiority against the toad's patrol manned, or I should say piloted, solely by the Twins. From the message the toads have been sending, and the limited English they understand, I don't think they intend to do much talking." His voice reflected relief that he would not have to test Ramsey's claim that the Korlah possessed superior weapons and armor.

"All right boys! Pull back and let the girls show us what they got," Colonel Ramos directed as he began backing his fighter away from the two Korlah vessels. When several of the other human fighters did not begin withdrawing in formation, Colonel Ramos spoke again.

"Gentlemen, this is not our fight. Do not interfere with the visitor's activities. Let's go! Keep it tight," Ramos demanded.

"They're wondering how they will sleep after this, Ramos," Captain Ramsey cried into the microphone. "Unlike you, you gutless little fuck, they know what they should be doing, and it's not what you're ordering them to do."

"Hey Hollywood, this is Hammer, what's my little sister's nickname?"

"Peggy Sue. As in, 'Pilots don't screw with your Peggy Sue.' Had any luck keeping her away from the fly-boys?" Ramsey replied, grabbing at the opportunity for an ally.

"Hollywood, my man! I'd like to say I missed you, but I can only handle one backstabbing career-focused prick at a time."

"Ouch!" Ramsey replied. "When the best fighter jock I've ever known is ordered to cover Ramos's ass, I'd have to say that your career has not exactly been blossoming."

Five of the human fighters sat motionless as the fifteen led by Colonel Ramos disappeared from sight.

"Captain Simpson! I am ordering you and the others to rejoin the wing immediately or I'll have you up for treason," Ramos screamed, his shrill voice testing the limits of the speaker.

"I never liked you, Ramsey, but I also never saw you make a bad decision. Can't say the same for Ramos. In about a minute the Twins are gonna open a can o' whoop ass on you. I'm giving you ten seconds to convince me I'm doing the right thing," Captain Ernest 'Hammer-Time' Simpson replied.

"Nice gesture, Hammer, but do as Ramos says. The bucket of shit your flying is a death trap, now get the hell outta here!"

"These aren't the rookies you remember, Hollywood. They've been training on their own for over a year now, and the sleds they're flying can crank turns that would mash us into jam. Communications with the toads has nearly ceased; it's like a friggin' cold war stand-off, nobody's talking. We've been trying to improve our weaponry and boost our numbers out here, but the toads ..."

The weapons console illuminated with multiple threats at the same instant as Hammer's fighter and the four other human-manned fighters with it lost all power. Responding with practiced precision, the pilot of Teela's freighter and Dooaugh accelerated their vessels from stationary positions to maximum gravitational drive speeds, while making multiple course changes in an effort to break the numerous weapon tracks that indicated the approaching craft were attempting to lock their weapons targeting systems on them. At the same time, the weapons technician was unsuccessfully attempting to obtain a weapons lock on one of the offending craft that was now pursuing them. A buffeting rattle and thump that sent Ramsey tumbling to the ground informed Teela that they had just taken a hit.

"Return fire!" Teela ordered.

"I can't get a weapons lock, Your Eminence," the weapons technician responded, embarrassed that she had been attempting unsuccessfully to do just that.

Another impact sent Captain Ramsey, who was trying to stand up, tumbling head first into Teela's lap. The gravitational effect of the seat intended to hold Teela firmly in place during battle maneuvers now held him securely between her legs with the side of his face pressed painfully against the buckle of her belt.

"Power cells exceeding maximum capacity!" shouted the weapons technician.

"Fire your weapons! Don't wait for a lock. Fire!" Teela grunted, trying to shove Captain Ramsey off her lap. Just as he managed to raise himself up, the next weapons impact sent him back down, this time sitting sideways on Teela's lap.

Dooaugh was surprised to find the enemy craft so agile and evasive. Without either a weapons or communications technician, Dooaugh was manipulating the weapons firing system utilizing the key on the new control stick, which had been installed as part of Challmara's modifications. Listening to the thoughts of her pursuers, Dooaugh anticipated their actions and dodged their weapons fire at the instant they directed it at her. With four fighters that were both faster and more agile pursuing her, it was all she could do to evade their thrusting spikes of concentrated energy.

"The assault pods are under attack by Kahshinki fighters," Teela's communications technician announced.

"Challmara is directing us to evacuate this sector before she initiates a defensive pulse."

"Instruct Director Challmara we are unable to comply and that ...," Teela began. Another impact shook the transport, followed by a pressure wave that crushed the air from her lungs. A brilliant flash of light emanated from the walls, floors, and ceiling of the transport causing the occupants to reflexively blink as electrical charges began arcing throughout the vessel and coursing through their bodies. Had her lungs not been devoid of air, Teela would have screamed from the painful muscle contractions the static electrical shocks were causing. As blackness choked her vision into a thin tunnel, she fought desperately to draw air into her aching lungs, refusing to release her grasp on consciousness.

As quickly as the paralyzing force had struck, the pressure dissipated, releasing its crushing hold on the occupants of the transport. Sucking air into her burning lungs in rapid gasps, Teela attempted to stand, her feet flailing without touching the floor. Reaching to touch the arm rests of her chair, she realized that she was drifting weightless a few feet above it. The sound of gasping and coughing informed her that the others were recovering as she was. She could see the thermal outline of the pilot who had wedged herself between the seat and her panel and was busily attempting to work the now inoperative controls at her station.

"What … is our … status?" Teela rasped between gasps as she pushed off the ceiling and sailed down behind the pilot's chair and grabbed hold of it to keep from rebounding off the floor.

"We have no power, nothing. I believe the power cells overloaded and discharged through the shield absorption array, completely discharged. I cannot detect even a residual charge, nothing. I should have taken it off-line. I am sorry, Your Eminence," the pilot answered, her exasperation evident in her furtive attempt at a palm display.

Remain calm, demonstrate confidence and maintain order, the inner voice said. With the words came knowledge and experience Teela could draw from.

"Pilot, it is not your fault. They will come for us when they can. Until they do, we can take this time to get to know each other. What is your name? Do you go by your sabat, or have you been given a clan name?" she asked.

"I am known by my sabat. Teaugh … Teaugh 20.10638."

"Ah, we have the same pre-name and are birth sisters. Not many from our birthing shift survived," Teela responded, recognizing that their birth number differed by little more than five hundred almost guaranteeing that they were born within a few shifts of each other.

"One hundred and three."

"What?" Teela asked, not understanding the significance of the number.

"There were 97,486 viable units produced during our birthing cycle. One hundred and three survived the attack. I don't know how many still exist, but I know we are fewer than we were," Teaugh replied, an edge of hostility creeping into her otherwise emotionless voice.

It never crossed Teela's mind to investigate how many of her birth sisters had survived the attack. She had always been so engrossed in her own existence she never considered those who lost theirs. The pangs of guilt these thoughts provoked were interrupted by a brilliant flash of light that illuminated the interior of the vessel through the viewing window.

"Plasma pulse! A particle wave will follow. Get down!" Teaugh shouted, using the lip of the control console for leverage to duck down below the viewing screen.

A bright blue ball appeared in the corner of the viewing window growing rapidly larger until it filled the screen. Grabbing Captain Ramsey by the pant leg, Teela pulled him down from where he was drifting motionless in the middle of the room. With one arm around his back and the other holding his head to her chest, Teela turned away from the screen just as a searing flash of particle energy swept over them. Traveling at sub-light speeds, billions of atomic particles per square inch struck the transport. Buffeted by the impact, the craft lurched violently, sending those occupants not secured hurling painfully against the interior walls. As the sub-atomic particles dissipated their energy into the hull, the subsequent molecular agitation translated into intense heat that radiated through the viewing window and into the exposed areas of the interior.

Teela shook her head in an attempt to alleviate the burning she felt on the crown tendrils at the back of her head. The communications technician was much less fortunate. Pressed against the viewing screen by the impact, the side of her face and one hand was instantly seared by the flash. As she regained consciousness she cried out pitifully at first, stifling the cries to a soft whimper as she regained her composure and sought to retain her honor.

Once the pulse dissipated, Teela searched the expanse of stars beyond the window, her thoughts on Challmara and Dooaugh. The heat produced by the plasma wave quickly cooled, and the chill on her face and the condensation of her breath reminded her that without power their ship would soon become a freezer.

"Shawlmon, the enemy fighters have been destroyed. The assault pods are undamaged," Dooaugh reported, the telepathic message received by Teela as clearly as if it had been spoken. *"Check your weapons pulse suppression cell. The energy wave has partially recharged mine."*

"Thank you. Thank you, my friend," Teela responded, speaking both verbally and mentally to Dooaugh.

"I'm not sure what I did. But you're welcome, I guess," Captain Ramsey said, lifting his head from Teela's chest.

Teaugh discovered the recharged power cell and immediately restored life support. When life support returned, so did gravity. Captain Ramsey landed on top of Teela as the two of them dropped to the floor. Rising up on his arms, he resisted Teela's immediate effort to throw him off, holding her arms firmly at her sides and smiling slyly not understanding why he was suddenly feeling so profoundly aroused. Before he could give it much consideration, he was roughly jerked up and off of her by two Korlah guards who slammed him forcefully into a nearby bulkhead.

"Hey now girls, take it easy," Captain Ramsey said.

"I am unharmed. Release him," Teela ordered.

Embarrassed and feeling oddly ashamed for his unusual reaction, Captain Ramsey returned to his post by the speaker, while maintaining a respectful distance from Teela's command chair.

"Whoa! I don't know what came over me," he said avoiding eye contact. "I was just a little dazed, that's all. What the fuck did they hit us with?" he asked, hoping to change the subject as Beth, Catherine, and Marsha emerged from the rear of the vessel.

Putting her hand up to acknowledge his question, yet inform him that she would not answer him at this time, Teela spoke to the Korlah crew instead.

"What is our status?" she asked, buttoning her vest while gingerly shaking her still stinging crown tendrils.

"We have power back, propulsion is functional. Shield system is damaged but not inoperative," Teaugh reported.

"Weapons systems charged and ready, Your Eminence." the weapons technician reported.

"Communications out, damaged. I will attempt repair," the communications technician reported, her voice strained and shaky from the pain of her burns.

Teela could see that the eye on the burned side of her face had already swollen shut and that she was unable to use her burned hand.

"The equipment repairs can wait. Have one of the warriors inspect the damage to your face and hand. Once field repairs have been made, you may attend to your equipment," Teela ordered.

Returning to her seat, Teela stared into the star filled screen ignoring the muttering voices of the minds around her as she listened for thoughts in the distance. Faint at first, feelings of fear and desperation preceded the words, angry words mixed with pleas for pity and forgiveness. Some of the words were clear, directed outward with the intent of being heard. Teela realized that she was hearing the thoughts of the human pilots trapped in their damaged and inoperative craft. More than just thoughts, she was listening to the prayers of men who believed with certainty that they were about to die. Flushing with embarrassment, she closed her mind to the private words and opened her eyes, ashamed for violating the sanctity of their final moments.

We would not hear their prayers if the Gods did not wish it to be so. By answering their prayers will we not be serving the wishes of our Gods? Dooaugh asked, reminding Teela that her own thoughts were no longer private.

Dooaugh's words made Teela feel even more uncomfortable.

There are no Gods, there is only us! Teela snapped, regretting the thought the instant it slipped into her conscious mind.

Through the long pause that followed, she strained to block Dooaugh's mind from seeing the conflicted thoughts racing through her own.

How can we answer their prayers? Teela finally asked.

We can save many if not all that have retained their existence. Tell your pilot what you wish, together you will know what to do. Collect the humans here, I will proceed to those in the distance and begin collecting them until you come. Roche Hah, Shawlmon, Dooaugh said, her words imparted with feelings of comfort and reassurance as the heavy fighter she was piloting raced out of view.

"Teaugh, proceed to and retrieve the nearest surviving human pilot," Teela commanded, not knowing how Teaugh would accomplish her task.

"What? How will I find it?" Teaugh stammered, surprised by Teela's request.

Considering the pilot's question, Teela rose from the command chair and moved alongside the pilot placing one hand on the back of her seat as she stared blankly ahead, her mind listening for the voices. Focusing on the nearest voice, she pointed down and to the right side of the view screen.

"That way," Teela commanded. The pilot deftly turned the craft and darted forward.

"Slow! He's close," Teela said.

The pilot slowed the craft as directed. Debris appeared in the distance.

"There. There he is," Teela said, pointing at the human pilot still strapped to the seat that had safely jettisoned him from his disintegrating craft.

The pilot continued her approach appearing as though she was going to impact the human that was now twisting in his seat to observe the approaching craft. At the last moment, Teaugh turned the vessel so that the bottom of the Korlah craft faced the human pilot. The floor behind Teela's seat rippled like liquid as the human pilot, still strapped in his seat, emerged through the floor as though floating up from a black viscous pool.

"Hammer!" Captain Ramsey shouted, cautiously approaching the chair once the floor appeared to firm back up. Kneeling alongside the ejection seat, he commenced removing the straps and disconnecting the hoses that the human pilot was struggling with. Releasing the pressure ring connecting the helmet to the pilot's suit, Ramsey helped him remove the cumbersome helmet.

Dooaugh circled the cluster of drifting fighters. Unlike the polymorphic metal that encased the frames of the Korlah vessels, these ships had thin plating that was now deformed and had ruptured from the impact of the particle wave. From what she could see, Dooaugh believed that Challmara's assessment of the fragility of their construction to be extremely conservative. A single high-energy diffused pulse from a heavy fighter like the one she was piloting would have had equal if not more catastrophic effect. Selecting the most severely damaged fighter first, Dooaugh piloted her craft over the dome of the smaller vessel. The floor in the cabin behind Dooaugh rippled like liquid as the dome of the damaged fighter emerged. With a grinding sound, the upward movement of the dome came to a stop as it contacted the immovable structure contained within the polymorphic skin of the Korlah craft. A few inches of the human fighter craft's viewing window emerged through the liquid floor. Although dimly illuminated within, Dooaugh could see the human pilot, and clearly hear the words of fear emanating from its mind.

"*I am here to help*," Dooaugh said projecting her thoughts to the pilot. "*We have little time before your sisters begin to cease their existence. You need to hurry. Exit your vessel, do not be frightened.*"

With a click and hiss of escaping pressure from within, a large rectangular portion of the dome popped up a few inches before sliding off the side with a thump. The pilot climbed out through the opening, and as he did, he pointed his arm at Dooaugh. An object in the human's hand, too small to be pulse weapon, shimmered in the dim light. Tilting her head and listening to the chaotic thoughts of the human, she sought to determine its intentions.

Dooaugh sensed that the human believed an enemy was capturing it, and the object in its hand was a weapon it intended to use to cease her existence.

"Do you wish to save your sisters, or continue to battle those who have come to be your allies?" Dooaugh quickly imparted, concerned now that this human, unlike the religious one, did not understand the words of her mind.

Anger mixed with excitement filled the human's mind once he established that Dooaugh had no weapon, and that there were no others onboard. He was angry that Dooaugh could speak with her mind, angry that the others he was with were being referred to as his sisters, and angry that his vessel had been damaged. But he was also excited, believing he had captured Dooaugh and her vessel. Dooaugh could sense no concern for the others of its group, this human was certain it would attain great honor for capturing and returning this vessel. Looking past Dooaugh, the human studied the controls, and in an instant, he made his decision. He would take the captured vessel and leave the others to die. Aiming for the center of Dooaugh's face the human pulled the trigger of his weapon.

Jerking her head to the side an instant before the weapon discharged, Dooaugh spun around to face her console. The projectile grazed the side of her head ricocheting off the screen and the console beneath it. The weapon barked a second time as Dooaugh actuated the controls that liquefied the floor causing the vessel it held to lurch downward with a grinding sound. The weapon discharged a third time as Dooaugh pressed the key that separated the two vessels. With a wet slapping sound, the floor sealed, moving inward and outward a few times before returning to a solid surface.

Teela lurched forward letting out a shriek of pain, feeling as though an invisible fist had slugged her in the shoulder. Falling from the command chair, she knelt on the floor clutching her right arm. Her eyes clenched tightly shut from the burning pain that immobilized her. She could feel blood pulsing from between the fingers of the hand she had clenched there. When she opened her eyes, she found herself sprawled across the pilot's panel and through the blood spattered window she saw a human pilot drifting away in space, writhing fervently at first, and then more slowly as the oxygen venting from the hose on its helmet dissipated in a swirling mist of ice crystals around him.

"Shawlmon! A projectile weapon. I am damaged, losing utility," Dooaugh's words rang in Teela's mind as the image she was seeing faded.

"Teela! Teela! What's wrong? Are you hurt?" Ruth shouted.

Teela found herself on all fours, staring at the floor. Sucking in a gasp of air, she sat up and examined her still aching shoulder. The details of what happened to Dooaugh flashed into her mind. Jumping to her feet, she drew her swords, the blades crackling with energy as she activated their pulse weapon capability. Ruth backed away as Teela leveled the tips of the swords at the human pilots who were assisting the last of the five out of his seat.

"Put your hands where I can see them," Teela screamed.

Freezing when Teela, followed by the two guards, directed their energized weapons at them, the pilots looked to Ramsey for direction.

"What the fuck is this?" Ramsey asked nervously.

"My friend, one of my pilots has been shot by one of the humans, one of your companions she was rescuing!" Teela screamed, her shoulder aching painfully.

"We don't carry guns. Do you see any guns? Did I have a gun when I was captured? No, I didn't. Throttle back before someone gets hurt," Ramsey said, talking slowly and evenly as he raised his hands.

"Colonel Ramos packs a .45, wears it in a shoulder holster attached to his pressure suit," Hammer whispered to Ramsey.

"Search us, tie us up. I don't care. But you gotta hurry and get the rest of my guys. They're freezing to death," Captain Ramsey said, looking down at the pilot they had just pulled aboard, still supported by the others, his blue lips and chattering teeth testimony of the validity of his statement.

"I want them strip-searched. Then pack them in the storage room. Ramsey, too," Teela hissed in English.

"Oh yes, oh my, yes. It would be my pleasure Capt'n," Beth purred with a pirate's accent, giving Teela a salute and handing her pulse rifle to Ruth before marching over to the nearest pilot.

"A word of advice, Gentlemen. Do whatever this ... lady asks. Don't fuck with her," Ramsey offered, recalling his painful experience at Beth's hands.

With Ruth, Marsha, Catherine and the two Korlah guards providing cover, Beth performed a thorough search of the human pilots. As she completed searching each one, she locked them all in the small storage room.

Confident that Beth and the others had matters in hand, Teela directed the pilot to proceed to Dooaugh's location. Searching the expanse of stars for Dooaugh's thoughts, Teela was unable to locate them. If it were not for the dull ache of empathic pain that persisted, she would have thought Dooaugh had ceased. Using the pain like a beacon she followed it. Arriving at the location, they found the Korlah fighter sitting motionless among the disabled human Fighters. Without direction from Teela, the pilot inverted and maneuvered her craft under the heavy fighter where the polymorphic metal on their undersides joined upon contact.

On Teela's command, the pilot opened a portal between the two vessels. With its charged pulse rifle at the ready, one of the warriors dove through the opening head first in a practiced maneuver that landed her on her feet inside Dooaugh's fighter. Once verified secure, Teela crawled awkwardly through the opening, her inexperience in dealing with reversed gravity fields evident.

Dooaugh lay sprawled across the pilot's control console, a pool of blood around her head and shoulder with a thin rivulet running down the skirt of the console and dripping into a large pool forming on the floor. Teela could see the entry wound just to the right of her spine. The fabric showed little blood with a small hole no more than a half inch across. The blood on the console, Teela reasoned, was coming from the exit wound. With the warrior's assistance, she lifted Dooaugh from the console and lowered her onto the floor. Kneeling over Dooaugh, Teela opened the front of the blood soaked cloak to locate the source of the profuse bleeding. Blanching with horrified shock, Teela stared into the gaping fist-sized exit wound. Sharp fragments of shattered collarbone jutted out from the sides of a ragged crater rimmed with shreds of torn flesh and skin. Feeling faint, Teela leaned back, her head rolling around to one side as her neck muscles refused to respond. With only a vague recollection of being lifted and moved, Teela regained her composure to find the warrior crouched over Dooaugh poking an object that resembled a small flashlight into the wound.

"What are you doing?" Teela cried.

The warrior stopped long enough to give Teela an annoyed look before continuing.

"This unit is badly damaged, and may not be repairable. I am stopping the loss of fluid to delay its cessation. Would you prefer that I dispose of the damaged unit instead?" the warrior asked without emotion.

"We have incoming, Teela," Beth called out as she jumped through the portal, imitating the warrior with moderate success. Clambering to her feet after tumbling into the fighter, Beth ran to the weapons console.

"Look! Ruth says these are incoming craft," Beth cried, pointing to the objects moving down the weapons console screen.

Teela reached across to the communications console and manipulated the keyboard with one hand. Korlah glyphs immediately began scrolling down the screen. Pressing one of her thumbs into the indentation for the microphone, she spoke.

"Lahsoon, this is Teela. Do you hear me?"

"Yes, Your Eminence. Challmara has directed me to come to your assistance," the speaker crackled.

"What is the status of the base?" Teela asked, fearful of what Lahsoon's response might be.

"The Kahshinki side of the base is secure. Minimal losses, however, we have suffered extensive equipment damage," Lahsoon responded.

"What of the humans?" Teela asked.

"Moderate weapons fire was directed against our vessels. A ground assault by approximately twenty human units was repelled without damage to our ground forces. It was reported that the attacking human force was completely destroyed. The humans have not launched any fighters other than the ones you encountered."

Rubbing her face in an effort to dispel the anxiety caused by the rising body count, Teela was unaware that she had smeared her face with Dooaugh's blood. Closing her eyes, she located the pilot of the transport's mind.

Pilot, the approaching craft are Korlah. I will have them finish collecting the human pilots. Follow me to the base, Teela ordered, speaking to the pilot telepathically.

A wet slapping sound announced the closure of the portal as Teela rapidly restored propulsion before taking the stick and pulling the heavy fighter away from the transport. Making a circumferential pass around the damaged fighters, she probed the craft with her mind. Most of the craft were now silent, only a few incoherent voices remained.

"Lahsoon, please assist with the collection of the human pilots from these damaged fighters. Exercise caution, as they may possess projectile weapons. Collect them whether they have ceased or not," Teela said, speaking into the microphone.

"Yes, Your Eminence," Lahsoon responded after a momentary pause.

Teela could sense Lahsoon's confusion from the strange request, but along with it, she felt a deep sense of loyalty. She was certain Lahsoon was someone she could trust to obey without question.

Thrusting first with the gravitational drive before jumping to light speed, Teela manipulated the controls of both the propulsion system and the navigational control system to direct the craft toward the Kahshinki base. Not until after she had reduced speed and was skillfully piloting the cumbersome craft though a dense cluster of asteroids did it dawn on her that she had never piloted a fighter. Glancing around the ship, she challenged her memory. She knew exactly what each indication meant, and how and when she would operate each of the controls for maximum efficiency and performance. Her memories were more than knowledge, they were memories of previous experiences she suddenly realized came from her contact with Dooaugh's mind. Distracted momentarily, she had to turn sharply to avoid hitting a bus-sized boulder tumbling much faster than the surrounding asteroids.

"Shit! That one was close," Beth exclaimed from her seat at the weapons console.

"Sorry. This is the first time, well, second time I've flown one of these things," Teela replied nonchalantly giving Beth a quick wink and a fanged Korlah smile.

The base was located on an asteroid which was enormous in comparison to those around it. As the rocky surface filled the screen, the size of the massive planetoid created an optical illusion making it appear as though impact was imminent. With her eyes scrunched down to slits, Beth placed her hands on the edge of the weapons console as though bracing for impact.

"Jesus, you're coming in fast!" Beth groaned.

Teela watched the distance read-out diminish to the appropriate value and then pulled back on the control stick to level the craft out a few hundred feet above the surface. At the perimeter of the base, she brought the vessel to a complete stop, leaned over to the communications panel, and answered the challenge to their arrival. Receiving approval to proceed, she piloted the fighter into the hangar entrance with the transport following closely behind. Moving through the battle-damaged hangar, Teela maneuvered the large craft into one of the bays designed for the much smaller Kahshinki fighters. With only a few inches clearance to spare, she glided in and hovered while the bay slid downward, scaling the outer hangar side before the inner hangar side opened. Cruising out into the inner hangar, Teela positioned the fighter over a gravity pad before opening the access portal and securing the propulsion systems.

"What now Capt'n?" Beth asked, cracking her knuckles loudly while stretching to relieve the tension from the white-knuckle landing.

"Good question. My plans are fucked! We killed people, American military probably. How am I going to convince them to trust me now?" Teela replied.

"Trust? Fuck trust. They never would have trusted you, and you sure as hell better not trust them. Just how naive are you?"

Beth asked with exasperation, continuing to speak before Teela could respond. "Listen, you need to get your head out of your ass fast. This isn't about trust; it's about mutual aid. Without you, they're dead, without them, you're dead. Am I right or what?"

"Yes, I know that. It's just that ... this is getting complicated. It seemed so simple at first. My original plan was so different. Now everything is changing and I can't control what's happening. I don't know what to do next," Teela stammered.

"Who the fuck am I talking to?" Beth shouted. "Where is Dade, he still in there? That cock-sure prick wouldn't be caught dead whining like this. Listen bitch, if you intend to run this show, you're gonna have to grow a pair."

The crackle of an energizing pulse rifle turned Beth's attention away from Teela. Correctly perceiving Beth's tone as threatening, the warrior who had just transferred Dooaugh out through the portal now stood pointing her rifle at Beth. With a gracious nod and silent mental command, Teela had the guard de-energize the weapon and lower it. After a momentary hesitation, the warrior saluted both Teela and then Beth before stepping into the portal and dropping out of the craft. Teela turned back to Beth and put her hands on her hips, lowering her head to match Beth's posture.

"I'm a cycle twenty birthing unit designated as Teela 10127. You're talking to me. Daedalus was an angry man who has helped me bluff my way this far. But he's dead, we're out of bluffs, and I'm all tapped out. Everyone seems to believe I'm something I'm not. And Earth's leaders, I don't know what they're going to believe. I don't need your shit. I need your help. So if you want to call that whining, then fuck you," Teela said calmly.

"Daedalus ... now there's a fucked-up name. If I had a name like that, I'd be angry too. Where is Dade? I see little tidbits of him on occasion. Like the 'fuck you,' now that sounded like him. What do you do, keep him in a little box and let him out once in awhile, or does he just slip out when you lose control?" Beth pressed the questions carefully, trying to match Teela's calm tone.

"It's not like that, at least not now. You need to drop this Beth. Once and for all, you all need to drop it. Dade is dead. When I begin to communicate with the military and governments of Earth, I'll be facing enough xenophobia without you and others telling them I'm a mind-sucking alien."

"But you are a mind-sucking alien. Quit bullshitting me, and tell me why that shouldn't scare me and everyone else on Earth shitless?" Beth demanded.

"Daedalus was invited to leave his failing body and join with me," Teela began, her voice soft and tired. "He didn't understand what was happening at the time, but he accepted and we have become one. This has not worked out well. I thought you understood how hard this has been on me. Our memories are like water and oil; the mixture keeps separating. Cooperation has acted as an emulsifier, but the strain is constant and I … we don't know how much longer we can keep this up and still retain our sanity." Teela turned away and relaxed her posture, signaling her surrender of the confrontation. "I need your help, not your condemnation," she said after a few seconds.

"You want to know how to deal with these assholes?" Beth asked.

"Yeah, that would make my day," Teela replied without turning.

"Carry a big stick."

"What?" Teela asked, turning back to face Beth.

"Political advice from the 26th President of the United States. 'Speak softly and carry a big stick.' You're good at the soft talk; now just back it up with some muscle. These military types respect strength. Although you don't want to threaten them, what you do want to do is make it obvious through attitude and action that you don't have to," Beth replied, relaxing her posture and moving close to Teela in an effort to see the human she was now certain was trapped behind the black alien eyes.

In the dim light of the fighter cockpit, the floor was obscured in dark shadows. Beth could not see what Teela bent over and picked up. Standing up she turned and held the object cradled in her hands for Beth to see. The object was a stainless steel .45

semi-automatic pistol with a barrel bore large enough to stick a finger in. A highly refined machine designed to kill with the touch of a finger; it looked all the more malevolent as the soft green light of the room reflected off its highly polished surfaces.

"That's one mean chunk of steel," Beth said, leaning down to examine the weapon more closely.

"My friend was shot in the back by the human whose life she was trying to save. How can I communicate rationally with people who would do such a thing?" Teela asked, cocking her head at the weapon as though by examination, the object might reveal the answer.

"May I?" Beth asked, reaching for the pistol.

When Teela acknowledged the request with a nod, Beth gingerly lifted the pistol and immediately released the ammunition clip, dropping the rectangular cartridge into the palm of her other hand. Slipping the clip into a pocket, she then pulled back on the slide mechanism and ejected the cartridge that was still in the chamber catching it in mid-air with skill developed through practice. Locking the slide back in the retracted position, she began to examine the weapon more closely while talking to Teela.

"You could have accidentally discharged it. Trigger guard has been removed and the safety modified so that it can be operated while wearing a pressure suit and heavy gloves. It was loaded with star slugs; hollow points with a star shaped hole that causes the bullets to open and flatten out with sharp edges when they hit flesh. A nasty messy ordinance designed for a single purpose: to kill. The paranoid asshole that carried this was scared of something or somebody, or maybe he was just a freaking psychopath. Your friend should never have turned her back on him. Here, it's safe now." Beth offered the dismantled pistol back to Teela.

"Get rid of it," Teela replied with a choked voice recalling the bloody crater in Dooaugh's chest. Stepping over the exit portal, she floated down and out of the fighter leaving Beth standing alone.

Beth released the slide mechanism closing the chamber. She then pressed the loose round back into the clip before sliding the assembly into the grip of the pistol with a snap. Thumbing the safety on, she slipped the pistol into an inside pocket of her Korlah vest and followed Teela out.

8 - Offering

Traveling near the speed of light, it took Shawaugh less than fifteen minutes to travel the 150 million miles to the area of the asteroid belt where the base was situated. It took another fifty minutes to navigate the last 60,000 miles using the gravitational drive. Arriving at the base a few hours after the battle, her group was intercepted by a contingent of Challmara's fighters. Not wishing to suffer the same type of surprise attack as the Kahshinki, Challmara ordered the fighters to assume defensive positions at a distance from the asteroid to extend the limit of the Assault Group's sensors. Shawaugh provided the necessary encrypted pass code and continued. Traveling a few hundred miles per second, her group negotiated the cloud of debris and damaged vessels surrounding the large asteroid.

Using the new control stick, Shawaugh rolled and turned her craft in tight curves and banks enjoying the fluid movement it provided. The sensation was dramatically different from the jerky angular course changes that were typical of the traditional key pad. To the dismay of those following her, Shawaugh purposefully took several turns through tightly packed debris areas to test the responsiveness of the stick. Finding it difficult to follow using the key pad, the craft following her began switching to the stick control. The group soon began to move as a smooth synchronized column through the debris field.

Seeing the troop carriers collecting and transporting the valuable debris back to the base, Shawaugh smiled at the efficiency with which this small battle group was operating. Her tour through the battlefield was more than an exercise of the new controls, she was also checking to see the extent of the Korlah losses. To her amazement, she had not been able to identify the remains of a single Korlah fighter. Reflecting on her earlier distrust of Challmara's battle plan, Shawaugh was certain she would have to re-evaluate the capabilities of this new Director and the weapons modifications that she was promoting.

The din of activity in the inner hangar of the captured Kahshinki base was deafening as Teela emerged from the fighter. Several warriors wearing formidable armored suits scarred by the recent battle stood at key locations covering the entrances leading in and out of the hangar area. Their energized pulse rifles held at the ready indicated that the security of the base was still questionable. The transport containing the humans was busy off-loading Captain Ramsey and his companions under the watchful eyes of a half dozen armored warriors. As one air lock closed, the rumbling and hissing sound from an adjacent air lock announced the arrival of another vessel.

At several locations, Teela could see armored warriors directing groups of human clones stacking bodies, breaking up and removing debris, performing structural repairs utilizing mechanized equipment on gravity-powered platforms, and repairing damage to several fighter craft and transports docked nearby. Dooaugh was put on a gurney, which was placed with a group of other gurneys containing injured warriors requiring repair.

"This unit must be repaired without delay," Teela said to the warrior in charge of the wounded.

"Roche Hah!" the warrior barked, saluting before turning and shouting orders to have Dooaugh moved to the area designated for biorepair.

Turning her attention to matters at hand, Teela marched over to where Captain Ramsey and the other human pilots stood under Korlah guard. Walking between the warriors and humans, Teela studied each of the human pilots in turn before stopping at a stocky black man with sparkling intelligent eyes. This man, she perceived through the thoughts of the others, was the one they believed to be the senior officer; the man they had followed before, and would follow again.

"Captain Simpson?" Teela asked, reading the embroidered patch on the chest of the pilot's flight suit.

"Captain Ernest James Simpson, serial number ..."

"Stop," Teela demanded. "You are not a prisoner. This is not an interrogation, and I don't have time for this bullshit. Until I can open a line of communication with whoever is in charge, people are going to keep dying. I apologize for the armed guards, but your Colonel Ramos has made it clear that you cannot be trusted to act honorably. However, I hope you can be trusted to act intelligently."

"The only thing Ramos and I have in common is that we came from the same planet," Captain Simpson shot back, "and I'm not entirely certain of that. I'll help you communicate in exchange for releasing my men."

Teela shook her head in exasperation. The thoughts of this pilot flowed out in waves of distrust and desperate concern to relay the tactical and technical details of his observations of Korlah vessels and weaponry to his superiors.

"You and all of your men are free to go. Tell your Superior I'll be able to talk for ...," Teela paused looking at the watch on Captain Simpson's wrist. "Does your watch work?" Teela asked.

"Yes," Captain Simpson replied sounding surprised.

"I'll need a watch," Teela explained, struggling with the Korlah etiquette of bartering, and the voice that told her to simply take it.

"Here, it's yours," Captain Simpson said, unclipping the hasp and sliding the thick watch, heavy from the shielding that protected it from the intense magnetic fields, from his wrist.

"Thank You," Teela said, taking the watch and examining it closely.

"It automatically adjusts for time distortion. Set to Eastern Standard Time to coincide with Earth communications, and will remain accurate to within a fraction of a second, even after doing a dozen faster-than-light missions. It also has an alarm function," Captain Simpson explained, showing her the illumination and setting features yet failing to mention the internal tracking device.

Unable to slide the watch over her hand, Teela put it into her pocket and turned to Captain Simpson. She sensed that he believed he had tricked her into accepting the watch. Straining to listen to his mind, Teela sorted through the chaotic thoughts sufficiently to gather that the deception involved a device that would enable them to track her location. Teela offered to shake hands. Hesitating at first, Captain Simpson took her hand and shook it with a firm grasp. Instead of letting go, Teela took his hand into both of hers and looked intently into his face.

Captain Simpson's eyes widened slightly revealing the xenophobic reaction to her proximity. Teela sensed that he was more concerned with appearing afraid, and allowed her to draw him closer.

"Would you buy a car without first test driving it?" Teela asked conspiratorially.

"What? No, I wouldn't," Captain Simpson replied nervously.

"I have been authorized to make an initial offering to the leadership of Earth of 1,000 fighter craft to be used for planetary defense," Teela said, speaking in a way that suggested she was confiding in the Captain.

"The craft you have are powered by components given to you by the Kahshinki, the ones you call toads have rigged the propulsion and weapons systems so that they cannot be used against them. That's why they lost power when the Kahshinki fighters attacked us. The materials used to fabricate the frames and coverings are weak and fragile." Stepping back, Teela retained a firm grasp of Captain Simpson's hand with her left hand. "Let's take a walk," she said, pulling the Captain along with her.

"What do you mean 'initial offering'?" Captain Simpson asked.

"Exactly what it sounds like. If things work out, we would be able to provide many more craft, as well as assist with the construction of your own production facilities." She led Captain Simpson to the fighter Dooaugh had piloted. "This is what we call a heavy fighter; its armor is extremely tough and its weapons exceptionally powerful. Our light fighters, however, are by no means 'light' as the title would imply. What they lack in armor and firepower they make up in speed and agility." Walking to the next docking pad, Teela gestured at the battle-scarred transport hovering over the gravity plate. "You and your men may take this transport to return to your base. You will find it equipped with an inertial suppression system that makes it possible for you to reverse direction, or take ninety-degree turns at any speed. Although seriously damaged, I think you will find it quite superior in comparison to any of your domestic fabrications."

Captain Simpson walked the length of the transport before turning and walking back to the front where he studied the multiple pulse weapon craters burned into the hull, and noted the fractured pulse pod splayed open as though it had exploded from within.

"This is merely a peace offering intended to open a rapport," Teela said, sensing his disdain. "You cannot expect me to turn you loose in our hangar with an armed vessel. At least not until we have negotiated an agreement."

"Let me contact my base, I'm really not authorized to make this kind of decision," Captain Simpson said. Swallowing nervously, he continued his examination of the underside of the craft.

"Examine the interior, use the communications console on board, I'll wait here while you confer with your superior," Teela offered, releasing his hand.

The Captain's brow furrowed with concern, he glanced around at the numerous armored warriors stationed throughout the hangar area.

"This is no trick Captain, I want to return you and your men to your base, and I want to open communications with your superiors as soon as possible. Don't trust me, trust your instincts, they have served you well so far," Teela said, pausing until he looked at her. "We mean you no harm, the offer is genuine."

Nodding his head almost imperceptibly, Captain Simpson stepped onto the gravity pad and floated upward into the opening on the underside of the transport. Teela watched him disappear into the fighter, twisting her hands nervously as she considered the risk she was taking. If the damaged transport were not as technologically superior to the human's fighter craft as she believed, the 'Big Stick' the Korlah possessed would not seem so big after all, and the human leaders may consider attack an option. By making an offer of one thousand fighters, she hoped they would realize that the number of fighters the Korlah possessed would have to be significantly greater in comparison.

The hissing and groaning of multiple hangar airlocks opening announced the arrival of another group of craft. Seeing the heavy fighters, Teela reasoned that this was the group belonging to Lahsoon's patrol. Technicians on hover carts darted under the fighters the moment they squeezed out of the airlocks. She could see limp human bodies being passed to the technicians on the carts even as the fighters continued to traverse the hangar to their docking pads. She counted seven bodies. As quickly as they had arrived, the carts and their Korlah operators raced from the hangar area and into an adjacent tunnel. Alarmed by what she saw, Teela took long strides to the nearest fighter to determine the destination of the carts and their cargo. As she approached, physically debilitated human pilots emerged from the underside of the craft. Staggering as they stepped from the gravitational field, each in turn stumbled to join the others. They formed a tight group, circled by the armored warriors waiting for them on the hangar floor.

"Roche Hah, Shawlmon," the pilot of the fighter called out upon seeing Teela's approach. Standing stiffly at attention, the slightly built pilot presented a double-clawed salute with such force as to nearly knock herself down.

"Roche Hah," Teela replied, returning the salute and bowing slightly implying that the pilot's greeting honored her. "Where have the damaged humans been taken?" she asked trying not to sound overly concerned. When the pilot seemed surprised by her question, Teela considered probing her mind, but resisted, feeling that the effort would contribute to the growing feeling of exhaustion that was beginning to plague her.

"Your Eminence, Lahsoon has ordered their repair and restoration. She ordered it as a priority command on your behalf," the pilot replied, her voice trailing off as she spoke, realizing that Lahsoon had made the order without Teela's knowledge.

"Lahsoon understands my needs; she is an excellent leader who is willing to make bold choices," Teela replied, opening her hands to show acceptance. "Confer my gratitude to Lahsoon and ask her to join me."

The pilot bowed deeply before turning and trotting off toward the adjacent heavy fighter. Turning her attention to the human pilots, Teela tried to ascertain their relative health. Suffering from hypothermia, several huddled together on the floor of the cold hangar while others marched in place and worked their arms in an attempt to restore circulation and body temperature.

Teela took the watch Captain Simpson had given her out of her pocket and noted the time. It read 1330. She wondered if time had any real meaning out here in deep space. Glancing back at the light fighter, she could see Captain Simpson walking toward her followed closely by two armored warriors.

"Were you able to contact your superiors?" Teela asked as soon as he was within earshot.

"Yes, Sir. One moment, Sir," he replied, walking past Teela.

"You guys all right?" he asked the group of pilots.

"S ... Seven ... dead," one of the pilots stammered.

"Yeah I know. I saw them being carted off. Right now we'll worry about the living. Hang on, you'll be taking hot showers in no time," Captain Simpson said before turning to face Teela.

"Sir, General Justin Hargrave of the United States Marine Expeditionary Forces has requested I inform you that he accepts your offer along with the return of his pilots, all his pilots, living and deceased. He would further like to arrange a meeting with you to discuss the unprovoked attack of this base, and the attack of a base on our home world. He is willing to meet with you here at a time of your choosing.

Captain Simpson delivered his message with cold unemotional precision. From the anger flashing in his dark eyes, Teela knew that whatever he had discussed with General Hargrave had convinced him that she was most assuredly his enemy. Teela straightened to her full height and met Captain Simpson's angry glare.

"I was once told that I should believe nothing I hear or read, and only half of what I see with my own eyes. Therefore it must be true that words may be lies and one must look to actions to ascertain the truth." Teela narrowed her eyes, her lips curling up to expose her fangs as she continued.

"Colonel Ramos shot one of my pilots in the back. Now Colonel Ramos is dead. Approximately twenty soldiers from your base attacked my forces. Those soldiers are now dead as well. Neither General Hargrave, nor you, or your pilots represent the people of Earth. At this time, your government is associating with our enemies. If I am unable to convince them to terminate that association, your government, and your government alone, will become our enemy."

"Sir, what shall I tell the General regarding the proposed meeting?"

Teela pulled the watch out and looked at it again. She reasoned that if she gave herself four hours she might have a chance to sleep for an hour or two and restore her diminishing mental strength.

"We can meet at eighteen hundred. Where would the General like to meet?" Teela asked dryly.

Concerned by the sudden change in Captain Simpson's demeanor, Teela opened her mind to his thoughts. A flush of adrenalin-pumped excitement mixed with the sketchy details of a plot falling into place exuded from Captain Simpson's mind like a pungent odor.

"Sir, the General would be willing to meet with you here in your hangar. I can bring him using the transport," Captain Simpson replied, his cool and even voice in sharp contrast to the murmurings of his mind.

Teela blanched, the details of what Captain Simpson and General Hargrave were planning shocked her deeply. The vision of what the detonation of a nuclear device within the base hangar would do filled Captain Simpsons mind. After pausing a moment to regain her composure, she replied.

"That is an extremely generous and trusting offer. But as a demonstration of my sincerity I will come alone and unarmed to meet with your General at his base."

"I'm sorry, Sir, but General Hargrave insists on meeting here."

"Then we will meet in space, where neither of us needs to fear that the other may be using the meeting as a ruse to smuggle a thermonuclear device into the other's base. Detonation of such a device would be a cowardly and shameful act of aggression," Teela hissed, her crown tendrils rising into an angry mane.

Captain Simpson did a remarkable job of controlling his surprise. Teela sensed that he believed that his communications with General Hargrave had not only been monitored, but the complex encryption and code name for the planned action had been compromised. Delivering a thermonuclear device into the toad's hangar had been planned months before as part of a neutralization plan when communications with the toads began to breakdown. The use of the plan at this time would have just been a convenient means of dealing with the current threat.

"Sir, I don't know the basis of your suspicions, but I assure you they are unjustified," Captain Simpson said, stepping back to open the distance between him and Teela's extended claws and bared fangs.

"I will see to the return of your remaining men. When they arrive, leave," Teela growled. "Eighteen hundred hours, above the base. Tell Hargrave I expect him to be on time."

"Yes Sir!" Captain Simpson said loudly, presenting a crisp salute.

Instructing the warriors as to the intended actions and planned departure of the humans, Teela issued orders to have the damaged human pilots delivered to the transport that would be used to return them to their base. Inquiring about the status of the seven human pilots taken to the biorepair facility, Teela determined that six of the seven had been stabilized and were currently having the frost damage to their extremities repaired. One of the humans was reported to be unsalvageable, even for spares. In a move that tugged at her conscience, Teela ordered the pilots delivered to the hangar whether or not their repairs were complete.

"Your Eminence," a brusque voice called, addressing Teela from behind.

"What?" Teela snapped, turning to find an armored warrior standing behind her.

"There is something in the Kahshinki feeding area you should see," the warrior growled from behind the heavy visor.

"What is it?" Teela asked, perturbed by the interruption.

Looking around suspiciously the warrior moved close to Teela, much closer than normal protocol would permit.

"Three Korlah, ceased no more than one or two shifts. From the remains of their uniforms and sabats, it appears that they were from our Campaign Vessel," the warrior whispered.

"What then? The crew of a reconnaissance patrol?"

"No, Your Eminence. The uniforms are from the Strategy Section, the boots of a quality worn only by senior officials … directors and leaders. It looks like a negotiation team."

"Afron! That fool," Teela hissed.

"You think it's Afron?"

"No!" Teela shouted rudely. "I'm sorry," she quickly countered, studying the warrior's name, rank and title markings, noting that she was the Assault Commander of the warrior group that had taken the base. "They are probably emissaries sent by Afron to negotiate a truce or a trade of some kind. What else did you find Commander Litnauh?" Teela asked respectfully.

"The Kahshinki have been feeding here for a long time. There are the remains of Korlah duplicates, human duplicates, human soldiers and many human originals, many more than can be counted. Even in the cold rock chamber where they lie, they generate a heat of their own. Without an atmosphere suit, the odors in the area are unbearable."

"You have done well to bring this to my attention, Commander," Teela said.

The sound of yelling and cheering turned their attention to the Transport where Captain Simpson and the other pilots were greeting the return of the comrades they believed were dead. The cart containing the injured pilots moved under the transport and began unloading them directly into the transport. With Litnauh in tow, Teela traversed the hangar deck to join Captain Simpson under the transport.

On seeing Teela's approach, Captain Simpson, who was talking to Captain Ramsey, stood at attention and snapped a flawless salute, holding it until Teela returned it with a Korlah salute.

"Thank you, Sir. I was told they were beyond resuscitation. Their arrival is a welcome surprise. I am truly grateful."

Ignoring his comments, Teela had the hover cart operator bring the cart to the ground. The Korlah technician graciously handed the cart over to Teela before departing on foot. Litnauh moved to the cart's control panel and climbed onto the platform in front of her.

"Ramsey, Simpson. Get on. There is something you must see before you leave," Teela barked.

"My men need to get back now. Some of them are in shock and need treatment!" Captain Simpson cried in protest.

"They're pilots aren't they? Tell them to go ahead and leave. I'll return you two when I meet with General Hargrave. Bottom line, you're not leaving until you see what I have to show you. Now make a decision, Captain," Teela growled unsympathetically.

Simpson and Ramsey conferred with each other and two other pilots preparing to board the transport. Within a minute, the two pilots boarded and Captain Ramsey and Captain Simpson joined Teela on the cart. Moving off the hangar floor, Teela had Commander Litnauh pause the hover cart until she witnessed the departure of the transport, after which they sped off into one of the tunnels adjacent to the main hangar.

The asteroid was composed primarily of iron. The walls of the tunnels were smooth, almost to the point of being polished. Streaks of orange-brown iron oxide created by condensing moisture striped the walls, giving it the appearance of a barred cage. Taking a turn the hover cart descended down a vertical tunnel. As it dropped, the air became pungent with the odor of decay. Teela noticed that Litnauh had already closed her faceplate and switched on her suit's life support. Teela pulled her crown tendrils back and tied them tightly together at the back of her head with a strip of cloth she kept in the pocket of her tah for that purpose.

"Jesus! What is that smell," Captain Simpson cried, pressing his nose shut with his thumb and forefinger while breathing through his mouth.

Teela recognized the predominant acrid smell as the acidic odor emitted by Kahshinki. But the odor of rotting flesh was so strong that she was uncertain if the air was breathable. Captain Simpson gagged, and moments later vomited over the railing of the hover cart. Ramsey stood swallowing repeatedly, fighting the urge Captain Simpson had been unable to resist. The tunnel ended at a heavy circular door that was open just enough for Litnauh to squeeze the cart through. On the other side of the door, the tunnel opened up into a natural cavern nearly 600 feet long and 150 feet in diameter. The end of the cavern was filled nearly to the top and half its length with bodies.

Located near the center of the asteroid, the inside of the chamber was nearly weightless. The bodies floated as a tangled mass against the area of the chamber that possessed the greatest gravitational attraction. Rippling like water under the hover cart, the bodies bumped and moved together releasing and stirring the gasses of decomposition trapped within.

Heaving violently over the side Captain Ramsey watched in horror as his vomit joined the pool of bodies, stripped of their muscle mass with only their heads, hands, and feet remaining mostly intact; their glistening bones and putrefying organs separating and hanging loosely from the carcasses in various stages of decay.

"Get us out of here!" Captain Simpson shouted between dry heaves.

Teela could not understand why she was not sickened as they were. The smell was understandably repulsive, but it no longer bothered her. Studying the bodies below her, she searched for something recognizable. Pointing out a specific body, she had Litnauh move the cart next to it. As the bodies bumped up against the sides of the cart, Captain Simpson and Ramsey retreated to the center, away from where the bony hands appeared to reach out for them. Grabbing a body by the boots on its feet, Teela pulled it up onto the cart. The fragments of cuffs at the boots and wrists were still recognizable as those of a human pilot's jumpsuit, but more importantly, the collar with a Captain's insignia pin still attached. Although the face was severely decomposed, the remains of bright red hair hung from shards of flesh still clinging to the top of the skull.

"This was one of your pilots, one of your men Captain Simpson!" Teela cried accusingly. "Now open your eyes and look around! The Kahshinki like their food fresh. Each of these people, yours and mine died screaming as they were eaten alive. To Kahshinki we are nothing more than cattle and your planet is ripe with their favorite food."

Teela had Litnauh move the cart to the area where she saw the Korlah emissaries. Stopping alongside the bodies as before, Litnauh assisted Teela drag the bodies onto the cart. Kneeling alongside the remains, Teela studied the faces and remaining fragments of clothing. Both the sabat and insignias of all three Korlah had been destroyed, either by accident or design. Regardless, Teela intended to have the remains studied to determine who they were, and more importantly, why Afron sent them here.

"You made your point, Sir. Can we leave now?" Captain Simpson pleaded, his complexion gray and his forehead beaded with sweat.

"Your Eminence, you are being summoned," Litnauh announced. "Challmara is requesting that you meet with her on the assault pod immediately. Shawaugh and several of our long range scouts have returned with information vital to the mission," she said, reading the message as it scrolled down the communicator on her forearm.

During the return to the hangar, neither Captain Ramsey nor Captain Simpson spoke. Each stared blankly ahead. On the flight deck, Teela found a contingent of technicians and warriors waiting to load her, the humans, and the grisly bodies onto a waiting transport. Making no effort to resist the efficiencies of the group, Teela found herself on approach to the waiting assault pod within minutes of arriving at the hangar.

Back in the hangar, Commander Litnauh relaxed for the first time since hearing that Teela had made the repair of the damaged humans a priority. Since it was her battle group that was responsible for the destruction of the human soldiers, she feared her actions would anger Teela and made it a point to find something that would demonstrate her efficiency as a leader. She would wait a while longer before reporting the capture of the additional Kahshinki in order to extend the duration of the positive image the capture would afford.

With Captains Ramsey and Simpson locked up in the storage room and under guard, Teela monitored the approach and docking with Challmara's assault pod. Technicians in pressure suits hovered over the surface repairing and making modifications to the defensive array that jutted out, forming portions of a geodesic dome over the surface of the craft. Once docked, she boarded the assault pod and made her way to the control room where she found Shawaugh, Challmara, and several pilots talking. Challmara was sitting up in her seat, the hover pack conspicuously absent. She rose to her feet and turned to face

Teela. Although her stance was awkward and unsteady, it was apparent to Teela that her paralysis had significantly improved.

"Greetings and great honor, Shawlmon," Challmara said, bowing with difficulty.

"Please, sit down," Teela cried, ignoring Shawaugh's and the pilot's salutes. She rushed to Challmara, "I ... I'm so pleased. You're so much better. You have been repaired?" she asked. Taking Challmara's hands in hers, she knelt before her chair.

"The symbiots have proven effective even in this case of extreme damage," Challmara said, "but my recovery is unimportant. There are serious complications that will affect the success of the mission that must be addressed."

Pulling her hands from Teela's grasp, Challmara straightened her tunic and assumed a posture consistent with her rank and title. Embarrassed, Teela blanched slightly as she stood and moved away a respectful distance. She knew little of the symbiots other than they were a symbiotic organism that provided healthful benefits to the Korlah. She wanted to ask more about them, but would have had to reveal her ignorance in the process.

"Report," Teela demanded. Rebuffed by Challmara's behavior, she resumed her role as Mission Potentate, feeling once again, alone and isolated.

Challmara outlined the successes and failures of the new technology she had employed in their weaponry. She then detailed the changes that would be employed to correct the problem associated with the overloading of the power cells, and promised that the reason for the failure of the weapon's locking systems would be found and corrected. She reported that the Kahshinki that were captured at the asteroid base, and those on Earth, were in transit to the Campaign Vessel along with news of their great victory. In closing, she listed the specifics of her request for additional fighters and troops needed for reinforcements at the asteroid base.

Shawaugh recalled the details of her mission, taking time to describe carefully the satellite weaponry they encountered and destroyed. She spoke of each of the warriors who had died by name and rank, describing their actions and honor with which it was performed. She pointed out how the Kahshinki were willing to detonate the molecular disintegrator, indicating that they would likely attempt to sterilize the planet again if given the opportunity. Finishing, she emphasized how vulnerable the planet was to attack, and that the Kahshinki would most certainly make another attempt.

The reconnaissance pilots spoke last, and it was their report that stunned Teela the most. Piloting stripped-down light fighters with a payload of charged power cells, they traversed the distance between Earth's solar system and another five light-years distant where the Kahshinki were in the final stages of completing their current harvest. Replacing the energized cells in mid-space as they were depleted, a dangerous task of great personal risk, they were able to reach the planetary system and observe the Kahshinki preparations. The Kahshinki were not preparing just one Campaign Vessel for harvesting Earth, they had prepared three, which were already beginning their slow acceleration out of that system.

"How long until they will be within striking range?" Teela asked.

"Technically, they could strike now," Challmara responded. "But they could only send stripped-down fighters that would arrive low on power with no place to recharge."

"Could they deliver a molecular disintegrator to Earth?" Teela asked.

"Yes," Challmara answered, expecting the question and the one that would follow.

"Then they will try," Teela said gravely. "What can we do to stop them, Director Shawaugh?" She met Shawaugh's eyes for the first time.

"We can station one assault pod at the planet," Shawaugh said. "It should be capable of gathering enough solar energy to keep a force of fifty fighters powered and patrolling. A thin shield at best, Your Eminence, but if they are carrying a disintegrator, we will detect it the moment it enters the planetary system. That will give us ample time and resources to intercept."

"Director Shawaugh, if you were going to deliver a disintegrator to this planet, how would you get it past the defenses you propose," Teela asked.

Recognizing the obvious logic Teela was using, Shawaugh frowned. This was logic that she had neglected to consider, certain the Kahshinki would behave as predictably as they always had.

"I would not send one. I would send many, as many as possible and all at the same time. I would have an automated program timed with the detonation sequence of the weapon, and I would deliver the weapon at hyper-light, dropping to sub light only after I entered the system, and braking by using the mag drive only after I impacted the atmosphere. An attack like that could not be stopped," Shawaugh growled.

"I disagree," Challmara said. "This planetary system has too much debris to enter at those speeds. I already have two teams dispersing sensors along the outer rim of this system. They will detect any passing craft and beam their speed and course ahead to where our defense force will be waiting for them. Once they drop to sub light, the signal from an active disintegrator will make targeting them simple."

"When you determine how they are jamming our targeting systems and counter it, targeting them will be simpler, but it will never be simple!" Shawaugh barked loudly, taking Challmara's comments as an insult.

"Director Shawaugh," Teela interrupted. "I believe we have an unacceptable reliance on the automated targeting features. Have your patrols begin practicing visual targeting techniques."

"The inaccuracies of visual targeting result in an unacceptable number of misses that waste valuable energy resources," Shawaugh argued.

"Correct me if I'm mistaken, Director, but the problems we experienced were associated with an overabundance of energy, not a shortage. If our weapons technicians had been targeting and firing their weapons visually, wasteful or not, the majority of the damage we suffered could probably have been avoided," Teela replied, raising her voice.

"That problem has been corrected," Challmara added quickly. "The power cells will automatically discharge through the weapons system before an overload condition is reached."

Clenching her fists tightly, Teela marched to the viewing screen and looked deeply into the field of stars beyond. Pulling Captain Simpson's watch from her vest pocket, she noted the time.

"Director Shawaugh, if anything happens to me I want your blood oath that you will personally deliver Beth and the other humans safely to Earth," she said.

"Nothing is going to …," Shawaugh started to say, pausing before continuing. "You have my blood oath, Your Eminence. The humans will be returned."

Teela remained standing at the window, saying nothing. Shawaugh believed that Teela was merely collecting her thoughts but Challmara noticed the periodic quaking of the fabric of Teela's tunic, indicating she was silently crying. Challmara had seen Teela cry before, quietly and always alone.

"Why are you refusing to train for visual targeting?" Challmara asked pointedly, intending to draw Shawaugh's attention from Teela.

"I did not refuse!" Shawaugh boomed angrily. "I … I only questioned its value."

"It just sounded more like a refusal than a question," Challmara taunted.

"I value all your questions, doubts, and suspicions. But most of all I value your advice," Teela said from where she stood at the window, using a cough as an excuse to wipe the tears from her face before turning around to face them. "Without your advice and guidance I am doomed. Please, never be afraid to question my orders," her voice cracking as she spoke.

"You do not sound well, were you damaged during the battle?" Shawaugh asked.

"I am preoccupied with a meeting I must attend with the leaders of the human base. I am exhausted and must rest for a couple sets before I go," she replied, pulling the watch from her vest. It read 1530; she had two and a half hours before the scheduled meeting, not much time to sleep.

"Then you will eat and sleep," Challmara said, standing. "Come!" she demanded, taking Teela by the arm and leading her out of the control room with small shuffling steps. From the force with which Challmara was leaning on her, Teela was keenly aware that Challmara could barely walk on her own.

Challmara's quarters were not much larger than a closet, providing barely enough room for a narrow bed. Sitting on the edge of the bed, they ate two biscuits each and shared a flask of water. Challmara had Teela help her remove her boots before lying down. Sitting on the edge of the bed Teela set the watch to alarm at 1745 and then stood to leave.

"Lie with me? Please," Challmara whispered.

Teela sat back down and removed her boots, swords, and vest. Lying down on the narrow bed, she had to press against Challmara to keep from falling off. Challmara snaked her arm under Teela, resting her hand between Teela's breasts. Teela could feel Challmara's warm breath against the back of her neck and slowly relaxed. With the physical tension within her body ebbing, her mind finally began to calm.

"I've missed you, little mother," Challmara whispered, her lips brushing the back of Teela's neck.

"I've missed you, too," Teela whispered, closing her eyes and wishing her life could be as clearly defined as it once was. Taking a deep breath, she let it out slowly and fell asleep.

Howard Lewis

9 - Suspicion

Acceptance and trust were not words used to describe the relationship between the humans and their Korlah escorts. For many of the Korlah warriors, especially those who just fought human clones during the base assault, seeing humans walking freely with pulse weapons was more than unnerving. If not for

Beth, this contradiction of logic might have been too much for them to bear. Stories had surfaced and were circulating regarding her handling of the human pilots. This, her advocates claimed, demonstrated her allegiance to Shawlmon and the goals of Campaign. With the majority of the warrior clan now accepting her into their sororal membership, the activities of Beth, or Bethaugh as the warriors now called her, was a popular topic of conversation. The accuracy of the reports were debated in detail and often exaggerated to either emphasize or downplay her now legendary prowess. As for the warriors occupying the base, the controversy of whether or not there would be a human alliance grew less and less passionate, with the subject shifting from "if" there would be an alliance, to "what" the alliance with these humans would be like.

I can't believe how fast I'm healing, Beth thought as she stretched shoulder muscles that had been severed no more than a week ago. *In a couple days, I'll be back on my game. It would be a bitch to get tore up again*, she pondered, stopping for a moment to check the progress of the cleanup activities.

Since leaving the Campaign Vessel, the division between the women was evident. Two distinct cliques developed; Ruth, Ann, Margaret, and Tiffany formed one group. Ruth led her group using a style incorporating discussion and consensus, the others following her lead eagerly. Beth broke away from the group early with Marsha and Catherine following soon thereafter. Without Crystal to lead the band, Marsha and Catherine accepted Beth's command and control style, hanging on her every word and action. Under Beth's rule, the young women assumed a noticeably mature and serious demeanor.

Beth and the girls were under the transport stretching in preparation to spar. Although focused on the training activity, Beth was acutely aware that all the warriors positioned within sight of the transport were obviously watching her activities.

"Take five," Beth said, giving Marsha and Catherine a much-needed break.

Stepping out from under the transport, she scanned the progress of the cleanup activities, giving a nod of acknowledgement to the warriors watching her. She was keenly aware the warriors had been encased in their heavy and confining armor suits for many hours and must be incredibly uncomfortable. Taking a head count, she noticed Rebecca had still not left the transport.

Rebecca belonged to neither clique of humans, choosing instead to sit apart from both groups. Initially, Ruth tried to coax Rebecca to join them, but Rebecca's fervent religious views and conversations with nonexistent people proved disrupting, so much so that Ruth quit trying. As a result, after the others left the transport, Rebecca sat alone in the transport engaged in a passionate discussion with a companion only she could hear.

Beth could see Ruth and the others watching the activities in the hangar. She noticed that the object of their interest was a pile of debris near an adjacent corridor. As they watched, transports would arrive and deposit materials on the pile while workers comprised of both human and Korlah clones disassembled the larger pieces and moved them out of the area using the hover carts, or more often, by hand. It appeared as though the workers, some no more than twelve years old, knew their task well, and the armored warriors did nothing more than stand and watch them, when they were not watching Beth.

When a young worker pulled on a sheet of debris, it caused a long beam to come sliding down the pile and hit a warrior in the side of her helmet. The automatic gravitational field of her suit reacted to the foreign object, stopping it before it took her head off, but not before causing the painful impact. Angrily shoving the offending debris to one side, the warrior stormed over to the young girl and butted her sharply in the center of the face with her pulse rifle. Falling onto her back and clutching her face, the girl began crying loudly. The warrior stepped over the girl and placed her armored boot onto the girl's throat ending the crying with a high-pitched squeak.

"Hey! Hey!" Ann screamed, sprinting toward the warrior.

Oh no, you freaking moron, do not interfere. Beth thought, having personal knowledge of what the military response would likely be.

Warriors within sight leveled their weapons at Ann as she ran to the girl's aid. The offending warrior removed her foot and stood pointing her rifle at Ann's approach. Ignoring the warrior, she slid to a stop next to the young girl and knelt protectively over her. A gash where the rifle butt had split the skin on the girl's forehead was bleeding profusely, but Ann's concern was the throat, which the child clutched with both hands while making a high pitched wheezing sound.

"Help ... Help!" Ann screamed.

"Wait here," Beth said to Marsha and Catherine as she began walking slowly toward Ann with her hands out and open to indicate to the warriors that her intentions were non-confrontational, hoping that she could keep the situation from escalating.

The child looked at Ann, her eyes fearful and devoid of understanding, her mouth gaping open, blue lips stretched over her clean white teeth. With one last whistling gasp, her eyes crossed and rolled up as the lids closed and she fell limp in Ann's arms.

"Her larynx has been crushed," Beth said as she walked up and stood staring provocatively into the visor of the warrior. "She's dead. Leave her before they smoke your dumb ass."

"She's just a little girl," Ann sobbed.

"She's a fucking clone," Beth said.

"She's human, Beth, are you?" Ruth growled as she joined Ann alongside the child.

"This is not our business. Get the fuck back where you belong," Beth said.

"We can give her a tracheotomy ... if we hurry," Margaret announced, ignoring Beth and joining the crowd forming around Ann and the girl.

"Have you ever performed a tracheotomy?" Beth cried angrily at Margaret, seeing the situation slipping from her control.

Margaret avoided Beth's glare, cringing when she looked at the young girl's bloody face, her silence the answer to Beth's question.

"I'll bet you have," Ruth said, confronting Beth.

"It's a fucking clone!" Beth shouted. She had never actually done a tracheotomy, but she had the training, and had seen it done. *This is so fucking insane,* Beth thought, looking around for something to use.

"Please, Beth. Please for the love of God help this child!" Ann screamed hysterically.

"Oh fuck me! Fuck … fuck … fuck," Beth muttered, marching away.

"You heartless bitch!" Ruth screamed at her.

Stupid fucking bitch is more like it, Beth thought, seeing the object she was looking for while lamenting her change of heart. She waded into the debris pile and grabbed a length of quarter-inch thick tubular conduit. Withdrawing her Korlah sword, she cut a length approximately six inches long, slicing one end of the tubing diagonally.

"Get out of my way!" she shouted, causing the group huddling around Ann to scatter as she stomped back toward them with her sword in hand.

"Stand up," Beth ordered Ann as she knelt on the opposite side the girl.

Ann stood as Beth offered her the handle of the sword. Reluctantly she accepted the handle, trembling and frightened of what Beth might order her to do next.

"Hold the weight, don't move it unless you feel my fingers directing the motion. And whatever you do, don't drop it," Beth said calmly, taking the tip of the blade between her thumb and forefinger and drawing it down toward the throat of the girl.

Carefully using the tip of the razor sharp blade like a scalpel, Beth made an incision into the trachea below the larynx. Leaving the blade in position like a shoehorn Beth slid the diagonal end of the tube into the opening. Feeling for a pulse and finding a weak one, Beth leaned back and addressed the group.

"Pay attention. I'm going to do this for one fucking minute and if she doesn't start breathing on her own, you patron saints of the human fucking race will have to take over."

Leaning down, she held the tube protruding from the hole in the girl's neck with one hand while placing her mouth over the tube. Using the air in her lungs, she inflated the young girl's lungs. She released her mouth and moved her head to the side as the air expelled through the tube. Several breaths later, she checked the pulse again. Finding a stronger pulse, she began delivering another breath. About halfway through, the child lurched, and her lungs began filling spontaneously with a loud sucking sound as she forcefully drew air into the tube. Anticipating what would happen next, Beth held onto the tube, but moved her head away. Ann however, leaned in to see what was happening. The air discharged from the lungs with the same force with which it was drawn, blowing out a mist of blood and mucus into Ann's face.

"Hold this in place," Beth ordered, drawing Ann's hand to the tube. "You're gonna need to tie it in place. When she wakes up, she'll try to pull the tube out. Don't let that happen, if it does, it's your fucking problem. Good luck kiddo." She patted Ann on the head as she stood and returned the sword to its scabbard.

"We need to get her to a doctor," Ruth said.

"Not my fucking problem," Beth replied. "This is your project, imperious leader, now handle it."

"They'll listen to you, Beth. I've seen how they act around you. Tell them to help her, please. After that we won't ask another thing, I promise," Ann pleaded, her blood spattered face streaked with tears.

"Look at them! Look at their eyes," Beth cried pointing at the group of clones gathered around them. "The lights are on, but no humans are home. They have been bred to take our planet from us. Before this is over we will have to kill thousands, or more realistically millions of these fucking things."

A loud clang of metal on metal interrupted Beth. Another warrior was by the one that injured the girl and was slamming the butt of her rifle into the offending warrior's visor. Shouting angrily, the warrior continued butting the other warrior in the visor as though punctuating her comments. When she finally finished, the offending warrior slung her rifle and marched out of the hangar. The new warrior approached Beth and from the palm display gestures she was making it appeared she was offering an apology. Listening intently, Beth finally gave the warrior a robust clawed salute. Grabbing Ruth by the shoulder, she pulled her over to the warrior and using sweeping gestures, she introduced Ruth to her.

"Ruth, I would like you to meet the asshole in charge of these soulless imitations of humanity. Asshole in charge, this is Ruth. She thinks I can somehow communicate with you ugly mother fuckers, but she is wrong, so I am turning that job over to her."

"You are such … an asshole," Ruth whispered.

"Better an asshole than a fool," Beth replied coldly.

Making one last palm display to the warrior, Beth winked at Ann, turned and walked away leaving Ruth standing alone with the armored warrior. Without looking back, she continued to the transport with Catherine and Marsha following closely behind.

"What if they need your help?" Catherine asked.

"Some people can't be helped," Beth quipped.

Taking a gasping breath of air, Teela opened her eyes, unsure of what had woken her. A tingling pulse on her palm, repeated by another, drew her attention to the source of disturbed sleep. The watch was emitting a low voltage charge, silently notifying her that it was 1745. Acknowledging the alarm with the tip of a claw, Teela gently lifted Challmara's arm from her chest and sat up on the edge of the bed. Challmara snorted softly, rolled over and resumed her slumber. Quietly, Teela dressed and returned to the transport. As she entered, Shawaugh stood at the weapons console and saluted her.

"Roche Hah, Shawlmon," Shawaugh barked.

"We need to leave soon. Where is the crew?" Teela asked.

"They are resting, Your Eminence. I will summon them directly," Shawaugh replied, tapping a message onto her communicator.

"I hate being called that. It makes me uncomfortable. Can't you just call me Teela?" she said as she sat down, stretched, and yawned.

"To treat you otherwise would indicate a lack of respect for your authority."

"Challmara just said that to … to make you leave me alone while I was making decisions."

"Challmara is right. I must not show disrespect or others will observe that and follow my example. Many doubt that you are Shawlmon, but they accept that you are the Assistant to the Potentate. Your position requires unquestioning loyalty and fear of immediate and severe punishment for failing to obey your will. As your Mission Director, how can I enforce that requirement if I do not obey it myself?"

"I don't want to be feared!" Teela exclaimed.

"You are Shawlmon. The Gods of Korlah reach out through your arms. As the Potentate of this mission, your words will control whether millions will continue their existence or cease. You deserve to be feared," Shawaugh barked. "Discard your birther shell and rise to accept the existence that has chosen you."

"Now you sound like Beth," Teela groaned.

"Then Bethaugh is as wise as she is formidable," Shawaugh replied.

The communications and weapons technicians entered and assumed their positions at their respective consoles. Shawaugh remained seated at the pilot's console.

"We need to get going. Where is my pilot?" Teela exclaimed, looking at the watch.

"I will be acting as pilot, Your Eminence," Shawaugh replied.

"Is the communications device on?" Teela asked, noticing the speaker was not emitting its telltale static signal.

"One moment Your Eminence," the communications technician said. She activated the device, a sputter of static announcing its operation. "It is now, Your Eminence."

Moving to the microphone, Teela thumbed the indentation to activate the sending unit.

"This is Shawlmon of the Korlah forces. I am proceeding to rendezvous with General Hargrave," she announced.

"Take us to an area between the two bases," she ordered.

With a slap, the access opening closed and the transport lifted away from the assault pod. Banking sharply and accelerating much faster than Teela expected, Shawaugh had Teela at a location directly between the bases and about 1000 feet from the surface within seconds. As they watched, a transport shot out from a hangar access opening on the human base, and rapidly climbed up to join them. Inverting as it approached, the craft joined with Teela's as the polymorphic metal on the undersides of the two vessels joined together.

"I will open the access on your command," Shawaugh said, her concern evident.

Moving to the chamber where Captains Simpson and Ramsey were, Teela opened the door.

"Your ride's here boys," she announced loudly, finding them asleep on the floor.

"Wha ... Oh! It's about time," Captain Simpson replied, eyes bleary from sleep.

Teela returned to the console and toggled the microphone.

"We're waiting. How would you like to do this?" she asked.

"Send my pilots first, then you, alone, and unarmed," the speaker crackled.

"Open the access," Teela commanded as she unbuckled her belt, placing it and her swords on the seat of the command chair. Without waiting for direction, Captain Ramsey, followed closely by Captain Simpson, exited the transport, clumsily crawling through the opening. Trusting the gravitational systems, Teela dove into the opening head first with her arms at her sides. Halfway through, her descent became an ascent in the opposing gravitational force and her movement slowed. Once she had passed completely through the access, but before she began to fall back, she leaned forward and stepped out from the access opening's gravitational control field.

The crew stations were filled with human pilots. A man in his late forties dressed in an ill-fitting dark uniform adorned with a chest full of medals stood alongside the command chair. Captain Ramsey and Captain Simpson stood rigidly against the center of the wall that divided the front and rear of the craft.

"Greetings, Shawlmon of Korlah. I am General Hargrave," the man with the medals announced.

The emotional tension in the room permeated Teela's mind like an overwhelming stench. Of all the emotions she sensed, fear dominated. Opening her mind, she searched for the sources. Focusing on the pilot and crew, she could feel their vulnerability, not from her, but the soldiers hiding behind the dividing wall at the rear. More specifically, they feared the bullets that would ricochet within the transport if the weapons were discharged. The General, who was not a General at all, feared that his communications system would fail and he would have to speak to her without the direct guidance of the real General. Both Captain Simpson and Captain Ramsey feared for Teela's life, believing that General Hargrave intended to kill if not capture her. The soldiers in the back were afraid that they would die as their companions had. The one soldier holding an explosive package knew that if the access between the transports was left open after he hurled it into the other transport, the occupants of both would be killed. Realizing the volatility of the situation, Teela sent Shawaugh a telepathic command to seal the hatch, depart to a safe distance and return fire if fired upon.

The access opening slapped shut and a slight shudder announced the departure of the other transport. Taking a deep breath in an effort to calm her racing heart, Teela walked to the man in the General's uniform. Scanning the uniform, she looked for the microphone and mini-cam. The miniaturized camera she was certain was positioned in the hat worn by the pilot who was posing as the General, a small black hole in the badge above its brim, the likely location. The location of the microphone she wasn't certain of, but believed it to be either a button that seemed slightly off color, or tucked into a buttonhole that looked oddly misshapen. Regardless of the details of the ruse, she was keenly aware of its existence.

"General Hargrave, I am the Korlah Ambassadress of Peace, a diplomat. The military contingent that is escorting me is looking at our meeting with acute interest. They are greatly concerned that your treacherous behavior is indicative of your species. Through my relations with the humans I am escorting home, I know that it is not. So I ask you to help me persuade them that you are an honorable species by engaging me directly and not through this poorly prepared puppet you have sent," Teela said, looking intently at the badge on the General's hat.

"I don't know where …," the mock general began to say before Teela interrupted him.

"Quiet! General, either have your man give me the earpiece or talk to me on the communications system speaker."

The mock general paused for a moment before quickly prying the hearing device from his ear and holding it out.

"Thank you," Teela said graciously, as the man dropped the earpiece into her hand.

Teela slid the device into her ear canal. Snatching the hat from the mock general's head, she looked inside and confirmed the location of the camera.

"Ambassador, it is difficult for me to believe your intentions are peaceful now that you have attacked our planet and this military installation," General Hargrave said via the earpiece.

"I'm not going to waste your time playing down the seriousness of what has happened. I regret the loss of life on both sides and offer my honest apologies that we were not able to accomplish the neutralization of our enemies without it. When I meet with the leadership of Earth, I will provide all the details. For now I will keep why we have come, what we intend to do, and what we expect from you brief and to the point.

"We are here to exterminate the alien species you call the 'toads'. Like you, we do not know their real name and call them Kahshinki, which is the name of a nocturnal blood-sucking parasite that once existed on our home world before the Kahshinki burned the planet and its remaining inhabitants into organic dust. We are escaped slaves, the Korlah equivalent of the human clones you call the 'twins'. It is our intention to protect your planet and its inhabitants from the Kahshinki. Your planet represents a rich food source to them and a strategic location to us. From this solar system, we can interrupt their harvesting route and drive them from this sector of the galaxy. In exchange for raw materials, food, and water, we will provide the governments of your planet with the advanced weaponry they need for a sustainable planetary defense.

"Until I can negotiate an agreement or alliance with the governments of your world, I need you to stay out of our way."

"You haven't explained the attack. If you come offering peace, why have you attacked?" General Hargrave asked.

"We believed the Kahshinki would attempt to destroy your planet rather than allow us to use it against them. They placed a device, a doomsday bomb, in an underground facility at one of your military installations. Twenty Korlah soldiers gave their lives to remove that device before the Kahshinki could detonate it. If they had failed, this asteroid would be your home and Earth would be uninhabitable."

"Why should I believe you?"

"You shouldn't, and I would be disappointed in your leadership skills if you did. But the two pilots I am returning to you, Captain Simpson and Captain Ramsey, have witnessed several events that should lend credence to my claims. This is not about trust General, it's about mutual aid. We need food, water, and raw materials, and you need weapons."

"To demonstrate your good faith, you could provide some of those weapons now so that I could appraise their military value and report the findings to my superiors."

"Forgive me for being suspicious, General, but in the last … six hours you have tried to nuke me and dupe me. And if my sources are correct, you have armed soldiers hiding in the back of this craft prepared to shoot me and drop a bomb into my escort vessel."

"Ambassador, I am a soldier not a diplomat. My actions have been enacted in response to a clear and present threat to the military presence under my command. Now that you have clarified your intentions I assure you that my actions will be strictly defensive in nature."

Taking a deep breath, Teela allowed herself to relax slightly, wishing that Hargrave was present so that she could actually evaluate his thoughts and emotions.

"I'm glad we had the opportunity to communicate, General, I only regret that it could not be face to face. With any luck, when I return we will be allies and our next meeting will be under more relaxed conditions," Teela said.

"We need to arrange channels of communication, a contact schedule, and a means for our vessels to pass through your blockade," General Hargrave said.

"The same methods you use to communicate with the Kahshinki should work with my military escorts. We have broken every form of communication you've come up with so far, so I don't think you should have any trouble getting through to us on any of your existing devices. As for your vessels, do not attempt to leave the base until I have had a chance to talk to your planetary leadership."

"Are you implying we're your prisoners?"

"No, General. Think of it as though we just showed up from out of town and we're blocking your driveway. Be patient and we'll eventually move out of your way. For you to make assumptions to the contrary would be detrimental to our mutual interests."

"Ambassador, I have spoken with numerous foreign dignitaries and military leaders in my career, and I have to say that you speak the English language with unexpected fluency. Tell me, how did you learn to speak our language so well?"

"It's Ambassadress, General, I'm a female. My training and education is a long and boring story that I will reserve for our next meeting. I regret that we don't have more time to talk, but I really must get going. With your permission I will use this vessel's communication system to call for my shuttle," Teela said as she handed the hat back to the man wearing the General's uniform.

"Ambassadress Shawlmon, it is I who regret that we don't have more time. Make your call, but before you go please tell me … how long have you had operatives in our government and military?"

"Now General Hargrave, what kind of question is that? Maybe I can answer your question with a question of my own. How long have you been communicating with the Kahshinki?" Teela asked, seeing the opportunity to feed General Hargrave misinformation that would hopefully send him off on a wild goose chase looking for Korlah spies.

Stepping between the pilot and communication consoles, Teela keyed the microphone and made a show of requesting to be picked up. Silently, she issued her instructions to Shawaugh with her mind while closely monitoring the thoughts of the soldiers behind the wall. Waiting until she was certain no attack was planned, she ordered Shawaugh to open the portal. Diving through the instant it opened, she had Shawaugh close it the moment she passed through. Breaking free, Shawaugh veered her vessel away from the General's transport and into the battered opening on the Korlah side of the base. Passing through the airlock, Shawaugh docked the transport alongside the one Teela would be using to return the humans to Earth.

We done good, I'm very proud of you, Daedalus said.

Thank you, Teela replied, blushing with pride.

10 - Faith

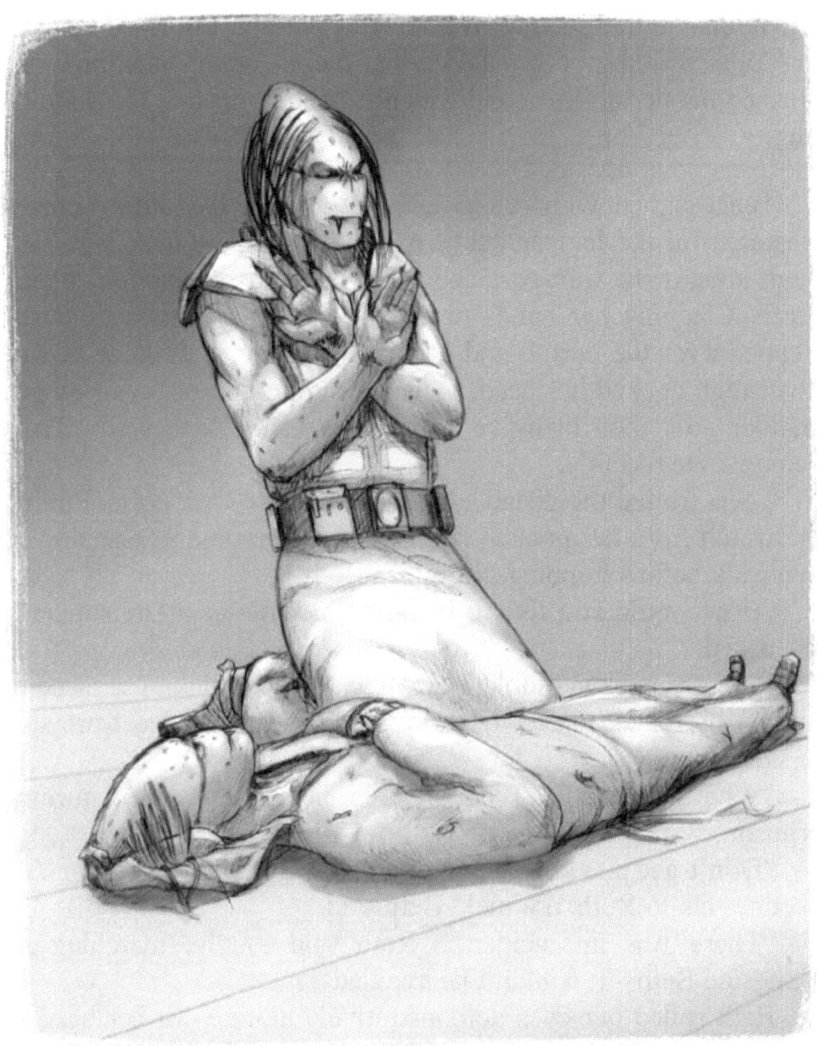

A feeling of trepidation caused Beth to pause midway through her 300th pushup. Exercise had always been her way of diminishing stress, but in the low gravity of the outpost it seemed a nearly useless endeavor. Passing the uneasiness off as a momentary pang of guilt for her earlier behavior, she continued her regimen, stopping again as the feeling grew stronger. She looked up just as a transport emerged from an airlock. Although she had seen numerous transports coming and going over the last few hours, an odd feeling of awareness within, informed her that this one would not be delivering more scrap. Standing, she brushed off her uniform and watched as it stopped at the docking ring.

Teela sighed with relief seeing Beth and the other humans clustered on the hangar deck. All she had to do now was load them aboard the transport and go, their next destination, planet Earth. Clapping her hands to signify her inner satisfaction, she stepped over the portal, and dropped to the hangar floor below. Shawaugh cocked her head, considering the odd behavior as just another of the many eccentricities she witnessed Teela demonstrate recently.

Teela trotted the distance between the two transports. Pulling the watch from her pocket, she looked at the time as she slowed to a walk before stopping in front of Beth.

"How would you like to be home in time for a late supper?" she asked.

Beth groaned and looked down at her feet, picking a piece of lint off her black tunic while slowly shaking her head from side to side.

"What happened?" Teela shouted, her crown tendrils turning crimson.

"Don't get pissed at me. I'm not in charge, remember? You need to talk to Ruth, not me!" Beth said.

"There was an incident," Ruth said loudly, marching up alongside Beth. "It couldn't be avoided

Beth rolled her eyes demonstratively along with her head as she turned and walked away.

"What kind of incident?" Teela asked slowly, straining to control her anger.

"Ann is tending to an injured … child, a girl, one of them," Ruth answered, pointing to the group of clones working at the scrap pile.

"Where?" Teela demanded, relieved that the incident only involved finding Ann.

"Well ... I'm not really sure. We had to communicate with sign language, pantomime really. But the soldier that helped us was real helpful. She went with the child to see a doctor, I think."

"Do you see the soldier you talked to?" Teela asked, looking toward the scrap pile where the human clones were working.

"The soldier left with them, but it talked to that one ... over there before they left," Ruth said, pointing to the nearest armored warrior standing at the scrap pile.

"Is everyone else here except Ann?" Teela asked.

"Yes," Ruth replied meekly.

"Get everyone inside the transport. Do not come out again," Teela demanded.

"There's a good explanation for what happened."

"Save it! Get in the transport," Teela ordered as she stomped off toward the warrior.

The warrior informed her that the Assault Commander had personally escorted the two humans to the repair facility. Using her communicator, the warrior spoke to the Commander and determined that the damaged human had been successfully repaired and was currently consuming a meal in the worker's dining section. With directions provided by the warrior, Teela proceeded to the workers section. As she traversed the corridor, she couldn't help but notice the similarities between the layout and construction of the base and the Campaign Vessel. It was as though they were formed from the same mold.

Teela could smell the food long before she reached the dining section. It was not protein biscuits, braddle, or rouk she smelled, it was something alien yet familiar. Sweet smells, savory smells wafted through the air. Shaking her crown tendrils loose she maximized the absorption of the scents, which produced sensations quite similar to taste.

Swallowing the abundance of saliva that filled her mouth, Teela stopped at the entry and surveyed the room. Long thin tables ran from one side of the room to the other. On each side of the tables were benches. Formed in the same material as the walls they flowed seamlessly into the floors. Capable of seating several hundred workers, the room contained no more than 50. Along the wall nearest the door, a dozen warriors sat hunched over their meals, their armor piled on the next table. Warriors still wearing their armor, stood on either side of the door, with another standing at a hover cart where the meals were being dispensed.

As she entered the room the warriors saluted, their armor, made a loud clattering sound that roused the attention of those eating their meals. On seeing the mission leader standing in the doorway, they all leapt to their feet, one of them falling backwards and knocking some of the piled armor from the adjacent table.

"You have fought hard today. Please ... sit ... finish your meals," Teela said making a brief salute to return the multiple salutes.

"Teela ... Teela, over here," Ann called, standing and waving.

Walking past the food cart towards Ann, Teela picked up one of the boxes piled upon it. The box was a military field ration, its contents of cans and packets packed neatly within.

"It's food Teela, real food! This is my second, beef stroganoff, I had chicken ... something last time. I think this is the best tasting food I've ever eaten," Ann said while spooning in another mouth full. The food smeared on her cheeks and chin emphasizing the abandon with which she was consuming it.

"It smells wonderful, Ann," Teela exclaimed in agreement, looking around at the other humans sitting at the table.

Wearing the dark coveralls of workers, the young women, their light brown hair cut to a few inches in length, ranged in age from pre-teen to mid-20's. Genetically identical, the only apparent differences between them were their size and weight. From their olive complexions and full lips, Teela figured them to be of southern European ancestry. The older clones, taller, heavier, and more muscular looked at her with expressions of concern. The younger ones, their coveralls hanging loosely on their thin frames looked blankly at her, their eyes devoid of fear. Most of the clones immediately returned to their meals once they confirmed that Teela was not there to make demands on them.

"Come on, Ann, it's time for us to go," Teela said.

"We have to take these children with us," Ann said.

"What? No … No! Everyone is at the transport. We're ready to go home. Back to Earth, Ann! Right now! Do you understand?" Teela exclaimed, flattening the box of food on the table in front of Ann with her fist.

"These are children. Humans like me. I will not abandon them here to be crushed under the boots of those thugs," Ann said gesturing to the table of warriors. "These are living breathing human beings who don't deserve to be murdered at the whim of these tyrants!"

Squeezing in between Ann and the clone next to her, Teela sat down on the bench. Ann sat rigidly facing the table, grasping the edge of the bench with her hands as though Teela might try to drag her away. Staring at the box of food Teela smashed, Ann began to cry.

"Ann, I promise I'll see about getting these kids back to Earth. I'll make sure no one hurts them again. I promise. But I can't take them back now. I just can't. I'm sorry."

Ann put her arm around the young clone sitting on the other side of her and turned her to face Teela.

"For no reason, no reason at all, one of them struck this child in the face and then smashed her throat with her boot. She would be dead if Beth and I hadn't saved her."

"Beth?" Teela asked.

"She didn't want to help, but she did," Ann quickly added.

"I'll make sure the warriors know these … young women are not to be mistreated. They'll be fine, really."

"How long do you think it will be until you can get them away from this place?" Ann asked.

"I don't know. A month or two maybe, it will have to be negotiated."

"Then I'll stay here and watch after them. Someone has to, and it may as well be me," Ann said, raising her head defiantly to meet Teela's eyes for the first time.

"No, Ann, No! I'm not leaving anyone else behind. Get up!" Teela ordered as she stood.

"You left Bill, and what good reason did he have to stay behind. Everyone could see what motivated him, and it wasn't his desire to teach English. My reason is just and right. These children need me. I'm not leaving without them."

"If you don't come with me now, I'll have one of these thugs butt you in the face and drag you back," Teela hissed.

Ann stood slowly lifting the young girl with her. Stepping away from the table, Ann held the child in front of her facing Teela. The wound on the child's forehead had been mended and appeared as a thin streak over the still bruised and discolored skin. Her throat slightly swollen was also bruised and showed evidence of a mended cut at the base of the neck. Ann affectionately brushed the short hair back with her hand before kissing the child on her bruised forehead. The child smiled and tilted her head back to look at Ann.

"If there's still a part of you that's human, then you know I'm right. Don't force me to abandon these children alone and unprotected," Ann pleaded.

Teela looked into the eyes of the child as her mind probed deeper. The young girl considered Ann to be like a Nursery mother, a recollection from her earliest memories. Communication by signing with a rudimentary verbal understanding learned in a training center … from someone who looked like Teela. She knew of the Kahshinki and feared them, but she did not know why. The battle at the base confused and frightened her, and she did not understand why everything had suddenly changed.

"Teela, what's wrong?" Ann asked.

"Nothing. I'm thinking," Teela answered, looking up. "What do you think you are going to accomplish here if we leave you?"

"Well I've given that some thought. There are quite a few of them so I figured I would break them into manageable groups and have classes to teach them to speak, play games, and be normal girls and young women of course," Ann said excitedly, recognizing Teela's response as acceptance of her demand to stay.

"Don't you want to go home?"

"More than anything, more than you can imagine. But if I did … if I left without these children, not a day would go by that I wouldn't be haunted by knowledge that I could have helped them. Do you understand?"

"More than you can imagine," Teela said thinking of Nerhala and the sisters she left behind.

Taking Teela into an embrace, Ann gave her kiss on the cheek.

"Thank you. I've always known you were a good person, and your looks don't scare me anymore," Ann said, releasing Teela.

"Good bye and good luck. I'll see you when I get back," Teela said, trying to sound positive when everything she felt told her surviving the next few days would be nothing short of a miracle.

Litnauh stood waiting for her in the doorway. The absence of her armored suit indicated that she was probably off-shift when the warrior at the scrap pile called her. Teela returned Litnauh's salute and then followed her outside the room where she moved far enough away from the posted guards to ensure that their conversation would not be overheard.

Teela stood impassively, waiting for Litnauh to speak first. The Warrior Commander stood before her staring at the floor carefully avoiding eye contact.

"Your Eminence, the warrior that committed the attack has been isolated and is waiting whatever punishment you believe suitable," Litnauh said.

"Commander, I hold my first line directors, supervisors, and commanders responsible for the actions of those under their command," Teela said, trying not to sound overtly threatening.

"Your Eminence, forgive me, I have failed you," Litnauh said solemnly, accepting the blame as Teela indicated she must.

"You haven't failed me Commander, just disappointed me on this single matter. You have already demonstrated exceptional leadership capabilities during the capture of this base. You are obviously a valuable resource to this mission and I respect and afford great honor to your success. I am well aware of the difficulty in dealing with these humans and that's why I've decided to appoint a mission assistant to work with you to oversee the care and handling of the human duplicates on this base," Teela said, gaining confidence that she had adequate leverage to manipulate Litnauh into accepting Ann's presence.

"Your Eminence, your honor is greatly appreciated. I am grateful to have this opportunity to serve during the first cycle of Campaign and will do everything in my power to serve you," Litnauh gushed, relieved that she was not going to lose her command. "When am I to meet with your assistant?" she asked.

"You already have," Teela said, gesturing toward Ann, who waved at them.

Litnauh's crown tendrils blanched when she realized that Teela had appointed the hysterical human she dealt with earlier into a position where they would be equals.

"She ... she doesn't speak our language. How am I to communicate?" Litnauh asked, dazed by the concept.

"I recognize this will be a considerable challenge. But I know that if any unit on this mission can handle it, you can. I am proud to serve the Korlah Mission alongside you, Commander, I am certain you will continue to earn great honor in this and every endeavor," Teela said, the trap now sprung with the Commander held securely by the warrior code of honor.

"I'll leave you to your duties then," Teela said, saluting the Commander.

"Yes, Your Eminence," Litnauh replied weakly, returning Teela's salute.

Teela took about a half-dozen steps down the corridor before turning around.

"Oh, I almost forgot to ask," Teela said, recalling the Kahshinki that Litnauh was holding captive. "How long do you intend to wait before you deliver the Kahshinki you captured to Director Challmara?"

"Ah ... ah ... immediately, Your Eminence," Litnauh stammered, surprised that Teela was aware of the capture, and shocked that she did not confront her for concealing it.

"Excellent! I will have Mission Director Challmara personally convey credit for your superior performance in these matters," Teela said turning and continuing down the corridor to the biorepair facility.

154

Since the original biorepair facility had been destroyed during the assault, a makeshift facility was set up in what appeared to be a dormitory. Instead of the larger permanently installed devices like those used on the Campaign vessel, smaller devices were set up on sleeping platforms with the pads removed. With the exception of two warriors having lacerations on their arms repaired, no other patients were in the room. Teela could see evidence of the recent repair activities in the form of blood and body parts that were being cleared and cleaned by a team of clones. Teela walked around the clones that seemed oblivious to her entry and approached one of the biotechs who appeared to be unoccupied. Upon seeing Teela, the technician rushed over, bowing deeply as she did.

"Roche Hah, Shawlmon. How may I serve you?" she asked, presenting a respectful palm display in lieu of a warrior's salute.

"A warrior called Dooaugh was sent here for repairs," Teela said.

"Yes, Your Eminence, has she ceased?" the technician asked.

"Why … what do you mean? Where is she?" Teela asked alarmed by the technician's response.

"The projectile that damaged her contained a toxic compound. I repaired the damage, but was unable to arrest the painful and debilitating effects of the toxin. The compound completely permeated her entire system, the effects permanent, irreversible, and ultimately terminal. I would have painlessly ended her existence, but she demanded that we return her to your transport, Your Eminence. I am sorry, but with this equipment I…"

Teela did not wait for the technician to explain further, she bolted from the room, and ran the entire distance back to the transport where she pushed through the humans to get to where Dooaugh was sitting alongside Rebecca. Dooaugh was sitting upright staring blankly forward, her mouth slightly open. Rebecca sat hunched over in the chair next to her clasping one of Dooaugh's hands in hers while she rocked slowly from side to side muttering incoherently. When Teela tried to touch Dooaugh's neck to check for a pulse, Rebecca started screaming hysterically. Surprised by Rebecca's reaction, Teela backed away, and Rebecca stopped screaming and continued rocking and muttering.

"We found them like this when we came back aboard," Ruth said softly. "I think it ... she is dead, but I can't see any overt cause, and Rebecca won't let us get close enough to make a more thorough examination."

"The bullet was poisoned," Teela said, sitting down in one of the chairs and putting her head in her hands. "I sent her out ... alone. I should have known. I should have been with her."

"Where is Ann, why isn't she with you? Ruth asked.

"She's staying, wants to look after the ... children," Teela replied, lifting her head and looking at her hands as though expecting to find something on them.

"We can't leave her here!" Ruth shouted.

"Yes we can, and we will. If you had stayed on the transport, this wouldn't have happened. But it did, and she's staying. As soon as I get this dead body out of here we're leaving," Teela shouted back, standing to face Ruth.

"Beth! Come here!" Teela demanded.

"Yes, Sir, Capt'n Sir!" Beth said pushing past Ruth.

"I'm going to remove the body. If Rebecca starts screaming again, shut her up."

"Yes, Sir," Beth replied snapping a salute.

Teela walked back to where Dooaugh was sitting and after skirting around Rebecca, leaned down to lift Dooaugh from her seat. Rebecca began screaming and Beth immediately slugged her, the dull crack of the impact preceding the silence that followed.

"Jesus, Beth!" Teela cried.

"What? You said shut her up. I shut her up," Beth said holding her hands up in mock surrender.

Teela shook her head with disdain as she lifted Dooaugh out of her seat and dragged her from between the row of chairs, laying her down in the aisle. Placing her hand on Dooaugh's neck, Teela noted that she was cold to the touch. Feeling for a carotid pulse and finding none, she placed her face over Dooaugh's and looked beyond the dull glazed eyes. Sensing nothing but darkness and silence within the shell, Teela leaned back on her heels gathering Dooaugh's bony and gnarled hands between hers.

"Warrior, hero, thief, swordsman, pilot, and prophet. You were a loyal follower, and I came to value your help and advice. My existence will be less without yours. Goodbye, my friend," Teela said in Korlah. "Requiescat in pace." she said in Latin, uttering Dade's favorite prayer for the dead as her voice trailed off to a whisper. "Someone … help me remove this empty shell," she said after a pause, pushing the eyelids down to cover the black orbs that seemed to accuse her of losing yet another life.

"I will remove the warrior's shell," Shawaugh said, kneeling down and effortlessly scooping the frail body into her arms. At the access portal, she positioned Dooaugh onto her feet while holding her under the arms. Together, they dropped out of the opening to the hangar floor below. Placing Dooaugh on her back Shawaugh saluted the fallen warrior with a two-clawed salute before stepping into the ring and riding the inverted gravity field back into the transport.

From the transport's communications console, Teela called for the removal of Dooaugh's body from the hangar deck, while the pilot began maneuvering the transport into the airlock. The communications console flashed a code indicating a high priority message had just been received for "TEELA20.10127." Entering her private code, Teela scanned the message, her crown tendrils blanching and her limbs feeling weak after reading the first few lines.

TEELA20.10127,
The Council of Leaders with the cooperation and agreement of the Leader Potentate has come to a consensus based upon irrefutable evidence and the combined faith in our many cycles of knowledge and experience that you are Shawlmon incarnate. As such, you have been named Campaign Potentate.

Glancing around to see who may have seen the screen, she found Shawaugh standing behind and to one side of her. Looking down when Teela turned to face her, Shawaugh kept her eyes averted, offering an apologetic palm display as she turned away acknowledging Teela's unspoken desire for privacy. Turning back to the screen, Teela read the remainder of the message.

Since your departure, new information obtained using the captured human/Kahshinki translator, combined with reports that are now coming in from our long-range reconnaissance of the Kahshinki-occupied planet, have found an overwhelmingly large Kahshinki force. The Kahshinki planet is heavily industrialized and the remains of other planets in the system appear to have long ago been stripped of their resources. Of the six Campaign class vessels in the system, three have begun accelerating in the direction of the human planet. The records from our vessel's map room indicate this is not a system that has been harvested, but rather it is the Kahshinki home world. The human planet is one of a few rich planetary systems they use as a laboratory for developing bio-organisms for seeding the planets they harvest.

With or without an alliance, our statisticians do not believe this Campaign can be won. The Council requests your immediate return to guide us during an evaluation of the alternatives that have been proposed.

Respectfully, your loyal subordinate,

Shyron, Assistant to the Campaign Potentate.

Teela cleared the message from the screen resisting the urge to slam her fists down on the panel in frustration. Wanting desperately to scream and vent the feelings that boiled within her, she could feel her crown tendrils burning crimson with the emotions she was barely able to control. Taking a deep breath she began to compose her reply, her hands shaking so badly, she was forced to make repeated corrections.

Shyron, Assistant to the Campaign Potentate,

For those with the faith that I am truly Shawlmon incarnate, it must be understood that I am obliged by edict to follow the path that I am on. For those with wisdom and knowledge of our Mission's bitter origin, it must be understood that the Campaign Vessel is equally obliged by edict to also follow the same path.

I do not believe those who feel our path is hopeless are any less honorable, or any less loyal to Korlah than those who do not. For those who wish to pursue a different path, I recognize there is honor in their continued existence and the continued existence of their beliefs. I pledge my honor to those who choose not to follow, as I do for those who will.

At this time, my presence here is critical. I will be negotiating and allocating the first shipments of food and water within the next shift. You may begin sending freighters and escort pods to collect and transport provisions. By the time they arrive, I will have planetary collection points designated.

By fang or by claw,
My honor, Shawlmon, Campaign Potentate

Taking a deep breath, Teela released the air through pursed lips as she passed her thumb over the control that sent the message to Shyron. Of the many superior technological devices, the communications systems permitted instantaneous messaging between locations up to a light-year distant. Beyond one light year, the messages began to corrupt, with the message being totally lost beyond two. With the Campaign Vessel now well below those limitations, Shyron received the message before Teela finished clearing her screen. Utilizing living tissue to create a form of electronically enhanced telepathy, this was one of the many aspects of biotechnology humans had not yet managed to comprehend.

Teela sat at the console, staring intently at the blank screen, waiting for the chastising reply she was certain would follow.

You are Shawlmon, the true prophesized Potentate. Your words are now Law. Since you did not request a reply, there can be none. Said a voice heard only by Teela's mind. Not the thoughts of Daedalus, this voice had obviously been projected into her mind.

Teela turned and scanned the room for the source of the words. No one in the room met Teela's eyes, and no source of the projection could be detected.

Did I really hear that? Teela asked herself. In response, she received a clear projection, not a verbal communication; it was a feeling of mischievous amusement.

"Who is doing that!" Teela shouted.

"Doing what? Your Eminence," Shawaugh immediately replied, turning to face Teela.

Scanning Shawaugh's mind, Teela looked for an indication of deception, but sensed only confusion caused by her outburst.

"No one. I was thinking of something else," Teela said while looking around the control room suspiciously.

Am I losing my mind? Teela thought. *No, I heard it and sensed it too.* Daedalus replied.

"Director Shawaugh, it's time to depart," Teela said in an attempt to mask her consternation. "Please coordinate with Challmara and arrange for one assault pod and every available transport to prepare for transit to the human planet. When they are ready, proceed with extreme caution using whatever means available to protect our assets. We can expect the human military to be prepared for our arrival, and we can expect a few tricks we have not yet seen. I will be with our passengers, notify me when we are ten bits from atmosphere contact. I will pilot us to the surface."

"You?" Shawaugh started to ask. "Roche Hah! Shawlmon," she quickly growled respectfully, making a two-clawed salute before turning to the crew and barking orders.

Moving to the back of the transport Teela found the humans seated at different places among the 12 seats that were there. It took a moment for her to realize that each person had assumed the same position they filled on the journey that took them from Earth. Rebecca smiled as Teela approached, turning her head to look at Teela with her right eye since her left had swollen shut.

"This is your seat," Rebecca said, gesturing to the chair next to her.

160

"No Becca, not this trip," Teela said, scanning the other empty seats. She looked at each seat in turn, silently recalling the name of each missing person. *Jimmy Bourke, Crystal Santos, Bill Jacks, and Ann Moore.*

When at last she looked down at the seat that belonged to Daedalus, she reached out and placed her hand on the soft seamless material of its armrest, a hollow, empty feeling, a feeling of irretrievable loss swept over her. Rebecca placed her hand on top of Teela's and gave it a reassuring squeeze.

"Seven angels and a woman with a crown having twelve stars. God has chosen the path for us that we must now follow," Rebecca stated with words firm and confident, forged by undying devotion to her faith.

"I'm sorry, I don't believe in your God," Teela replied, avoiding Rebecca's fervent gaze.

Pulling her hand from Rebecca's uncomfortably moist grasp, Teela left the passenger area and returned to the forward compartment, more to escape Rebecca's disquieting stare than to accomplish any specific task. After Teela had left, Rebecca whispered in Korlah, "You will believe, because you cannot deny the miracle of your existence."

Howard Lewis

11 - Return

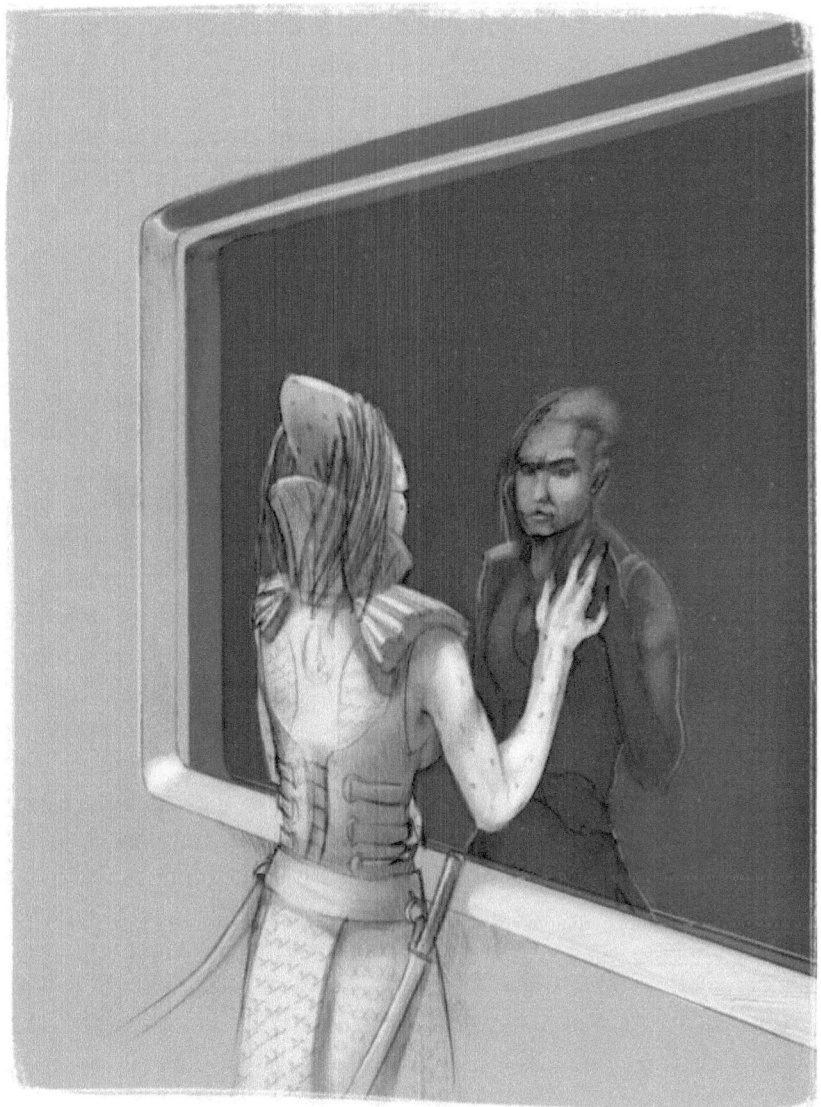

The Korlah task force assembled into a conical shaped wedge formation with the assault pod and Teela's transport at the core. The five heavy and five light fighters from the assault pod formed the leading edge of the formation, with thirty transports, most of which were commandeered from the base, making up the bulk of the group. Due to the greater number of vessels, and the tight proximity of the defensive formation, the group was forced to transit out of the asteroid belt at a much slower pace than Shawaugh did during her first visit to the planet.

Teela spent the long hours pacing the aisles, speaking only as needed to answer questions and, in most cases, with a single syllable response or unintelligible mumble. Stopping her incessant pacing, she looked into the darkness of space at the one source of light which was growing in size and intensity, drowning the other specks with its brilliance. To one side of the boiling sphere, a crescent of reflected light with a half orb adjacent to it glistened like a polished gem among the myriad of stars. With her face nearly touching the cold surface of the viewing port, she leaned heavily on the pilot's control console, devouring the objects ahead with the intensity of her gaze. The polished gem was her destination and source of her tortured thoughts since the first moments following transfer.

She placed her hand on the surface of the viewing screen. A halo of condensing moisture formed around it, tendrils of vapor rising and dissipating above. Contact with the ice-cold surface conjured a recollection that was more than a memory, in that moment she flashed on Dade's experience aboard the damaged transport and shuddered involuntarily. The anesthetizing effect of the freezing temperatures helped to diminish the intense aching of Dade's burned flesh, soothe his fears of re-capture, and introduce the bittersweet promise of death with minimal pain.

Teela struck the viewing port with her fist to break free of the effect, murmuring to herself, and receiving an uncomfortable glance from Shawaugh. Teela was aware she was behaving oddly, but felt it was insignificant compared to the issues at hand. Taking a deep breath, she listened to the voice that she and she alone could hear. The memories were not supposed to come with a voice; they should only have contained the experiences and subject matter content of the creature from which they were salvaged. She knew his voice should not be there, and that its presence would be considered a failure of the experiment and a threat to her assigned mission. A whisper at first, barely comprehensible, his voice had grown loud and clear. It was more than a voice, she was now intimately aware that he could control her actions if she allowed it.

I will never force you to do anything, Daedalus announced the instant following her moment of concern. *Their relationship being a marriage of the minds, secrets and deception cannot exist.*

You have nothing but contempt for this planet and everyone on it, Teela responded. *Your memories show me that they are selfish, wasteful, dishonest, dirty, disrespectful, and without honor. You were thrown out before you were given a chance to demonstrate your utility. You have suffered greatly and only attained marginal utility. You hate this planet. You hate everyone on it and have repeatedly wished it destroyed. I don't understand why you are so intent on prolonging its existence.*

I don't hate everyone on the planet, Daedalus replied with plaintive tinges of guilt combined with images of his wife, Julie.

Yes, the female, Teela acknowledged, her thoughts dripping with jealousy. She knew the emotion was not rational; the voice in her mind was nothing more than the disconnected essence of a creature long deceased and incapable of showing her the physical and emotional affections Daedalus had experienced with Julie. But the companionship, the deep understanding that came with the shared memories, she now realized sated the loneliness suffered throughout her adult life and she could not bear the thought of sharing him with anyone else.

You exist because of me. This female will not accept me as your replacement. I know this, because you know this. You have me pursuing this insane plan for the existence of a single female on a planet that is likely doomed regardless of whether or not we negotiate a 'strategic alliance' with these technological primitives.

Teela would have continued, but the angry voice in her mind shouted its dissatisfaction with her thoughts.

You would be nothing without me! They would have you scrubbing feces and filth from the floors in the Nursery section, or worse, you would be reclamated. Why do you care if your people win this war? Why do you really care? They were going to kill you, part you out, grind up the remains, and dump it into a digester. Honor and dedication? Don't even start to try to feed me that party-line bullshit! Sisters? They're not your sisters, they're duplicates of you, clones, hundreds of thousands of copies of you. They treat you like shit and work you like a borrowed mule.

Teela did not respond immediately, her mind digesting the barrage of thoughts, smiling when she finally related Dade's memories with the meaning of being "worked like a borrowed mule." She liked his use of metaphors and found these discussions enjoyable and strangely fulfilling. However, she did not like it when he was angry, and changed her tact to calm his angry thoughts.

It is not a matter of caring. It is a matter of purpose. When I worked, even when I scrubbed floors, I had purpose. My utility is defined by my purpose, and now my purpose is this mission. Your memories will provide the basis for the success or failure of this mission. I apologize for my doubts, but your memories and thoughts do not engender confidence in the probability of a successful alliance. We exist together now, we are one, and together we have purpose. This planet cannot be allowed to fall to our enemies. This is my chance, our second chance, would you have us risk our existence for this planet you hate?

Look at us. Daedalus said, observing Teela's reflected image peering back at them from the viewing screen. *Can you see me?* he asked.

Teela studied the image and dredged forth the memory of Daedalus looking in a mirror. For a moment, the image melded with hers and she could see their combined images looking back, looking within, gauging and demanding they be more introspective of themselves in relation to the universe around them. It was at that moment of self-evaluation that Teela experienced his need, and Daedalus in turn experienced hers. This chance encounter, this brief moment in time, and for as long as it lasted, they knew that if they had nothing else, at the very least, they would always have each other.

Teela was not the only one engaged in a debate over the possibilities that awaited them. Beth and Ruth were having a heated argument over how they would be treated upon their return. Beth was convinced they would be taken into custody and quarantined for both medical and political concerns. Their story, she believed, would never be told the way it actually happened, and they would be lucky if they were not locked away for life, or eliminated for what they now knew. Ruth agreed that they would be quarantined, that would be standard protocol, but was adamant that they would not be in any danger as long as their return was public and incontestable. Disengaging from the debate with a wave of her hand, Beth stood and approached Teela.

"Hey Dade, what's the plan for dropping us off?" Beth asked.

Teela's eyes warned Beth that her interruption was not welcome. Teela hissed her words out slowly and ominously.

"What is left of Dade is in the storeroom with Crystal and Jimmy. He's dead Beth. Please accept it … I have."

"Sorry … *Teela* … I didn't come over to start a fight. I want to warn you, I know how the military operates, and you know as well as I do, the government will not want the public to hear what we have to say. If you're expecting to be welcomed, you got another thing coming. Ramsey wasn't bullshitting when he said they would destroy us. You can bet they're gonna give it a try. Out here, it looks like you have the edge. Earth side, it may be another story. You need to make contact if you intend to negotiate an alliance; I understand that, but you need a backup plan in case things don't go as expected," Beth said.

"And I suppose you have a backup plan in mind," Teela said, listening to the details of the plan flowing from Beth's mind.

"I'm thinking you should drop me off, separate from the others, quiet-like. If things don't work out for you I could take our story to the international press," Beth said.

"Okay, sounds good. I'll arrange it," Teela replied without hesitation. "Don't worry, you will be dropped exactly where you specify. You won't have to walk far," Teela added.

It was not the quick response that surprised Beth; it was the comment about her being worried about how far she would have to walk. That was exactly what she was thinking a moment before Teela commented on it.

"I understand now why your crew is afraid of you," Beth said, lowering her voice. "I thought it was respect at first, but it's not. They talk when you're not around, and it's obvious to me that you scare the shit out of them. They have a name for you. I thought it was a name like 'Big Boss', but my translation 'head-mouth' was wrong. What they call you is 'mind talker.' I know you just read my mind. You can read theirs, and they know it."

Closing the gap between them, Teela stopped when her face was inches away from Beth's. She spoke softly and without any hint of hostility.

"Although they may not be readily apparent, I do have ears. For the sake of this conversation, let's just say I hear very, very well. I hear what goes on around me and I make assumptions based on partial information. I will undoubtedly be dealing with species xenophobia, and that alone will present enough of an obstacle to open negotiations without there being fears I can read minds, so I would like you to keep that suspicion to yourself.

"I also overheard concerns regarding quarantine. I don't know what concerns or precautions should be taken for diseases or parasites. None of you ... humans and none of us Korlah have gotten sick, so I believe the risk of introducing an alien pathogen is probably unlikely. But I admit it is a great risk and I ... well ... I can only hope returning you separate from the others will not be one that you or I will regret," Teela said.

"I was planning on asking Marsha and Catherine to go with me," Beth said.

"You're not a team player, Beth. I believe you would do better alone. But I understand that you wish to ensure they at least will get home safely so that your debt to Crystal will be paid," Teela said.

Beth stepped back, the pale skin of her face and neck flushing with surprise and embarrassment. She looked down at Teela's feet to avoid eye contact, clearing her throat before she spoke.

"Yes ... you're right. Um ... damn good assumption," Beth said, feeling as if Teela had just reached into her mind and pulled out the one thing that made her feel weak.

"Beth, you do whatever you think you have to do. I don't want to know what your plans are, and you shouldn't tell the others either. They will be interrogated and it must be assumed that they will tell the authorities everything they know. I will package the evidence you will need and make arrangements for your delivery. If your fears are justified, then it will not be long after the others are returned that the government will begin looking for you. If I fail, the responsibility to inform the people of this planet of what is happening will fall upon your shoulders. Do you accept this responsibility?" Teela asked.

"Sir, yes, Sir!" Beth cried, snapping a clawed Korlah salute, before turning on her heel and marching back to where Ruth stood leaning on her seat watching them.

With Beth well out of ear shot, Teela said, *I'm not your enemy, I hope one day you will accept that,* telepathically projecting the words to Beth. With a jerk of her head, Beth turned and looked directly at Teela with a look of surprise. A moment later, she smiled a crooked smile and nodded her head slowly. Teela did not attempt to scan her thoughts, but rather nodded unspoken understanding before leaving the rear area to speak with Shawaugh about arranging transport for Beth and the girls.

After providing her instructions, Teela watched as Shawaugh responded with astute efficiency, developed through years of service in both subordinate and supervisory roles. Delegating the orders and the multiple activities that were culminating with their approach to the planet, Shawaugh stood back merely monitoring and advising when needed, allowing the crew to perform with the speed, quality and accuracy they were specifically selected and trained for. But it was more than the designed utility of their positions that ensured their flawless performance. Each was imbued with great pride to perform at a level equivalent to flawless perfection based on the deep respect and admiration they had for Shawaugh as their immediate leader. The true import of "Mission" and "Campaign" had eliminated any and all dissention that may have existed among those present. With the fearless and undefeated Shawaugh leading them, Teela was certain that the concept of failure was incomprehensible, theirs was a common cause and they embraced it with a single-minded conviction; defeat was not an option.

Unlike the humans who clustered into a knot and talked more and more excitedly as the moment of their return neared, the Korlah spoke only when necessary, manipulating the panels and monitoring the instrumentation with intense concentration. Shawaugh patrolled the control room, assessing the panels and progress as the formation began multiple course and speed changes, jumping in and out of high velocity travel in an effort to both prevent and disrupt their detection. From the direction of their approach, the Earth was now on the far side of the sun. Placing the burning orb between Earth and the formation of Korlah craft, Shawaugh notified Teela they were in position for the final approach.

Teela found Beth, Marsha, and Catherine waiting at the partition that divided the front and rear of the transport. Setting down a slim box she was carrying, she took each in turn, into a close embrace, touching her forehead to theirs before releasing them with a respectful bow.

"This is a communications device," Teela said, picking up the slim box and handing it to Beth. "It has been modified to permit the use of spoken communications. To talk to me you put this where the log bars go." She handed Beth a device that, when placed in the cradle where the log bars went, acted as both speaker and microphone. Turning the device over, Teela opened an access panel in the bottom to reveal its inner workings. The pulsing blobs of living flesh, laced with hair-sized connections flashing with bio-chemical charges, presented a dramatically alien technology.

"Yuck! God almighty, shut that thing would you?" Beth cried, stepping back the moment the stench reached her nostrils.

Teela closed the panel and unconsciously shook her crown tendrils to clear the noxious smell that was offending their sensitive olfactory nerves. Reaching into a pocket, she withdrew a number of log bars as well as a portion of the dog tags and uniform patches removed from the human soldiers that participated in the assault on the Campaign Vessel. Taking the evidence from Teela, Beth pushed it into a pocket.

170

"We're taking rifles, too," Beth said, patting the pulse rifle cradled in her arm, like the ones Marsha and Catherine were also holding.

Without commenting, Teela turned and walked to the center of the control area. An access hole had opened in the floor leading to a light fighter docked with their transport. Diving through the opening, Teela waited until Beth, Marsha, and Catherine joined her. The three-person crew had been reduced to only the pilot. Moving to the empty seat at the navigation panel, Teela deftly manipulated the controls causing a view of Earth to fill the entire window of the ship. With a motion of her hand, the view shifted bringing the American continent into view.

"Point to where you want to go," Teela said, demonstrating by pointing to the west coast. In a flash, the view zoomed to the area where she had pointed. Pointing again, the view zoomed further and further until the intersection of a residential street filled the screen. When a car passed through the intersection, Beth realized she was viewing the planet in real time.

"Jeeze! Is that- like-... live?" Catherine asked.

"Yes," Teela answered matter-of-factly, restoring the image with a wave of her hand. "You try it," she said to Beth, stepping aside.

Beth stepped forward and selected an area in Arizona near the Colorado River. Zooming into a desert wash near a small cluster of buildings a few miles away from Lake Mohave.

"Here, put us right here."

Issuing orders to the pilot, Teela bowed deeply to each of the women in turn, finishing with Beth. From her pocket, Teela withdrew a creased and tattered scrap of paper. Pressing the paper into Beth's palm, she looked down as she spoke.

"If I fail, find her, tell her ... Hell, tell her everything," Teela said, turning away and exiting the vessel without giving Beth a chance to respond.

After the floor sealed, Beth looked at the scrap of paper, it was a photograph. Beth recognized the picture as one that had been in Dade's wallet. A candid, un-posed photo of a woman with long brown hair, the image captured as she turned. Beth studied it closely before turning it over. On the back, a name and address had been carefully scribed. Looking up, she realized that the pilot had already detached the fighter from the transport and was banking sharply away from the cluster of vessels. A moment later, the fighter began accelerating directly toward the sun.

Watching the fighter blink out of sight, Teela sat down at the central control panel. With skill and expertise borrowed from Dooaugh's memories, she deftly manipulated the controls bringing the transport onto the heading that would take it to Earth. Moving out from behind the sun, the formation of vessels followed Teela's lead and proceeded toward Earth, making no effort to mask or hide their approach. As intended, she would draw attention away from the craft delivering Beth. Still well beyond the orbiting defenses of Earth, all vessels in the formation except Teela's transport dropped back and formed a defensive grouping in a stationary orbit above the east coast of the North American continent.

"Transmit the signal," Teela ordered. A message based on the coded signal the Kahshinki were using notified the humans of Teela's intentions to approach. Modifying the signal, Teela included a greeting expressing her peaceful intentions and desire to communicate with a government representative.

"Done!" the communications technician replied, sending the message on cue.

"Signal received. Twelve hits," the communications technician announced a moment later, indicating the coding in the signal had functioned properly, automatically generating a signal from each listening station that received it.

Bringing the transport to a stop, Teela closed her eyes and listened with her mind. The thermal images produced by the hisnah contributed little to directly illuminate the darkness and silence of the area before her. Focusing her mind as Dooaugh had taught her, she slowly moved her head and opened her mind like a receiver centered through the hisnah. The satellites began to appear in the darkness like small blue spheres, each babbling with thoughts composed of electronic computations and communications. Each satellite was producing simple thoughts, mechanical and rudimentary in their purpose, the computer intelligence of each was busy performing dozens of functions, repetitive and predictable. But then, as she listened, she heard something else, something new. Automatic systems switched off and new systems, controlled from remote locations, began energizing in many of the satellites before them. Like following strands of wire, Teela traced the signals with her mind, following them to the planet's surface and the minds that were sending them.

The entire evolution took less time than was required for Teela to sharply expel the air from her lungs as she realized what was about to happen. Grunting with urgency, she slammed the controls to the side while initiating a momentary hyper-light jump. The area where they had been sitting ignited into a dazzling flash of light and raw energy as the simultaneous emissions of more than a dozen particle beam cannons discharged their powerful beams of densely focused protons and neutrons. The colliding particles momentarily coalesced forming a ball of burning atomic plasma that provided its own fuel in the vacuum of space. Like the glowing embers of fire blown by the wind, the highly ionized particles of atomic matter sparkled briefly before fading as the cloud of molecular waste expanded and dissipated in all directions from the impact site. To the instrumentation on Earth and in orbit, it appeared that the satellite defense system had obliterated Teela's transport.

"Shit!" Teela shouted as the transport shook violently in and out of hyper-light. Even after the transport had returned to normal space, the shaking and vibrations continued. Through the front window, all that Teela could see was a spinning deep dark blue. She realized that they were plunging through the atmosphere toward the open ocean in a spiraling, uncontrolled descent.

Unable to control the vessel's speed or direction, Teela watched as the absorption arrays began to crumble, melt, and disintegrate from the atmospheric friction. In the final moments as the surface details of the ocean became visible and clearly indicated their imminent impact, Teela abandoned the traditional controls on the panel and pulled back on the joystick that was added as one of Challmara's improvements. The instant Teela pulled back on the stick and applied directional force to counter the spin, the rapid descent curved into a stable horizontal trajectory a few yardss above the surface of the water. The craft, still traveling in excess of mach-3 creased the surface of the water, skipping across the peaks of the swells, the multiple impacts pounding the hull of the transport violently. If not for the inertia suppression system, the pounding would have beaten the occupants of the transport senseless. Easing back on the joystick, Teela lifted the craft from the surface, allowing it to glide through the atmosphere by virtue of its momentum alone. Finding the gravity drive unit off-line, Teela held her breath as she initiated a restart, the power blinked once before climbing to optimum.

Banking right and left, and up and down while changing speed, Teela verified the craft was undamaged and responding normally. Breathing a sigh of relief she leveled the craft off at a few thousand feet above the surface of the water, turning onto a southwest heading so that the sun, now low in the westerly sky, would not be in her eyes. Using the global positioning viewer, she adjusted the settings until the transport was positioned such that she could see the east coast of North America. She scanned the cities and roads that appeared as tumor-like growths connected together by arteries that surged and pumped as the vehicles moving along them glistened in the afternoon sunlight. Her hand directing the images, Teela worked her way down the coast toward her intended destination.

"New York, Philadelphia, Baltimore, and there you are, Washington!" she exclaimed, adjusting the controls of the transport.

Teela directed the vessel's gravitational drive unit to proceed to the location. The device reached out to the planetary magnetic lines of flux that flowed past that location, and by a process of gravitational magnification, the vessel allowed itself to be pulled to the location rather than being propelled. In what appeared to those who had spotted the craft off the coast to be a rapid burst of speed, the craft actually fell to its destination by virtue of the forces of gravity multiplied many times.

In a fraction of a second, the transport appeared several thousand feet above the ground on the northeast edge of Washington DC. Surveying the city, Teela could see the unmistakable dome of the United States Capitol building, and further down the Mall, the spire of the Washington Monument.

"Multiple threats, surface, and atmospheric," the weapons technician reported.

Anticipating the report, Teela dropped the vessel's altitude from several thousand feet to less than a hundred feet before the technician had finished speaking. Below them, the Southwest Beltway 395, already packed with afternoon commuters, came to a grinding stop as numerous vehicles slammed into one another at the sight of what appeared to be a large object falling from the sky. Hoping to use the crowds and buildings as a deterrent against attack, Teela followed the busy road to South Capitol Street and on towards the Capitol Building.

Teela concentrated on the building that would soon be directly under them. The multiple thoughts of the building's occupants co-mingled like a buzzing sound. Picking through the droning noise, listening more for emotion and intent rather than content, she found one sound, one mind that rang out loudly above the others.

Conflicting orders, confusion, and panic harried the mind she had found. Listening rather than probing, Teela understood the confusion. An order had been sent out to fire upon the unidentified object entering restricted air space, only to be rescinded moments later in the form of a Presidential directive, a directive sent from the White House. "Unless confirmed by hostile act, no hostile actions shall be taken." The order was repeated and relayed to the civilian and military forces that were rapidly taking positions on the roofs and grounds of the buildings beneath them. Glancing at the weapons console threat display, the screen had completely filled with identified and targeted threats, the technician frantically attempting to adjust and coordinate the weapons fire that she anticipated would be requested should the forces below, or above, attack.

"Secure all weapons and targeting systems," Teela said calmly and slowly to make certain her words would not be questioned.

The technician, true to her training, immediately secured the systems. The glowing tip of the pulse cannon that appeared to those on the ground as a light on the front of the transport, slowly faded as the transport's power cell reabsorbed the energy within the pulse chamber.

"Secured!" the technician reported.

Banking sharply left and with a burst of speed, Teela guided the transport down the Mall toward the Potomac, banking right as they passed within feet of the Washington Monument, she proceeded directly towards the White House. Wishing to ensure contact with the media and public before the military forces on the ground could intervene, Teela passed over the front of the White House, which appeared devoid of the vehicle and pedestrian traffic that choked the streets beyond. Turning the transport so that it would be parallel to Lafayette Street, Teela began a slow descent into the center of the avenue, allowing the crowds of people to clear the area beneath them. Taking the gravitational drive unit off-line, the transport slowly settled onto the pavement with a loud buzzing sound as the magnetic fields in the drive unit dissipated their electrostatic energy.

"All weapons and armor are to remain inside," Teela said, facing Shawaugh and the other Korlah warriors who were in the final stages of donning their protective armor and shoulder-mounted cannons.

With an indignant grunt of acknowledgement, Shawaugh ordered the other warriors to remain in their armor and assume defensive positions around the area of the hull where the access door would open. With movements and mannerisms that reflected her disapproval of Teela's order, Shawaugh removed her weapons and armor, throwing them haphazardly onto the floor rather than stowing them in their proper locations. Teela directed the pilot back into her seat before addressing the entire crew and delivering orders that she believed might be the last of her existence.

176

"If I am attacked, you are to depart immediately. You will use only the force necessary to protect this craft and retain your existence. No retaliation or revenge shall be implemented. Is this understood?" she asked.

The silence that followed indicated that although it was understood, the concept of being attacked without retaliating was difficult for the warrior caste to accept. As the true leader of the transports crew, Shawaugh replied to the order and question, her approach cautious and respectful.

"Yes, Your Eminence, we understand the order, but we do not understand your logic. If they attack and we do not retaliate, we will appear weak and without honor."

Putting her hand on Shawaugh's heavily muscled shoulder, Teela gave it a tight squeeze. Releasing her grip, she looked at Shawaugh without seeing her, her eyes focused on something beyond Shawaugh, beyond the moment and far into the future. When she spoke, it was with empathy and sorrowful disagreement of the application of Korlah warrior ethics.

"How we appear is unimportant, for even with our help their existence is likely forfeit. This planet will probably be harvested or sterilized by the Kahshinki. I cannot conceive of a punishment you could possibly inflict that would better preserve our precious honor."

12 - Message

Riding the invisible magnetic lines of flux emanating from the sun, the saucer-shaped fighter traversed the sun's equator within a few hundred thousand miles of the turbulent surface. Within the vessel, Beth and the girls stared in awe at the filtered view of the churning granules of short-lived cells of plasma that appeared as bubbles the size of Texas carrying heat from the Sun's core to its surface. At a predetermined point where the ship was centered directly between the Sun and Earth, the vessel rocketed away from the Sun using the gravity of both planetary bodies to accelerate. Raising the vessel to near light speed, the pilot engaged the hyper-light drive, compressing the plasma from the sun's solar wind and traversing the ninety-three million miles in a little over thirty seconds.

With the gravitational drive system controlling their descent, the pilot brought them straight down to within a few hundred feet of the planet's surface. Unlike Teela's uncontrolled decent, the fighter's drive system utilized the combined electromagnetic fields to slice through the atmosphere by guiding the molecules of atmosphere around the ship. In the case of atmospheric travel, the faster the craft moved, the less detectable the effect of molecular compression and decompression was. In the dry desert air, no contrail formed, and no sound emanated as the fighter appeared and descended to within a few yards from the ground.

"Let's go!" Beth shouted, jumping through the opening in the floor. Marsha quickly followed, with Catherine so close behind that she nearly landed on Marsha's shoulders causing her to tumble onto the ground. As silent as it had arrived, the fighter leapt skyward leaving an artificial dust devil swirling around the three women standing in the middle of a sand-covered wash.

"I hope you know where we are," Marsha said, her eyes nervously scanning the foreboding desert landscape.

"Sure do," Beth answered, glancing about the area and confirming that they had been dropped exactly where she asked.

"It feels funny to walk," Catherine said, shifting her weight from one foot to the other.

"Yeah, I noticed that," Beth replied, bouncing up and down on the balls of her feet. "This is real gravity. We've been living with artificial gravity, a lot more than this, so this feels like less, but it's actually normal. Excellent! The entire time we've been gone, we've been receiving the best well-rounded exercise program possible. Let's go soldiers! We have places to go, people to see, and things to do."

Setting out at a determined pace, Beth headed down the wash toward a settlement she knew to be about a mile away. Without question, and without further comment, Marsha and Catherine fell in step close behind. The wash passed through a narrow gap in the low lying hills and spread out into numerous dry bed rivulets through the rocks and brush down a gentle grade toward the Colorado River, which could be seen glistening in the distance four or five miles to the north. Climbing out of the wash, up and over one of the many small knolls, Beth spied the destination she sought. A trailer with structures attached to one side and across the front, stood in an otherwise undeveloped field of rocks, brush, and cacti. As they neared the structure, Marsha could see that a road had once snaked across the high spot to where the trailer was sitting, but was now nearly obscured by the growth of brush, erosion of wind, and the seasonal rains that were known to produce killer flash floods in the same wash they had just hiked down.

At the back of the trailer, Beth popped off one of the faded taillights and shook the key within it into her hand. She unlocked and removed the padlocks from the trailer and then the storage building doors. The doors of the shed opened with a low groan. She stepped inside and pulled a canvas cover from a portable generator near the door. The gas can was right where she left it. Shaking the can, she hoped that the fuel had not gone stale. Checking the fuel level, Beth topped off the tank on the generator. After repeated priming, and a half dozen pulls on the manual starter cord, the unit coughed, sputtered, and begrudgingly rumbled to life.

With the flip of a switch, the inside of the windowless garage illuminated. An old van covered with a dusty tarp filled half the garage. The other half was filled with six-foot steel storage closets, each with its own padlock. Pulling the tarp off the van, Beth popped the hood and connected a charger to the terminals of the van's battery before plugging it into one of the spare outlets on the generator. After opening the closets, she instructed Marsha and Catherine what would be loaded into the van and, most importantly, how to wrap and where to conceal the pulse rifles.

With Marsha and Catherine busily loading the van, Beth returned to the vintage 1950s trailer. Once inside, she locked the door behind her, turned on the lights and walked to the back where a sliding door separated the front from a small bedroom. Claustrophobic at best, the contents of the room consisted of nothing more than a bed, an end table, and a small lamp that was missing its shade.

From a small drawer in the end table, she withdrew a long, thin, letter opener. With a kick, she knocked the mattress off the bed frame, tilted it on end and shoved it through the narrow door to get it out of her way. Feeling the far corner of the plywood bed frame, back beneath the window in the area where the low curvature of the trailer's round aerodynamic shape created a dark cavity, she found the narrow slot for which she was searching. Sliding the letter opener into the slot, she climbed off the platform and opened the cupboard door beneath the bed. Inside the narrow storage space was a suitcase, its handle facing outward. As she slowly pulled the suitcase out, she listened carefully for the sound of a snap that would give her five seconds to evacuate the trailer. Since no snap was heard, she took the lamp from the end table. She held it down and into the opening under the bed; in the back, she could see the blocks of C-4 neatly stacked around the hand grenade whose handle would have flown off when she removed the suitcase had she not inserted the letter opener to hold it in place.

This ain't exactly what this joint is for, but it will do, she thought as she folded down the kitchen table and placed the suitcase on it. With her thumb, she entered the combination: 0507, the month and day of her discharge from the Marines. Grinning at the irony, she popped the release latches and opened the suitcase.

One betrayal deserves another, she thought.

Inside the case were a number of passports with matching driver's licenses, two half-inch-thick stacks of fifty-dollar bills, and a small overnight bag. From the stack of documents, she selected two sets of identification, and all the money. Before closing the case, she withdrew the overnight bag. In the narrow alcove that served as the dressing area, Beth sat the bag down on the counter and propped up one of the identification pictures at the bottom of the dusty and age-mottled mirror. Taking a barber's shear from the bag, she plugged it in, set the tip for about a quarter inch and switched it on.

Marsha was holding a box of camping gear near the back of the van while Catherine was inside the van trying to make room for it. Movement at the opening of the garage caught her eye. A portly man, with a shaved head and a thick mustache, wearing a Hawaiian shirt, baggy pants, and pilot-style sunglasses stood holding a suitcase in one hand and a large silver pistol in the other.

"What the hell are y'all doing in mah garage?" the man boomed in a thick southern drawl.

Marsha dropped the box and stepped from behind the van, raising her hands.

"Answer mah question, God damn it!" the man shouted angrily.

"I'm just loading the van," she answered cautiously, noticing out of the corner of her eye Catherine sliding serpentine-like out of the van and onto the floor.

"Why you loading mah van, sugar plum?"

"I was told to, asshole," Marsha growled, feeling more confident as she saw Catherine slide a pulse rifle off the front seat.

"Oh my! You are a feisty little fireball, ain't you?" the man asked, setting down the suitcase and pushing the pistol into his belt, before walking towards Marsha.

"Freeze, Dick Head!" Catherine shouted stepping out from behind the van and pointing the pulse rifle at the man.

Pulling the pistol from his belt, the man leveled it at Catherine's head.

"Bang your dead. Those weapons are useless unless they are energized," the man said in a voice that was unmistakably Beth's, lowering the pistol and winking at Catherine.

"Beth?" Marsha asked, looking more closely. "You Fucker! You scared the shit out of me."

Catherine laughed, walked up to Beth and poked her in the sculpted padding that transformed her lean waist and breasts into the barrel chest and belly of an out of shape man in his late-fifties.

"My name is Burton Portenski. But y'all can call me Burt. Now we gotta git this here van loaded up and on the road post haste. Ah spect the Feds will be crawling all over this joint in a couple a days if not sooner. Now I mean it when I tell ya to call me Burt. From now on that will be who ah am, you understand what I'm telling y'all?"

"Fuck'n A!" the girls shouted in unison, laughing.

"We'll get some miles between here and where we're going, then we'll do some shopping and get us a hotel room with hot and cold running water near a restaurant that serves great big juicy steaks," Beth said. She slid the suitcase under the driver's seat and tucked the pistol into a hollow cavity hidden behind the armrest of the driver's side door.

"Where are we going?" Marsha asked.

"To the last great bastion in the war against Federalist aggression," Beth replied.

"The South?" Catherine asked

"No darling, Montana."

Washington was cool and damp, made even cooler by the long shadows of the late afternoon. The crowds that fled in panic down Lafayette Street and into the park as the transport descended began to return in groups of two or three once the vessel settled onto the avenue and became motionless and silent. Emboldened by the few that ventured forward, the crowds began to surge toward the craft, cameras snapping and flashing as they approached.

An oval opening appeared on the side of the craft, the material of the hull seemingly melting down and forming steps as the opening grew in size. A Japanese man ran forward taking pictures. Teela exited first, followed by Shawaugh, Rebecca, Ann, Tiffany, and Ruth. The crowd surged forward even closer when Rebecca and the other humans emerged. Questions were shouted by the tourists and answers shouted back by the disembarking humans, the noise level rising to a chaotic cacophony within a few minutes. Police in riot gear materialized from staging areas on either end of the street, sweeping through the crowd and funneling groups of people toward windowless black vans that began arriving at the intersections of Pennsylvania Avenue and 17th Street, and New York Avenue and 15th Street. With Shawaugh following close behind, Teela made her way to one of the gated driveways that led to the back entrance of the White House.

They approached the guard shack situated on the left-hand side of the driveway, intended for a time when vehicular traffic had been allowed on Lafayette Street. The small building was now used primarily as a security outpost. Behind the thick bulletproof glass, two guards stood staring wide eyed at Teela's alien visage as she approached the window. One of the guards stood in the far corner of the small room talking on the phone. The second guard stood near the window with one hand on the counter and the other behind his back in an attempt to conceal his un-holstered revolver.

Teela bowed respectfully to the guard. He just stared at her, his face an expression of shock. Sparkling flashes of light reflected on the glass around her silhouette drew her attention away from the guard at the window. Turning, a bright light struck her cyc causing her to shade her brow with her hand to block the painful beam. From the dots of light that danced on Shawaugh's head and chest, Teela realized they were being targeted by numerous laser-sighting scopes.

"Return to the transport and remain there," Teela ordered.

Shawaugh stood silent, neither moving nor speaking. Teela held her hand up to block the point of light that she could see was being purposefully played across Shawaugh's eyes.

"Please, permit me to do this my way," Teela pleaded.

With a grunt of disapproval, Shawaugh turned and marched back to the transport, entering and then closing the access portal. Standing in the driveway, Teela could see that police and military

185

personnel were nearly finished clearing the streets and establishing barricades at all the access points to both the street and Lafayette Park. Movement drew her attention to the rooftops; she could see soldiers taking up positions on all adjacent buildings, the heat from the faces and the laser beam sights marking their positions. The combined drone of three unmarked military helicopters replaced the shouts and noise of the crowds.

Beth was right, they're going to try to squelch this, Teela thought.

Turning back to the guard shack, Teela considered what to say and how to say it. Everything she had rehearsed in her mind during the journey, everything she had wanted to deliver in this critical moment seemed to be slipping from her grasp. Speaking more for the benefit of the recording she was certain was being made, than to actually communicate with the guards, she addressed the microphone set in the thick bulletproof glass at the window.

"I have no weapons. I am here to see the President. I have critical information regarding the safety and security of both this country and planet," Teela said.

"Yes ... ahhh ... S ... Sir, arrangements are being made," the guard nearest the window stuttered, making furtive gestures toward the other guard still on the phone.

Standing in the shadow of the guard shack, Teela savored the dim light. Unaccustomed to sunlight, her eyes ached from the bright white light and the skin of her face already felt as though it were sunburned. The chill of the late afternoon air relieved the discomfort, while at the same time it caused her to shiver. Closing the top clasp on her vest, she plunged her hands into the pockets of her tunic. Through the gate, nearest to the driveway where she stood, she could see activity in the form of people and vehicles. With a screech that caused Teela to jump, the gate began to move, rolling on tracks it opened and then stopped.

"Someone is being sent to meet you, Sir. You may proceed through the gate," the guard's voice instructed her via a speaker above the window.

Out of habit and good manners, Teela made a courteous gesture of appreciation with her hands before walking through the gate. As she passed through the threshold, the gate began closing. Walking down the center of the road towards her, a person wearing a biohazard suit was coming. Stopping a few feet in front of her the person bowed as she had done at the guard shack.

"Greetings from the President of the United States," came a muffled voice from within the suit.

Teela stared at the man with incredulous dismay. There was no logical basis for the insult she was feeling. There had never been a negotiation with another sentient species during the entire history of Campaign. Yet, this behavior, this distancing and isolating that these creatures were displaying struck a chord of anger in that part of her that was still Korlah.

"I have come unarmed and unprotected. My vessel was nearly destroyed by the unprovoked hostile actions of this country. Even now, your soldiers hide like frightened rodents as they point their weapons at me. Ask your President, what kind of greeting is this?" Teela railed, unable to contain the anger that was swelling within her.

"Yes, Sir, I'm sorry, Sir. I … uh, we … have a procedure for this … and we are trying to follow it. I am truly sorry … if … if we have offended you," the muffled voice stammered.

"Do you fear that I am unclean? Is that why you are hiding within protective garments?"

"No … No, Sir. It's procedure, Sir."

"I am called Shawlmon. I am the designated representative of this peaceful mission. It has been clearly demonstrated that I am in great danger, yet I honor my species by demonstrating that I am unafraid. Do you have no one who can honor your species in the same manner?" Teela asked, shaking her head in disgust.

After a momentary pause, the man in the suit pulled off the hood. A young man in his late twenties, his hair closely cropped to the point of nearly being shaved, smiled politely as he tossed the hood onto the ground. He had the non-descript appearance of the typical Secret Service agent, his tanned complexion pale only around the eyes from the dark glasses he normally would have been wearing. Pausing he turned to one side and spoke for the benefit of a microphone in his lapel.

"No, No! It's called diplomacy," he whispered tersely before continuing to remove the rest of the biohazard suit.

"My name is Cooper, Special Agent Richard Cooper," the young man said, straightening the jacket of his black suit before extending a hand to Teela.

Taking his hand, Teela returned the firm grasp as they shook hands. Scanning his thoughts, Teela was only able to gather that he was genuinely excited and pleased to be where he was at that moment. Nowhere in his thoughts did she detect any hostile intent or planned malfeasance. Releasing his hand, Teela gave him her most human smile.

"You have not been trained in diplomatic protocol, why is it that they sent you to meet me?" Teela asked.

"I'm sorry, Sir, I'm being told to bring you inside where they will have someone answer your questions," Agent Cooper replied.

"You have honor, this I can respect. I will deliver my message to you. The others and your President can listen from wherever it is that they are hiding."

"Sir, they want me to bring you in. Inside ... um ... a meeting room is being prepared."

"First you will tell me why they sent you out to meet me and not a diplomat."

Looking Teela up and down, the Agent bit his lip, trying to make a decision. Nervously clearing his throat before speaking, he looked over his shoulder and back at Teela before replying.

"Everyone except security headed into the shelters when your ... vehicle was sighted. I'm part of the White House security detail, so when things like this happen we stay put. They needed someone to come out and bring you in. I volunteered, didn't really think about it, it just sounded cool."

Teela looked into his eyes, the contrast of the iris against the miniscule dark pupil of humans usually made her feel uncomfortable. His eyes were warm and sincere, renditions of the thoughts Teela felt emanating from within. In an instant, she knew this individual could be trusted to behave honorably.

"You make me believe that there is hope for this day. Your superiors would be well advised to emulate your candor. As long as you remain with me, as my escort, I am prepared to go with you," Teela said as she bowed and displayed her palms.

"Follow me, Sir," Agent Cooper said, appearing visibly relieved.

Walking down the driveway toward a small group that awaited them by one of the side doors, Teela stayed closely behind Agent Cooper. Shaking out her crown tendrils, she sampled the multitude of odors that filled the air; fresh cut grass, damp pavement, flowers, automobile exhaust and an overwhelming smell that made her mouth water and stomach growl with memories suddenly awakened.

"Did you just eat a pastrami sandwich? I can smell pastrami, rye bread, dark mustard, lettuce, tomatoes, and maybe, mayonnaise," Teela said.

"Wow! Yes, Sir … that's exactly what I ate. You have a good nose. If you would like, I'll have one sent from the kitchen."

"Oh … yes, yes I would like that," Teela wheezed, swallowing to drain the saliva that began to fill her mouth. "And six more, no, make that twelve more to go."

"To go?" Agent Cooper asked with surprise.

"Yes, to take with me when I leave. For my crew, not just me."

"Yes, Sir, of course," Agent Cooper replied.

With the exception of Agent Cooper, all the personnel along the way were wearing biohazard suits. Entering the building through a basement doorway, they went down a short flight of stairs, through a plain unimposing hallway to an alcove with an elevator. The elevator took them down several levels opening up to a richly decorated foyer. From the foyer, Teela was led into a large room with an ornately carved oval oak table positioned at its center. Despite the many fascinating objects and decorations in and around the room, it was the soft spongy feeling of the carpet beneath her feet that Teela found the most intriguing. Knowing what it was and having memories of it did not quell the intense desire to kneel down and run her hands over the soft velour-like surface. She had never walked on anything but hard cold surfaces, the appearance and feel of carpeting seemed bizarre. It took effort to resist the urge to touch it; she contented herself by shifting her weight from one foot to the other, marveling at the soft flexible surface.

"Sir, if you'd like to sit down, the President and several members of our government will be ready to speak with you in just a few minutes," Agent Cooper said, drawing Teela's attention away from the carpeting.

At Agent Cooper's beckoning, Teela accepted an offered chair, as well the courtesy of having it pushed in as she sat down at the table. Withdrawing a distance behind her, Agent Cooper stood quietly as the wall across the table from Teela slid open to reveal an array of viewing screens.

"You're going to teleconference this meeting?" Teela spat out, rising from the chair and pushing away from the table. Pacing the length of the table and back, she turned to the only other person in the room and marched over to him. Agent Cooper swallowed as the obviously angry alien stopped in front of him. Pausing, she took a deep breath, clenching her fists to regain control of the anger she felt.

"You have courage. I will honor you with what I have come here to say. The others can continue hiding, if that gives them comfort. I do not blame them for being frightened; I understand their fear. I've lived with the fear of death most of my life and only recently have come to realize that there are things in this universe much more worthy of fear than death. What I have to offer this world could save it and its inhabitants from a fate that is far worse than death. Those who accept fear and allow it to lessen their value of life are already dead. I will not waste my honor on the dead."

Teela turned away from Agent Cooper and returned to the table, taking a chair on the opposite side with her back to the screens.

"Join me, Special Agent Richard Cooper. As the only official representative for this government and the human species with honor. Please … join me. You are needed here … now," Teela said, leaning back in the chair her hands held out before her with palms up as a gesture of openness.

Agent Cooper, his concentration divided between what Teela was saying, and the message he was receiving, put his finger to his ear and asked for the message to be repeated.

"What? Are you sure? How was I supposed to know it's a woman? Now?" he whispered, his head jerking to look at the door, then back to Teela, he straightened as the door opened.

"Ah ... Madam Shawlmon, the President of the United States," Agent Cooper announced.

The president was a tall man, with wavy, graying hair, combed back to cover a thinning crown. He wore a dark tailored suit that although exquisite in its form and fit, showed the wrinkles of a day's usage. From the stubble on his face to the creases of worry around his eyes, Teela knew his arrival was unprepared and unrehearsed. Walking boldly into the room, the man walked around the table, approached Teela, and offered his hand. Having stood as he entered the room, Teela took his hand and shook it as she had Agent Cooper's. As they stood shaking hands, the moment undoubtedly being recorded, four additional Secret Service agents took positions within the room.

"Madam Shawlmon, I do not like being placed in a position of having to offer apologies. I am here now against the persuasive advice of my staff and everything I know to be sane and logical to personally greet you on this historic day."

His hand, wet with perspiration, left her hand feeling cold and clammy when their extended handshake ended. Anxious to scan his thoughts, but reluctant to risk the chance that her effort would be detected, she opened her mind to his emotional and subconscious feelings—those thoughts least guarded and often the most informative. His calm demeanor and smiling face, she discovered, belied a tremendous feeling of anger and betrayal. His subconscious thoughts raged against those who he felt had lied to him. His conscious mind, loud with unrestrained indignation, cried out against her inference that he was a coward. Marveling at the restraint that he portrayed, while raging within, Teela took the initiative to try to quell his unrest and build a solid foundation on which she could present her proposal and the difficult terms required for its implementation.

"We, Korlah, place great importance on honor when perhaps it would be wiser to consider the virtues of that which is sane and logical. So please allow me to offer you an apology. Mr. President, great effort has been expended to keep us apart and although unwarranted, my inference that you were being cowardly was intended only to bring us together," Teela said, bowing and offering a palm display.

"Thank you … Madam Shawlmon, it is Madam, isn't it? I was informed on the way here that in addition to the many other blunders in protocol and etiquette, that we have also incorrectly addressed your gender," the President said while inappropriately emulating Teela's palm display for the context of his statement.

"Yes, it is. However, my gender, and how you address me is the least of my concerns. Let us sit and I will tell you why I am here. If my suspicions are correct, what you believe you know, and what you will eventually discover to be true, will place you in great peril. Not from me, but from those whom you believe have sworn to protect you and this country," Teela said, gesturing to the chair across from hers. Once the President stood by his chair, Teela sat down.

"You cannot imagine the awe that I feel," the President exclaimed as he seated himself. "You are from another world and I … well … I am in awe. I know that's not a very Presidential thing to say. But, there it is."

Staring at him, Teela opened her mind to the conscious and unconscious thoughts that flowed from the man. In the time it took for him to round the table and sit down, she had ascertained that he was genuinely unaware of the events preceding her arrival, including any knowledge of his government's activities in space. He was angry that their arrival had been met with unprovoked hostile action, and was appalled to learn that the authorization for commencing the attack was buried within an anti-terrorist directive that he himself had signed. In the moments before he entered the room, he viewed a full body scan they took of Teela in the elevator that indicated she neither carried any weapons nor devices on or in her, but more importantly, it clearly showed that her cranial and skeletal structures were definitely non-human. It was at that moment of realization that he insisted he would risk a meeting.

"Mr. President," Teela began, opening her hands in a gesture of commencement. "I have returned four of twelve of your citizens that were abducted from this country by our enemies. Five have freely elected to stay with us until issues I am presenting are resolved. Three are dead, and at the end of this meeting, I will transfer their remains to your care.

"My enemies are in contact with members of your government and have developed an agreement that allows them to abduct your citizens without interference. I understand how this is possible because it follows the same methodology of technology for compliance that was used against my people prior to the ... destruction of my world.

"We assisted your citizens when they escaped from their abductors. With their assistance, we learned the location of this planet. We have also determined that this planet, and specifically the governing body you claim to represent, is the source from which a cowardly attack was launched against my people. Our first inclination was to seek revenge while at the same time eliminating this planet and its inhabitants as a threat to our mission. However, in the short time that we have spent with your citizens, we have learned that individually they are courageous and capable of great acts of honor. To destroy such a species, without first exploring alternatives to genocide, would be a criminal act by the laws that govern my people. Therefore, I am here before you as the leader of this mission to present the accusations, demands, and proposal of our Council of Leaders. I do not expect you to respond at this time. It is known that such things require discussion and debate. The information I am sharing with you I intend to share with the other governments of your planet. I suspect that there will be a great outcry of anger and indignation when it is revealed that your government has been in contact with an alien species for decades, and that it has withheld this information and the technology obtained from the global community. Just as I suspect there will be an even angrier outcry from the citizens of this country when it is learned that they have been pawns in a game of fear, greed, and deception.

"Mr. President, the Korlah have always followed behind the Kahshinki, liberating the planets after or during the invasion and harvest. This planet is the first in more than a thousand years and twelve military campaigns where we have arrived before the Kahshinki invasion. For that reason, and that reason alone, the Korlah Leaders have allowed me to attempt to negotiate an alliance that will be mutually beneficial. I believe that your government or the entities within it have acted out of fear and desperation. To believe and understand does not mean that we condone the actions that have been taken. Ours is not a forgiving culture, for us to develop a meaningful relationship of mutual trust will take a great deal of action and reform before we, together, would be capable of preventing the annihilation of your culture and existence as you know it. If you wish to be a part of this alliance there are some conditions that must be met.

"First, your government stands accused as having participated in an unprovoked attack against the Korlah resulting in more than 2,633,000 deaths. The death toll, however, pales in comparison to the misery and suffering that has since followed. Additionally, by purposeful complicity, your government has been permitting the abduction of your citizens for use as slaves, food, and both genetic and biological experimentation. Your government must publicly respond to these accusations by either admitting or denying responsibility.

"Second, these crimes are violations of Law, both yours and ours and must not go unpunished. Those who are currently cognizant of these criminal acts are considered responsible and must be neutralized and punished for their crimes. Additionally, we seek reparations in the form of food and water to alleviate the shortages we are currently suffering as a result of the attack.

"If you are willing to meet these demands, your government will be included with the rest of the global community in the sharing of technology that will provide this planet with the capability of defending itself. If you fail, our technology will be withheld from this country, your military will be eliminated, your borders will be sealed, and your survival will no longer be within your government's control.

"I have evidence, records, and testimony to support all of these claims. Denial, although tempting, will be met with contempt."

With a bow of her head, Teela placed her hands palm down indicating she was finished speaking.

The President did not speak at first. His clasped hands and thoughtful expression camouflaged the hostility of his emotions. He was not angry with Teela or her demands. He had good reason to believe that everything he had just heard was true. He was angry because when he took the office of President he was told there was an organization that was dealing with potential threats of an extraterrestrial origin, but the threats were described as only theoretical in nature, and he had been reassured that no physical contact had ever been made. This all made too much sense; the urgent advice to attack rather than communicate, the whispered conversations and activities that he sensed were intended to keep him out of the loop.

I'm the President for Christ's sake! This is unacceptable, he thought, rising to his feet.

"You appear to have an intimate understanding of our language and culture. So when I say to you that I am giving you my word as a man of honor, do you understand the importance of what that means?" the President asked solemnly.

"In our culture, an individual's word is a legal contract. I understand and accept your word as honorable," Teela replied.

"Madam Shawlmon, you have my word that I will do my best to resolve the issues you have presented. I cannot promise a resolution to your satisfaction, only that I will do my best. Without admitting any guilt on the part of my government in the crimes you have mentioned, I am prepared to offer immediate aid in the form of food and water to help sustain you through the shortage you are suffering. What do you need?"

"Thank you, Mr. President. Most of our sustainable food production facilities were destroyed and will need to be restocked with a carefully selected compilation of plants and animals. This will take time and consideration. Although restoring our self-sufficiency is my prime concern, I have nearly three million citizens surviving on quarter rations, who need immediate relief. Processed and prepared rations would be the most realistic form of augmentation at this time. I have immediate capacity for transporting 50,000 cubic feet of cargo. Although an insufficient quantity to meet our current needs, the pre-packaged meals and bottled water rations like those that have been supplied to your General Hargrave's base on the asteroid outpost would provide an excellent start to offset the famine."

General Hargrave's ... asteroid outpost? the President thought, recognizing the name. Smiling at his ignorance, pleased only with the fact that he would be figuratively ripping hearts out until he got some answers from the Joint Chiefs of Staff, he nodded to indicate acknowledgement before speaking.

"Do I understand correctly that you are prepared to come and get these supplies?" the President asked.

"Yes, of the forty craft positioned just out of effective range of your orbiting particle beam weapons, thirty are transports like the one I came in."

"My particle beam weapons?" the President asked incredulously, slipping from an intended position of not revealing what he knew, or more importantly did not know.

"Well, I assumed they are yours because they are in a synchronous orbit over this country. After announcing our arrival and peaceful intentions using the same frequencies utilized by your military, these weapons received instructions that originated from this city, moments before they fired on me," Teela replied, her vehemence of the hostile act fully illustrated by the sarcasm in her voice.

Exercising a nervous habit he had never been able to break, the President laced his fingers and bending them back as he flexed his arms forward, the knuckles of his hands made loud popping sounds. The muscles of his jaw visibly tense, he looked directly at Teela with an intensity that made her uncomfortable.

"Madam, I'm going to need some time to get my house in order. Do you understand what I mean?" the President asked, straining to sound calm.

196

"Yes, Mr. President, I believe I do. But time is something we must not waste. My enemy, the Kahshinki, have an invasion force that is already in transit. This planet will need every minute to prepare its defenses. How much time do you need?" Teela asked, trying to sound sympathetic.

"You say 'invasion force'. Isn't it possible that this force is being sent as a result of your arrival and not as a prelude to invasion of this planet?" The President asked, trying to make sense of what had been proposed.

"Yes," Teela replied. "It is certainly in response to our arrival, and invasion is probably no longer their intended purpose. A few days ago, we removed a weapon from one of your military installations. This weapon was a doomsday device. It was intended to destroy this planet rather than allow it to fall into our hands. The Kahshinki guarding the weapon activated the device, but my forces were able to remove it from the planet before it detonated. Had they failed, this planet would effectively be sterile and strategically worthless to us. Although I believe the Kahshinki originally intended to invade and harvest this planet, I now believe they are frightened by what an alliance between our species could accomplish. Rather than risk an alliance that would create a military advantage in our favor, in all probability they will now attempt to destroy the source of the threat; your planet and the human species."

"There must be a way that we could negotiate a peaceful solution to this situation," the President stated.

Teela smiled. Not a smile of happiness or amusement, but one acknowledging the historical irony of the President's statement.

"They will negotiate, they will agree with your demands; they will promise peace and even give you more weapons and technology to protect yourself. Then when you believe you are safe, they will invade. The weapons they give you will fail, just as they were programmed to. Your populations will be harvested, and the planet seeded for the next cycle. If you somehow manage to rebel and successfully wrest your planet from their grasp, they will again want to negotiate. They will agree to your demands and again promise peace. Then at their first opportunity, they will sterilize your planet and hope for a better harvest next cycle … just like they did to my planet," Teela said.

"You have repeatedly mentioned a harvest and cycle. Would you mind clarifying what this means?" the President asked, his thoughts suggesting that he already knew and was merely validating his suspicions.

Teela looked at her hands, studying the mortality of the flesh, trying to imagine her body the bounty of a Kahshinki meal.

"We are cattle, Mr. President; humans and Korlah. We are their food. The invasion is the round-up, and the harvest the slaughter. The beauty of the Kahshinki methodology is that they use selected genotypes from the same species they consume to perform the invasion and harvest. When the harvest is complete and the work force no longer needed, they just add it to their larder and move on to the next planet."

"How long … how long until this … attack force arrives?" the President asked, his composure visibly shaken by Teela's explanation.

"They are within range now. However, with the defensive perimeter I have established, any attacks at this time would be suicide. The journey would deplete the power cells on their attack craft, and without a source to recharge, they would be incapable of attacking or defending. My strategists have calculated that the earliest they could send the first fully functional strike force would be in a little more than one-half of this planet's solar revolution.

The President worked his jaw muscles while otherwise appearing to be calmly considering his options.

"I'm going to need at least four weeks to resolve the issues you have presented," he said finally.

"You may take as long as you wish. However, you must be aware that my arrival did not go unnoticed. It would be to the advantage of your government if you began introducing me to other government leaders of this planet. Arming and training may begin immediately with those governments that will agree to the alliance. To delay global defense preparations while you are getting 'your house in order' would present an unacceptable hindrance," Teela responded.

"My advisers are not going to like the idea of me arranging meetings for you to begin disseminating advanced technology to foreign governments while we bicker about the accusations you have made," the President replied.

"As difficult as it may be for your advisors to comprehend, military supremacy is a fleeting dream from which they must awaken. Have your advisors ask General Hargrave how well the advanced technology provided by the Kahshinki performed when it was put to the test. It was the same when my planet was conquered. The dominant clan had established military supremacy with the technology the Kahshinki gave them. When the Kahshinki invasion forces arrived, the valiant Korlah defenders were annihilated in a single day. The existence of your species is at risk. Put aside the petty politics of the past and realize that you must fight as a species, or you will cease to exist as one."

The President looked at the area where he knew a camera was focused at them before looking back at Teela and speaking.

"I will have my staff set up a timetable for meetings. Naturally, I want to review the evidence you spoke of during the first of those meetings, then, I will begin making introductions. How will I contact you?" the President asked, his calm demeanor restored.

"You could use the same method and encrypted codes your military has been using to communicate with the Kahshinki. Or I could provide you with a device that would allow you to speak directly to me whenever you wish," Teela replied, jabbing the President with another accusation rolled up neatly with an implied offer of assistance.

"Let's plan on both," the President said, a flush of color in his complexion combined with the rapid tensing of his jaw muscle exposed his lack of confidence in being able to determine who had been talking to the extraterrestrials.

"I will no doubt have many questions for you in the days ahead," he said, studying the details of Teela's face.

You ... are not what I expected, the President thought, his brow furrowed in consternation. *This is too bizarre to be real.*

I'm not really certain I fully understand the full width and breadth of what is happening. What am I missing?

"I am pleased that we were able to meet," Teela said with a bow. "Without this meeting, I would not believe what I now believe. You see Mr. President, I no longer believe you are my enemy. Therefore, to those who are my enemy, you have just become a threat. If you are true to your word, as I believe you are, you will need to be exceptionally careful in the days that lie ahead."

"No doubt we will both need to be careful," the President said, leaning back and folding his hands in front of him.

During the few moments that they sat looking at each other, Teela scanned his thoughts, again listening unobtrusively. He was wondering how justified the concern over alien disease was. He felt dirty, contaminated, and longed to wash. He wanted to vent his anger on those responsible for his ignorance, but was now truly concerned with both his and Teela's safety. He knew that a government entity capable of keeping a President on his second term in office ignorant of such globally important activities would be an entity capable of assassination. Looking at his hands as Teela had, he thought again of the alien bacteria that were probably, right now, multiplying in the moisture of his palms.

"Mr. President?" Teela asked.

"Yes?" the President replied looking up from his hands, feeling embarrassed by the momentary lapse.

"I would like to say that I was impressed by your willingness to meet with me today. I know that you will probably be quarantined as a result of our meeting. Would it not help assuage the concerns of your medical advisors if I were to allow them to examine me and verify that I am not carrying any harmful microbes or pathogens?"

"Yes ... I ... think that would ... be a good idea," he replied looking again at the camera and nodding, the action an unspoken demand for action.

"Good! When they have finished I will have Special Agent Cooper escort me back to my vessel, I will transfer the remains of your citizens to his custody, and I will give him the communications device I spoke of," Teela said standing to signal that the meeting was over.

Taking her cue with a sigh of relief, the President stood and walked to the end of the table where Teela met him and they shook hands. This time the President took hers in both of his and held it while he spoke. Teela sensed that he was doing this because he believed that her comment regarding the medical testing was somehow related to some visual indication he had given her of his fear, and he would not tolerate being perceived as fearful.

"For many reasons, Madam Shawlmon, this has been a momentous day for me. It has been a pleasure and I look forward to our next communication," he said, releasing her hand.

"As do I, Mr. President," Teela said bowing her head. "Before you go, Mr. President, I have a special request of a personal nature."

"What would that be Madam?" he asked, his brow furrowing with concern, knowing full well the danger of dealing with off-hand requests.

"On my future visits, I would like Special Agent Cooper assigned to coordinate my personal protection. A familiar face in an unfamiliar land."

"I think that can be arranged," the President said smiling broadly, relieved by the innocuous nature of the request.

"As Special Agent in charge of my security, he would receive additional compensation, wouldn't he?" Teela quickly added.

"Yes, yes he will," the President replied, stopping at the door to give Agent Cooper a long hard look.

"More compensation and substantially more responsibility," he added quietly, wagging his finger at Agent Cooper as he departed the room.

Soon after the President left, personnel in biohazard suits brought in a covered tray and large white box with handles on the sides. Setting the tray and box on the table, the delivery personnel removed the polished silver cover from the tray before departing the room, leaving Teela alone in the room with Agent Cooper. Teela examined the contents of the tray, her expression and posture one of awe. An ornate china plate, fine silverware, a glass of ice water and a neatly folded linen napkin sat neatly arranged on its polished silver surface. But it was what was on the plate that mesmerized Teela. She stared at the large pastrami sandwich, dill pickle, and liberal serving of potato salad. Everything seemed both familiar and incredibly alien at the same time. Swinging her crown tendrils over the plate of food, she basked in the heavenly aromas rising from its contents, a rivulet of drool dribbling off her chin. Tearing off small pieces of the sandwich, she pressed them into her mouth and began to masticate the pieces between the bony plates on the back of her tongue and the roof of her mouth, swallowing between deep sighs of joyous sensory rapture. Without looking up from the tray, she consumed all of its contents, including the garnish and the ice left in the glass. Wiping the residue from the potato salad, Teela licked her fingers clean before straightening from her hunched-over position.

Two people wearing biohazard suits stood behind her with trays of medical test equipment. They and Agent Cooper were all staring at her. She immediately sensed their revulsion of her behavior. Embarrassed, she wiped the drool and remnants of food from her face with the linen napkin, muffling an unexpected belch with the wadded fabric before speaking.

"I have been starving my entire life. Forgive my crude manners," she said, unsure why she cared what they thought.

"No apology needed Sir ... er ... I mean Madam," Agent Cooper said correcting himself with a warm and genuine smile.

Spying the racks of vacuum tubes intended for blood samples in one of the cases that the two suited individuals carried, Teela took a moment to perform a more invasive scan of their thoughts. They had been rushed here from a nearby government laboratory. One a xenobiologist, the other a virologist, both held PhDs. Neither had any thoughts of causing her harm, and both were eager to begin gathering samples and test data. The biologist, a female, early twenties, young to have a PhD in such an unusual field, was distressed by the short notification, lack of equipment, and inadequate preparation for this moment that she was certain would be a defining day in her career. The virologist was a male, twice the age of the young woman. His thoughts were openly skeptical as to the validity of the allegedly extraterrestrial origin of the visitor. He was primarily concerned with ensuring that the samples he took would be sufficient to prove his suspicions correct while at the same time he was trying to think of ways to make an impression on the young female biologist whom he found sexually attractive. Teela found the thoughts amusing yet they lacked personality and she wished she could better see their faces through the reflective material of the biohazard suit's faceplate.

"You may obtain your samples and perform your tests," she said.

For the next twenty minutes, Teela patiently submitted to a battery of tests and samples. They took her blood pressure, temperature, drew blood, scraped her skin in several locations, and swabbed her mouth, eyes, and ears. They pricked, poked, and prodded her while taking turns asking questions about Korlah physiology, diet, reproduction, health, and diseases. On the subject of reproduction, Teela realized she was quite knowledgeable and took pleasure in detailing gestation, pre-natal care, and child rearing. When asked her age, she replied that she was twenty-two, pausing to clarify that she was twenty-two by the Korlah calendar. Showing the doctors the watch she had been given, she explained that she recently calculated the differences in their perceptions of time. The Korlah day was longer; approximately forty-two Earth hours. Although the Korlah year (cycle) was shorter (333 days), the difference amounted to 1.6 Earth years for each Korlah year. Therefore, she estimated, she was a little over thirty-five in Earth years.

Even though Teela already explained she had little training or knowledge of Korlah medicine or medical practices, the virologist continued to press for answers about how the Korlah treated sickness and disease. Unable to recall a time when she or anyone she knew had ever been sick, she explained that she had no knowledge or recollection of either any childhood or adult diseases, and knew of no one ever being treated for anything other than injuries. The virologist's openly skeptical attitude toward her answers finally struck a nerve and Teela brought the interview to an end.

"Agent Cooper, I am ready to return to my vessel," she said, rising to her feet without responding to the last question the virologist asked.

"A few more minutes, please," the female biologist pleaded.

"I must return ... now," Teela replied firmly.

"I've waited a lifetime for this moment. Please, just a few more questions," the biologist persisted.

Teela cocked her head, the thoughts of the young woman emanated like a ringing bell. To her, Teela and the Korlah culture represented a dream that she never really believed would be realized until she walked into this room and faced a species that was not of her world. The woman believed that this was the singular moment in her existence that would have meaning, and it was slipping from her grasp; her heart was racing and with each beat, her thoughts pulsed with the anxiety of opportunity lost.

"What is said, and what is seen and experienced are totally different renditions of that which is perceived as truth and reality," Teela said, trying to see beyond the reflective lens of the biohazard suit.

"I'm sorry, I don't understand," the biologist said after a momentary pause.

"You can't truly understand something without experiencing it. Please, accompany me as an observer. See firsthand that which cannot be described with words."

"What? Go with you?" the biologist gasped.

"Precisely," Teela replied. "Are you ready Agent Cooper?"

"Yes, Madam, whenever you are."

"I depart in ten minutes," Teela said looking at her watch. "You are welcome to join me ... if you can get permission. You will be returned on my next visit. I should warn you though, people on your planet have been shooting at me," she added with a smile.

With the box of sandwiches under one arm, Agent Cooper led Teela out of the room and out of the White House the same way they had entered. However, when they exited the basement entrance, a black van had pulled up tightly to the entrance so that when they stepped out of the door of the White House they were able to step directly into the van. Inside and outside the van, Secret Service agents stood facing potential threats in all directions. Once Teela and her entourage of agents were aboard, the door of the van slid shut and the driver whisked them out of the grounds and to the side of Teela's craft within seconds. With a thought, Teela notified Shawaugh of her arrival and the door in the side of the transport flowed open. Stepping out of the van Teela looked into the night sky at the wispy clouds surrounded by twinkling stars. Pausing, she marveled at how different they looked, how surreal and unmistakably alien, compared to the clarity of space. Taking the box of sandwiches from Agent Cooper, she climbed into the transport.

Teela retrieved a portable communicator and passed it out to Agent Cooper. After briefing him on how the device operated, she coordinated moving the remains of the deceased humans from the transport to the black van. The expressions of the Secret Service agents spoke volumes as to the horror they must have felt seeing the eviscerated remains of Jimmy, the faceless dissected remains of Daedalus, and Crystal with her clawed body and slit throat. Once loaded, Agent Cooper, the van, and its grisly contents sped away, replaced by another. When the door on the side of the van opened, a slightly built young woman dressed in a rumpled mid-length black skirt and white blouse stepped out carrying a polished aluminum case in one hand and a jacket in the other. She paused before the transport, her head scanning its length from front to rear and back again.

"I see you have been allowed to join us," Teela said, after the doorway in the transport flowed open.

The young woman looked at Teela. Swallowing with difficulty, she said nothing as she moved with halting steps toward the transport. Teela scanned her thoughts and found that she was worried about the aluminum case. It had been handed to her just after she was briefed on what to say and more importantly what not to say. When she asked what was in the case, she was told it was a computer and recording device for documenting her experiences, but there was something about the man who brought it into the briefing that she did not like. She felt certain that she was being placed in jeopardy by being told to bring it with her.

"Do you really need that case?" Teela asked.

"I … uh … no, I don't think so," the young woman replied.

"Then leave it," Teela said.

"Okay," the young woman said, setting the case on the ground. With a look of relief, she entered the transport, the door closing behind her.

"It has an active transmitting device, Your Eminence," the communications technician called out, indicating the source as the young woman.

Teela looked the young woman over. She appeared nervous and frightened, a scan of her thoughts revealed no deception or malicious intent. None of her thoughts contained any details of a transmitting device. It would have to be something that had been planted on her. Teela looked at the coat draped over the young woman's arm. It appeared too large for her petite physique.

"May I see your coat?" Teela asked.

"Yes, certainly," the young woman replied nervously.

Taking the coat, Teela opened the hatch and threw it out. Closing the hatch, she looked to the communications technician.

"The signal is gone, Your Eminence," the technician announced, turning back to her panel.

"I … I'm … sorry … what … what was wrong with the jacket?" the young woman stammered.

"Bugs. Do not be frightened," Teela said soothingly, emanating calming thoughts. "I know the deceptions were not yours. It was wrong for them to place you in such a tenuous position."

"I'm not - sure what deceptions you mean," the young woman stammered, visibly shaken by the events.

"It is truly unimportant. What is important is that you are here. My friends call me Teela, what is your name?" Teela asked, smiling graciously and gesturing for the young woman to follow her toward the forward portion of the transport.

"Doctor Erin Marshall, but … uh … my friends call me Erin," she replied, studying the dimly lit interior of the transport.

"Well, Erin, I intend to return to space where I can get some distance between us and the hostile elements of this planet. We should have plenty of time to talk while we wait for your President to arrange the next meeting. I was thinking … maybe we could go to the moon. What do you think?" Teela said with a smile.

A little before midnight, the transport rose slowly into the night sky. It glided upward, at a low incline, clearly visible to the swarms of media trucks and vans that formed a barrier equally as impressive as the one formed by military vehicles and soldiers surrounding the nation's capital.

13 - Landfall

The eastern sky was beginning to change from inky black to milky purple over the peaks of the Rocky Mountains. Beth yawned and glanced at her watch, it was approaching 6:00 AM.

She had been driving eleven hours and was planning to drive for at least another sixteen. The fuel tank indicated less than a quarter full, but her stomach felt as though it was already running on empty. The sun had just started to send shafts of light through a gap in the mountains when she pulled into a truck stop on the northeastern outskirts of Salt Lake City. Driving to the back of the restaurant, she parked the van where it could not be seen from the road. She released a catch above the driver's side door handle. The panel flipped open revealing a concealed compartment in which Beth had hidden her .45 caliber semi-automatic pistol and a small vial of tiny white pills. Beth dispensed two of the tiny pills into her palm, tossed them in her mouth and swallowed them with a slug of cold coffee, the last of the thirty-two ounces she purchased during their last gas stop. With a soft click, she pushed the panel shut and the door once again looked as any well-worn vehicle door should. Tilting the rear-view mirror over, she examined her face. The mustache and stippled look of a 5:00 o'clock shadow appeared intact. Rubbing her hands over the stubble on her head, she closed her eyes, pinching them shut tightly as the burning sensation caused by eleven hours of driving slowly dissipated. She would feel the effects of the amphetamines in a few minutes, and the addition of food would help eliminate the jittery and edgy sensations she knew were coming. In the back of the van, curled up in down sleeping bags, Marsha and Catherine were sound asleep. Beth turned on the overhead light in the back.

"Time to rise and shine ladies!" Beth shouted, enjoying the grumbling response that followed.

The crisp Utah morning was a sharp contrast from the warm desert of Arizona. Beth pulled on a burgundy corduroy jacket, the kind with leather patches on the elbows and right shoulder. Marsha and Catherine wore only thin cotton tank tops and jeans that they purchased the evening before. Stepping into the cold air, they exchanged a silent look of regret for ignoring Beth's recommendations to buy coats. Although there was nothing available that met with their fashion approval last night, anything would have been welcome now. Running ahead to get out of the cold, the girls rushed into the restaurant. Warm air scented with the heady aroma of fresh coffee and bacon greeted them. The restaurant was nearly empty with the exception of a small group of truck drivers clustered around the television. The conversations hushed for a moment as the truckers eyed the two young girls, but much to the surprise of Marsha and Catherine, the men returned their attention to the television and resumed their conversations. On the television a recording of the Korlah transport rising into a night sky over the White House was playing, the screen caption read "ET's land in Washington." Beth came in behind them and directed them into a booth away from the men and the TV.

The waitress, a woman in her mid-fifties, graying auburn hair pulled back into a bun, wearing a well-worn pink uniform and modest lacy apron, immediately approached them as they were sitting down.

"Can I get y'all something to drink," she asked, handing out menus.

"Coffee, lots of it," Beth said in a low baritone.

"What's everybody watching?" Marsha asked innocently.

"Well supposedly a space ship landed at the White House yesterday. The news has been playing the same pictures over and over. The President made an announcement, but he didn't sound too excited. If you ask me, it's some kinda hoax. Hell, we got enough illegal aliens as it is, sure don't need any from outer space," the waitress groused.

The waitress took their orders and brought Beth a cup of coffee.

"It won't be long now until they start looking for us. You two need to change your appearance, and try and make an effort to avoid being noticed," Beth said quietly.

"It's on the news like Teela said it would be. Everyone knows about it now so why would they look for us?" Catherine asked.

"I've been listening to the news all night. Media feed was cut off less than five minutes after they landed. The President hasn't said anything about the abductions, or even about the return of the others. By now the CIA, NSA, and who knows who, have had over twelve hours to interrogate Ruth and the others. That means they know we were part of the group, and that we were also returned. Right now, they're searching our backgrounds to try and figure out where we'll go. They'll go everywhere we've ever been, watch everyone we've ever known, and within a few hours our pictures will be out to every law enforcement agency along with a federal arrest warrant to apprehend and detain us. This is why you two are going to undergo a bit of a makeover this morning."

Marsha and Catherine did not have to say anything for their opinion of Beth's idea to be known. They looked at what Beth had done to change her appearance and imagined the worst. People tend to notice the unusual and ignore that which is common. An overweight middle-aged man traveling with his wife and teenage son would not attract much attention, especially if the authorities are looking for three women. Beth smiled at their discomfort and rubbed her bristled head while scrutinizing Marsha, trying to visualize how she would look in a buzz.

Two thousand eight hundred miles to the east, the President of the United States was sitting down to his second meeting with the Joint Chiefs of Staff since Teela's departure the day before. Although clean-shaven and wearing a fresh suit, the man had not slept in nearly thirty hours and it showed in the dark rings under his eyes. The creases around his eyes and forehead, however, were the result of a deep sense of dissatisfaction that had been building throughout a night fraught with surreptitious double-talk and abject denial by those he depended on for information.

Rising from his chair, while leaning forward on fingertips pressed against the table, he glared at each person sitting around the table in turn. The expressions of those around the room varied from stoic to nervously guilty. Without relaxing his posture, the President addressed the group.

"Six hours ago, I presented this group with a number of questions. The answers I received were anything but illuminating. In the span of time between then and now, I spent the first four hours analyzing who could possibly be operating a government organization capable of such incredible deception, and then I spent the last two hours with Legal Counsel. I was assured that if anyone in this Administration is found to be willfully withholding information from me that is pertinent to National Security, they can and will be arrested for treason. Considering the grave consequences of the clandestine activities that I have already verified preceding yesterday's arrival, those who persist in perpetuating them will be held accountable. From this moment on, if you are not cooperating with this administration, then you are working against it, and that gentlemen, is treason of the highest order. I want everyone in this room today to know that if you are charged and found guilty of treason, I will not request the death sentence, I will insist on it.

"Before entering this room, I implemented a Presidential directive reserved for situations involving internal military threats. As I speak, trusted elements of the Federal Bureau of Investigation are isolating the top ranks within our intelligence and military elite. Without exception, it is my intention to determine whom and what organization is operating outside recognized legal channels. For a few of you, this meeting may be the last opportunity you have to convince me of your loyalty.

"Six hours ago, I presented a number of questions; I want some answers and I want them now!" He slammed his fists down on the table.

The desert wind, hot and dry, blew the powder-fine dust up the road toward the small trailer and shed where a group of six men in black suits searched the now abandoned structures. With the sun at its zenith, the men continued their activities suffering silently in the intense midday heat. The dust soon turned their suits a dull gray, and mottled the skin of their faces and the collars of their white shirts with muddy sweat as it trickled down their necks and evaporated from their collars.

Sitting in the air conditioned cab of one of the black vans, a man in his late fifties, hair cut into a flat-top so short as to nearly pass for a buzz, sat thumbing through a red binder labeled 'Porter, Bethany'. One of the men exited the trailer and trotted over to the black van, tapping on the window where the older agent sat. Rolling the window down the man inside spoke without looking up from the dossier.

"What'd you find?" the older agent groaned.

"C-4, Sir, two pound block and a hand grenade," the man answered.

"Was it rigged?" the older agent asked.

"Negative. Could have been, everything was there. Had a note on it, it's addressed to you, Sir." The young man held out a folded piece of paper, the hint of a smirk indicating that he enjoyed delivering the note.

"What?" the older agent looked up for the first time and snatched the paper.

"You got anything else?" he growled.

"No, Sir," the young agent replied.

"Then get back to it!" the older agent snapped, as the window closed to seal the cool air in the cab of the van.

The paper, white at one time had yellowed around the edges with age. A printed document, the paper was a military procurement chit that had portions typed and others filled in by hand. Reading the document, he saw that it was for a number of items including C-4, hand grenades, small arms, and other sensitive military weapons provisions. His face twisted into a grimace when he realized that it was he who had signed for the provisions fifteen years ago. Turning the paper over, he found a note neatly written on the back.

Hello Chris,

What a surprise it was to find all my gear still safely tucked away where I left it. This site should have been cleaned immediately after I disappeared, unless, of course you were certain I wouldn't be coming back. But how is that possible?

If you are reading this, and I expect that you are, it will mean that you know exactly how it is possible, and all about what I intend to do, and it is now your job to stop me, or die trying. Come on, Chrissy, catch me if you can, I'm looking forward to kicking your ass … again.

Sincerely, B3

Chris Johnson lit the bottom of the note with a pocket lighter and held it while it burned. He dropped the last corner into the van's ashtray and watched it shrink and darken into ash as the flames finished consuming it. He placed the tip of his index finger on the photograph of a much younger Bethany Porter. On the next page, he ran his finger down to the last line that read, 'Terminate Asset.' Closing the folder, he used it to fan some of the cool air flowing from the dashboard onto his face.

"I know you. I know you better than you know yourself. I'll find you, and when I do, I'll 'bring it on' like I should have fifteen years ago, you fucking muff-diving cunt," the agent growled as he shoved the red folder back into a brief case that he locked, before sliding it into a cabinet in the van which he closed, giving the combination dial a spin. Exiting the van, he began shouting orders to the investigating team.

Ruth opened her eyes only to close them immediately. The light in the room reacted with her dry, blurry eyes to create a piercing ache at her temples. Placing her hands on the sides of her head in an attempt to contain the throbbing mass and prevent it from exploding, she slowly sat up, her head spinning and her stomach threatening to disgorge whatever contents it contained. With one hand, she felt around, establishing that she was lying on a narrow bed. Opening her eyes slowly, and just enough to focus, she took stock of her surroundings. She was in a small room, no, a confinement cell, eight feet by ten feet at most. The head of the bed was against the wall next to a small corner table on the right. At the other end of the cell was a polished metal door with a window about head high that was covered on the other side. To the left of the bed was a lidless, stainless steel toilet with a matching sink. In the center of the ceiling was a large mirrored dome surrounded by the illuminated panels that were causing her eyes to ache. She found that she was wearing a type of paper fabric smock, and nothing else. Moving to a sitting position, she swung her feet off the bed and onto the cold linoleum floor, her toes curling by reflexive response.

"Good morning, Ms. Tuman. How are you feeling?" said a pleasant female voice, emanating from a source Ruth could not identify.

Ruth ignored the question. She stepped to the sink and turned on the cold water allowing it to flow over her hands for a few moments before splashing the water onto her face and into her parched, dry mouth. The insides of both of her arms showed evidence of needle marks and the soreness deep in her throat convinced her that far more invasive examinations had been performed. She was acutely aware that she had been drugged and was systematically attempting to recall the events that had preceded her present situation.

She remembered leaving from the transport and talking with people, tourists, and reporters. She recalled the group of uniformed police that separated her, Tiffany, and Margaret from the crowd and pushed them into the back of a van. The van had taken them on a short trip, somewhere nearby, and when the back doors of the van opened, people in biological hazard suits sprayed something into the van, and that was the last thing she could remember clearly. Beyond that she had only vague recollections of talking to someone, a man, but she could not remember who, or about what.

Although the nausea was dissipating, Ruth felt as though her head were stuffed with cotton to the point of splitting open. She thought about Beth's comments regarding the probability that the returnees would be imprisoned to prevent the truth of their abduction and the details of what they knew, from becoming public knowledge. With that thought, she suddenly recalled telling someone that Beth would make sure the truth would get out, and God help anyone foolish enough to get in her way. With that thought, she looked up at the mirrored dome that she was certain had a camera in it and smiled for the benefit of whoever was watching. While still looking at the camera she spoke, and although her thoughts were clear, her mouth refused to completely obey and she slurred her words like a belligerent drunk.

"I want to speak to someone in charge."

"Would you like something to eat or drink?" the voice asked.

The smile on Ruth's face faded to scowl. She turned away from the dome and began examining the bed and table. Both were of a modular design, no nuts, bolts, or pieces that could be removed, and like the sink and toilet, they were firmly attached to the floor. A rectangular seam in the wall above the table indicated a likely opening. However, the seam was tight and she had no tools to try to pry it open. Jumping, she slammed the mirrored surface of the dome with a clenched fist. The solid, unrelenting surface was built to withstand much more force than she could hope to deliver with her bare hands. Unlike the room she escaped from on the Korlah vessel, this room had no other outlets or panels that she might somehow access. After pacing the room several times, Ruth concluded the cell was well designed to prevent escape.

Retiring to the bed, she sat with her back against the wall and stared at her distorted reflection in the dome on the ceiling. A soft click and quiet sliding sound drew her attention to the table alongside her bed. A box, four inches deep, twelve inches long and twelve inches wide had emerged from the wall. Like a drive-up bank window, the box had a lid, that when opened revealed an enclosed space within. The lid then had to be closed, in order to be withdrawn, preventing any access to the outside through the opening. Inside the box, she found a plate containing standard breakfast fare of eggs, hash browns, sausage links, toast, jam, orange juice, and coffee. The aroma of the food caused Ruth's mouth to begin watering. After a moment's reflection, she closed the lid without removing the contents.

"I'll eat when I'm free," Ruth said to the dome.

"Ruth, my name is John, Dr. John Rost. I'm the Senior Physician at this facility. I can see that you are upset, and I empathize with your position. I have your records in front of me and it is obvious that you are an intelligent, educated woman and must be aware of the seriousness of this situation. I ask that you behave in a professional manner congruent with your professional background and experience. I want to help you and your companions, but in order for me to do that, I will need your complete cooperation. You have been quarantined for the safety of the general public and will not be released until we find a way to safely remove the parasites from your body."

Ruth listened patiently to the smooth loquacious introduction of the doctor, visualizing an older man from the sound of his voice. Upon hearing an inference of parasites, she bolted into an upright position and swung her legs off the bed, her eyes reflecting the alarm that sent a cold chill through the depths of her chest.

"Don't be alarmed Ruth," the doctor continued, seeing her distress. "Other than being mildly dehydrated and mal-nourished, you are in excellent health. But the organism we are concerned about has spread throughout your tissues and organs to a cellular level. At this time, we don't know anything about this organism, how it is transmitted, and most importantly, how to eradicate it from your system without hurting you. We are still trying to establish if it is in fact parasitical, or possibly symbiotic, providing enhanced immunity to bacterial and even viral infections. And that's real good news Ruth, but you need to realize that this is going to take time … and cooperation."

"How much time?" Ruth asked, turning her attention from the dome to her bare feet, embarrassed by the disarming effect the doctor's words had on her resolve.

"I honestly wish I knew. You do understand the potential dangers this organism could have on the ecology of this planet?"

"Yes," Ruth replied dryly, rubbing her feet together, feeling suddenly guilty.

"We need your help with finding the others, hopefully, before they infect the general public," Dr. Rost said.

"Why bother asking? Why don't you just drug me again?" Ruth snapped, the throbbing of her temples reminding her of the previous night's treatment.

"The drugs were not my doing. Those responsible have a duty to obtain information, and obtain it fast. Although interrogation drugs used today are excellent by comparison to those used in the past, they still cannot replace lucid cooperation. Will you cooperate?"

Ruth felt nauseous again and swallowed the saliva that filled her mouth. She rubbed her hands over her face to relieve the prickly sensation as much as to remove the cold perspiration on her forehead. She honestly had no idea where Beth, Catherine, and Marsha would have gone, so offering to cooperate could only help her current position without compromising their mission.

"Yes ... but I don't see how I can be much help."

"Hello, Ruth," a coarse, deep, and raspy male voice announced. "I have a few questions for you. Now it's very important that you don't think about the questions. I will say something and you will immediately say whatever comes into your mind. You have to answer quickly. Do you understand?"

"Yes, I think so," Ruth said, lying.

"Rebecca," the coarse voice said.

"Becca ... um, she prays a lot ... she's ... um," Ruth said, puzzled that she suddenly could not remember any details about the woman.

"Where is she from? Answer quickly!" the man blurted out.

"I don't know, the South maybe," Ruth said as even the surety of Rebecca's existence faded from her memory.

"Age?" the man shouted, the desperation in his voice apparent.

"I don't know," Ruth gasped, astounded by the fact that she could not even remember who he was talking about. "What was her name again?" she asked, embarrassed by her memory lapse.

After a long pause, Doctor Rost's voice broke the silence.

"That's alright, Ruth, both Tiffany and Ann are having the same problem. We believe that some of your memories may be repressed, we'll talk some more about Rebecca after you eat and rest. Doctor's orders."

In the facility's observation room, the coarse-voiced agent pushed his sunglasses up on the bridge of his narrow, flat, almost non-existent nose, which looked oddly out of place on his wide pockmarked face. Rising to his feet, he fastened a button on his jacket before smoothing the fabric over his shoulder holster.

"It's a form of post hypnotic suggestion," the agent rasped with dubious certainty. "Programming agents to forget sensitive information is nothing new and neither is the method needed to break through it. My team will start with the weakest of the three.

Move the young woman … uh, Tiffany, back to the examination room, strip her and strap her down. My people will be here within the hour; give them your full cooperation."

"Agent Willis, there will be no more interrogations. This is a medical facility, my medical facility, not your personal torture chamber. These women are in my care now and I will not permit you or anyone else to traumatize them further," Dr. Rost replied.

Agent Willis approached Dr. Rost, moving so close that the doctor backed away. Finding himself cornered against the wall, Dr. Rost cringed as Agent Willis pressed into his personal space and pushed his face so close that the oily tip of his acne-pocked nose grazed his cheek. With breath that competed with body odor from wearing the same suit for the previous thirty-six hours, Agent Willis strained his words through clenched teeth, yellowed by years of black coffee and unfiltered cigarettes. Although even and unemotional, the man's words had a menacing intensity that drained Dr. Rost's bravado along with what little color he had in his already pallid face.

"This is now my facility, and you work for me. The lives of these three women mean nothing! Not when the lives of billions are at stake. I will get the answers I need, and I will get them today. You are going to help, or you're going to find yourself in a cell next to theirs."

Agent Willis turned and strode toward the door speaking in a normal voice as he walked.

"My team will be here within one hour. Thank you for your cooperation," he said as he closed the door behind him.

The four-lane highway curved through the lush green hills of Delaware, creating the appearance of a snake writhing from the bronze light of the late afternoon sun. Rudy Hayes tapped the brakes of his Freightliner as another car cut in front of him, making its mad dash away from the city, now only visible by the gray smudge of smog that hung over it, a few miles behind them. He did not think about his action, after forty years of driving big-rigs, such actions were instinctive. He did not curse the driver like he normally would have, the smile on his face replaced the scowl he had worn for so long that the lines formed by it permanently creased the skin around his eyes and mouth. For a reason he could not recall, he thought of his wife and the many years of happiness they had spent together. But as usual, the smile quickly faded and the frown returned, and with it came the depression that had plagued him since her death.

It was his wife, Maria, that he thought of when he saw the skeletal frame of the woman walking on the side of the road. Cancer had taken Maria, slowly devouring the robust woman, draining her health, spirit, beauty, and finally without any mercy, her life. As he was driving by, the frail woman turned and looked directly at him. Then he did something he had never done in over forty years of driving; he stopped to give her a ride.

It took over a mile to stop the truck and pull it off the road and onto the narrow shoulder. He sat and watched her in the rear-view mirror as she slowly walked the distance to the truck. He nearly pulled away a couple of times, but something drew him back to the mirror and the image of the woman. Climbing the steps molded into the cab of the large truck, the woman opened the door, and climbed in. She sat motionless and looked straight ahead. Without turning to face Rudy, she spoke.

"Do you cherish life?"

"Yes," Rudy answered, his voice choked with emotion as he vividly recalled the precious life of his wife.

"Do you reject despair?" she asked.

"God, I'd like to!" Rudy sobbed, tears now flowing freely down his face as he suddenly and inexplicably released emotions repressed for years.

"God would like you to," the woman said turning and smiling at him, her voice and smile and something else, a feeling deep within the center of his chest, replaced the choking sorrow with joy.

For the next eighteen hours and one thousand miles, the woman talked while Rudy listened. She described in intricate detail every sin he had ever committed and reasons each had been forgiven. Everything she told him he was certain was true, every explanation for the events that shaped his life finally made sense. His life was not a failure, it had meaning, it had purpose, and he finally knew and understood why things had happened as they did. The death of his wife had tested his faith in God. His state of depression and despair caused his business and health to suffer, yet he persevered without understanding why … until now. This frail wisp of a woman, God's Oracle as she described herself, found him and defined his place in the universe and the events that would follow. He accepted his role as a disciple of God's Oracle and the archangel Shawlmon who, like the Oracle, was chosen by God to battle the demons of Hell that were corrupting the world, and if not stopped, would bring about the end of days; Armageddon. He was a soldier now in a war of good against evil; others would join them, this the Oracle made clear.

Traffic slowed to a crawl, forcing Rudy to downshift into the lower gears. As the truck crested the next hill, he could see the source of the congestion. Cars were stopping to pull off the road and into a field where a makeshift parking lot had been set up. The meadow beyond was filled with crowds of people forming into a semi-circle around a stage that was erected in a natural amphitheater formed by two small hills. Banners set up on either side of the stage proclaimed the event as a Christian revival concert. The Oracle told him hours ago that they would be at their destination before his truck ran out of fuel, after which he would no longer need it. Looking at the truck's fuel gauge, he could see that it was near empty. "The children of God will gather and we shall lead them to salvation," she told him. Rudy smiled, laughed, and shouted, "Halleluiah!"

After departing Washington the day before, Teela's craft rendezvoused with Challmara's assault pod on the far side of the moon. Once on board Teela resumed her role as leader, reading and responding to the numerous communications and issuing orders to coordinate the transport of food and water. Dr. Marshall stayed busy following Teela around, asking questions and taking notes in a small notebook.

Challmara, Shawaugh, and all others aboard the assault pod treated Teela or Shawlmon as they now referred to her, with the greatest respect. With this respect, came a distancing and isolation that neither Teela nor Daedalus had experienced in either of their previous lives. Touching others and being touched, the reassurance of physical contact that was common practice among the birthing units was not an acceptable behavior for a leader. In the close confines of the assault pod, where little privacy existed, Teela maintained the expected image of an omnipotent leader while suffering silently with the chilling loneliness that continued to nag at her subconscious needs.

Finished with the tasks of immediate concern, Teela deferred those of lesser importance to Shawaugh before retiring to get some rest while she waited for the President's anticipated communications. Refusing Challmara's cabin, Teela claimed an unoccupied sleeping niche in the assault pod's central corridor. With her head in the corner of the narrow coffin sized shelf and the communicator on her lap, Teela closed her eyes. Without conscious intent, she stroked one hand with the other for the tactile stimulation it produced. Eventually she clasped one hand tightly, squeezing it firmly and finally with painful intensity as she recalled holding the hand of a dying sister whose name she never knew. Past and present collided as she cried silent tears of loneliness and loss. She eventually drifted off to sleep, mourning for those who had ceased since the beginning of her ordeal, and those she feared would soon follow.

Howard Lewis

14 - Resurrection

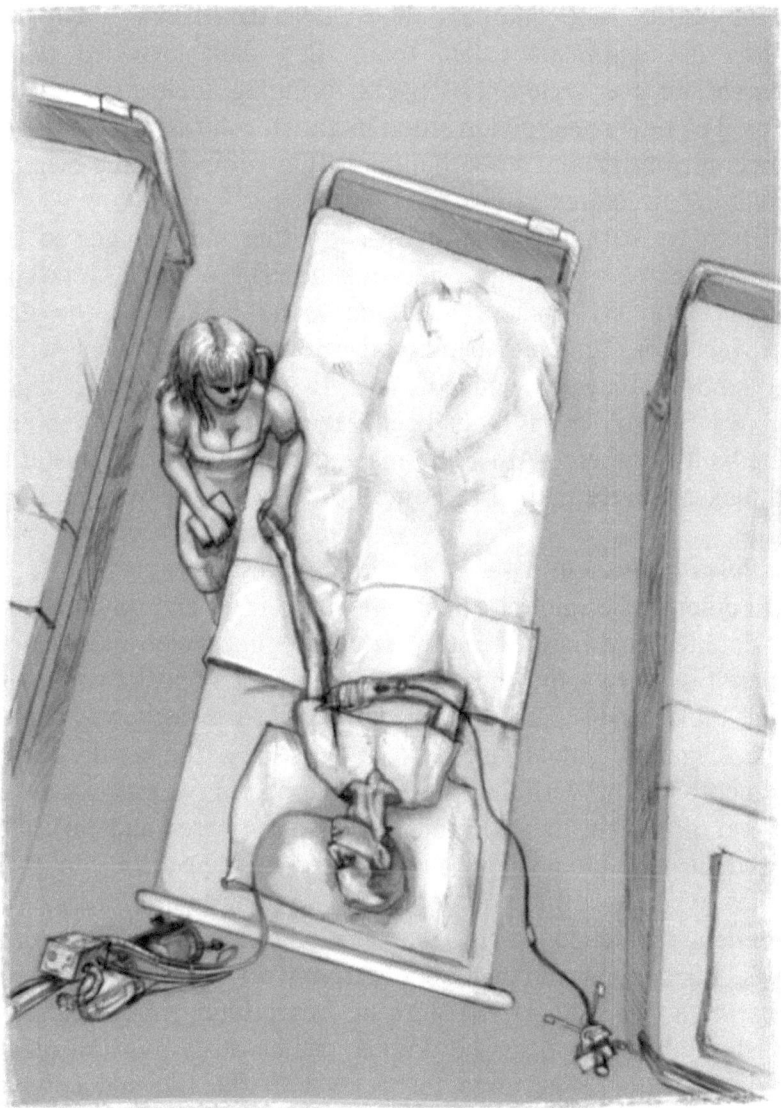

Spirals of dust whirled and turned, dissipating and dropping their cargo of litter mixed with shards of dry grass from the surrounding hills only to whip them up moments later and carry them further down the potholed road that was both, the main highway and Main Street of the small Montana town. After nearly becoming a ghost town following the corporate consolidation of smaller independent ranchers, the town had only recently begun renovation and regrowth as the PIBs, or 'people in black,' as the locals called them, fled their crowded urban lifestyle for the wide-open spaces, bringing their money with them. The new construction stood in garish contrast to the turn of the century brick and stone buildings that composed the original remaining structures.

Beth walked down the sidewalk noting the changes to the little town, new and old, side-by-side. BMW SUVs and the highly favored Hummers could be found parked by the new hardware store, grocery, bank, and restaurants. However, where the smooth sidewalk ended, and the cracked and chipped walkway and older buildings began, the vast majority of vehicles were well-weathered American made pick-up trucks. A cluster of old pick-ups were parked in front of the Hole in the Wall Bar and Grille.

Pushing through a set of traditional western swinging doors Beth entered the saloon. The room was narrow and dingy with a bar counter running the length of one side lined with fixed stools covered in worn and torn red vinyl. Along the opposite wall were small tables and stools, and all the way in the back was a pool table. Cigarette smoke hung like a dense fog, the acrid odor of tobacco blending with the smell of stale beer. Five men sat at the far end of the bar, their weathered Stetsons creased and curved to suit their individual styles. They were in their fifties to mid-sixties, whereas at the pool table, three young men in their early twenties were engaged in a game. Long sleeve western shirts, vests, faded jeans, and dusty boots were worn by all, except Beth. Wearing a wrinkled flannel shirt, new dark blue jeans and highly polished, black boots, she looked ridiculously out of place. Taking a stool adjacent to the nearest of the five old cowboy types, Beth smiled in response to the hostile glare the gray-haired gentleman gave her.

"Whisky," Beth said loudly to the bartender.

The bartender, who sat across from the five men at the end of the bar, made no effort to stand.

"We're all out," he said flatly. "There's a steak house across from the gas station that has a bar. You can get your whisky there." Several of the other men sitting at the bar snickered.

"Well, if you haven't got any Whiskey, maybe you can help me find a fella, an old time local boy," Beth said, staring at the shelf of full whiskey bottles.

"I'm looking for James McClellen, also known as General McClellen or Jimmy Guns. Hero or traitor, depends on who ya ask." The bar became stone silent, the sneers and scowls turned expressionless and deadpan, even the young men at the pool table, who, until a moment before were ignoring the exchange, stopped playing, and at that moment all eyes in the small silent bar were appraising Beth with predatory intent.

The bartender picked up a shot glass and set it down in front of Beth.

"Haven't seen or heard from Jimmy since his Brother Jo's death, bad business that was. How is it that you know Jimmy?" he asked, never removing his gaze from Beth's face as he filled the shot glass with Jack Daniels.

"Don't really know Jimmy," Beth said scooping half the peanuts from a small bowl on the bar and pouring them into her mouth. "I knew his little brother, George, or Jo as you call him. That Jo was one tough kid.

"Guns for the revolution; noble cause. Dangerous though, making plans to overthrow the United States government, more so now, than before I'll bet." Beth chased the peanuts with the shot of whiskey.

As soon as she set the shot glass down, the Bartender refilled it.

"General McClellen is a patriot," he stated flatly.

"Yeah, I know," Beth said knocking back the second shot, setting the glass top down, as she stood. Pulling a thick roll of fifties from her coat pocket, she peeled one off and put it on the counter making certain that the thick wad of money was seen before tucking it away.

"If you know any other - patriots, buy them a drink for me," she said as she turned and walked to the door. "Y'all have a nice friendly town here, I think I'll stay for awhile," she said as she pushed through the swinging doors, exiting the bar.

The crackle of static emanating from the crude speaker on the communicator in Teela's lap, jolted her awake.

"Hello? Hello?" the communicator crackled loudly.

Teela fumbled with the device, her eyes and hands mirroring her drowsy state of mind.

"Yes? This is Teela," she croaked, coughing and swallowing forcibly afterwards. After a long pause of hissing and crackling, the communicator continued.

"I have a message for Ambassadress Shawlmon from President William McCormick," the communicator crackled, the message scrolling onto the screen in the light patterns used by the Kahshinki.

"Proceed with your message," she replied, glancing at her watch trying to gauge how long she had slept. It was a little over eleven hours since she had departed Washington, six since she had laid down to rest. Rubbing her throbbing temples, she listened to the itinerary as it scrolled out and was recorded on the communicator's log bar. She was impressed that President McCormick had been able to put together such a comprehensive timetable of meetings in such a short period. Only the first meeting included a time, location, approach trajectory, and verification code. Once the communication had concluded, Teela took the log bar to the assault pod's navigation station and input the location information. With clarity that was nearly three dimensional, the technician provided a simulated approach identifying the location of the first meeting as Camp David. With a heavily protected remote location and a nighttime arrival, there would be no press coverage of this meeting.

Teela went to the bridge of the assault pod to meet with Shawaugh and Challmara to plan her meeting with President McCormick.

"Teela!" Challmara began as she approached, breaking protocol by speaking first, and most inappropriately by using her birthing section name with no title or rank.

"There are urgent matters you must address. The situation on the Campaign Vessel has grown worse. Word of 'New Korlah' has spread and the clans are divided between those who wish to continue Campaign, and those who wish to abandon it. Shyron has forbidden the allocation of anymore resources for the journey to New Korlah until you return. This has resulted in an armed standoff in the supply section."

Teela signaled her to stop with her hand, and stood mute while she fought to maintain her composure. When she finally spoke, it was with a calm dignity.

"Director Challmara, I appreciate your concern, but I have issues I must deal with before I can return. I will prepare a directive to resolve the issue until I can handle the situation first hand."

"You must return now!" Challmara demanded.

Shawaugh huffed to demonstrate her disapproval of Challmara's apparent disrespect for Teela's authority.

A moment of silence followed. Teela, who had grown accustomed to the respect and courtesy her new position demanded, was shocked by Challmara's behavior. Challmara realized her indiscretion and blanched white with embarrassment; she dropped to her knees and offered an apologetic palm display.

"Your Eminence, please forgive me, I have forgotten my place."

In that instant, Teela sensed Challmara's deep concern for the viability of the Mission. She completely distrusted the humans and was certain that the proposed alliance was wasting valuable time that should be spent unifying and preparing the Campaign Vessel for an attack that could occur at any time.

"Don't … please," Teela said, bending to draw Challmara to her feet.

Challmara rose slowly, keeping her head and eyes downcast.

"Your place … is providing me with accurate information and honest advice. I am not concerned with titles and protocol. You, as well as every member of this mission need to understand what my position is. Without this planet, without an alliance, our mission, everything we have fought for, every individual that has sacrificed their existence for the honor of Korlah for the last one thousand cycles will be wasted, and our existence will end without purpose, utility, or honor. I know who I am and what I must do to achieve victory, and I will fight anyone that gets in my way, human or Korlah. Any Korlah that is unwilling to accept our role in this Campaign will only act to weaken our chances for success, therefore, as the duly appointed Mission Potentate I am issuing the following directive." With a glance and a projected command from Teela, the communications technician snapped a log bar into the console and stood ready to transcribe her directive.

"Any who are unwilling to make a blood oath of loyalty to this Campaign and the Korlah Mission shall be included in the transit to New Korlah. It shall be the Mission of those who flee this engagement to establish and fortify a Korlah colony. They must relay the history of our culture, and the honor earned by those of us willing to continue the Mission to the generations of Korlah who survive.

By fang or by claw, by the blood of my existence I accept my place in this Campaign and will not waiver in my determination to see justice served finally and for all time. TEELA20.10127 Shawlmon, Mission Potentate"

"Send it!" Teela growled.

"To whom, Your Eminence?" the technician asked politely.

"Everyone!" Teela hissed.

"Shawaugh, Challmara, come with me," Teela ordered as she walked briskly from the control room and into the first transport she came to. Dismissing the crew, she closed the access portal once Shawaugh and Challmara had entered.

"How many will leave?" Teela croaked, turning away from them and blinking her eyes in a failed attempt to prevent the tears that began to well up from flowing down her cheeks.

"Many. A third or so ... maybe," Shawaugh said.

"Shyron has estimated higher percentages, perhaps seventy to eighty percent," Challmara countered.

"Shyron is wrong. Not a single birthing unit has left, or has requested to leave. They have great influence over the education section and together they represent over half of the vessel's compliment," Shawaugh growled.

"The concern is operation and defense of the Campaign Vessel and you can't count the birthers in … that group," Challmara said, realizing the verbal blunder as she spoke it.

"Do you wish to leave, and go to New Korlah with the others?" Teela asked slowly, wiping the tears away before turning to face them.

"No!" they replied in unison. Shawaugh glared at Challmara before quickly adding a comment intended to smooth over Challmara's insult.

"You will be proud to know that as shortages developed, your birth sisters have been filling positions in every section. There is no job they are afraid of or unwilling to undertake. What they lack in training they make up for in effort and determination."

"Will they be able to fill the vacancies?" Teela asked.

"No," Challmara said, glaring defiantly at Shawaugh as though expecting another contradiction. "It is true that they put forth great effort, but no amount of effort can make up for their lack of technological comprehension. They are attempting to fill positions that require two cycles of training and three of apprenticeship. Forgive me for saying this, but it is true; it is not that they are unafraid, it is that they are ignorant of the dangers they face."

"They are fearless," Shawaugh growled.

"Only when they are in groups," Challmara countered.

"It doesn't matter, I have an idea, something that I have been thinking about … for some time now," Teela said remembering something Daedalus had thought about, or maybe it was something he feared.

"With or without the help of birthing units, we can restore our defensive and even our offensive capacity," she said squinting, rubbing her palms on her temples to soothe an ache that suddenly formed in her head. And just as quickly as the pain appeared, it dissipated, and the idea appeared to her as an intricate and detailed plan in her mind, the specifics and complexity developing with astonishing clarity.

"You see?" Shawaugh growled, grinning at Challmara, who immediately nodded her head in acknowledgement and offered Shawaugh an apologetic palm display.

"See what?" Teela asked, curious as to the nature of the exchange.

"When events create insurmountable obstacles, you do not despair nor do you proceed with foolish optimism. You come up with ideas that are … unique. Or as Shawaugh put it, 'You have a plan for every problem,'" Challmara answered, offering Teela the same palm display.

I do reject despair and cherish life, Teela thought, considering the implications of her plan.

Are these your words, thoughts, or God's will? a voice within Teela's mind asked. A cold chill flowed up her spine as she recognized the thought as you might recognize the sound of someone's voice.

"Dooaugh?" Teela whispered, speaking both audibly and telepathically.

Challmara looked at Teela who was staring in her direction, but her eyes were glazed, unfocused, looking through and beyond where Challmara stood.

A tittering snicker of amusement, an emotional feeling preceded the next thought as it was relayed to Teela.

Those who serve shall live forever in the Kingdom of God. You have thought it and your words have confirmed it. It is God's will Shawlmon. The crippled shall walk, the sick cured and dying rejuvenated. The army of God shall rise from the forgotten discards of Earth to become the 'Soldiers of Shawlmon', and together we shall strike down the minions of Hell! The words crashed into Teela's mind with an intensity that caused her to clutch the sides of her head and stumble backwards. Shawaugh caught her by one arm and around her waist to support her.

"What is it? What is wrong?" Shawaugh asked, concerned by Teela's near collapse.

"Dooaugh! She is speaking to me, I hear her thoughts," Teela gasped as the telepathic onslaught continued.

As Daedalus ceased, so has Dooaugh, I am reborn as was Shawlmon, I am the Oracle Rebecca; together we are the voice and hands of God! Your thoughts prepare me for your words. When you voice your wish, so shall I endeavor to make it reality. My followers and I are poised to recruit the pilgrims you need; we shall have no less than ten thousand within the next seven days. I hear you, my Lord Shawlmon, your servants await your words. Speak to us and we shall act. Roche-Hah! The final thoughts were projected not only to Teela, but Shawaugh and Challmara as well.

Silence hung like a thick fog as they listened with their minds, expecting more. After a long pause, Teela broke the silence.

"There are great risks with this plan, but I see no other alternatives available. Dooaugh will obey my wishes, I am certain of this. There are many tasks that will need to be accomplished.

"Shawaugh, prepare transport for me to the planet. Challmara, coordinate as many additional transports as possible to support ... the Oracle's activities."

Turning her back to Shawaugh's and Challmara's astonished stares, Teela walked slowly to the viewing window of the transport and stared blankly into the infinitesimal expanse beyond as she engaged Dooaugh in an in-depth discussion of both a theological and political nature.

A white sedan pulled into the parking lot of the Kansas City Veteran's Hospital. Five young people emerged, the oldest no more than twenty-five, the youngest eighteen by no more than a few months. Dressed in blue and black business suits and white shirts, clean-cut with hair neatly combed, they entered the lobby where the eldest approached the desk and spoke with the receptionist while the others waited, smiling pleasantly. Like soldiers with rifles, each clutched a bible in their right hand, standing straight and proud. Within a few moments, the eldest returned and spoke with the others and they moved to the elevators.

Two of the five, a young man and woman, exited the elevator on the third floor while the rest proceeded to the upper floors. The young woman continued down the hall and into one of the wards. The ward, dedicated to respiratory complications, provided each of the patients with a bed, oxygen, breathing devices where needed, and three televisions for the entertainment of the twelve men in the twenty-by-ten-foot room. The smell of stale urine, ammonia, sweat, and antiseptics hung heavy in the poorly ventilated space. The young woman's smile never faltered as she passed the coughing and gasping patients. Reading the names posted by each of the beds, she located the first on the list of ten men she was seeking. Picking up a chair between the closely spaced beds, she turned it toward the patient before sitting down.

"I told ... 'gasp' ... you fucking ... 'gasp' ... bible thumpers ... 'gasp'... to let me ... 'gasp' ... die in peace!" The man rasped between breaths ravaged by advanced respiratory disease. A once handsome and vain man, he turned his head away from the woman, embarrassed by his sallow wasted appearance.

The young woman calmly opened the bible in her lap and removed some papers that had been folded and inserted within it.

"You are Colonel Zachary Jacobs. You served in both the Korean and Vietnam wars, a fighter pilot and decorated veteran. You were one of the first pilots to engage in aerial combat in a jet fighter," she said, reading from the paper. "Did you enjoy flying in combat?"

"Please kid ... leave me ... alone," Zachary replied, angry that this soul saver would use his military record as leverage to engage him in conversation, yet he was too weak to rudely dismiss her as he would like.

The young woman replaced the paper in the bible and closed it. Reaching out, she took the man's cold hand between her warm, soft hands and rubbed it gently. She waited patiently until he finally turned his head and met her gaze.

"I have been sent by the Oracle Rebecca to offer you a commission in the Korlah military as a fighter pilot for the defense of Earth," she said.

Zachary stared at the young woman holding his hand. He squinted his bloodshot and watery eyes to get a better look. No more than a teenager, blond, neatly combed hair, and a peaches and cream complexion; she was the picture of health and youth.

Smiling warmly, she gazed down at him with clear blue eyes that were devoid of any hint of deception. He continued staring for a full minute, punctuated by twelve painful gasps, while he wondered if he had really heard what he thought he had heard.

"What?" he finally asked, unsure if his fragile reality was suddenly coming apart.

"I have been sent by the Oracle Rebecca to offer you a commission in the Korlah military as a fighter pilot for the defense of Earth."

Zachary stared a little longer at the pleasant face before he responded.

"You kidding? Look at me kid ... I'm dying ... can't pilot ... shit!"

"In exchange for your services, you will be reborn in a young and healthy body. But I am required to tell you that you will be fighting a desperate battle against a determined enemy, your new life may be short lived," she replied, her voice soft and controlled.

"I'd fight ... the devil himself ... to just fuck'n ... breath again," Zachary said, before having an extended coughing fit, his heart racing from a feeling deep within, that told him, this unusual offer was genuine.

Releasing Zachary's hand, the young woman took some tissues from beside the bed and tenderly wiped the blood-streaked spittle from the corners of his mouth and straightened the oxygen tube in his nose before standing.

"That's a good thing, Sir, because it is the army of Satan we are fighting. Blessed and holy is he that hath part in the first resurrection: on such the second death hath no power, but shall be priests of God and of Christ, and shall reign with him a thousand years.

"My brothers and sisters will come for you tonight. God bless you, Zachary Jacobs," the young woman said before moving three beds over to the next name on her list.

In over a thousand different hospitals, retirement homes, and hospices across the United States and around the world, similar scenarios played out as the disciples of the Oracle Rebecca recruited soldiers, mechanics, engineers, physicians, technicians, and specialists from all walks of Earthly life to join their holy cause.

15 - Salvation

Teela leaned heavily on the Communications console as she selected the last name on the long list of people the Oracle provided. The conversations varied from individual to individual, some open and positive, others skeptical and negative. All in all, she had developed a great appreciation for the capabilities of the Oracle Rebecca and the work that she was performing to help establish an alliance. She did not question how Rebecca managed to get the list of delegates that would be attending the emergency meeting of the United Nations Security Council, nor did she question how she managed to get their private cell phone numbers. However, she insisted that Rebecca not preach or prophesize during their discussions.

Their telepathic communications were at first uncomfortable for Teela. With the soft voice that was clearly Rebecca's came an image of her face. The face imparted was distinctly different than the haggard one she remembered. The face appeared to her young and smooth. Recalling the transplant of Dade's face on Bill, she imagined the flesh of Rebecca's face stretched and pinned onto something, something inhuman. The face imagined was both beautiful and disturbing. Clearing the image from her thoughts Teela made her last call.

"Ah-lo?" a deep voice announced over the console speaker.

"Ambassador Leblanc?" Teela asked.

"Yes?" the voice responded.

"I am Ambassadress Shawlmon of the Korlah Mission. My assistant informed you that I would be calling?"

"Yes. We are eager to learn more of your Mission and intentions. A team is being prepared as I speak to you now. Once we have inspected your facilities we will evaluate your offer. Let us be clear on this matter; you are offering us access to your Spacecraft Carrier and weapons technology in exchange for resources and assistance with mining and production activities?" Ambassador Leblanc asked, carefully enunciating his English.

"We are offering much more than that. We will be taking bids on construction and operation of the mining and production facilities. We will provide the technology, tools, training, and access so that you may build and operate the facilities yourselves. Interested governments and corporate entities will be competing to provide the necessary personnel to support these joint ventures. Our negotiations will be handled in the language of International Corporate Law, contracts will be drafted that will define the rules of profit and eventual ownership of the facilities. You need to understand how serious the time constraint involved is, if we are not in full production within six months ..."

"Yes, yes I know," Ambassador Leblanc interrupted. "Your assistant was quite descriptive on the implications of the timeline. My advisors have informed me as to the activities of the Americans, and we have no reason to disbelieve your claims. Their military forces are behaving provocatively, and their intelligence community is suppressing information coming out of the country. The European Union is greatly concerned with these ... and ... er ... other developments.

"I must ask you Ambassadress; if you believe the Americans cannot be trusted, and I do not disagree, why then have you agreed to meet with them at a location where they will be in control?"

"Because they are not, and will not, be in control, and my behavior must demonstrate confidence of that fact," Teela replied.

"You no doubt are privy to information that I am not. However, my experience with Americans has been similar to dealing with stray dogs; they are friendly as long as you leave them alone and let them take what they want. If you interfere with their activities, they get mean and vicious. When you try to chase them away, they will turn on you, and if they find themselves in a corner, they will attack," Ambassador Leblanc said gravely.

"Your advice is greatly appreciated, as is your support. Do not concern yourself with the Americans. If they do not wish to take part in this joint alliance, they will be excluded from the security and benefits that it will provide. Now, please excuse me, Ambassador, but I must prepare for our meeting. I look forward to meeting with you in person," Teela said, refraining from entering into a discussion of her concerns, of which there were many.

"Ambassadress Shawlmon, on behalf of the French Government, thank you for your open and candid approach to this crisis. It will be my honor working together with you and the other delegates of the United Nations toward an agreement that will be mutually beneficial to all of us."

"Thank you, goodbye," Teela said quickly severing the communication in an effort to avoid the niceties that unnecessarily prolonged several of her earlier conversations. She looked at her watch. She would be early, but she longed to feel the openness of being on the planet's surface and out of the confines of the transport.

"Proceed to the designated coordinates," she ordered, speaking to Shawaugh who was sitting at the pilot's console.

Like a rock dropping from the sky, Shawaugh piloted the light fighter straight down to the surface of the planet. Unlike Teela's flaming entrance, Shawaugh was able to fully utilize the shield and inertia suppression technology to move through the atmosphere with minimal disruption and friction. Arriving at over

Mach-4, the craft stopped instantly only a few feet above the center of the target painted on the asphalt of a helicopter pad at the Camp David compound. To those on the ground, the ship seemed to silently appear followed by a muffled thump and outward rush of air. Warmed by the arrival of the craft, the moisture on the asphalt under and around it formed a low fog in the brisk afternoon air.

Although Teela arrived nearly an hour early, Agent Cooper was already waiting at the edge of the helicopter pad accompanied by several other Secret Service agents. Additional military personnel, and a special aide assigned as spokesperson for President McCormick, quickly joined Agent Cooper and his entourage as Teela disembarked.

Carrying a portable communications console slightly larger than a briefcase, Teela stepped into the open portal in the spacecraft's floor, floated down to the ground, and walked out from under the light fighter an instant before it rocketed skyward disappearing from sight in a fraction of a second. Against Shawaugh's wishes, Teela carried no weapons and wore no armor other than that afforded by the ornate vest and robe she was wearing. Having refused an escort as well, she finally relented at Shawaugh's insistence and agreed to carry a tracking device that also would allow her to request assistance if needed. Since her outfit, unlike a modern warrior's, lacked the attachment point for the locator, she carried the device in the pocket of her robe where it rattled annoyingly against Dade's pocket knife as she walked across the tarmac of the helicopter pad.

Even with her eyes reduced to mere slits, the bright sunlight caused them to ache and the pale skin on her crown and face to sting. Much to her relief the presidential aide quickly introduced himself and ushered her into a nearby van, which whisked the group to the center of the compound and into an underground parking structure. From there they took an elevator to the second floor of the main structure and into an area that had been prepared to accommodate her between meetings.

The aide had the loquacious demeanor of a tour guide, as he provided details of the agenda for the first meeting with President McCormick and his advisors that would precede the meetings with NATO and members of the United Nations Security Council. Outlining an ambitious schedule that would span the next few days, he specified the proposed meeting times and the names and titles of those who would attend. Citing the dangers associated with gathering too many of the world's leaders in one place at one time, he explained that for security reasons some of the participants would be teleconferencing. Seemingly without stopping to breathe, he provided a written itinerary and then verbally outlined each meeting, the meals, some of which would be combined with meetings, a brief history and some of the specifics of Camp David; and even the location, function, and particulars of the well-appointed accommodations he led her to.

"As you can see, the next few days will be quite busy. If you have any questions, need anything, anything at all, all you need do is pick up the phone and someone will be there to help you. Before I leave, is there anything you need?" the aide asked.

Teela had stopped listening long before they reached the apartment and was currently engrossed with the fire crackling within the hearth of the apartment's stone fireplace. Without responding, she moved her attention to a painting on the wall. The aide cleared his throat and was about to repeat his closing statement when Teela's mouth opened to speak.

"Nope, no questions, we got it from here," Daedalus said, responding for her when he realized that Teela was not listening to either of them.

"What?" Teela said, surprised by her own voice.

"Ah … very good then," the aide said uncertain how to respond. "If there's nothing else …"

"No, nothing else," Teela said turning her attention back to the blended colors of the paintings brush strokes.

With the first meeting several hours away, she examined a large leather recliner that sat in front of a floor-to-ceiling picture window overlooking the scenic wooded area outside the apartment. The thick bulletproof glass and large overhang of the roof provided ample protection from the sun. Moving to the window, she watched as the wind gently rustled the branches of the trees and provided the medium through which the birds were able to swim like rouk through water.

To see these things, to touch them, smell, taste. It ... it's not the same as your memories! Teela exclaimed completely engrossed in the act of experiencing each perception with her own senses; birds in flight, the soft texture of leather, a wooden table warmed by sunlight. Exposure to each sensation, whether visual, tactile, or olfactory congealed the disassociated memories that were both familiar and alien, solidifying piece by piece the puzzles of a distant life into raw memories personally experienced. Of all the memories that resisted comprehension, it was the abundance of water that Teela found most astounding. The bathroom, by itself, was twice the size of Challmara's quarters on the Campaign Vessel and contained a sunken bathtub that would require at least one hundred gallons to fill.

"*One hundred gallons!*" Teela thought with utter disdain of the waste. "*To cleanse in what would be approximately two hundred shifts worth of water rations.*" The concept was beyond her comprehension.

It was the eventual need to use the toilet that drove the realization home. Within her combined memories, she had experienced both decadent opulence and abject poverty with regard to this life-giving substance. And now, her thoughts were embattled in an effort to logically rationalize its use as a means for waste removal. She stood staring down into the bowl of the commode, her reflection staring back at her from what constituted more than a shift's water ration. She loathed the idea of fouling the life-giving fluid with her excrement.

After pacing the room for several minutes debating her options, Teela succumbed to necessity, and finally relieved herself, finding the use of toilet paper and the need to cleanse her hands with additional water, equally offensive.

There is no shortage of water here. Soon there will be no shortage on the Campaign Vessel. Relax and enjoy the moment. It's okay, Daedalus said, urging Teela to open the valves on the sink.

The sensation of warm water flowing over her skin was intoxicating. She reveled in the sensation for a few minutes before shutting off the water at the sink and turning the water on at the bathtub. Moments later, her robe and vest sat in a pile on the floor, and she sat in the tub playing with the flat stream of water flowing from the custom faucet like a waterfall. For the next two hours, she played in the tub like a child, inspecting and sampling the shampoo, soaps, and lotions, lining them up on the edge of the tub like toy soldiers in a row.

A knock on the door interrupted her bath, bringing the exquisite experience to an abrupt end. The dark sky and artificial lighting, which now illuminated the area outside her window, indicated that several hours had passed; a glance at her watch confirmed that it was nearly time for her first meeting. Quickly toweling off and dressing, she donned her robe and vest. Picking up the package she brought with her, she opened the door to find Agent Cooper and the presidential aide waiting for her.

Carving off another thin sliver of steak, Beth put the bloody chunk of meat into her mouth and chewed it slowly, savoring the flavor before washing it down with another sip of scotch and water. The ice in her drink had melted long ago, watering the whisky down even further. Having finished their meals over forty minutes earlier, Catherine and Marsha fidgeted uncomfortably on the sticky vinyl of the booth's seat across the table from Beth.

"How much longer are we gonna sit here?" Catherine whined.

"Well … let me see," Beth murmured glancing at her watch. "They should have had enough time, let's go find out."

"Who had enough time … for what?" Marsha asked.

"The people I came here to find. People who may already know what's going on, and might just be willing to help us get the word out when the time comes," Beth said before slipping back into her role as Burton Portenski.

"Now you two just behave yourselves and don't do nothing less I say so. These are some dangerous fellas, they ain't gonna want ta believe a word I say. Might get a little rough, but if I can convince em to help us, we'll be a whole lot safer than if I cain't."

With Beth in the lead, the trio walked the quarter mile from the restaurant to the motel. The sun now completely set, the town lay immersed in the twilight between day and night, the chill in the air growing with each passing moment. The streetlights came on as they approached the motel, all except for the one on the side of the motel parking lot where they had parked their van. Crossing the street, they passed under the darkened streetlight, the freshly broken glass from the lens crunching noisily beneath their shoes. Beth paused mid-stride and changed direction, walking toward a phone booth on the other side of the parking lot. Silently following Beth's lead, the girls trailed her to the phone booth, their slower pace indicative of their disapproval. Positioning themselves on the leeward side of the booth, they did the best they could to get away from the cold breeze that was threatening to become a numbing wind.

Beth dialed the number for the motel and asked for their room. After allowing the phone to ring for a while, she hung up and leaned against the side of the booth obviously intending to wait.

"It's getting cold!" Catherine whined.

"Yep," Beth replied, nodding her head in agreement while continuing to watch the front window of their bungalow intently. She intended to wait a few minutes and call again, believing that eventually the people waiting for them inside the motel room would answer the phone. The sound of tires turning on the gritty surface of the road drew Beth's attention from the bungalow.

Two local Sheriff's patrol cars turned into the parking lot. Accelerating, the cars turned and raced towards the phone booth. Their blue and red lights began flashing as the headlights kicked up to bright. As the cars squealed to a stop on either side of the phone booth, the doors of the cars flew open and two deputies emerged from each car and leveled their weapons at Beth and the girls.

Offering no resistance, they were quickly handcuffed and patted down. The four deputies asked no questions nor offered any explanation for the detainment. Hustling the three women into the back of one car, the deputies got back in their cars, and drove out of the parking lot away from the motel.

Driving through town, the two cars proceeded past the Sheriff's station and out of town, turning not onto the highway, but off onto a dirt road and into a secluded area shrouded by trees and dense bushes and brush. Stopping in a clearing, the deputies in the lead car where Beth and the girls were being held, exited the car and proceeded to the rear of the other patrol car where they climbed in the back seat. The other car then backed out of the area, the lights of the vehicle quickly disappearing into the darkness, leaving Beth and the girls sitting in the dark.

They did not have to wait long, light intermixed with the shadows of trees and bushes dancing around the patrol car indicated that a vehicle was approaching from the direction the other car departed only minutes before. A black van, its windows tinted so dark as to appear opaque, looked suspiciously like a government vehicle, so much so that Beth flushed with unease, realizing that if it was, her mission would be a failure, and they would likely find themselves in shallow graves not far from where they were sitting.

The moment the van pulled alongside the patrol car, the side door slid open and two men in black ski masks jumped out. Opening the car door, the men grabbed them roughly and threw them into the van where they were forced onto the floor on their stomachs. Beth felt a sharp pinch on the cheek of her butt and realized that the restraint of choice was to be drugs, moments later she felt a momentary giddiness before drifting off into a chemically induced abyss of garbled sounds and voices.

The secret service agent pressed the bridge of his nose with his thumb and forefinger in an effort to quell his throbbing headache, the result of too much coffee and way too little sleep. His forehead wrinkled and his brow furrowed as a scream pierced his ears. The scream, if you could call it that, lasted the entire duration of the exhalation and included a choking and gurgling sound during the inhalation that would have been a scream had it been made during the exhalation that followed. From the darkness outside the area of light that illuminated a stainless steel table in the center of the room, he spoke. His voice was unemotional with a rough and raspy sound caused by too many years of smoking unfiltered cigarettes.

"Okay, Tiffany, I want you to try again. If you can't remember her name, then tell me something about her."

"I don't know, I don't know, I don't know. Please God, help me remember, please, please stop, please," Tiffany panted in a hoarse whisper, her vocal cords raw from screaming. Wisps of smoke rose from the skin around the electrodes attached to her body and several of the numerous blisters ruptured by her convulsions spilled their liquid contents down her naked body like tears. Her muscles still contorted by the electrical current continued to spasm even though the source had been removed.

"You can remember. You spent a long time together, you must remember something," the man rasped.

"I can't remember, I'm sorry, please, please, please don't hurt me anymore, please," Tiffany begged, her eyes wide with pain and terror, searching the dark for the man, begging for mercy.

"I'm running outta time here," he growled loudly. "Move the contacts to fresh meat and crank up the goddamn voltage!"

"Nooooo!" Tiffany screamed, anticipating the next round of pain.

"Listen, we're already marking her up," a different voice replied, one younger, but no less cold and emotionless than the agent's. "The shocks alone should have bumped through any hypnosis, any more juice and she'll start ripping tendons loose, probably blow out her heart, and then you won't get jack shit."

"We're out of time, what would you suggest?" the other agent asked with unveiled contempt.

"You said not to leave marks, whoops! Too late for that now. Her memories are much more repressed than I've ever seen. You want me to get through? I'm gonna have to cause some serious damage. And even then, there are no guarantees. So ... Sir, just how far do you intend to take this?"

"You're the fucking expert. Do what you have to, just get me what I need!" the raspy voice replied.

"Yes, Sir," the younger voice said. A clicking sound could be heard until a butane flame ignited with a hiss. The torch illuminated the face of the younger man as he rolled forward on the office chair in which he sat, and positioned himself next to Tiffany's right foot.

"Please God! Please ..." Tiffany moaned.

The raspy-voiced agent lit another cigarette not so much because he wanted one, but because he really disliked the smell of burning flesh.

Suddenly a crackling sound, like cellophane being crumpled, rose in volume. The younger man looked up to see the ceiling above and to the rear of him glowing. The illumination rapidly changed from a dull red glow to bright yellow an instant before a flash of blinding white light filled the room. A neatly cylindrical column, approximately four feet across and white hot, vaporized those portions of the younger man that were unfortunate enough to be engulfed. His arms from forearms down, and legs from mid-thighs including the front portion of the chair he was sitting on tumbled forward onto the floor smoking, his dead hand still holding the butane torch. The light blinked out, the only illumination in the room being the torch, a smoldering ring on the scorched floor, and the open hole in the ceiling.

Three armored warriors dropped through the opening, their rapid descent slowed only a fraction of an inch before they landed on the floor with a loud thump, their knees bending deeply to absorb the impact. The raspy-voiced man drew his pistol and fired twice in rapid succession, both rounds striking the center of the face shield of the warrior nearest him. The warrior's weapon, already energized and glowing, flashed. The pulse struck the man in the center of his chest, slamming him backwards with sufficient force that he snapped like a rag doll over the edge of the steel counter behind him. Stunned and broken, he fell to the floor, his pistol clattering across the linoleum.

As the other two warriors marched out of the room, the warrior that had been shot in the visor approached Tiffany. She released the seal on one glove. The seam that connected the glove to the jacket separated and the glove relaxed sliding easily from her hand. The hand that was revealed did not belong to a Korlah, it was human, thin with pale skin, the nails on it neatly manicured and coated in a bright red polish. Reaching out she gently caressed Tiffany's anguished face.

"Rebecca! I remember now. Your name ... you're Rebecca," Tiffany sobbed, closing her eyes tightly.

Rebecca pulled the helmet off, leaned over and placed her forehead against Tiffany's, cupping the crying girl's head between her gloved and ungloved hands.

I am so sorry, little sister. I had no idea this would happen. The Gods have heard your prayers and sent me to take your pain and heal your damaged soul, Rebecca said with her mind.

With Margaret and Ruth liberated from their cells, the warriors paused, alerted by an unusual sound. A low moan punctuated the silence, rising in volume to a piercing siren of a scream. Lasting no more than fifteen seconds, the scream peaked and ebbed back into silence. Single file, with the women between them, the warriors resumed their course back to the location where they had entered the medical facility, and the source of the scream.

"And they shall see his face; and his name shall be in their foreheads," Rebecca said after lifting her face from Tiffany's. She cleared her throat; the scream was unexpected, as was the intensity of Tiffany's emotional suffering. She released Tiffany's bindings and helped her stand. Although marred by numerous burns and shaking with palsy-like tremors, Tiffany stood up straight, the terrified look replaced with one of deadly intent.

"Tiffany! Rebecca?" Ann cried as the warriors led them into the room. As they got closer, both Ruth and Margaret gasped in horror seeing the severity of the burns on Tiffany's naked body. Rebecca held out her ungloved hand, nodded, and with an unspoken telepathic transference, she imparted to them everything that had occurred since their quarantine, along with an offer to join her at a place where they would be safe. Rebecca knew their responses without the need for words and gave the warriors their instructions as she smiled warmly and silently, welcoming her new recruits.

Awed by the exchange, Ruth and Margaret departed in silence, rising upward through the opening in the roof and into the waiting transport. Tiffany looked around the room as if seeing it for the first time. Cauterized body parts lay on the floor along

248

with a man who was folded backwards, his spine clearly broken, groaning in pain by his attempts to reach a pistol that was just out of his reach. Tiffany stepped over him and kicked the gun into the far corner. She walked from cupboard to cupboard examining the bottles of chemicals in each. Finding what she was looking for, she extracted a bottle and removed the glass stopper. A white wisp of vapor flowed from the bottle as the moisture in the air reacted with the concentrated sulfuric acid within. Rebecca smiled and nodded her approval imparting her words telepathically to Tiffany in the same way that she was controlling her thoughts and actions.

Vengeance is ours sayeth the Lord Toma. By your loss and suffering, you Tiffany, have been chosen. Through you, God's vengeance shall be delivered to those who have sinned against mankind. I shall guide your hands as you bathe in the blood of their corruption and cleanse the despair from your soul with the sins of their existence.

"There will be others?" Tiffany asked.

"Yes child, many more." Rebecca said.

Tiffany smiled pleasantly as she turned and knelt next to the man writhing on the floor.

The screaming started out as a low and deep yelling, it rose in volume and octave to become a shrill scream that alone would have been enough to unnerve her. But it was laughter, not maniacal or hysterical, but Tiffany's joyous laughter combined with the man's screams that caused the hair on the back of Ruth's neck to rise as a chill moved slowly up her back.

Howard Lewis

16 - Betrayal

The remnants of daylight projected upward from behind the silhouettes of the trees and buildings at Camp David, creating a flat two-dimensional appearance. Without the sun's warmth, the air temperature was dropping quickly.

Aboard the Campaign Vessel, the temperature was relatively stable, varying on the average no more than a few degrees. Although a reasonably comfortable temperature to the Korlah, humans considered it a bit too warm, if not outright hot. For

251

Teela the cold air was uniquely uncomfortable. Having failed to consider the possibility of exposure to the cold, she wore nothing more than the robe, vest, and boots, which provided minimal insulation. Her breath, like that of the others she was walking with, came out as visible vapor, trailing out and back from the corners of her mouth. But Teela, in contrast to the humans, had the unique feature of crown tendrils, which, due to being warm and moist, were also generating a plume of condensing vapor. An involuntary shudder, combined with the burning sensation of her crown tendrils, made Teela wish she had accepted the armored suit and helmet Shawaugh wanted her to wear.

The procession of agents and the aide came to an abrupt stop. Agent Cooper, who was leading the procession, was speaking to a group of men, other Secret Service agents, Teela presumed from their appearance. Although wishing to hear the details of the discussion, the voices were too low to comprehend. The tone of Agent Cooper's voice indicated that he was not pleased. Too absorbed in her own discomfort, she declined to gather information telepathically, instead, she moved as close as she could to the nearest agent, hoping to tap some of the radiated heat she could see emanating from his body.

"The meeting location has changed," Agent Cooper announced as he turned the group around and headed back toward a small building on the perimeter. "I apologize for keeping you out in the cold, I'll have you indoors in just a minute," he added, noting that Teela was shivering.

True to his word, Agent Cooper led them to a building and into a room near its center. The warm air was a welcome relief. Teela shook her head to distribute the warm air around her stinging crown tendrils, and by doing so found the odor of the room to be stale and dusty with none of the pleasant odors she had experienced previously. The odor was the first indication that something was amiss. The room, small and plain had none of the opulent amenities that earmarked all of the accommodations she had experienced thus far. Agent Cooper turned around, the look on his face confirming that her suspicions were well founded. A shove from behind caught her off balance and she stumbled forward into Agent Cooper. Catching her with his left arm, his right hand darted into his coat. However, the two agents standing inside the door, both of whom already had their weapons drawn and pointed in his direction, caused him to pause and reconsider.

"What the hell is this?" he shouted angrily at the two agents while slowly withdrawing his open hand from inside his coat, but not before he had deftly palmed the pistol into the sleeve of his jacket. Showing his open empty hand, he raised his arm slightly allowing the pistol to slide down the inside of the coat along his forearm where it came to rest at the crook of his elbow. The second and much more difficult part of the maneuver would be getting the gun from the elbow, back into his hand.

"Calm down, Agent Cooper. You are being relieved of your security assignment," a voice announced.

On a small desk-sized table opposite the door, a laptop monitor illuminated and displayed a man seated at a like-sized table facing the screen. Agent Cooper turned and stared at the screen incredulously. Richard Parkhurst, the Director of Homeland Security, smiled smugly at him from the screen. Tapping the microphone on his lapel, Agent Cooper verified that the lack of sound in his earpiece was not due to equipment failure, but rather, the room they were now in was 'hardened' to ensure communications could neither enter nor exit the room unless the people monitoring permitted it.

"What's going on Dick?" Agent Cooper asked, having argued with the Director about the evening's security preparations only a few hours before, and President McCormick had ultimately established Agent Cooper's authority, much to Director Parkhurst's chagrin.

"The creature you are protecting has the ability to control minds. It can make you see and believe whatever it wishes. Both you and the President have been affected. The room you are in is specially insulated against all known forms of transmission signals. If I told you of this protective measure, the creature would have been alerted and my attempts to protect the President compromised. You do understand?" the Director asked.

"Yes, Sir," Agent Cooper replied, assuming a more relaxed posture.

Her senses now alert and operating at a heightened level, Teela probed the minds of the two men standing at the door behind her. Their intentions were clear and unburdened by politics or conscience; they would kill her or Agent Cooper with a single word from the man on the screen, and if it came to killing her, she sensed that they were hoping that order would come. Probing deeper, she was distressed to discover the intent of the evening's activities; actions that would bring an end to her plans for an alliance.

Teela looked at Agent Cooper who appeared outwardly relaxed. However, she sensed that he was, in fact, highly agitated and tense. Warmed from the heat beneath his arm, the silhouette of the pistol glowed faintly through the thin fabric of his black suit coat. Teela smiled, as Agent Cooper shifted the gun from his elbow, to the wrist of his coat sleeve, with an innocent cough and shrug of his shoulders. Clasping his hands at his waist Agent Cooper stood ready to take action if needed. Like the others, his thoughts were clear. If needed, Agent Cooper would kill to protect her.

"You are misinformed Director, I cannot control minds," Teela interjected, moving to the table and sitting down in the chair in front of it. "And even if I could, I would have no need to control Agent Cooper's mind, he has honor, a trait your species generally lacks. Now what is it that you would like to discuss?"

"Well, this actually won't be much of a discussion. I'm going to ask questions, and you're going to provide me with answers. I know you think you have us by the short and curlies, but I'm here to tell you that you do not! For you, this conflict is over; you are now a prisoner of war. Cooperate and I'll see that you get a nice cell and three square meals a day. If you do not cooperate, well … this discussion will get a little unpleasant," Director Parkhurst said.

"You have no need to threaten me. In fact, it is a foolish thing to do. Have your superiors actually agreed on this course of action?" Teela asked. The screen on the monitor blinked as the image of the Director was replaced with a grainy enlargement of a woman's face in partial profile. It was unmistakably Rebecca.

"Who is this?" the voice of Director Parkhurst asked, demonstrating that he would be the one asking the questions.

Teela smiled broadly. Rebecca was obviously causing them problems, and was apparently proving difficult to locate. Dooaugh managed to avoid the Council's Security Guards for nearly one thousand years on a ship the size of Manhattan. On a planet, she would be impossible to catch. Teela knew there was nothing she could say that would betray Rebecca, and answered as honestly and openly as she could.

"That is the Oracle and Prophet Rebecca. She can speak with God and has ordained that our arrival here, at this planet, corresponds to both Korlah and human biblical prophecies," Teela replied as though it were a well-known matter of fact.

The screen changed to a series of video clips of their arrival in Washington. From various angles with arrows superimposed to direct your attention to the figure of Rebecca, it followed her as she walked through the throng of spectators, past the lines of police and through a military roadblock unchallenged. In fact, at the military roadblock, the soldier saluted and lifted the barricade so that Rebecca could pass. The screen changed to a clear and crisp image of Rebecca standing at a podium, her arm raised with a finger pointing skyward, her mouth open in mid-sentence. She looked wonderful, Teela thought. Her hair showed no gray, but instead was a brilliant and lustrous auburn, contrasting the intensity of her blue eyes. Her nails were painted to match her hair, and her dress, formal, with a high neckline and low hem a brilliant hue of lime green. With no trace of the pallor or sunken cheeks Teela remembered, Rebecca appeared a picture of health.

"This woman, this creature, whatever it is, controls minds. This we know to be a fact!" the Director's voice railed. "It ... she walked out of the quarantine area and no one she passed or encountered has any memory of her. The other returnees, women who allegedly spent months with her, cannot remember her. Agents that I sent to apprehend her disappeared, and now it seems they are working for her and are protecting her. We have recently determined her identity from fingerprints obtained from a safe house she was hiding in. Her name was Rebecca McCabe.

Over two years ago, Rebecca McCabe was diagnosed with an inoperable brain tumor and given three months to live. She spent her final days in a hospice in Northern California; she was schizophrenic, bi-polar, and delusional. After lapsing in and out of a coma for several days, she got up one night, dressed, and walked out of the facility and into the nearby woods. She has not been seen since ... until now.

"This creature has formed a religious cult that, with remarkable speed, is garnering incredible interest among numerous religions. This woman, creature, whatever it is, is clearly a direct threat to national security.

"Who or what is Rebecca McCabe, and what is her mission?" Director Parkhurst demanded.

"Do you believe in miracles?" Teela asked; her tone serious.

"No," Director Parkhurst replied dryly.

"Neither do I, but Rebecca does. I know that you will not believe me when I tell you that I cannot explain Rebecca's unique abilities. All I know is that she does in fact have them, and they are quite powerful. I don't really think you realize just how powerful. She has recently told me all about the Quorum, and your agenda. I regret having not released the information earlier, for I doubt you would have done something as foolish as kidnap an Ambassadress during negotiations and make declarations of war without the President's consent." Teela said.

"What Quorum?" Director Parkhurst asked.

Teela would like to have seen the man's face, knowing that the release of the information would strip the shield of secrecy that protected the clandestine organization, and along with it, the security the man believed protected him from prosecution for his many crimes.

"Please, Director Parkhurst, you are holding me captive. The Quorum, and your affiliation with it, is no longer a secret. What do you want me to say?" Teela replied slowly, pausing for effect. "I hoped the President had some notion of your existence and would find the means to eliminate your influence. I am certain that you are aware that it has been my intention from the beginning that those of you involved in the numerous criminal activities that are being perpetrated will be punished.

"I am aware that you are just a stooge. The true members of the Quorum are primarily wealthy corporate entities who hire men like you to be the men behind the men, a secret government within the government, 'The Keepers of Continuity' as you call yourselves. Your organization formed during the years of reconstruction following the Civil War, and has positioned its members strategically throughout the private and political sectors to ensure the wealthy and powerful remain wealthy and powerful. Civil war is bad for business, so political stability is imperative. You perpetuate an illusion of democracy to ensure the populace will have someone to vote out of office when decisions do not meet the expectations of the masses. You maintain a two-party political system to simplify the transition and maintenance between administrations. You, yourself, are actually a low ranking member of the organization, and considering your actions today, you are at great risk of being eliminated to protect those you serve. I have a membership list of the inner circle, a small number; a little over three hundred. It includes the names, occupations, accounts, activities, dates, and other trivial details that will certainly facilitate the investigations that will follow our discussion today. A much bigger list is tied to the first, by transfers of money, property, and influence. It looks more like a payroll or payoff list than a membership.

"I can understand how it is that you accept wealth and power for your services. I can even understand that you do not believe in government by the people and for the people. But I cannot understand that you actually believe the Kahshinki will spare you and the Quorum elite when they harvest this planet," Teela stated gravely. A long pause preceded the next question. Teela hoped this indicated that her knowledge of their organization was rattling a few nerves.

"The returnees claim that you possess the mind and memories of a man called Daedalus Rimes, they say he was murdered for that purpose," Director Parkhurst said.

"Yes, that is true, except Dade and I don't believe murdered would be an appropriate term," Teela said slowly, taking and releasing a deep breath, the admission feeling like a long overdue burden being lifted from her shoulders.

"Really? What would be an appropriate term when someone's life is prematurely brought to an end?" Director Parkhurst shot back with practiced vehemence.

"I have given this subject much thought," Teela replied, bowing her head and clasping her hands. "This is a difficult concept, as each of us is quite understandably obsessed with our corporeal existence. Consider what life is, other than that which is acquired by the senses and stored in the mind and memories of the bodies in which we reside. If life, the essence of who we are, is this stored information, then Daedalus Rimes is not dead, his existence continues. If it is the body, and not the mind that represents life, then he is dead and I am responsible for his murder."

"You are claiming to be Daedalus Rimes?" Director Parkhurst asked skeptically.

"No, of course not," Teela exclaimed, frustrated by the question. "Listen to what I am saying. This body, is a shell, a receptacle for the essence of Daedalus Rimes as well as that of Teela 20.10127, together we form a new and unique essence. I now call myself Shawlmon, but I am Daedalus as much as I am Teela. If it were not for the sacrifice of Daedalus and Teela, we Korlah would lack the ability to communicate this offer of help your planet needs to defend itself from a terrible enemy."

"You can't even help yourselves, how can you help us?" Director Parkhurst replied dryly, his image replacing that of Rebecca on the monitor. "We have no intention of waging war against the ... we call them Ganglicans, at least, not on their terms. We're going to deal with them like we dealt with you.

"We are much more prepared for them than you may realize. Think about it ... forty years ago with much less technology than we have at our disposal today, while you were still light years away, we delivered four nuclear bombs to your vessel along with enough nerve gas to wipe out an entire continent. Your spacecraft carrier is little more than a ghost ship, and you and your companions nothing but a handful of starving refugees. You have nothing to bring to the bargaining table," the Director sneered.

Teela struggled to contain the raging anger that threatened to spill out with uncontrollable fury. Without conscious thought, her claws raked the top of the small table as she straightened and pushed herself erect in the chair. Thin curls of oak formed as she carved deep grooves into the polished wood, the spiral shaped pieces rolling off the tabletop and onto the floor as her hands slipped off the edge and dropped to her sides clenched into tight balls.

"You … will … be held responsible for your actions," she hissed.

"As will you!" Director Parkhurst shouted back. "When you released Bethany Porter, Catherine Purcell, and Marsha Clarke, you released a plague. They are infected with a parasite that could destroy the entire ecological balance of this planet. Is that their mission? Is that what you have programmed them to do?"

"No! They were afraid that the government … you … I guess, would kill them rather than allow their story to be told. I granted their request to be returned … privately. I know nothing of any parasite," Teela replied weakly, feeling guilty at the recollection of Challmara's mention of a symbiotic organism, and Ann's emphasis on the importance of quarantine.

The image on the monitor changed again. This time a video taken of an electron microscopic examination of a tissue sample displayed small nearly transparent worm-like objects wiggling in the cytoplasm of a cell.

"Do you recognize these organisms?" Director Parkhurst asked.

"No," Teela replied with honest sincerity.

"What of these?" Director Parkhurst asked as the screen changed to depict a fat grub-like worm and several scarab-like beetles.

"We call them Scrum. They are harmless consumers of waste," Teela replied.

"They are anything but harmless. Their reproductive spore infests living tissue down to the cellular level. They consume viruses and restore cancerous cells back into their pre-cancerous state. Do you realize what this will do?" Director Parkhurst cried angrily.

Teela did not immediately reply as the realization of why Korlah did not have colds, flu, or diseases became clear. Putting the situation into perspective on global level, she replied.

"Save millions of lives, bankrupt pharmaceutical corporations, and disrupt biological weapons programs?"

"This planet is already grossly over populated. The culling that the Ganglicans have proposed would solve that problem for more than a thousand years. This ... this parasite will have us back at the same unsustainable population levels within a few hundred.

"This must be quarantined before it becomes pandemic. Tell me where Bethany Porter and her companions are hiding and I will ensure that you are returned to your people unharmed," Director Parkhurst offered, his smiling image reappearing on the monitor. Teela smiled back before responding.

"I am amused that you think I care what happens to me. If I really cared, I wouldn't be here now. I don't know where Beth is. But I have a feeling that when she finds out who you are, she'll find you," Teela replied, her voice tapering off into a low undulating growl.

"Very well, we're out of time and this discussion is going nowhere," Director Parkhurst exclaimed with finality. "Special Agent Cooper, do you stand with or against the United States of America?"

"Sir!" Agent Cooper replied crisply. "First and foremost I am American, for America."

This was apparently what the Director hoped to hear as he smiled broadly and opened his mouth to speak.

"America ... by the people and for the people," Agent Cooper added, his hands sliding together and back as he chambered a round, and switched off the safety of the sleek, nine millimeter semi-automatic pistol concealed in the sleeve of his jacket.

The sound made by the weapon's slide mechanism, unmistakable to the men standing behind Teela, triggered a simultaneous reflexive response. Thoughts, intentions, and actions collided, and in that instant Teela knew what would happen next. Using the table for leverage, she kicked the chair she was sitting in back into the man standing behind her with as much force as she could muster. As she ducked and spun around to face the man behind her, multiple loud pops and concussions caused by the explosive powder ejecting lethal cargo from the small weapons reverberated within the close confines of the room. She turned in time to see the man closest to Agent Cooper fall backwards into the man behind her, the two of them falling together onto the floor in front of the door. Two neat round holes clearly visible in the forehead of the man on top, his eyes staring blankly forward, his mouth slightly open and lax, giving his face an expression of surprise. The other man, underneath the first, twitched this way and that, a dark patch forming in the light colored hair at his temple, the shadow flowing down around his ear to stain the collar of his white shirt. As the dark stain on the collar grew to encompass the front of his shirt, the twitching slowed and finally stopped. Agent Cooper stood flat against the wall, his pistol pointed at the men at the floor. Slowly he lowered his gun, grunted twice and stumbled forward. Teela grabbed him by an arm and provided support to prevent him from falling. Turning him, she sat him on the edge of the table. Behind him, the monitor emitted wisps of smoke from a hole in the shattered glass, and Teela noted two additional bullet holes in the wall to the right of the screen that marked the path her head had taken as the man behind her had attempted to put a bullet in it.

Agent Cooper continued to take in shallow gasps of air and let out short grunts of pain while leaning back and gaping repeatedly as though unable to breathe. On close inspection, Teela found three neat holes in the left center area of his starched white shirt. Using the claw of a thumb, she split the shirt down the front and pulled it open. Gray smudges marked the area where the bullets penetrated the outer layer of Agent Cooper's vest and impacted and penetrated the steel plate in the pocket beneath it. Releasing the Velcro straps, she lifted away the front of the protective vest. The Teflon coated, armor piercing projectiles, flattened by their impact, protruded through the reinforced Kevlar fabric stretching the inner lining like obscenely large blood soaked blisters. On his chest, the area of impact was framed by dark bruising, with three distinct areas of crushed flesh, each oozing a thin trickle of blood.

"How bad?" Agent Cooper gasped, his complexion beginning to pale noticeably.

"Your vest stopped the bullets, but you have at least two, maybe three broken ribs."

"Is that all?" Agent Cooper exclaimed, wincing from the intense pain he was experiencing.

"You are lucky to be alive. If he had shot you in the head as planned, we would both be dead, and you would not have the opportunity to prevent the assassination of the President and delegates of the United Nations.

"What?" Agent Cooper gasped in disbelief.

Teela studied her watch for a moment. "We have ... ten minutes before the Quorum will stage a mock attack using spacecraft and pulse weapons to make it look like an alien attack. If they succeed, the world will be outraged by the cowardly attack, and my efforts to form an alliance will be thwarted."

"When did you find this out?" Agent Cooper exclaimed, forcing himself onto his feet.

"The big guy with light-colored hair was worried about getting out of here; the attackers will kill everyone in the compound, no exceptions. Now let's get this door open," Teela replied coolly. Turning to face the door, she began examining the area where the inner doorknob had been removed and replaced with a blank plate.

"So you can control minds?" Agent Cooper asked, his tone accusatory.

"No, of course not, I can hear what people are thinking. And by the way, I think you're attractive as well, although not really my type," Teela replied, giving Agent Cooper a sly wink.

Agent Cooper blushed on recollection of the erotic thoughts that seemed to plague his mind whenever he was in her presence. Clearing his mind quickly and concentrating on how to get out of the locked room, he moved forward toward the door and lifted his pistol.

"Step back, I'll shoot the lock," he announced.

"Not likely," Teela replied, as she pulled out the Swiss Army knife in her pocket and leveraged out the large blade using the tip of her claw. "This is a heavy-duty, all-steel security door, probably made by Ameri-Steel. The latch mechanism and hinges are both tool steel. You shoot at it, and the bullet will ricochet and probably kill one of us."

"How would you know that? And what ... you're going to open it with ... what is that? A Swiss Army knife?" Agent Cooper asked in amazement.

"This door is designed to keep people out, not in. The pick-plate is on the outside. Inside there is nothing to stop me from reaching in ..." Teela said, sliding the blade of the knife into the narrow gap between the door and its frame where the doorknob should have been. "And manually actuating the solenoid release mechanism," she said as a faint click was heard and the door moved slightly outward.

"Shit! Not yet, don't open it," Agent Cooper whispered, keeping his weapon leveled on the crack of the door. "Kill the lights ... no wait ... get their guns, then kill the lights."

Picking up the guns, she handed one to Agent Cooper, who took it with his left hand. Unable to fit a fingertip through the opening in the trigger guard, she resolved to hold the remaining pistol with her right hand and if needed, she would actuate the trigger with the tip of a claw. Stepping to the side of Agent Cooper, she reached over and switched out the lights. For Agent Cooper, the room was pitch black, whereas for Teela, it was shades of gray, the room and its contents outlined and defined by the various thermal gradients around them.

Director Parkhurst watched as the screen on his monitor went dark. A few moments later, images on the screen returned in silhouette illuminated by light outside the door of the room as Agent Cooper kicked open the door and jumped out with a pistol in each hand.

"Fucking cowboy!" Director Parkhurst cursed, pushing away from the monitor and rushing to the door of the office. In the next room, a group of men were coordinating activities using similar monitors and communications systems.

"Who's left on the ground?" he shouted as he charged into the room.

"Anderson's team is waiting at the chopper for Billings and Hardesty," a man at console replied without turning around.

"Billings and Hardesty are dead! Cooper and that fucking creature are loose and heading for the conference center. Send Anderson's team back to intercept, and take them out," Director Parkhurst shouted.

"Sir! The attack craft are on final approach," Parkhurst's aide exclaimed, unsure if the Director realized that Anderson's men would be trapped on the ground during the attack. Director Parkhurst just stood and glared at the man, defying him to question his order.

"Yes, Sir!" the aide replied after a momentary pause. Switching on the microphone at his console, he relayed the orders to Agent Anderson.

Agent Cooper and Teela ran across the compound. Everywhere they looked, Marines and Secret Service agents lay strewn upon the ground. Cooper thought they were dead at first, but Teela reassured him they were merely unconscious, drugged by a fast-acting gas, that although mostly dissipated, was beginning to make them both feel light-headed and euphoric. Crossing diagonally through an ornate garden courtyard, they headed toward the main entrance of the Conference center, a large three-story building where the upper floor windows overlooking the courtyard were illuminated brightly from within. Grabbing Agent Cooper's sleeve, Teela pulled him to a stop just before they were about to enter the building.

"What is it?" Agent Cooper gasped, his chest aching painfully with each breath and every beat of his heart.

"Four men with automatic rifles are coming, from that direction," Teela said, pointing to a dark gap between two buildings across the courtyard.

"I hear their thoughts. They're coming for us," she said, grabbing Agent Cooper and throwing him through the door as flashes of light from the dark gap between the buildings preceded a hail of bullets, which blanketed the doorway they were standing in. Knocked to the ground by Teela, Agent Cooper rolled to the side and kicked the heavy door shut.

"Are you hit?" he shouted as he secured the deadbolts at the top and bottom of the armored door.

"I'm okay," Teela lied, struggling to pull herself to her feet, knocking over a table and sending the bronze sculpture on it crashing onto the marble floor. Her left arm hung limp, dangling by connective tissue where the elbow should have been, her right hand clutched at a place on her neck that burned painfully and prevented her from lifting her head fully. After standing, she stepped forward and collapsed, screaming in pain as her shattered arm, twisted beneath her.

Agent Cooper slid over to where Teela was laying. The back of her robe and vest were mottled with dark smears where the unique material had deflected or absorbed the impact of more than a half dozen bullets. Rolling her over, he placed the shattered arm across her waist and scooped her up into his arms.

"Leave me!" she screamed as he lifted her, the reason unrelated to any noble gesture, but simply because of the excruciating pain it caused. Agent Cooper ignored her demand and carried her to the elevator. As the elevator doors were closing, they could hear gunfire and rattling at the door of the conference building.

"Tool steel latches?" Agent Cooper asked, smiling reassuringly into Teela's pained grimace as soft music played from a small speaker in the ceiling.

"Yes," Teela groaned, trying to smile back.

As they exited the elevator, an explosion shook the building. Agent Cooper knew the men below had blown the door and would be up the stairs in less than a minute. He pushed through the doors into the conference room and looked around. Agents, delegates, aides, and associated support staff lay slumped in chairs, on tables, or on the floor where they fell. Many, however, were beginning to stir. Seeing a man sitting up on the floor, rubbing his face with his hands, Agent Cooper took Teela and set her on the ground and put her head on the surprised man's lap.

"Take care of her!" Agent Cooper demanded.

The man looked down at the head resting in his lap and began rubbing his face and slapping his cheeks in an effort to wake up from what he could only imagine was some sort of a dream or hallucination. Agent Cooper went to the two Agents lying unconscious by the doors. From each of the guards, he unclipped and removed the machine pistols that hung on straps over their shoulders and were concealed under their jackets. Running to the front of the conference room, he looked for the President.

Teela pulled the pistol out of her pocket and fumbled with it in a futile attempt to take it into a hand for which it was not designed. The man whose lap she was in pulled the gun from her grasp. Taking it in his, he released the clip, counted the shells, ejected the chambered round, reinserted it into the clip, reinstalled the clip, and re-chambered the round.

"You are Shawlmon … No?" the man asked with a thick French accent.

"And you … are Ambassador Leblanc?" Teela gasped, finding it difficult to breath. The man nodded to affirm her response. Removing his necktie, he gingerly secured it above the elbow of Teela's shattered arm to slow the flow of blood that had already formed a substantial pool at her side.

The conference room door burst open and two men with machine guns stormed in. At the podium in the front center of the room, Agent Cooper fired two machine pistols simultaneously using the podium with its ornate Presidential Seal as a shield. Ambassador Leblanc fired the pistol twice and the two men dropped to the floor like rag dolls.

"Two shots left. You see? This was maybe … not such a good place to meet … No?" Ambassador Leblanc chided.

The courtyard outside the window lit up with a flash-like lightning followed by a thunderous crash that shook the building and caused the lights to go out. Within a few seconds, backup lights came on bathing the room in an eerie twilight where the beams of light shone down like miniature spotlights through the smoke from the gunfire. More and more people were waking; some began shouting, others screamed in terror as additional flashes of light and thunderclaps began shaking the building.

266

"What is happening Joseph?" the Austrian delegate asked, speaking to Ambassador Leblanc while staring intently at Teela.

"The Americans are pulling some bullshit no doubt. I think the only reason we are still alive is because Ambassadress Shawlmon and her friend at the podium are keeping them from coming in and shooting us," Ambassador Leblanc replied.

"Oh! Thank you," the delegate replied politely. "I'll call for help," he added, pulling out his cell phone.

"Help," Teela gasped, not as a request, but as acknowledgement of a thought that struck her with the force of ignorance realized. In her pocket was the device that Shawaugh had given her in case she needed to call for help and she had failed to utilize it. Her left arm useless, she reached across her waist and clawed at the fabric of her robe unable to reach the pocket.

Ambassador Leblanc removed his coat and rolled it into a ball. Easing Teela's head off his lap, he placed the coat under her head and knelt over her to better examine her condition. Teela was taking air in tiny panting breaths, the area around her mouth tinged blue from lack of oxygen. She continued to claw at the pocket while trying to explain in a mixture of incoherent English and Korlah to the Ambassador that all she needed to do was press the button on the disc in her pocket and everything would be all right. But the Ambassador continued with his examination, determining that the wound on the neck was only superficial. He could find no bullet holes in the chest area of her clothing that would explain her difficult breathing. As he prepared to roll her over, he noticed a small puddle of blood under the upper portion of her damaged arm. As he raised the arm, a slurry of frothy blood and bubbles surged out like wet belch. Teela gasped loudly taking in a partial breath as the pressure collapsing her lungs was momentarily relieved.

"Pocket!" Teela cried, the vise-like sensation crushing her chest preventing her from saying more.

Exhausted from struggling, drowning in her own blood, she unwillingly relaxed, her arm falling to her side. A loud ringing in her ears replaced the sounds around her as she stared up into the questioning expression on Ambassador Leblanc's face. The ringing faded to silence as the image of Ambassador Leblanc blurred. Her eyes fluttered open and shut as she fought to remain conscious. Losing the fight and dreading the journey, her eyes closed and she could feel the now familiar embrace of unconsciousness dragging her down into the abyss that exists somewhere between life and death.

17 - Setback

Beth woke to the suffocating smell of stale scotch and bad breath only to discover it was her own. She shook her head to detach the fabric of the bag over her head from where it was sticking to her cheeks and chin from her own perspiration and saliva. She ascertained that she was seated in a chair, her arms and legs tightly bound. She strained to see or hear what was beyond the black bag over her head but detected only the sound of her own breathing and flitting shadows from light leaking up from beneath her chin that indicated the room she was being held in was brightly illuminated. She tested each restraint, one arm, one leg at a time checking for weakness. Her hands were free, but her forearms were fastened down to the arms of the chair with what she believed to be reinforced duct tape. This did not bode well; she recognized this as a specific position favored by certain interrogators who were known as "palm readers" because of the skill with which they could inflict sufficient pain from the hands alone to obtain complete cooperation from their unfortunate subjects.

A dull thump and the sound of muffled voices drew her attention away from potential threats and on to more immediate ones that just entered the room where she was being held. With a snap, that threw her head forward and removed a substantial amount of hair from the top of her scalp, the bag was jerked from her head. Bright light from a lamp that was no more than eighteen inches from her face caused her to squint and grimace as her dilated pupils strained to constrict. The fresh air, however, felt heavenly and she took in a deep breath through her nose and expelled it through her mouth. Musty dampness and the smell of earth told her that they were underground, in a basement, cellar, or more likely one of the many abandoned mines found in the mountains of Montana.

Before her eyes could adjust, something shiny came between the light and her face, the end of it catching her under the nose and forcing her head back. With sufficient force to tear the skin without tearing the cartilage at the base of her nose, the .45-caliber pistol held Beth's head back to the extreme extent that the chair and her neck would allow. Something touched her cheek, and then an instant later, her false mustache was ripped off with the same disregard as the hood had been. The gun was withdrawn, the tip dragging down her chin, chest, and coming to rest in her crotch. She could see the silhouette of a man and smell the tobacco from cigarettes on his breath as he leaned in close.

"Bethany, Bethany, Bethany," the man said whispered. "You can't imagine how much time and money I have spent trying to put you in this chair. When I finally located you, it was after an anonymous call to one of my cousins. The only reason I didn't have you killed then is because I wanted to do it myself. By the time the job was set up and dialed in, you dropped off the face of the earth, according to your friends, Marsha and Catherine ... literally. But here you are, and I'm having a hell of a time trying to decide how I'm going to kill you."

"General, listen to me for one minute. I did not kill your brother. The reason I'm here is because of what he told me before he was murdered. I didn't realize then what I know now, if I had, he'd be alive and I'd be working for you" Beth said.

"Murder? That's interesting. Your report said it was self-defense. Why don't you tell me about my brother's murder," General McClellen asked, his voice barely a whisper.

"I was following your brother to get to you. Your file stated that you were suffering from paranoid schizophrenia and were a threat to national security, so it was my job to find you, and retire you ... permanently. Rumor had it you were buying guns to arm your mercenary organization with intentions to overthrow the government, top quality military grade shit. When I heard about an attempt to hijack some shoulder-launched surface-to-air missiles from an army base, I figured it was probably you or someone hoping to sell them to you. So I arranged to have some moved around from armory to armory using the excuse that it was to improve security. It wasn't long before four cases of stinger missiles up and vanished off a transport.

"A week later when the tracking devices that I planted on them activated, it was no surprise that they were in Montana, less than an hour's drive from your hometown. I took a four-man team and staked out the mineshaft where the suspected arsenal was located and put your brother under surveillance, expecting that he was going to lead me to you. His behavior was really strange; every night he would drive out to the mine and load a box of missiles into the back of a pickup, pitch a tent, and go to bed. In the morning, he would get up, put the missiles back into the cave, drive back into town, and go about his daily activities. I figured he was planning to shoot a plane down. Then I made my first mistake; I reported his nightly behavior and requested instructions on what I should do if he were to attempt shooting a plane before he made contact with you.

"That night, without any forewarning to me or my team, my controller, sixty agents, and a helicopter showed up at the mine loaded for bear and posing as A.T.F. Your brother couldn't help but hear and see this fucking circus coming his way. He was out of his tent, rifle in hand, and headed into the thick cover of the canyon. I could have dropped him right then and there, but I figured the chopper would just track him using thermal signatures and night vision. I wanted him alive, that way, with enough drugs and coercion, I figured he'd let something slip that would take me to you. Unfortunately, the order I received that night was to 'terminate the subject.' This pissed me off and I had a little argument with my controller, I may have said a few disrespectful things in front of his team leads, and as a result, I was relieved of my job assignment and directed to return to my interim post until further notice.

"I had a pretty good idea where Jo was going. I thought it was odd that your armory was located in a box canyon. It appeared that the only other way out was to come up and over a low trough where the two ridges that formed the canyon intersected, and at that location, he would be exposed and vulnerable to sniper fire from the chopper and all the shooters coming up the canyon. But early on during this stake out, I figured your brother was smarter than that and I sent for a mine claims map from the Bureau of Land Management. I'll bet you already know what I found. Yep, there were three mines listed in this canyon, two on the inside of the canyon and one on the other side of the ridge, right next to the river bank almost directly on the other side of the ridge from a mine located near the back of the canyon.

"While the other sixty assholes were tripping over the booby traps your brother set up along his escape route, I hiked over and waited outside the entrance of the mineshaft by the river. I didn't have long to wait. He was either confident that he had pulled off his escape or realized that it wouldn't matter if he hadn't, because he came out of the mine with a kayak and headed for the water without so much as a cursory glance around the area. When he was well out in the open, I put a bullet in his leg, just above the knee, and shattered the bone. Much to my surprise, as he fell, he tossed the kayak and sprayed the area where I hid with a machine pistol. My next round hit him in the right shoulder and he dropped the pistol. But he wasn't deterred, he rolled down the bank and into the shallows, sat up, and pulled out a pistol from his boot and emptied the clip where I had been sitting a moment before. I put another round in his left shoulder. Unless he could have fired a gun with his left foot, he was no longer a threat.

"So he's sitting there in forty-something degree water staring at me as I walk down the bank towards him. I figure he's going to give me the silent treatment, so I was just planning on getting him out of the water and making sure he didn't bleed to death. But he starts talking to me, actually he started questioning me, wanted to know if I knew what he was planning to do with the missiles. So I give him the silent treatment, just to see if he would keep talking, and he did. He apologized for shooting at me, said he knew that I was just a soldier and was just doing my job. Real calm and collected, he says the government is helping aliens take cattle and people, that they have been sending space ships into this area and have been performing experiments on the cattle, mutilating them. One of the ranchers and his entire family disappeared and the government suppressed the story, allowing the man and his family to be listed only as 'missing persons.' He said that he was going to shoot down another space ship, and this time you would make sure the world finds out what's going on. Then, just as he's starting to mention you, bam! The top of his head explodes and he drops back into the water … dead.

"I don't know which one of the assholes shot him, doesn't really matter, I know who ordered it, so I charged the mother fucker and would have beat him to death for screwing up my capture, except some of the assholes with him pulled me off and cuffed me. I know how the report read, it said I killed him, but that was bullshit. I got a reprimand and one shitty job after another that left me open and exposed. I knew you would probably try to have me killed, I was ready for it, and that kept me sharp. It also kept me looking for you. If I got to you, before you got to me, I could have put an end to this.

"You know, I found out some interesting things about you during those years. Back in 1980, you were awfully young to make General, must have been running with the right crowd. But in 1986, something happened; you went underground and took a good number of your staff and associates with you. Rumor had it you went mercenary and were running guns and drugs. This was a big embarrassment for Uncle Sam, so they sent me to ... well, implement your retirement. Funny thing is you weren't selling guns; you were buying them.

"So there I was, in a Podunk town in the middle of nowhere-Oregon, assigned to the FBI and working undercover as a bank manager, waiting for a bank robber that was working the Northwest. For a frigging year, I'm waiting for this asshole to show up, until one night I get this high-level communication to go out at two in the morning and meet some un-named source on a logging road in the middle of nowhere. I figure that this is it, I had asked one too many questions and they were going to take me out. And that's exactly what happened, I was taken ... out," Beth said, ending her dissertation by letting out a sharp breath through pursed lips. A moment of silence followed as the man studied Beth's face, and she in turn stared defiantly at the shadowed face and the eyes that glinted at her from the darkness.

"The man ... the one responsible for ordering my brother's murder ..." General McClellen started to say.

"He's mine. It's not open for debate. You help me and you can watch me kill him. You kill me, and you kill any chance you will ever have for avenging your brother's death."

"I have no intention of killing you. Leaving you alive will be much more gratifying," General McClellen whispered into her face as he grabbed the index finger of her right hand and bent it back to the painful point near where it would either dislocate or break. A scraping sound announced the departure of the General's hunting knife from its sheath. Holding the blade up for

274

Beth to see, he then placed the razor sharp edge against the side of the tightly stretched skin at the knuckle of her index finger. Slowly he pressed the blade into the skin, which pulled apart and separated exposing the joint beneath.

"Did you notice that the particle beam weapons I brought you are fired using the thumb and not the index finger," Beth groaned.

"Who are you working for?" General McClellen asked drawing the point of the knife slowly around the periphery of the finger severing the outer layer of skin like you would the peel of an orange.

"I like to think I'm working for myself. But you could say I'm doing a favor for this guy I know, or knew. A real asshole. In fact, you remind me of him," Beth answered, her voice losing its calm and taking on an edge. The General chuckled to himself at her bravado as he placed the tip of the knife at the base of the finger and began to draw it up the side toward the tip.

"Fuck you! You mother fucker!" Beth shouted as General McClellen drew the blade under the edge of the cuticle and began peeling the skin off the top of her finger. "This is nothing compared to what they're going to do to you. You dumb mother fucker! They're going to eat you alive, you and everyone else on this shit-hole planet!" Beth screamed angrily, straining impotently at her restraints.

"Tell me something I don't know," General McClellen said, the tip of his knife pausing momentarily from its task of skinning her finger.

"There are two types of aliens, each wants the other dead. The Kahshinki have been here for some time now and our government is helping them in exchange for technology. The Korlah just arrived and want to eliminate the Kahshinki.

"The weapons I have, I got from the Korlah, they are BB guns compared to the weapons that are available for ground troops, not to mention stationary and vehicle mounted versions. I assume you have been watching the news. That's the Korlah trying to get Washington to shift their loyalties. When the negotiations in Washington fail, as I expect they will, I'll be able to get you anything the Korlah have in their arsenal," Beth answered, trying not to sound as desperate as she felt.

General McClellen released Beth's finger. With the tension removed from it, the finger began to bleed profusely. Wiping the tip of the knife off on Beth's sleeve, General McClellen straightened and returned it to its sheath before disappearing into the darkness behind the spotlight. A moment later, fluorescent lights turned on overhead and General McClellen returned and switched off the spotlight in front of Beth's face.

The room they were in was approximately twelve feet in length and width, and no more than twelve feet high. Carved out of rock, the walls had been smoothed with concrete and plaster, shelves carved into the walls held bottles of liquor, glasses, and books. Electrical wiring was tacked to the surface with anchor bolts and ran from a switch near a large wooden door to several outlets and the lights overhead. On the floor lay large red clay tiles. The area beneath the heavy steel chair where Beth sat was covered with a plastic painter's drop cloth that was currently preventing the blood from her peeled finger from staining the grout. A well-worn rectangular table, probably an old dining table that would seat six, was tucked tightly into one corner of the room. Lying on the table were two of the pulse rifles, the polished stainless steel pistol, the communications case, and Beth's Korlah uniform and sword. Another man was in the room, sitting in a chair with both hands resting on a small black valise that was sitting in his lap. Looking to be at least in his late seventies, the old man had short white hair and skin that was as creased and wrinkled as a dried prune. Although dressed in casual clothing, jeans and a flannel shirt, his posture and the clean and neatly pressed condition of his apparel provided him a respectful appearance.

General McClellen knelt before the chair once again, this time Beth could see his face and was surprised to find that his features had been surgically altered. His complexion, smooth and well-tanned, made him look at least ten years younger than he actually was. Dressed in an impeccable gray pinstriped suit, he looked like the proverbial business professional. It was apparent

276

that he had not been hiding in the woods as she had expected, but instead, was hiding in plain sight, using an alias no doubt.

"I would never have recognized you," Beth stated honestly.

"Can't say the same for your disguise," General McClellen replied as he removed a folded piece of paper from his pocket, unfolded it, and held it up for Beth to see. An 8-1/2 inch by 11 inch sheet of paper, it was an 'All Points Bulletin' containing her, Marsha, and Catherine's pictures, their real names and physical descriptions. It offered a $250,000 reward for information leading to their capture. It specified that they were wanted in connection with the murder of two United States Federal Marshalls. At the bottom in bold print it said, 'Armed and extremely dangerous, do not attempt to apprehend, notify the FBI immediately'. Someone had penciled a moustache onto the picture of Beth that provided the distinct likeness of Burton Portenski.

"This was circulated the day after the DC-ET landing; initially in the Las Vegas, Phoenix, and Los Angeles areas. By the second day it went national, and by the third, international. They want you real bad Agent Porter, more than me maybe. Why is that?" General McClellen asked.

"I guess you could say that I'm now an agent for the opposition. I have the evidence needed to prove that our government is trading lives for technology, and has engaged in acts of war against a foreign government without-" Beth was saying before General McClellen's laughter cut her short.

"Agent Porter, do you hear yourself? For Christ's sake woman, you're one of their assassins. You know better than most how governments have been trading lives and engaging in unlawful acts of war since the beginning of time. Our government is no different. The gizmos and gadgets you have are impressive, but I can tell you from experience, if the government doesn't want this shit to go public, it will disappear, fake devices will replace those presented and whatever dumb bastard breaks the story will die of natural causes, or have an unfortunate accident. What the fuck do you think I've been doing the last twenty years?" General McClellen asked, grabbing the hunting knife off the table and drawing the blade from its sheath.

"You tried. But you didn't have me and my new friends to help," Beth replied, wincing when she tried to close her bloodied hand as he approached.

"What makes you think these new aliens are any better than the first?" General McClellen asked, moving the knife towards her face.

"The Korlah eat rats and snakes, the Kahshinki ... well, they eat people," Beth replied.

General McClellen knelt in front of Beth again, resting the hand with the knife in it on her shoulder while he studied her face intently.

"I received a phone call about ten minutes after my boys picked you up, on my cell phone, my personal, private fucking cell phone," General McClellen said as he watched Beth's face.

"And?" Beth replied defiantly, meeting General McClellen's intense gaze.

"It was a friend of yours, she told me everything you just told me, said that if I killed you as I intended, God would not forgive me. She told me that she was working with you, said her name was Rebecca."

"Rebecca? No, I ... uh, I don't know why ... hell, I don't even know how she would be calling you," Beth replied with visible surprise.

"She gave me a phone number, said it was someone that would be willing to listen to me now. I called the number, it was not your typical phone number. President McCormick answered."

After studying Beth's face for a few moments longer, he ran the knife through the tape holding her chest, then down the tape securing her right arm, and along the waist.

"Doctor, would you please come suture this finger and administer something for the pain," General McClellen said as he continued to cut the remaining tape.

"Tell me Agent Porter; are you here to betray the government of this country, or because you believe you are defending the Constitution against domestic enemies?" General McClellen asked, sheathing and tossing the knife onto the table as he walked to the shelf where the liquor resided.

278

"I was a loyal soldier and they sold me out, same as you," Beth replied.

"You still consider yourself a soldier then?" General McClellen asked as he filled two glasses with whiskey.

During the silence that followed, the doctor set up a rusty old TV tray next to Beth's chair and removed a suture kit from the black valise. His dark eyes folded into the deep creases of his face and reminded Beth of the old Korlah warrior that died on the transport. He was already injecting Novocain into her throbbing hand by the time General McClellen handed her the glass of whiskey.

"Yes, Sir, I am," Beth finally answered, taking the glass of whiskey and meeting the General's piercing gaze with one of her own.

"Welcome to the United States Militia, Lieutenant Porter," General McClellen said, holding his glass out as if to toast.

"I don't think so General, I have ..." Beth started to say, lowering her glass.

"Who does that uniform and sword on the table belong to soldier?" General McClellen demanded gesturing to the Korlah uniform on the table.

"Me ... but ..." Beth started to reply, but was again interrupted by the General.

"Are you going to tell me that you would serve in a foreign, hell, alien military but not one that defends the Constitution of the United States of America?" the General growled disdainfully.

'No Sir ... I ..."

"We are at war, you said it yourself. You have indicated your choice of the side you intend to support. So ... are you going to be a conscript or a volunteer?" the General demanded.

Beth glowered at the General, and General McClellen glowered back, his tumbler still raised. Slowly Beth lifted her tumbler to meet the General's, the glasses clinking together with sufficient force to nearly shatter them.

"Sir, a volunteer, Sir!" Beth hissed through clenched teeth, realizing that she was not being given a choice in the matter.

"To we the people," General McClellen said, raising his glass again.

"We the People," Beth repeated before downing the full tumbler in three gulps.

"Now Lieutenant, I would like to hear your perspective of these new aliens. Start from the beginning," General McClellen said, filling Beth's glass with more whisky.

Now that her hand was numb, the doctor began sewing up the General's handiwork. Although resentful of the injuries inflicted, Beth reasoned that General McClellen could have used far more damaging methods to secure the reassurance he needed before drawing her into his organization. The first glass of whisky gone and the second soon to be, Beth relaxed and proceeded to tell General McClellen everything she could recall of the events following her abduction.

Ten, eleven, twelve. The words seemed to come from everywhere and nowhere, the counting stopped and something touched her mouth. Teela opened her eyes to see Agent Cooper, his face over hers, their open mouths together. She frowned as his face moved away, her mind questioning what was happening. She was cold, freezing cold, and so tired that she physically ached with exhaustion. She fought to stay awake. *Am I dying?* She wanted to ask, but her mouth would not respond. Agent Cooper spoke, but she could not understand the words, they seemed muffled and muted, the image of him blurred, and like her fear, it faded into nothingness.

Agent Cooper saw her eyes open and grow wide with fear formed by the comprehension of her condition. The physical response spurred him in his efforts to resuscitate her. She was still alive, he was sure of it. She opened her eyes slowly and for a fraction of a second looked directly into his eyes before the focus shifted, looking through and beyond him. No pulse, still not breathing on her own. Another breath, chest compressions and another breath, repeat. He was vaguely aware of the transfer to the shuttle. They pulled her away, but he followed. No more than a minute or so elapsed before he was able to continue providing the lifesaving actions. Why were they not helping? They moved her onto a low table in the forward end of the shuttle and stood watching him. Where were their doctors? His lungs burned and his arms ached with fatigue. How long had it been? More of the aliens crowded into the shuttle. Agent Cooper did not look up from his task, he looked only at their legs and odd feet clad in wide-toed boots as they crowded around. The group included a young Korlah with feet much smaller than the others, wearing slippers instead of boots; Agent Cooper reasoned that it was a child. It was escorted up to the table that Teela was on and once at the table it immediately screamed, its ear-piercing shriek drawing Agent Cooper out of his trance-like state to stare at the child with his blood-smeared face. The child recoiled from the table, her head and body thrashing wildly as the Korlah soldiers attempted to restrain her. The room, which had previously been nearly silent, erupted into a cacophony of shouting and screaming. Undeterred, yet more aware than before of the intense emotion that filled the room, Agent Cooper returned to his task, ignoring Teela's parchment white complexion and dull glazed eyes that pleaded convincingly of his failure.

Howard Lewis

18 - Beyond

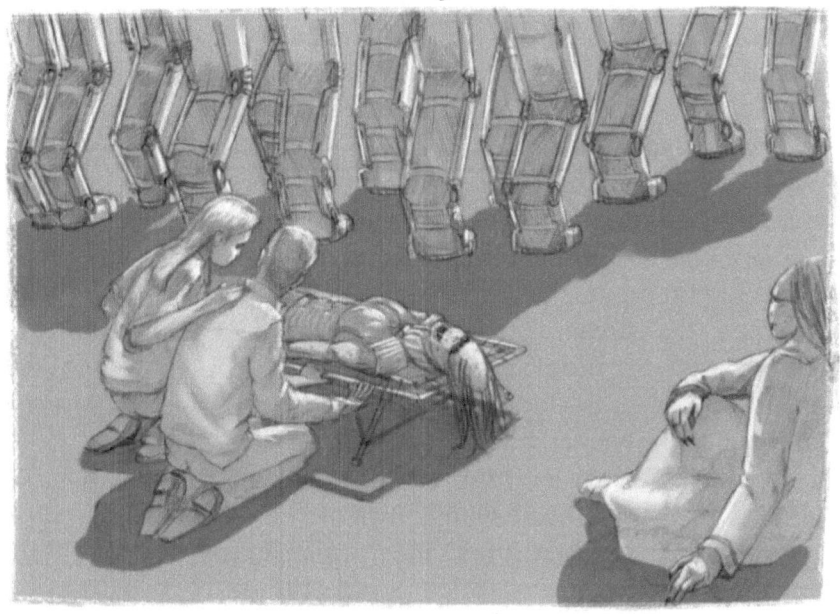

Black upon black, silence beyond all nothingness enveloped them, yet their minds stirred within the abyss that held them prisoner. *Listen with your mind*, Teela cried, and Daedalus strained to obey her command. The silence faltered, a soft murmuring of voices echoed in the darkness beyond the blackness around them. Barely discernable, the thoughts came, blending from an incoherent droning to concise conversation making splashing and tinkling sounds like flowing water; rising and ebbing, becoming more and more distinct the more intently they listened. Their thoughts spun slowly around creating a feeling of dizziness that grew into an awareness of physical form that moved and flexed to the rhythm of the sounds. The darkness faded to gray, and they found themselves, or more aptly the physical form they had come to accept, sitting on a seat of wet mossy stone overlooking a stream, in the distance, a waterfall, the source of the sounds created a fog that blurred the details around them with its thick mist. Droplets of water formed on their face running down their arms and off their fingertips onto the stone where they joined the rivulets of water that in turn flowed down into the stream where they were carried away. As they sat and watched, they reasoned that each droplet was a memory, each distinct and intricate in its individual detail, each belonging to a part of a universe of thoughts and memories that comprised all that is or ever would be. They looked at their hands, indistinct, neither Korlah nor human, like the hands of a cartoon, they were mere representations of a physical existence that their mind created in its attempt to rationalize what they were experiencing. As they watched, their hands became translucent as the droplets formed upon them, flowing together and down the mossy rocks and into the stream. As the corporeal image dissolved and merged with the droplets of thought, the voices all around and within saturated their perceptions, they could feel themselves joining the flow that moved and carried their memories with them, down and away from where they had been, taking the essence of who they were with it.

The elements of their individual essence proved to be firmly fused together and they traveled as one with the flow that carried them. There was no sense of control, no concern over where they were going or why, the idea that this was the end of their existence seemed inconsequential and wholly acceptable. Releasing the concerns of the present, together, they relived their past, experiencing the memories and emotions of each, considering for the first time how wildly different their hopes and dreams had been. It was upon consideration of their regrets, that they each found the one true common ground between their vastly different personas.

We would have liked to have children. Yes ... we ... would, they thought.

"Mother?" a voice called, coming from somewhere outside the stream.

Their thoughts working together like eyes, searched for the voice that came to them so clearly. The stream above them shimmered at the point of separation between water and air, a shadow above, cast its silhouette onto the surface of the stream flowing over them. The ripples smoothed and the image became clear. A young birthing unit reaching down toward the stream appeared like a reflection in a mirror.

Is that ... us?

Yes.

The thoughts conversed as together they recognized the identifying mark, the sabat "Teela" on the birthing unit's face.

Their minds reached like a hand to touch the one being offered to them and in the instant of that choice, the image flipped. Instead of looking up, they were now looking down; only it was not a stream that met their eyes, it was a pallid, blood spattered face. A moment of disbelief followed, as realization and the wish to deny it paralyzed their thoughts. It was an older, emaciated version of Teela's face. They had not realized the extent to which Teela's physical condition had deteriorated. Looking down on the gaunt remains, they gasped in horror at the visage of their final condition and the realization of their own mortality. Physical pain followed the instant of visual recognition. Blinding in its intensity, the pain was unbearable and together they screamed as their thoughts, memories and emotions were forcibly torn and ripped from the flow, like bloody ragged bits of flesh with nerves exposed and inflamed, dragged out of the continuum and thrust back into physical existence.

With her hands covering her face in a useless attempt to stop the incipient flow that was searing and burning its way into her mind, Teela fought to turn away from the source of the pain, but others grabbed and forced her toward it. The room spun around her as the realization of what was happening became evident. This was the transfer occurring. It was not as expected, not as Shyron and Nerhala had described, and not at all as they had experienced it before. Unsure of how long the event lasted, Teela was finally able to relax as the pain began to subside, and as it did, she opened her eyes and drew a deep breath through a throat that stung from screaming. Hands gripped her arms tightly just below the shoulders, no longer struggling against their grip, she looked for a familiar face. Her gaze met the scarred and scowling face of Shawaugh. Their eyes met and just as Teela opened her mouth to speak, Shawaugh swung her thick muscular arm across the narrow gap that separated them, the back of her hand striking Teela firmly on the side of her face, snapping her head painfully to the side. The impact, a white-hot flash of pain, was followed by a sensation of tumbling into darkness as she slumped limply in the grip of the warriors holding her.

The sound of people arguing and shouting roused her from her stupor. Teela realized that she was sitting on the floor, her back against the cold bulkhead of the transport. She dimly recalled the realization of transfer.

"Who am I?" she whispered, trying to gather a realization of self. "I am Teela," she replied to herself with dubious certainty. Since receiving the transfer of Daedalus the confirmation of self, had been her hands, their familiarity, the pain her claws could produce, like a pinch, it would inform her that she was not dreaming. These were her hands, she was certain. But they were youthful, smooth and only lightly callused with no indication of the self-inflicted wounds on the palms. Although she had managed to stop clawing her palms, she had begun to perceive the healing punctures as an indicator of her healing sanity. The fingertips of one hand played upon the palm of the other as she fought to come to grips with what had happened and who she was.

We are Shawlmon! Her thoughts demanded. *Yes ... Teela and Daedalus. Together ... we are Shawlmon,* she rationalized, before looking at the unblemished palms. *How can these be my hands?* she asked.

Teela 20.1507210, she whispered, stunned by the realization.

Although Teela was not a common name, of the roughly three million Korlah aboard the Campaign vessel, several thousand units shared the "T-E-Ela" designation. However, the unit Nerhala had provided Shyron with was quite unique. She was a birthing unit, not only from the same section as Nerhala, she had been birthed and raised in the same nurseries and dormitories as Teela 20.10127. The similarities of their individual experiences, so alike, that without conscious deliberation, one was nearly indistinguishable from the other. This made it clear to her why the leader shells were isolated and deprived of unique or specific stimulation, and given only the names of the eleven section leaders. Without the numerical designator, it would have been difficult to separate the memories of the one Teela from the other.

Her neck and chest ached from the gunshot wounds. With her hands, she explored the areas of injury confirming that the pain was only a remnant of her past existence. During the examination, Teela noticed blood on the front of her tah. From the dull ache, emanating from the side of her face and mouth she reasoned it was hers. Upon examining her face with her hand, she found that her lip was split over her right fang, and her eye was beginning to swell. She wiped the congealing blood from her face and chin.

Her posture shifted as the awareness of who she was became clear. As she scanned the room with her eyes, it became evident that no one, except her, was aware of what had occurred. If she told no one, they would likely return her to the birthing section and she would be able to shed the burden of her previous responsibilities as she had her previous shell. She was both elated and dismayed, the emotions twisting their way through her conjoined consciousness. To be the Teela, the "Warrior Mother" as her sisters in the birthing section now referred to Teela 10127, was an honor of unbelievable proportions for the young Teela. To be the Campaign Potentate, Shawlmon, was the position that would best facilitate the plans Daedalus had for establishing an alliance between the Korlah and humans. Yet it was Teela's intense desire to return to Nerhala and her sisters in the birthing section, that creased the young face with a frown of disappointment, as the realization that the life she once knew was no longer hers alone.

Teela leaned against the wall and climbed to her feet. With her back against the bulkhead, she observed the chaos around her while listening carefully with her ears and mind. Afraid at first that she had lost her telepathic capabilities, she discovered that if anything, they were much more refined. It was with subconscious effort that she was able to shut out the overwhelming cacophony of mental noise, isolate her own mind and focus on the specific thoughts and emotions around her. If fear and trepidation possessed an odor, the closed confines of the transport reeked of it, causing Teela to shake her head as if that would free her crown tendrils of the stench. She scanned the group, which consisted mostly of warriors, many of which were wearing heavy armor and pack-mounted pulse cannons. The armor on many of the warriors was pockmarked by projectile weapons fire, and Teela reasoned that this was the group that rescued her.

Filling the transport to capacity, the warriors tried to stand out of the way, their armor and weapons knocking into each other and the walls, making a clacking sound as they bumped nervously together. Nervous, because although they had retrieved Shawlmon as demanded, they believed Shawlmon was dead and their mission a failure. Across the transport, Shyron was speaking telepathically to Shawaugh. Shawaugh's head was down in submissive acceptance of what Shyron was saying. Shyron's communication was direct and specific to Shawaugh and as such, Teela could not hear Shyron's thoughts without revealing the intrusion, so instead she had to feel, or more aptly experience Shawaugh's response to what Shyron was saying. Shawaugh's emotions were plagued by feelings of hopelessness and regret. Another defeat, another failure, a doomed campaign, and an overwhelming desire to end an existence that no longer seemed to have any meaning or honor emanated from Shawaugh's mind. Teela physically winced at the intensity of Shawaugh's emotional suffering and was about to announce that she had not failed, when the warrior to her left moved and Teela saw Rebecca kneeling next to Agent Cooper, who was sitting on the floor staring blankly at the low table and the lifeless body upon it. The thoughts that emanated from Rebecca were not those of consolation, as the words she spoke to Agent Cooper would suggest. Rebecca was distraught, confused, and dismayed by what she considered to be an impossible contradiction of expectations. She was trying to rationalize why, if Shawlmon had not yet led them to victory as the Gods told her, how then could Shawlmon have ceased? As Rebecca spoke her soothing words, Teela could feel her scanning Agent Cooper's mind, certain that Shawlmon's essence was somehow hiding within it.

Glancing down at her blood smeared hands, Teela clenched them tightly into fists, careful not to let her claws pierce the palms.

Is it possible, Teela thought, relaxing the fists and turning the hands over and extending the claws, *that these are the claws of Shawlmon? Will it really be me that brings an end to this conflict?* When she looked toward Rebecca, she found Rebecca staring back at her, their eyes meeting and locking. They both stared, Teela knew that it was not a challenge; Rebecca had felt Teela's telepathic probe and was now attempting to scan her mind. If Teela's eyes truly were the gateway to her soul, Rebecca found the gate closed and locked, her efforts to see beyond, merely rattling the latch. A mental blockade now encased and enclosed Teela's conscious and unconscious thoughts, insulating her from Rebecca's probe. Unable to proceed beyond the young birthing unit's intense glare, Rebecca cocked her head, questioning her efforts. Teela nodded her head to affirm Rebecca's suspicions, breaking eye contact, she wormed her way through the crowd to where Agent Cooper was sitting. Kneeling next to him, Teela noted that his shirt and a pant leg were soaked with blood. His pale complexion and the little round hole halfway between his shirt pocket and belt line confirmed what she suspected.

"You were hit!" Teela exclaimed reaching for the shirt to examine the extent of the injury. With speed and strength that belied his deteriorated appearance, Agent Cooper intercepted her hand and held it firmly by the wrist in his grip.

"Who are you?" Agent Cooper asked, retaining control of her hand but relaxing his grip. Teela smiled at the irony of the question and the fact that he knew nothing of its significance to the event that transpired only minutes ago.

"Thanks to you, I am Shawlmon. You kept that body alive long enough that I was able to transfer from it, to this one. You saved me Agent Cooper, thank you," Teela answered, speaking slowly, relearning how to enunciate the words with her new body, the split lip causing her to wince from the oral movement some of the words demanded.

"What? How? It ... it's ..." Agent Cooper stammered, looking first at the body on the table and then back to Teela and shaking his head in disbelief.

"It's a miracle!" Rebecca exclaimed as she bowed her head and knelt, while offering Teela a palm display above her head, to demonstrate acceptance of Teela's authority while offering her unconditional servitude.

Transfer succeeded! The essence of Shawlmon continues, Rebecca announced telepathically, the volume and clarity arriving to every person on the transport and in the nearby fighter escorts as clearly and loudly as if someone had shouted it into their ear. The transport immediately became silent, heads turned in search of the source of the announcement. Finding Rebecca kneeling, her palms upturned in Teela's direction, the warriors in the area stepped back, their eyes, along with all others in the transport looking first at Rebecca, then at Teela in disbelief.

"Impossible! There was no transfer," Shawaugh shouted, glaring at Teela.

Locking eyes with Shawaugh, Teela rose to her feet and walked with slow purpose toward Shawaugh. Those caught between pushed into the crowd, or pressed themselves against the bulkhead to clear her path. Diminutive, even in comparison to the original Teela, the young birthing unit had been raised during the peak of the famine and at twelve cycles, she could easily have passed for a unit of seven or eight. Stopping directly in front of the huge warrior, she had to tilt her head far back to maintain eye contact. When she spoke, she did so only with her mind, and only to Shawaugh.

One of my first memories is of your face. The memory both haunts and comforts me. You have been my savior, protector, friend, and advisor. I have ignored your advice, and nearly paid with my existence. How may I regain honor in your eyes?

Even as the young birthing unit was approaching, Shawaugh knew it was not a child, at least not the one that she had met when it arrived. The eyes bore into hers with an intensity borne not of malice, not of challenge but rather of intent. Wishing immediately to break eye contact with this non-child, it was Shawaugh's conditioned response to maintain it. When the thoughts came to her, they came with honest sincerity as a spoken word might, but unlike words, these thoughts were laced with emotions that held more meaning than spoken words ever could.

290

Shawaugh broke eye contact the instant she received Teela's first thoughts and she realized the truth of Rebecca's declaration. Looking nervously around the room, Shawaugh could see that all within the confines of the transport were watching her intently, waiting for her response. She opened her mouth to speak, but when she looked back at the young face bloodied by her own hand, her voice caught in her throat. With an unintelligible grunt, Shawaugh made a two-clawed salute, followed by an open apologetic palm display.

With Shawaugh's challenge of Rebecca's announcement successfully countered by the young Teela, the existence of Shawlmon was officially confirmed and documented into the ships log by the communications technician. No one else offered a challenge as Teela made her way through the transport, thanking each warrior and every member of the transport's crew personally and individually for the role they played, not only in her rescue, but also in the Campaign as a whole.

In keeping with the Korlah culture of utility, Teela watched as the empty and useless shell of her previous existence was unceremoniously stripped. The gaunt and scarred carcass was then placed out of the way in a corner for later reclamation. Once cleared of the useless remains, Agent Cooper was then lifted onto the low platform, and under Rebecca's watchful eyes, two biotechs tended to his gunshot wounds. Shyron made no attempt to speak to Teela, as there really was no need. She had already told the young Teela all of the things she needed to tell Shawlmon, and although the young Teela may not have understood all that Shyron had told her at the time, Teela was now keenly aware of all that was said and how it would affect her plans. They were in transit to the Campaign Vessel, her anticipated protest already acknowledged and addressed. The Council made its decision, and when they arrived, she would do what was expected of her. She was after all, a servant of the Korlah Mission.

Some inner need pulled her over to the corner where the naked body that was once hers was laying. She knelt and took one of its hands in hers. She pried the partially clenched fist open and massaged the damaged palm with the soft pad of a thumb as she stared at the hated scar that crossed from one leg to the abdomen. The scar and damage beneath it had been a source of intense shame and embarrassment. She could not understand why, now that it was no longer a part of her, and like the body before her, she felt naked without it. She gently kissed the cold hand before laying it down.

"Roche-Hah, Teela of generation twenty, birthing unit 10127," Teela whispered.

She sensed that the majority of the transport's occupants feared her. Moreover, they feared that she could read and reveal their thoughts, their fears, and their lack of conviction. To them she was all-powerful, and if they knew how terrified she was, it would destroy the fragile remnants of control she retained. She bottled her thoughts, emotions, and fears, drawing them deep behind the façade she knew she would need to maintain. She stood, straightening her posture; she followed Dade's advice and held her head high with a display of confidence that belied the dark content of her thoughts.

19 - Rebirth

Sahanga filled her lungs with air, exhaling while relishing and truly appreciating the excellent health she enjoyed. She smoothed the fabric of her pilot's uniform taking pride in the rank that she had been awarded in recognition of her decision to volunteer for the newly formed flight section that would be composed of Korlah-human transfers. It had only been a few hours since they began the process and her group had already been briefed and assigned to their new areas. Sahanga stared at her reflection in the polished surface of the briefing room wall. The image perceived was both familiar and at the same time oddly foreign.

"Man or woman?" a voice from behind her asked in English.

Sahanga turned toward the source of the question. A pilot dressed as she was, a genetic duplicate, it could have been her own reflection if not for the sabat on her face that identified her as Rowanga a birth sister and close companion she grew up with.

"Don't ask, don't tell, and things won't get too weird," Sahanga replied in Korlah, smiling slyly.

"Maybe we knew each other. Tell me who you were Sahanga!" Rowanga demanded in English.

"It doesn't matter," Sahanga replied, speaking again in Korlah. "We were told not to speak of it, and I think it's a good thing. It doesn't matter who we were as humans or Korlah. This is a new chance, a new beginning, an honor and an opportunity for the future."

"Don't parrot that propaganda bullshit! We were all pilots, human pilots. Who's running your shell, Korlah or human? Can you even speak English?" Rowanga hissed with frustration.

Sahanga ignored Rowanga's outburst and instead surveyed the room. It appeared that everyone was present and although talking, had assumed their ranked positions in preparation for the flight briefing. She proceeded to the elevated dais at the front of the room and waited until the talking tapered off. She addressed the 450 units that represented the pilots, navigators, and communication technicians that comprised the crews of the 150 spacecraft that formed the ten fighter groups assigned to her.

"Many in this room are not transfer recipients and therefore do not speak English. For this reason, I am issuing the following directive: only Korlah is to be spoken while you are on shift. What you do off shift will be up to you, but I would hope that you will exercise consideration and respect for others around you," she said firmly, ensuring her gaze settled on Rowanga.

The composition of the non-transfers was primarily birthing units, with a few technician and soldier genotypes included in the mix. Of the ten flight groups of fifteen fighters each, only a third of each would be manned with human transfer units. Like Sahanga, the transfer units were technically young, inexperienced Korlah pilots, most of whom had never flown anything other than flight simulators. It would be the skills and experience from a past life that would make them the ace pilots they needed to be.

Immediately following transfer of the human essence, Sahanga had been briefed on the desperate condition of the defense forces. This wing would be the only long-range patrol force that would be used for the defense of Earth, the bulk of the fighter craft being dedicated to the protection of the Campaign Vessel. There would be no relief until more transferees or human pilots arrived. She knew that a Kahshinki attack was expected and actually considered overdue. She also knew, not from her Korlah experience, but from her human memories, that this wing was intended to be the sacrificial first line of defense. In a word, they were … 'expendable.' She took in a deep breath, taking a moment to appreciate her good health and clear lungs before continuing her address.

"Until we receive adequate reinforcements, I am dividing this fighter section into two groups. I will lead fighter groups one through five and Assistant Section Leader Rowanga will lead fighter section groups six through ten. One group will be on-shift, while the other group will be off shift, and we will be turning over on station."

A murmur of disapproval rose from the group increasing in volume. Hands among the group shot into the air, as pilots waited to be recognized. The human influence was immediately apparent. No Korlah would openly voice disapproval, and there was no protocol among Korlah pilots for asking questions during a briefing.

"Put your hands down and listen!" Sahanga demanded. The room grew quiet as the pilots reluctantly lowered their hands.

"We are Earth's shield. Until more reinforcements arrive, we will train on location. We will sleep in the hangars next to our craft. We will eat, drink, and breathe combat principles and strategies, both on and off shift. We will fight when asked, and we will cease when we have no other choice. We will employ a combat strategy called dogfighting. For those of you that don't know what a dog is, it's a big mean hairy beast with fangs and claws. Look around. You may not know it, but some of the best pilots in the universe are sitting in this room. In my human life, I fought as a pilot in three Campaigns humans call Wars. I helped define, develop and master dogfighting techniques. My style of combat was so aggressive that I was called 'Mad Dog.' Korlah pilots have always been fearless, but now we will fight with methods so fearsome that the Kahshinki will shake with fear when the Mad Dogs of Korlah attack!" Sahanga shouted the last words, holding an open clawed hand in the air.

A group of ten to fifteen pilots jumped to their feet and began clapping and shouting their approval, the remainder soon stood and joined the enthusiastic response.

"That's Mad Dog Jacobs, Ace fighter pilot ... twice over. He's a fucking legend!" Rowanga exclaimed in English, to the pilot next to her. Noting the pilot's confused expression and the white ring that circled the collar of her uniform, Rowanga realized that she was one of the non-transfer volunteers, who did not speak English. Switching to Korlah, she rephrased her comments.

"Good pilot. Sahanga has the essence of a good pilot."

The pilot nodded deeply and began clapping enthusiastically again.

When the room quieted, Sahanga continued with a briefing on changes to standard Korlah formation and engagement strategies. She took questions from the group and together they discussed the changes, entertained scenarios, and developed contingencies for the unique situations that were integral to spacecraft combat. With less than half a shift, or six hours Earth time remaining, she dismissed Rowanga's section and directed her section to launch and rendezvous outside the Campaign Vessel in preparation for proceeding to their patrol station.

Within two hours of departure, the seventy-five fighter craft were on location a mere ten billion miles from earth on the outskirts of the Kuiper belt. From there, they would get a clear view on their sensors of any enemy craft approaching from the direction the Kahshinki were known to be coming. For the next three and a half hours, Sahanga led the group through numerous attack and defense formations. Placing her craft in the forward-most position with its sensors probing the vast emptiness of space, she coached the groups through some 'follow the leader' strategies in hope of improving the desperately feeble dogfighting skills of the untrained Korlah volunteers.

"Hyper-light trace, deep space, coming directly at us," the navigation officer announced.

"How many?" Sahanga asked calmly.

"Many … very many," the navigation officer shot back.

"I need numbers. What is their course, how many, and how long until they pass this region?" Sahanga demanded sternly. The navigator adjusted her panel, and made some calculations before responding.

"They are on course for Earth, about … a hundred, and they will pass us in less than ten bits," the navigator groaned.

"No worry, that's less than two to one. We'll kick their asses," Sahanga replied with confidence.

"Commander! One hundred groups … that's one hundred groups of fifteen each … 1,500 mixed craft in a standard assault wave," the navigator clarified. "Twenty to one." she added with unmasked panic.

"Fuck me!" Sahanga exclaimed in English switching her screen to the long-range sensor and confirming her navigation officer's claim.

"Notify Campaign Command of the numbers and course. Rowanga is en route to this location, direct her to hang back and intercept whatever enemy craft get past us," Sahanga said to the communications officer.

As the communications officer relayed the information, Sahanga recalled the fighters in her section and had them regroup in preparation for the first defensive battle of the Campaign. Forming a single file line behind Sahanga, each group of fifteen formed up with the heavy fighters split ahead and behind the light fighters. This was contrary to the standard Korlah practice of meeting the enemy head-on, which would have required her group to split and spread out, to meet the vastly greater number of approaching craft. If the attack wave dropped out of hyper-light before it reached them, Sahanga's plan was to drive through the front of the wave and take out the Kahshinki command vessels that traditionally trailed the assault wave, and then engage the enemy fighters which were not trained in how to fight independently. If the wave blew past them, Sahanga would have the Korlah flight section jump to hyper-light and follow, engaging them from behind when they dropped to sub-light speeds.

Adjusting the sensors to relative space, the navigator of Sahanga's light fighter aimed the forward sensor array in the direction of the approaching armada. As she did, the image of the Kahshinki craft began to appear on Sahanga's targeting screen as a thick phalanx, 1,600 miles long, several hundred wide, and several hundred deep, moving steadily down the screen as they rapidly closed the distance between them.

"Good, good ... they are spread out. We will use this to our advantage," Sahanga announced. "Notify Rowanga that we will attack their center and attempt to break their formation. Her flight section will be able to mop up the formation as it tries to regroup."

"All craft, including ours, are being recalled to defend the Campaign Vessel. Rowanga's group has already acknowledged the order. Our leaders are apparently not as fearless as we are. So tell me Mad Dog, shall we tuck our tails between our legs and run for home?" the communications officer asked.

Sahanga did not respond. She stared at the mass of dots growing larger and larger on her screen, and realized that as she was assessing the enemy, the enemy would be assessing the threat value of her column of seventy-five defenders. Even if every one of her fighters was manned with a seasoned pilot, a frontal assault would be suicidal; the new pulse absorption shields, as impressive as they sounded, had encountered serious problems during the first engagement. Even if the overload glitch was fixed, they were still rated at only ten to fifteen direct hits before their effectiveness would quickly degrade. To hold a frontal position at twenty to one was not an option. She could split the section into five groups, break off, and harass them from the sides and behind as they continued on course. But that, she knew, would just delay the inevitable. At twenty to one, unless they retreated, they would most certainly be destroyed. Unfortunately, for Sahanga, to retain her honor, retreat was not an option.

Sahanga engaged the audible communications system and although limited in its range, she believed it to be faster and more effective than the communication panel readouts that had traditionally been used by the Korlah and were still being used by their enemy.

"You all received the same order as I did. If you want to break formation and run, now is the time. Otherwise ladies, on my lead, match course and speed. We will drive through the front line, weapons on narrow beam, constant fire. Do not let your power cells exceed 75 percent. Once we are through the front line, split into sub groups of three and spread out within the center of their wave. Ignore the fighters; concentrate your attacks on assault pods and transports. If you lose your group, join another," she said calmly, her voice emanating from speakers in each of the seventy-four spacecraft behind her. "Roche Hah, warriors!" she cried, as she pushed up the speed of her fighter and nosed it toward the approaching wall of enemy craft.

Fourteen hours later, astronomers at the Palomar Observatory in Southern California attempted to train the massive lens of their telescope onto an unusual grouping of flashing lights emanating from the depths of space. Unfortunately, twenty minutes after it started, the frequency and intensity of the lights diminished and finally ceased, long before the telescope could be repositioned and focused. An odd event, it was later documented by those who observed it as an "interesting phenomena."

20 - Miracle

The tumbling masses of iron-laced rock were nearly imperceptible to the naked eye. Every now and then, if Teela stared long enough, a moving shadow within the star field or a glint of reflected light from a facet of ice crystal would divulge the location of the dull gray-black giants that threatened their transit through the asteroid belt. The pilot was not studying the myriad of stars beyond the window as Teela was, but instead had her attention fixed on the monitoring screen in front of her that was displaying a three dimensional rendition of the objects ahead of them. When Teela asked to look out the window, the pilot obliged, even though she would have preferred to have the window morphed to match the much more durable molecular density as the rest of the transport's hull.

As she stood there staring intently into the star field, a cold chill swept through her. If Daedalus had succeeded in bringing the transport back to this point during their escape attempt, he and the others with him would undoubtedly have died here in the asteroid field, obliterated in the cold depths of space by his ignorance. She shook her head and exhaled forcefully in an attempt to clear her mind of such dark thoughts, her breath condensing on the cold surface of the viewing window. She was no more in control now, than Daedalus had been then. Only now it was not ten lives at stake, it was billions. She ran a trembling fingertip through the condensed breath on the screen, slow circles moving slowly inward, her mind racing through the events that had brought her ... them to this point.

"System defense forces report an incoming Kahshinki attack wave," the communications officer announced. "1,500 mixed craft on a course for the human home world."

"Where are we in relation to their approach vector?" the pilot asked.

"Well outside their relative scanner range. If we skirt the debris zone, their long range scanners will not be able to differentiate us from debris," the navigator replied.

"Where will the system defense forces intercept the wave?" Teela asked.

"System forces are being recalled to defend the Campaign Vessel," the communications officer replied.

"On whose authority?" Teela shouted.

After a long pause with no response from the crew, Teela ordered the communications officer to issue an order in her name.

Although she did not refuse, the communications officer remained silent, her face turned away from Teela's glare. When someone put a firm hand on her shoulder, Teela spun defensively, grabbing the hand at the wrist. It was Shyron, with eyes and head downcast, her embarrassment of what was happening plainly evident.

"You should have read the reports, answered our messages. You should have returned when we asked you to," Shyron said accusingly.

"Am I a prisoner?" Teela gasped.

"No, Your Eminence, but it has been decided; there is no hope for this planet. It cannot be defended with the forces we have. Authority aboard the Campaign Vessel is being challenged from one shift to the next. We are on the verge of another armed insurrection. You must return and restore order. We must save ourselves before we can hope to save the humans," Shyron said, emphasizing her words with waves of telepathic sincerity.

Teela scanned the faces in the room; none would look at her except Rebecca, who in the instant of eye contact imparted her thoughts and plan as she moved toward the center of the transport. Teela glanced at the pilot's control panel, gauging what it would take to initiate Rebecca's plan. Focusing on Shyron, she spoke directly into Shyron's mind hoping to avoid the proposed action.

Give me a ship. Let me go, you don't need me. Shawlmon's robe was made for you, not me. Return as Shawlmon, restore order, no one here will question your authority. Please sister, let me go, Teela pleaded.

Shyron's head jerked upward in response to the message, her eyes meeting Teela's. She did not need to read Shyron's thoughts to know what she was thinking.

If we are to be Shawlmon, then who will you be? Shyron asked skeptically.

I will be free to be whoever I wish. Eventually I will find a name that fits. For now, I will be this Teela, a Teela nobody cares about.

I accept your offer, but we cannot implement it until after we return to the Campaign Vessel, Shyron replied, breaking eye contact, indicating there would be no negotiation on the subject.

"I can't wait that long," Teela said as she took two steps toward the pilot's console, reached over and pressed the control that opened the portal between the transport and the heavy fighter attached to its underside.

Having positioned herself over the portal, Rebecca dropped through the instant it opened. Teela ducked and dove between the legs of the warriors that separated her from the opening. As she flew through the opening, her angular trajectory carried her out of the portals gravity field. Up instantly became down as she flew through the opening and crashed into the rear bulkhead of the fighter falling into a rack of pulse weapons before dropping into a twisted heap on the floor. The opening in the floor closed with the expected sloshing sound, but was then followed by a dull thump. Lifting her head from her prone position, Teela could see Rebecca lying on the floor. Shawaugh was standing over Rebecca glaring at Teela.

"Do not use your mind against me!" Shawaugh ordered, pointing a clawed finger at Teela. The intense anger emanating from Shawaugh frightened Teela. She looked at Rebecca, wondering if Shawaugh had killed her.

"It has not ceased. But I believe we should end its existence now, before it regains its senses," Shawaugh growled, placing her foot on Rebecca's neck.

"She carries the essence of Dooaugh!" Teela cried.

"That is why it must cease! Dooaugh is insane, she … she believes she speaks for the Gods. This creature, this Korlah-human abomination has abilities that no living being should possess. Dooaugh without these abilities was dangerous, this creature … I can't describe the threat it poses to both humans and Korlah. I tricked it this one time, I deceived its mind probes; it won't give me a second chance," Shawaugh cried.

"I am the same abomination as she," Teela replied coldly. "Let us take this fighter and do what we can to protect this planet. At 1,500 to one, we won't be a threat for long."

"Are you really without fear for your existence?" Shawaugh exclaimed in exasperation.

Teela looked down, the question all too familiar in her mind. She studied her feet embarrassed by the question. She wiggled the exposed portion of her toes nervously like a child caught in a lie.

"I have been prepared to end my existence for a long time. I think, since long before my first transfer," she finally replied, whispering the words as a confessor would to a priest.

Shawaugh grunted with disapproval, causing Teela to cringe with regret for voicing her thoughts without editing them for content. Removing her foot from Rebecca's throat, Shawaugh turned and toggled the communicator on the panel before re-opening the portal.

"This is Director Shawaugh requesting Mission Potentate Shyron join me for a brief consultation on my vessel."

Accompanied by Agent Cooper, Shyron joined Shawaugh, Rebecca, and Teela on Shawaugh's heavy fighter. Shawaugh closed the portal after Shyron entered. From the perspective of those on the transport, less than a half hour later the portal re-opened and Shawlmon left the heavy fighter dressed in the ornate blood-stained robe that had been stripped from the body of her last shell. Then, by order of the Mission Potentate, the transport containing Shawlmon and the escort fighters departed the asteroid belt en route to the Campaign Vessel, leaving the single heavy fighter on the fringe of the asteroid belt as the sole defender of Earth.

110,000,000 miles away in Geneva, Switzerland, a contingent of six Korlah representatives exited a transport vessel at the helicopter pad adjacent to the United Nations Security Council building. The entire area for miles had been cleared of all non-essential personnel. An intense military presence secured the area and implemented a media blackout. With briefcases in hand, the Korlah representatives dressed in identical black robes marched into the Council chamber. Meeting them at the entrance, a middle-aged man, stocky and muscular with thick black hair and a matching thick black mustache, smiled pleasantly offering his hand and shaking each of theirs in turn. The last Korlah paused and studied the face of the man greeting her. Somewhere beyond the dark eyes, ringed with shadows and perched above puffy bags formed by the ravages of time and insufficient sleep, a spark of recognition flashed into the mind of the Korlah representative.

"Joseph? Joe Leblanc? Is that you?" the Korlah asked, holding onto the Ambassador's hand.

"Yes, I am Ambassador Leblanc," he replied politely, repressing his surprise.

"I'm sorry!" she replied, releasing his hand. "It's been so many years. I saw your name on the list ... but this is so strange, so surreal to actually ... see you again."

The other representatives continued into the room leaving them standing by the door. Instinctively, Ambassador Leblanc took the Korlah representative by the arm and led her into the room, smiling pleasantly in an attempt to mask his unease. He studied the arm, hands, and face. It was neither mask nor makeup, of that, he was certain.

"How could you know me ... from years ago?" Leblanc asked skeptically as he delivered her to a chair at a table in the center of the room facing the raised and tiered seats where the assembled members of the United Nations were also busy taking their seats.

Setting her briefcase on the table, she turned and faced Ambassador Leblanc, her ebony black eyes again studying the details of the man's face.

"I am ... well, actually we are all ghosts from the past, here in the present, trying to help preserve the future," she finally said, smiling as she did, feeling witty and somewhat mischievous. "I will explain in my opening presentation ... what we are. Trust me Joseph, there will be no secrets," she added with a wink as she took her seat and opened her briefcase, removing the stacks of carefully drafted legal documents within and spreading them on the table before her.

Ambassador Leblanc paused briefly before proceeding to his seat four rows above the Council floor. As he sat down, he took a deep breath through his nose; all he could smell was leather and furniture polish, whereas, moments before, when he had been standing next to the Korlah he was sure he could smell the sweet scent of honey, and the physical response it produced caused him to blush. He smiled at the thought, looked at his watch and silently wished the meeting were over so that he could stand next to her again.

The formalities of the session proceeded to the point of the Korlah opening statement. During that time, Joseph had not been listening, instead he sat staring at the Korlah representative sitting at the end of the long table. When she stood, she looked right at him, and in that moment, he felt as though she was aware of his erotic thoughts and he blushed deeply. To his relief, her gaze moved beyond him and around the room as she began speaking.

"Ladies and Gentlemen, thank you for this opportunity to address the Nations of Earth. As you are aware, this is our second attempt. I understand many of you were present at our first attempt. For those of you that were at that meeting, I bring news, both good and bad. The good news is our alliance representative Ambassadress Shawlmon will survive her injuries." The news of Shawlmon's recovery received a round of standing applause.

"And the bad news," she shouted over the applause, bringing the room rapidly to a state of dead silence.

"You have been placed under a tremendous burden. I cannot imagine what you could possibly do to make this meeting more exciting than the last," she said her demeanor and expression serious and deadpan. She stood there patiently as a few of the members chuckled, followed by some restrained laughs and soft clapping.

"Yes … that was a joke. I apologize. But if we cannot laugh at the obstacles facing us, then we are doomed to cry." With that said, the chamber again erupted with applause. This time, she waited until the applause stopped before proceeding.

"Thank you, thank you very much for your warm welcome. We have already been in communication with each of your governments and in many cases with some of you individually. You have been informed what it is you are facing as a planet, what it is that we are offering as an ally, and most importantly, why we are offering it. We have made no secret of our intentions, and negotiations are already underway with those countries. The reason we are here in this room, the reason you have agreed to remain in this room until a decision has been reached, is the understanding that if our two species do not stand together against this threat, then apart, we will fall.

"At this time, fear and distrust are our greatest enemies; fear of each other, and fear of the unknown. If we can overcome this first obstacle, the next will seem less intimidating. Honesty and truth will lead to trust. But the truth can sometimes be frightening. What I am about to tell you, until now, has been a closely guarded secret. The secret has great military value against the enemies of the Korlah. But you are not our enemies, and to make you our allies and win your trust, it has been decided to reveal this secret now.

"My name is Mary Zeera. I gave myself that name yesterday ... after I was reborn. We, Korlah, possess a unique ability, where under the right circumstance we can accept the essence or, as I like to think of it, the soul of a person when their body dies. The ability to transfer, as it is called, has been traditionally used by our religious leaders to perpetuate and preserve knowledge. During our war with the Kahshinki, we have used this ability to infiltrate our enemy's ranks. We have recently discovered that due to our genetic similarities, we are able to accept the essence of humans as well. Before yesterday, my name was Rehzeera 20.77935. Like my sisters with me, I am a clone, designed and trained to fill a specific purpose within our spacecraft carrier's organization. Rehzeera's area of expertise was to be information and communication.

"My other name was Dr. Marylyn Daniels. Many of you here today knew Marylyn. For those who didn't, Marylyn held a PhD in International Law from Harvard. She worked as a law professor, and either drafted or contributed to the preparation of the majority of the current international agreements and treaties on record today. Marylyn was diagnosed with breast cancer a year ago, treatment was unsuccessful and she was near death when she was offered a second chance at life. She willingly accepted," she paused, as a murmur of disapproval rose in volume.

"Before you condemn me, before you condemn us, try to comprehend what a miracle this is, and grant us the respect we deserve for the sacrifice we are making. Each of us, both Korlah and human, volunteered for this. We are tools that have been forged for a limited purpose; beyond this purpose, I cannot foresee how we will fit into either the human or Korlah societies. In the meantime, however, it is my privilege to facilitate this offer of an alliance between our two species and to draft the first intergalactic laws, and God willing, witness their successful implementation," Mary implored. The words had not been rehearsed, not drafted like the speech she held in her hand, and as she spoke the words, she felt their truth, and with it the isolation it implied. She continued with her introductions, no longer deviating from her script. The giddy feelings that her rejuvenation engendered faded as the difficulty of her task became evident during the questioning that followed.

The meeting lasted for sixteen hours. As agreed beforehand, the doors were locked and all members remained sequestered in the building during the meeting. Only water was distributed and bathroom breaks were limited. In the end, following protests and repeated disruptions of the proceedings by members of the delegations from the United States and Britain, a new global entity was formed which excluded those nations. The final draft of the alliance between the United Nations of Earth (UNE) and the Korlah Liberation Forces (KLF) was signed in the last few minutes of the sixteenth hour.

The basic outline of the alliance document was a concise twenty-six pages and included the most heavily debated portion that required a thorough investigation into the attack on the Korlah spacecraft carrier and the recent assassination attempt of Ambassadress Shawlmon by human forces. The Korlah delegates refused to alter the wording of that section, stating that if the results of the UNE investigation failed to locate, arrest, prosecute, and punish those responsible, the KLF would. In addition to the document, there were a number of attachments. One attachment outlined a program of military aid that involved personnel, equipment, and technology exchange. A second attachment outlined provisions for establishing a Korlah military base on Earth in exchange for establishing a UNE military force aboard the Korlah spacecraft carrier. Additional attachments outlined the protocol for coordinating communications, a chain of command, and rules of engagement for joint military operations.

A few hours following the historic signing, a formal celebration was held. The celebration was attended by the Korlah delegates and most members of the newly formed UNE. Although the celebration, like the meeting, was held under the strictest secrecy and security, a day later the event was published in a British tabloid with the headline; "Galactic Alliance derailed by French." The associated story provided vivid and accurate details of the meeting including the alliance document as well as allegations that during the party, the French Ambassador sexually assaulted a member of the Korlah delegation, and had to be physically restrained as the Korlah delegates fled the party. The French Government immediately issued a press release stating the incident was a misunderstanding caused by too much alcohol, and too little sleep, and that no provisions of the alliance had been violated by the unfortunate incident.

What was not released to the public was that within hours of the incident, the Korlah received a lengthy apology from the French government, including an offer of an island in the Mediterranean off the south coast of France for the Korlah to use for as long as they like. The response from the Korlah alliance representative was immediate. The French apology was graciously accepted along with their island offer. Included in the response from the Korlah was the request that in the spirit of the alliance, no punishment be afforded the French Ambassador as the apology had implied.

Mary Zeera and her team of delegates continued to work on refining the Alliance documents as additional lawyers and government specialists joined her team. Coordinating with the delegate assigned to medical and health issues, Mary identified the issue of pheromone effects as requiring the highest priority. Rebecca had warned them all of the potential reaction and Mary was now intently aware from first-hand experience that if this effect could not be controlled, it could easily become the greatest threat to maintaining the alliance.

21 - Requiescat

A string of thirty disc-shaped fighters skirted the outer boundary of the asteroid belt in staggered groups of two, rising and dipping, over and under the boulders in their path. Inside the lead craft, the navigator relayed computations and readings to the other vessels, alert for any indication of enemy craft that might appear in the clutter of signals produced by the tumbling rocks.

"Unidentified craft, two o'clock!" the navigator shouted.

"Light em up!" the pilot cried, energizing the light fighter's pulse weaponry at the same time the navigator brought the fire control tracking system on line.

"This is Captain Ramsey of the Earth Defense Force. Identify yourself," Captain Ramsey demanded, transmitting the message using the short-range communications signals on all frequencies.

"Hello James. This is Rebecca McCabe, thank you for coming," Rebecca replied from the pilot's console aboard Shawaugh's heavy fighter.

"Yeah, I got it and all the other chatter as well. What's going on Rebecca, where'd all your buddies go?" Ramsey asked skeptically, scanning his sensors intently.

"They've been recalled to protect the Korlah spacecraft carrier. We are all that stands between the Kahshinki and Earth," Rebecca replied calmly.

"Yeah, right. 1,500 ships you said, running on empty. It's a suicide mission, what do they hope to achieve?" Ramsey asked.

"They're delivering bombs, planet killers. Four got through the initial defenses. The bombs are being carried on transports and are being escorted by 223 fighters. If they get through the asteroid belt, they will jump to hyper-light as soon as they get Earth's coordinates. One bomb detonating in the atmosphere will burn Earth to a lifeless desert that will be uninhabitable for several thousand years," Rebecca answered unemotionally.

"How do you know that?" Ramsey asked.

"I will enlighten you later brother James. May God protect you. Here they come," Rebecca replied, as she accelerated forward.

Captain Ramsey instinctively fired his weapon when her ship moved, hitting it with a pointblank broadside. Her craft veered away, knocked sideways by the blast. Shaken, but otherwise undamaged, the craft curved back onto its original trajectory. With its absorption array still sparkling with residual static charges, Rebecca discharged her fighter's main pulse weapon as groups of enemy fighters began dropping out of hyper-light all around them. The density of the arriving craft appearing before them grew so thick that the first two narrow beam bursts that Rebecca fired destroyed two enemy craft each; the debris buffeting them as their gravity shielding deflected it. By the time the transports dropped out of hyper-light, Rebecca had personally destroyed seventeen fighters and unfortunately received an equal number of high-energy pulse blasts. As her absorption shielding failed, Rebecca spotted a transport moving into the asteroid field. Banking hard, she fired at the transport and accelerated in pursuit. At the same instant, an enemy fighter crossed her path, the high intensity beam of her pulse weapon split the ship in two. The larger of the two pieces plunged through the gravity shield of her fighter and ripped off a section of her absorption array as the enemy transport disappeared from view. Continuing to accelerate, Rebecca followed, leaving a trail of sparkling debris in her wake.

Staring intently at the monitor, Rebecca's hand jerked right and left, up and down, as asteroids seemed to fly at the heavy fighter. Accelerating to nearly the speed of light, the small craft suddenly bounced between three asteroids as the field of the vessel's gravity shield grazed the mass of the stones.

"Slow down! We've lost it," Shawaugh shouted.

"No ... it's just ahead," Rebecca whispered as she nudged the speed even higher.

Wisps of glowing plasma appeared ahead of them, looking at first like dots and dashes of light, the trails grew solid as they got closer until finally the back of the transport was clearly visible ahead of them. Rebecca closed the gap, as Shawaugh adjusted the focus of the pulse cannon. When Rebecca finally fired, she was less than 200 feet behind the enemy transport. The resultant explosion caused the adjacent asteroids to bounce off one another like billiard balls, their paths disconcerted and unpredictable. Rebecca veered away and decelerated rapidly to a more manageable speed.

"Good! Excellent job," Shawaugh shouted.

Rebecca did not respond. She stared intently into the asteroid field. She closed her eyes and trembled slightly before speaking in a mechanical monotone.

"There is another one. It slipped past Ramsey's fighter group. It's past us, too far, too far. God help us ... please."

Taking her left hand, she placed the palm on the screen in front of her. Shawaugh watched intently, trying to determine what she was doing. Rebecca pursed her bright red lips as her pale blue eyes opened, and rolled up, leaving only the whites exposed. Releasing the flight controls with her right hand, she reached up and placed it on the hyper-light controls.

"No!" Shawaugh screamed as Rebecca engaged the engines that would drive the small ship forward in multiples of light speed.

The flux accelerators screamed in protest as the heavy fighter surged forward, climbing from sub-light velocities to hyper-light, in a fraction of a second. Shawaugh said nothing more, wincing as the screen in front of her blurred, and then blackened. She turned away from the screen and closed her eyes tightly anticipating the impact that would disintegrate their vessel and them along with it. Long seconds passed without an impact. Shawaugh slowly opened her eyes and looked at the screen; it was still black, indicating that they were traveling at hyper-light velocities through the asteroid belt.

"How is this possible?" Shawaugh whispered.

"It's not ... possible. It's a miracle," Rebecca said as she switched the hyper-light drive off, dropping the fighter back into sub-light speeds. Flipping the craft over, front to rear, she turned it to face the direction she had come. The asteroid field they just passed through now lay spread before them. From their stationary position, the rocks and boulders were visually imperceptible, yet on the tracking screen the quantity and density of material was plainly visible.

"It is coming. The bomb has been activated. They will need to calculate the jump to Earth. We must destroy them before they jump. Energize our weapons," Rebecca said, straightening on her seat and taking the control stick firmly in her hand.

"No charge! Our weapons will not charge!" Shawaugh shouted, both hands racing over the controls on her panel as she attempted to diagnose the cause. "The pulse chamber is damaged, dissipating energy, draining our power cell," Shawaugh continued, her voice dropping in volume as she realized there was no way to restore the system, no way to fire their weapon.

"Ram it ... I've done it before, it works," Teela said as she stepped between.

Both Rebecca and Shawaugh looked at the young birthing unit who had not spoken since Shyron assumed the role of Shawlmon and departed.

"Yes ... we shall ram it," Rebecca agreed, knowing full well that this impact would be significantly greater than the one Teela had delivered in her previous life.

"To our honor!" Rebecca shouted as she accelerated the fighter toward the enemy transport now visible on her scanner. With the slightest manipulations of her wrist on the control stick, she brought the fighter onto a head-on collision course with the approaching transport.

At a combined speed approaching 100,000 miles per second, the pilot of the enemy transport noted the suddenly accelerating object, but had no time to react before the two vessels collided. At the moment of impact, the combined momentum of the two spacecraft pressed their protective magnetic shields together to the point of collapse, caving the dense polymorphic skin of each vessel and shattering the underlying support structures. The leading edge of the disc-like fighter sliced into the front of the transport, flipping and ripping off the front edge. The two objects bounced apart at reduced velocities, the intense impact having absorbed a portion of their momentum in the collision. Venting atmosphere and trailing globules of polymorphic metal from the embedded section of fighter, the enemy transport corkscrewed away, one engine still generating propulsion. The heavy fighter flipped end over end, trailing a shower of sparks, as the fuel cell vented the remains of its stored energy through the large semi-circular area ripped from the smooth edge of the disc.

A few minutes later, the bomb detonated ninety million miles from its intended target, Earth. With an invisible flash of energy rivaling the most powerful atomic bomb ever built, the explosion bathed an area of space for over a 100,000 miles in all directions. The energy would have caused the molecules of organic material it contacted to explode as the atomic structures within them released their electromagnetic bonds in a self-perpetuating chain reaction. Without the presence of the critical elements oxygen and hydrogen in a planet's atmosphere, the blast initiated and dissipated in the vacuum of space with a minimal release of photon energy.

Although the occupants of the heavy fighter were protected by the effects of the inertia dampening field during the collision, the system failed soon after impact along with the artificial gravity. In the darkness, Teela wedged herself between the base of a seat and the adjacent wall to keep from floating weightless. She could hear Rebecca praying but could not make out the words over the heavy breathing and moans of Shawaugh and Agent Cooper. No one spoke, yet Teela could clearly sense the feeling of helplessness and dread they each felt.

I'm sorry. We should have let them burn the planet. It's a lost cause no matter how you slice it, Daedalus said soon after the rapidly dropping temperature caused Teela to begin shivering.

What about Julie? Teela asked, referring to Julie by name for the first time. *I know it is her and not the others, or the planet that concerns you. Your message, what about your precious message?*

Lost, like me, like you, gone, Daedalus said, despair evident in the emotion of the thought as well as the words.

I have a plan, Teela said, repeating the Daedalus adage as her idea formed and congealed in the region between conscious and unconscious thought.

You want to pray! Daedalus said, having only partially understood the forming thoughts.

Like a prayer, a projection of our thoughts, with all of our combined strength. Like you always tell me, I cannot succeed, if I fail to try. If Rebecca can create miracles, then so can we.

Teela clasped her hands together and pressed her chin down tightly against the interwoven fingers and thumbs while focusing her thoughts on the one individual she hoped would hear her final hope and prayer.

In the aftermath of the attack, when the numbers were tallied, it was estimated that the enemy sacrificed 4,500 soldiers and 1,500 craft in their first, and unsuccessful attempt to destroy the resource base, Earth, which they anticipated would prolong the impending conflict. The Korlah defenders lost 432 soldiers and 144 fighter craft. The human defenders lost 36 soldiers and 12 craft. Strategists estimated that the astounding ten to one success ratio was attributable to the depleted energy reserves of the enemy craft, and a combination of technology and training that could be improved, lending hope in the face of growing uncertainty.

Sahanga was unsure how long she was unconscious. It was hunger that woke her, and although her body was bruised and battered, she felt rested. Her confinement cell was dark and unheated, the door, warmer than the adjacent walls, glowed faintly, indicating that the room beyond was heated. She recalled the events following her return to the Campaign Vessel and cringed with regret. She would no doubt be brought before the Council of Leaders and confronted with her actions, and there could be no other punishment possible than immediate reclamation; a bitter end to her short-lived advancement for accepting Zachary's essence. She tried to stand, but her right leg gave out and she fell to the side of the sleeping platform, landing face down on the floor. Unable to block her fall with her hands bound securely behind her back, her head hit the juncture between wall and floor with a painful reminder of her vulnerable state. It was then, as she was lying there on the floor with her face in the corner that the door to the cell opened. Light flooded into the small room and from the shadow on the far wall of the cell, Sahanga could see the shadow of someone enter the cell and bend over her. The person released the bindings on her arms, dropping them on the floor before sitting on the edge of the cell's sleeping platform.

Sahanga rolled onto her side and looked at the hemline of the person's robe. Neat rows of ornate glyphs decorated the robe, each depicting and detailing the historic events of the occupant's past, the events detailing the life of the arbitrator; Shawlmon. Sahanga gasped with surprise, momentarily looking down instinctively as any Korlah would when meeting the Mission Potentate. But then, something else, feelings alien to her Korlah past, made her look up past the hem, past the belt and swords, and into the eyes of Shawlmon. Defiantly meeting the eyes looking down on her, Sahanga challenged the Potentate's authority. Shawlmon smiled and broke eye contact before the act could officially be considered a challenge. Folding her hands in her lap, Shawlmon spoke without meeting Sahanga's defiant glare.

"You remind us of someone ... someone we admire. However, your actions have placed us in a difficult position. First, you defied the orders of your direct superior. Then you returned and attacked her. She was severely damaged and nearly ceased. Three of the warriors that came to her defense also required repair and will have diminished utility for several shifts. We would like to hear what you have to say before we rule on this matter," Shawlmon said, her voice even and unemotional.

Sahanga lowered her eyes and clenched her jaws tightly together before speaking.

"I apologize, Your Eminence, for damaging the three warriors. They did what they were trained to do, and they did it honorably. I also apologize that I failed to cease the existence of the scrum-sucking sack of worm roe that is superior to none!" Sahanga hissed, spitting on the ground to emphasize her disgust.

"We have spoken with Director Rhetga. She claims you took her comments out of context," Shawlmon replied.

"Bullshit!" Sahanga growled in English.

"You would argue the logic of sacrificing unskilled pilots to determine the strength and capability of the enemy is not the best use of their limited utility?" Shawlmon asked.

"Yes! I would argue that. But that's not why I attacked Director Rhetga. I attacked her because she said that my pilots, who she referred to as birthers, would not receive honors for their part in the battle, because they were only there to draw fire away from the real warriors," Sahanga cried, her voice choked with anger of the recalled insult.

"We have been told that you were strongly against the idea of admitting birthing units into the pilot ranks. So why is it that you would throw away your existence to defend the honor of these ... unacceptable pilot volunteers?"

"They fought bravely. They ceased honorably. They deserve recognition. I don't care how you rule on me. But if you let that fat overfed scrum grub steal their honor, then you have none," Sahanga replied looking away and down, realizing that as she issued the insult, it would most likely convince Shawlmon to end her existence.

320

Shawlmon rubbed her hands together, massaging the backs and palms as she contemplated Sahanga's words. Placing the palms of her hands together, as if praying, she touched the tips of her fingers to her forehead before separating them and sliding them down her thighs and onto her knees. She took a deep breath and let it out slowly before speaking.

"Director Rhetga is leaving, as are most of the members of the Council. It has been decided that the best chance for saving the existence of Korlah culture is to proceed to New Korlah and establish a colony of Korlah-human hybrids. The Campaign Vessel is being divided as we speak. Two of the five sections will split off, taking the propulsion system with them. Two shifts from now, it will begin its journey to New Korlah. The remaining three sections will be divided between the Korlah purists, the humans and those ... like you, which fall in between," Shawlmon said gravely.

"You can't allow that. The open sections will be vulnerable to attack. How would we defend it?" Sahanga asked, shocked by Shawlmon's statement.

"We no longer have any authority over the Council," Shawlmon replied.

"And what does Shyron say of this?" Sahanga asked.

"Shyron, Director Shawaugh, and the Oracle were in transit from the asteroid base during the attack, with only two fighter groups of human pilots to assist them; they faced the remaining Kahshinki attack wave. They were lost during the battle, they ceased with honor," Shawlmon answered.

"What ... Shyron has ceased? Who will lead? You? You are nothing more than me, another clone with human memories." Sahanga gasped, shocked by Shawlmon's news, her tirade over, issues of honor seemed suddenly insignificant.

"Some believe that I am something more. With the help of those who believe, I will arbitrate between the three sections of this vessel. Together we will rebuild the vessel as we prepare for the next attack," Shawlmon answered.

Neither of them spoke for several minutes, the room remained silent with the exception of their breathing. It was Sahanga who spoke first.

"And what will you do with me?"

"What would you have us do?" Shawlmon asked.

"Let me do what I do best. Let me fly, let me fight, let me cease with honor," Sahanga quickly answered.

"That would not be much of a punishment," Shawlmon chuckled, making a low clucking sound that caused Sahanga to swallow nervously, as she contemplated the painful and degrading possibilities.

"We have found that when someone cannot follow orders, it is best that they give them. With Rhetga's departure, I am without a Director, and I have no suitable replacements. Your punishment will be assignment to the Directorship of one section of the Campaign Vessel. This may not sound like punishment, but eventually you will come to realize that it is. You will be responsible for those Korlah and humans that choose to work together and of course the transfer volunteers like yourself."

Sahanga froze in disbelief. Unsure if she really heard what Shawlmon had offered her. "Thank you, Your Eminence, I will not dishonor your decision," Sahanga finally cried, astounded by the incredible honor being bestowed upon her.

"There is this one thing though. We have a task we need performed ... before you assume your duties. It will require discretion and secrecy," Shawlmon replied.

Sahanga swallowed deeply. *Ah, the catch, there's always a catch,* she thought.

"Whatever it is, Your Eminence, I will perform it without question," Sahanga replied solemnly.

"Good. You will not speak of what we are going to ask of you beyond this room. When you have finished the task, it will be as though it never happened. Do you understand what I am asking?" Shawlmon asked.

"Yes, Your Eminence," Sahanga replied, anticipating a request that would require her to perform a dishonorable action that would violate Korlah Law or Ethics.

"Sit over here," Shawlmon said, indicating the far end of the sleeping platform. Sahanga rose to her feet and hobbled over on her bruised legs to sit across from Shawlmon. Shawlmon stared at Sahanga as she withdrew a polished metal circular container and set it between them.

We need you to deliver this, and a message to someone who will meet with you on the planet of humans, Shawlmon said, speaking with her mind as she slid the silver container toward Sahanga.

22 - Twisted

Time seemed to suddenly stop, the rapid deceleration threw Julie out of the trance-like state she was in, only a few minutes after the memory transfer began. She sucked in a deep breath and let out a long soft moan. The room seemed to expand and contract in waves as her eyes refocused.

"But it was Dade, he came back. It was him," Julie said, unwilling to accept the final details of the message.

No Julie, it was just a messenger. Teela is dead and when she died, your husband died with her. You are all alone and always will be. There is nothing left, nothing left to live for. This planet is going to die. There is no hope, the voice said. With the words came overwhelming feelings of despair and hopelessness flooding her mind with a suicidal depression.

"No hope," Julie groaned.

Nothing to live for, the voice said.

Julie stood and walked over to the kitchen counter. She stared at a block of wood that served as a holder for a selection of knives. She pulled a carving knife from the block and felt the razor sharp edge with her thumb before raising it to her neck. The tip of the blade entered the flesh just below her left ear. It stung, and she paused. A feeling of warmth flowed through her and the sting of the blade felt exquisitely good. As she was about to draw the blade across her throat, she saw her reflected image in the glass of the kitchen window, but the reflection was not of her. The woman in her reflection was pale with long red hair, with eyes equally pale and cold with lethal intent.

"Rebecca," Julie whispered. The image smiled before fading leaving only Julie's reflection. Julie wanted to drop the knife but her arm would not respond.

"Nothing to live for", Rebecca said. But it was Julie's voice and mouth that spoke the words.

Someone began pounding on the front door. Julie fought to move her arm, but again it refused to obey. The tip of the knife pushed deeper as her eyes widened in terror. Her dog began barking wildly.

"Help me!" Julie screamed.

With a sound like a thunderclap the front door burst open. Her left hand was suddenly hers and she grabbed her right hand and attempted to pull the hand with the knife away from her throat with all her will. The agent who had been there earlier charged into the house. Ignoring the dog, he grabbed Julie's knife hand and twisted it away from her throat. Julie screamed again as the man continued to twist her arm up behind her back until the knife dropped from her hand and clattered across the floor. The dog was now firmly latched onto the back of his leg viciously attempting to pull him off of Julie. With his free hand, he slammed the cover on the communicator shut, knocked it from the table, and smashed it with his foot. Julie immediately went limp and he released her, turning his attention to the attacking dog. The dog dodged a blow to the head by releasing his leg. Squaring off with the agent, she prepared to lunge at him again.

"Candy! Come girl! Now!" Julie shouted. The dog immediately stopped barking and cautiously skirted the agent to get to Julie's side.

"Are you okay?" the agent asked.

"I don't know," Julie said, touching the bleeding wound on her neck.

"Your mind, is she out of your head?" the agent shouted.

"Yes. It was Rebecca, wanted me to kill myself. She told me Teela died. She doesn't want me to talk to Dade. Teela's alive! They didn't die, did they?" Julie asked.

The agent reached to help Julie up. The dog began growling. Julie took his hand and allowed him to guide her to a chair at the table. He sat down in a chair facing her. Ignoring the growling dog, he examined her neck. Confident that it was superficial, he leaned back and relaxed.

"My name is Richard Cooper. I am a friend of Shawlmon, Teela or whoever the hell she is."

"Agent Cooper, from the White House?"

"Yeah that's right. Listen Julie, Rebecca just declared war. Six of my agents are dead, four wounded. She took Teela."

"Why would she do that?" Julie asked. Agent Cooper frowned, and looked away before answering.

"I screwed up. I owe Rebecca my life and I violated her trust. We were freezing in space, minutes away from death, and she used her mind to bring Captain Ramsey and his patrol directly to us. We met up with a messenger who brought your husband's personal effects. She asked me to help Teela deliver her message and had me promise not to tell anyone I had seen her.

"Listen, I don't usually break promises, but that lady is … well I'm not sure what she is. The government is looking for her and it was my duty to report her whereabouts."

"You turned her in?" Julie asked.

"First chance I got," Cooper replied.

"That was Teela who visited. I spoke to Dade through her, didn't I?" Julie asked.

"Yeah, I guess so," Cooper replied.

"What happened? How did Rebecca take Teela from you?" Julie asked.

Agent Cooper looked at his watch. "We don't have a lot of time. I don't think Rebecca is done with us." He rubbed his face, unsure what he should do next.

"Tell me what happened damn it!" Julie cried, and Candy punctuated the demand with a bark.

Agent Cooper looked at his watch again. If Rebecca had the power to reach them, he figured she would have had him kill her and then himself by now. With a groan of defeat, he proceeded to tell her the events that transpired following his earlier departure.

The caravan left the residential neighborhood, making its way back to the highway. This was not the only caravan of vehicles on the nation's highways that morning. Long lines of olive green and camouflaged trucks, personnel carriers, and an assortment of military vehicles were either en route, or had arrived at their destinations. Since mid-afternoon of the previous day and throughout the night, military installations around the country had begun deploying troops from the National Guard, Army, and Marines. By the time most people were sitting down to their morning coffee, heavily armed military contingents had set up, or were busy setting up, field installations in most of the metropolitan areas throughout the United States.

Inside the limousine, Teela sat between Cooper and Beth.

"You really think there are going to be riots?" Agent Cooper said to no one in particular as the limousine passed a large column of Army trucks.

"McCormick is just shaking up the military until we have a chance to weed out the opposition. That way he'll have less a chance of a military coup," Beth said.

Teela did not appear to be listening to the exchange; she was looking down at the golden medallion resting in the palm of her hand. She made no effort to conceal the tears flowing down her face.

"I can see you're upset, but we need to talk," Beth said.

"I didn't ask you to come so that you could interrogate me," Teela said, wiping the tears from her face.

"Alright then, I'll cut to the chase. The only reason I went along with this meeting is because Agent Cooper insisted that this meeting was sanctioned by the President himself, and from what I can tell he's a good, honest, standup guy. But I can't help feeling like you just mind-fucked that poor woman right in front of us. And what about Rebecca, do you really expect me to believe that woman is the same Rebecca I was abducted with? Shit! How fucking stupid do I look? McClellen's right, you get in people's minds and do something to them."

"I've done nothing to harm or influence Rebecca or Julie. But I don't really care what you or McClellen believe. I'm finished, done, and complete. I didn't ask you to be here because I like you. I'm passing you the torch."

"What are you talking about?" Beth asked.

"From the moment he escaped the Kahshinki, Dade has been on a mission to return you to Earth. When he became a part of me, I inherited the mission. But now, you and the others are back, Dade's message has been delivered, my obligation is complete. I'm leaving. No more Daedalus, no more Teela, no more Shawlmon. We are going to disappear and let those who really care about this shit-hole of a planet deal with it. This is goodbye, Beth."

"I have a mission of my own," Beth said. "McClellen wants Rebecca ... neutralized. And he wants me to bring you in for questioning," Beth said.

"McClellen would be wise to cancel those plans. In the last two weeks, Rebecca has done more than anyone to help this planet prepare for attack. I agree that she's dangerous, but right now you really need someone like her, and McClellen needs her as a friend. He certainly doesn't want her as an enemy, I know that I don't," Teela said.

"Teela, you know I'm your friend," Agent Cooper said. "We know Rebecca is not the same person she was. We have documented evidence that she can read minds and alter the thoughts and perceptions of those around her. McClellen just wants to know who she really is and what she's up to."

"I'll tell you who she really is, and exactly what she's up to, but I doubt McClellen will believe it. Hell, I'm not sure I believe it myself. At one time, there were priests on Korlah whose job it was to preserve the religious beliefs, scripture, and prophecies of Korlah culture. One such priest survived the holocaust of our planet by transferring into the mind of a female. Unfortunately, religion interfered with military doctrine so our leaders banned all religious teachings. For over a thousand years, the priest preserved his memories by transferring from one person to another.

"He was in the body of a pilot called Dooaugh when we met. I thought she was crazy, claimed she could talk to God. So when Dooaugh met Rebecca it was a match made in heaven. They immediately connected; I think they were able to converse telepathically. Dooaugh was shot during a rescue mission and later died while alone with Rebecca. The priest simply transferred into Rebecca's mind when Dooaugh's body died."

"That explains a lot," Beth said. "McClellen will believe it. But what is she, he, or whatever it is up to? Right now it appears that she's forming a militant religious organization that stands to threaten not only national security but global security as well."

"I owe her my sanity," Teela said. "Dooaugh got into my mind. She didn't do it to alter my thoughts or take control of me. She did it to keep me from going insane. She taught me how to cope with telepathy, how to turn off the noise of everyone's thoughts. But while she was inside me, I was inside her. Skills and abilities I never had before just sort of rubbed off and became part of me. I learned of the prophecies and I understand why the priest transferred into Rebecca's mind. To understand the priest is to understand Rebecca.

"The Korlah prophecy predicts a final battle between good and evil at a time when there is no respect for life, and despair has choked out the last remnants of hope. The conditions on our ship fit the precursors of the prophecy to a tee, and there is no doubt that a battle will be fought at this planet. Rebecca is simply attempting to prepare the world for Armageddon.

"Tell McClellen to accept whatever help he can get from Rebecca. I told you I'm finished with this. All of it," Teela said.

"If you know Rebecca, or this Korlah priest as well as you say you do, McClellen needs you more than ever now. You and I really don't have a choice in this," Beth said.

A few blocks in the distance a woman stepped from the curb, walked out into the center of the lane and turned to face the approaching caravan. Without warning, the driver in the lead vehicle slammed on the brakes, the helicopter peeled off to the right and continued away at full speed.

"What the hell?" Beth said as the limo ground to a stop. She leaned forward and looked out the front window. The van in front of them had skidded to a stop, resting slightly askew across the lane. She could see flashes of light from gunfire within the van. The backdoor of the van opened and an agent stepped out, took two steps toward them, put the gun to his head, and fired.

The agents including Beth drew their weapons. The driver and agent in the front seat turned to direct their guns at Beth and agent Cooper. Beth grabbed the gun directed at her, and twisted it from the agents grip. Agent Cooper was not as quick and the driver's gun discharged as he attempted to take it. Beth's head snapped to the side and she slumped forward.

"I was fighting for my life," Cooper said. "Then as suddenly as it started, it was over. Teela was gone, most of my agents were dead. Beth has a head wound, I don't know how bad it is, but it doesn't look good. I called for help. While I was waiting, I had this feeling Rebecca would go after you. It was more than a feeling. It's like I could feel what she was thinking. I don't know

... this is just crazy. You must think I'm nuts," Cooper said, rubbing his face with both hands.

"No, I don't," Julie replied. "After you left, I felt Dade's sadness, his conflicted thoughts. I say felt because I can't find the right word. Connected maybe, connected to his ... I don't know what ... his mind? I think she realized that he would try to make contact again. I could sense that she considers me a threat to her control over Teela," Julie said.

"Connected, yeah, that's a good description. I think Teela connects to the people close to her. I think Rebecca does too, but in a bad way. You got a cell phone?" Cooper asked.

"Yes, a company phone," Julie replied.

"Get rid of it. We have reports that Rebecca can get to people through them. I believe she used that alien communication device to control you. Unless she is nearby, she can't hurt you. Don't worry, I'll get you someplace safe."

"What does Rebecca want with Teela?" Julie asked.

"I really don't know. Whatever her plan is, whatever she intends to do, she's made it perfectly clear that she will kill anyone that gets in her way."

23 - Revelations

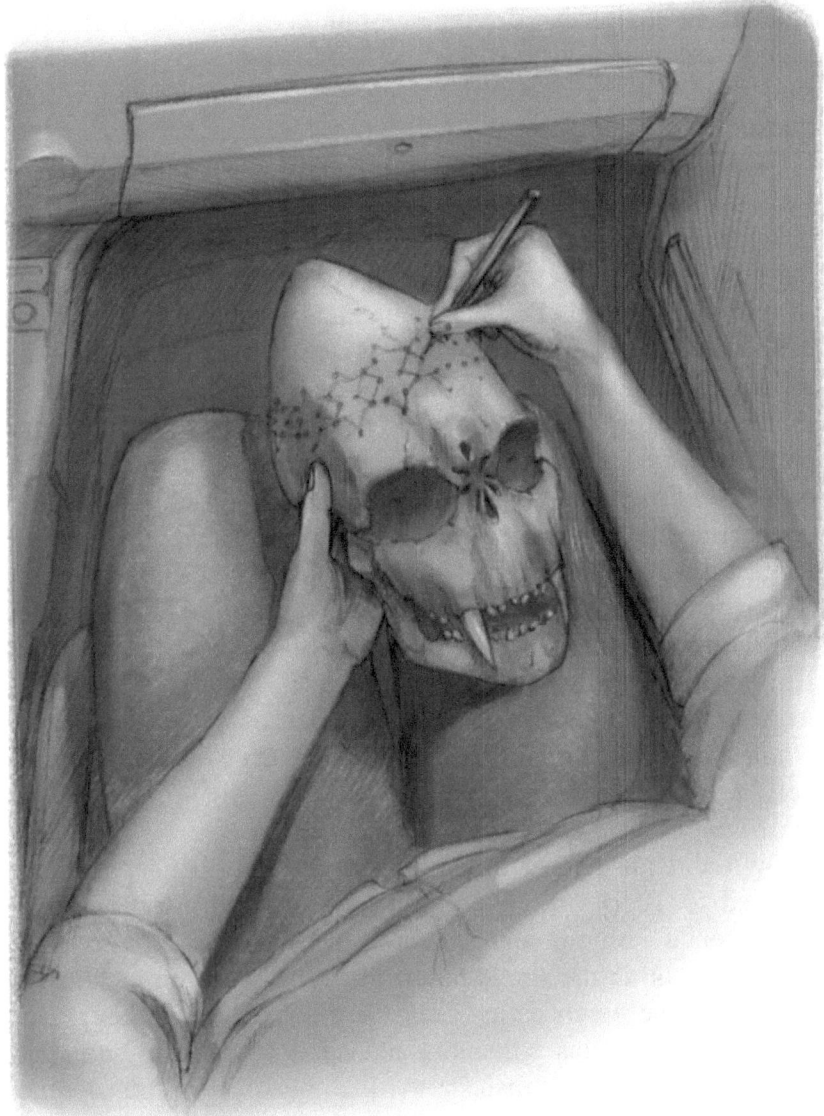

Pulling the edge of her hood down to block the burning rays of sun stinging her face, Teela walked to a large motor home parked at the side of the road. Rebecca opened the door for her and helped her in. A few moments later, the motor home drove away.

To the soldiers and police at the roadblocks and checkpoints, Rudy, who was driving the silver motor home, appeared to be a soldier in uniform, driving a military vehicle with valid identification. Rebecca worked her magic to ensure the guards all saw whatever they needed to see so they could pass without question.

From the back of the motor home, now sixty miles southwest, Rebecca shook her head as her link to Julie was interrupted. Her brow furrowed in thought as her pale eyes drew in the images before them in the same manner as her mind drew in the sounds of millions of minds flowing around and through her. She would deal with Julie later. She had her prize and no one could take it away. Looking down, she silenced the sounds and focused her thoughts on the Korlah skull she was holding in her lap. Small patterns of round holes marked the areas where the nerves of the crown tendrils had passed through the skull. Rebecca finished connecting the last pattern of holes with a pencil. Each pattern formed a perfect six-pointed star. In total, twelve stars encircling the crown of the skull. She placed the skull in a box by her feet and returned to the bookmarked page of her bible. She traced the words with her finger as she silently read.

And there appeared a great wonder in heaven; a woman clothed with the sun and the moon under her feet, and upon her head a crown of twelve stars: and she, being with child cried travailing in birth and pained to be delivered.

Without raising her eyes from the Bible in her lap, Rebecca listened to Teela's thoughts with great care to avoid detection. She listened with rapt amazement at the two distinct personalities contained within the single mind. There had been no melding, no joining of the essences as Teela would have her believe. Both Teela and Daedalus somehow managed to achieve something never before accomplished in the history of transference. Together they were sharing the new shell, the essence of the younger Teela absorbed by them both as it normally would be. As she listened to the conversation, Dooaugh considered the difficulty she had absorbing Rebecca's essence. If Beth had not knocked Rebecca unconscious, she would have failed to dominate the transfer. But now, with Rebecca's essence evicted, this new shell provided her with unprecedented abilities her Korlah shells never had. From Rebecca's memories, she discovered distinct ties between Korlah and human theologies, as she and her followers studied the incredible similarities, the gaps in the scripture began to fill, and their prophetic meaning was beginning to become clear.

In a conversation that only Rebecca could hear, Daedalus assured Teela that they would soon go swimming and walk barefoot through grass, smell the many flowers, and listen to the birds she saw flying in the atmosphere of this marvelous planet. Certain that she was safe and with friends, Teela closed her eyes and much like a couple in love, together in an emotional rather than physical embrace, she and Daedalus fell asleep comforted by each other's presence.

Rebecca released a sigh of relief. Creating the illusions necessary to control Teela required tremendous effort and it was exhausting her. It was now clear to Rebecca; Shawlmon would rise from Teela as foretold, but not as she initially envisioned. Focusing her mind on Teela's abdomen, she could hear the rustle of sentient life growing within. Teela's donor had been unaware of the implantation, knowing only that she had been examined to ensure fertility. Even Shyron was unaware of the experiment's success. Rebecca was concerned how Teela would react when she found out. This child was the future, and she was dedicated to ensuring that nothing and no one, especially Daedalus, would be allowed to contaminate or endanger it.

Rebecca frowned, her thoughts turning dark as she considered Teela's future. Daedalus was a non-believer and his lack of faith had poisoned Teela. They could not be allowed to poison the mind of the child. She realized that Teela's mind was too powerful to control indefinitely, so all she could do for now was to perpetuate the belief that they were friends. Once the child was born, Teela's purpose would end, and with the end of her purpose, she would no longer have utility toward the mission. Rebecca knew she would have to end Teela's existence.

Purging the disturbing thoughts from her mind, Rebecca clasped her hands tightly together, bowed her head, and prayed for the health and safety of the unborn prince. She thanked the gods for the miracle of Immaculate Conception resulting from joining of the ovum of a T-series birthing unit and the salvaged gametes of the human known as Daedalus Rimes.

Glossary of Humans

Bourke, Jimmy. Abducted; student at USC, physical education major.

Clarke, Marsha. Abducted: musician, drums, member of the band Metal Maidens; Seattle, Washington.

Cooper, Richard. United States Secret Service, assigned to White House security detail.

Daniels, Marylyn. PhD International Law, Harvard Professor.

Hargrave, Justin. General USMC Expeditionary Forces.

Heckart, Margaret. Abducted; elementary school nurse: Southeast Oregon.

Jacks, Bill. Abducted; security guard at Mill Valley Industrial Center; Central California.

Jacobs, Zachary, aka Mad Dog. Veteran pilot of both Korea and Vietnam wars. Pioneer in jet fighter combat techniques.

Johnson, Chris. Prior member of the Central Intelligence Agency, and associate of Bethany Porter. Currently working for clandestine organization called the Quorum as a lead agent within the National Security Agency.

Leblanc, Joseph. French Ambassador to the United States.

Marshall, Erin. PhD Xenobiology. Research analyst and consultant for the United States government.

McCabe, Rebecca. Abducted; self-described missionary of the Christian faith.

McClellen, James, aka Jimmy Guns. Rogue US Army General. Allegedly the leader of an American Militia with intentions to overthrow the United States government.

McCormick, William P. President Elect of the United States.

Moore, Ann. Abducted; day care center manager; Northern California

Parkhurst, Richard. Director of Homeland Security USA.

Portenski, Burton. Alias used by Bethany Porter while disguised as a man.

Porter, Bethany. Abducted; ex-Marine, undercover federal agent working as a bank manager.

Purcell, Catherine. Abducted; musician, bass guitar, member of the band Metal Maidens.

Ramos, John, aka Rambo. Colonel USAF, Wing Commander asteroid outpost.

Ramsey, Jason, aka Hollywood. Captain USAF, asteroid outpost fighter pilot.

Rimes, Daedalus. Abducted; maintenance supervisor at Mill Valley Industrial Center; California, USA

Rimes, Julie. Wife of Daedalus.

Rost, John. MD, researcher, Center for Disease Control (CDC) Washington D.C.

Santos, Crystal. Abducted; musician, vocals and lead guitar, member of the band Metal Maidens.

Simpson, James Ernest, aka Hammer. Captain USAF, asteroid outpost fighter pilot.

Steiner, Tiffany. Abducted; student at USC, performing arts major.

Tuman, Ruth. Abducted; electrical engineer.

Glossary of Korlah

Afron \ˈaf-rän\ Strategy Section leader, tactics and navigation.

Challmara \ˈchäl-mä-rä\ Senior technical unit; Arms Section, assigned to weapons maintenance, research, and development.

Dooaugh \ˈdü-ə\ **also "the Oracle."** Warrior; designated for reclamation; outlaw Non.

Gremensh \ˈgrə-mench\ Director of Biological Repairs, Health Section; performs memory transfer experiments for Afron.

Lahsoon \ˈlö-sün\ Senior Resistance soldier; laborer; soldier genotype that was never apprenticed.

Litnauh \ˈlit- nä\ Assault Commander, close friend of Challmara, assigned by Shyron to lead ground forces on Earth mission.

Nerhala \nər-ˈhäl-ə\. Senior birthing unit; Teela's Birth Section mother; friend and mentor who cared for Teela when she was injured.

Plefauna \ˈplö-fä-nä\ Senior guard; Security Section; officer in charge of Teela's security following transfer.

Rahfoon \ˈrä-fün\ Biological Technician; Health Section; leader of cooperative interested in acquiring Bill Jacks as their mate.

Rehzeera \ˈreh-zë-rä\ Security Unit, information and communication apprentice who received the essence of Marylyn Daniels.

Rhetga \ˈret- gä\ Director of Warriors and Pilots, Warrior Section, Khranga's replacement, assigned to Campaign Vessel and Earth's defense forces.

Rowanga \ˈrö -waŋ gä\ Assistant Commander, Warrior Section, assigned to Earth's defense force.

Ruwaugh \ˈrü-wä\ Warrior; Spectacle pugilist; archrival of Shawaugh; mercenary willing to work for the highest bidder.

Shawaugh \'shä-wä\ Warrior; deposed director of Campaign Warrior Forces; "living shame of the Warrior Section"; blamed for failing to prevent devastating Kahshinki attack; found Teela in wreckage following attack.

Shawlmon \'shȯl-män\ Famous arbitrator and bladesman of ancient Korlah; Korlah legend states that Shawlmon will rise to defeat the Kahshinki in the final battle for those that cherish life and reject despair.

Shyron \shī-rän\ Potentate; Campaign Vessel Council leader; one of the original survivors of the Kahshinki holocaust; essence passed down from shell to shell for over one thousand cycles (Korlah years).

Teaugh \'tē- ä\ TEAUGH20.10638; T-series, Group E, Augh clan, generation 20, unit 10638; birth sister of Teela, one of the remaining 103 survivors from E section.

Teela \'tē-el-ə\ TEELA20.10127; T series, Group E, Ela clan, generation 20, unit 10127, birthing unit damaged during Kahshinki attack, designated for reclamation;-reassigned to Health section for memory transfer experiment;- received the essence of Daedalus Rimes.

Zeera \zë-rä\, **Mary.** Leader of Korlah delegation to Earth, received the essence of Marylyn Daniels.

Glossary of Terms

afterdeath. 1. An existence after death. **2.** A later period following one's death.

assault pod. Cylindrically shaped spacecraft transport vessel. Fitted with twenty recessed docking bays for smaller craft; each bay provides access to the mother craft. The smaller craft are comprised of five heavy fighters ringing the forward end, five troop carriers ringing the center, and ten light fighters filling the back. When joined together, the craft appears to be one vessel. The mother ship provides the means to travel the vast distance to the target so that the attached fighters could be built without the large and bulky plasma conversion components they would otherwise need for long-range travel. This allows the fighter craft to be more compact and maneuverable, an especially important consideration for planetary atmospheric activities.

birther. (derogatory). Birthing unit; usually taken to be offensive; genotype assigned duties of surrogate mother for clone embryo gestation.

bit. Measure of time; one three-thousandth of a Korlah planetary rotation; 100 bits = 1 set.

bladesman. Mercenary warrior skilled in the use of bladed weapons; associated with ancient Korlah tradition for settling armed disputes and clan warfare when arbitration fails.

braddle. Small rodents similar to mice or rats, possessing a long snout and prehensile tail; food source of Korlah; prepared for consumption by removing fur and purging the digestive system; served live.

cease. 1. To cease existence; to die. **2: ceased.** Dead; without honor.

crown tendrils. Olfactory organs that project out in long strands from twelve patches around the crown of the Korlah skull. They swell with blood when the individual is agitated or in a state of heightened sensitivity.

cycle. Measure of time; one Korlah solar revolution.

duplicate. Of or relating to clones or groups of clones and clone genotypes.

Ganglicians. Name given to Kahshinki by humans, associated with the theory that they are individual neural beings, which are part of a collective organism.

grav-reflector. Gravitational reflection amplification generator; sublight form of propulsion. Also used with gravity reflection plates (grav-plates) for personnel, material and equipment handling devices.

hisnah. 1: Organ that provides a form of thermal vision. **2:** A series of pits located in the center of a Korlah face where the nose on humans would be.

hyperlight. Transit stream propulsion capable of achieving up to three hundred times the speed of light.

Kahshinki. 1: The race that enslaved the Korlah and is the current target of their quest for revenge. **2:** Blood-sucking parasite found in stagnant pools on the planet Korlah.

log bar. Record-keeping device that stores written and visual records.

non. 1: Measure of time; one one-hundredth of a bit. **2:** Something without merit; inconsequential. **2: Non.** (derogatory). A unit that has been slated for reclamation.

Pulse-rifle. A shouldered Korlah weapon that discharges an energy pulse.

reclamation. The collection and processing of organic materials for reuse.

Rouche Hah. 1: Warrior greeting or farewell; to my honor, to your honor. **2:** Battle cry to honor those who will cease.

rouk. Aquatic snakes. Food delicacy. Care must be taken to remove paralyzing slime that the creature exudes. Consumption produces a form of intoxication.

sabat. 1: Tattoolike marking of the face of all Korlah that is used for individual identification. Indicates the genotype, birth cycle, and production number. **2:** Stenciling or embroidered or embossed markings on Korlah uniforms and equipment to identify the individual wearing it, especially when it hides or obscures the facial marking.

scrum. 1: Scarab-like beetle that consumes decaying organic material. Used in reclamation digesters. **2:** Food source comprised of ground scrum beetles and grubs that is made into protein bars. **3:** Someone that is dirty and disgusting. **4:** Someone that is dishonorable.

scrum worm. Grub of the scrum beetle.

set. Measure of time. One-thirtieth of a Korlah planetary rotation; 10 sets = 1 shift

shell. The physical body without regard to the individual's essence. An individual is not considered to exist until they have been assigned rank and status.

shift. Measure of time. One-third of a Korlah planetary rotation; 1000 shifts = 1 cycle.

Spectacle. Pugilistic honor dispute involving unarmed combat, historically using only fangs and claws, nonlethal methods involve the use of riz.

tah. Loose-fitting floor-length gown or robe, usually worn without a belt. Standard apparel of the birthing units.

Toma. Korlah God which embodies greed, cruelty, dishonesty, strength, and bravery.

transfer. The act of moving the essence and memories of one individual into the mind of another.

transit-spoke. Portals for access and egress within the Campaign Vessel that utilize gravitational adjustment to allow falling up or down through the conduit at controlled rates.

wave compressors. Light speed propulsion devices used to gather and compress light into a stream of plasma energy.

COVER ARTIST
Oliver Wetter

S T I LL L I F E 2003 Resurrection

1999, Original plaster sculpture, ca. 55 X 60 X 10 cm

Currently there are three official digital derivations from 2002, 2003 and 2005

Oliver, also known as Fantasio, is intrigued by every kind of mythology. The majority of the works he has produced deal with this fascination.

His artistic approach involves mixing the common with the uncommon. In the case of the Still-life series, he initially created a plaster sculpture that was rendered photographically to capture the element of emotion. The final digital derivation is Oliver's version of what could be compared to the 'directors cut' of a movie production.

To create a sense of soul in what would otherwise be merely a "Still-life-being", traditional sculpture and digital experimentation have been specially combined as the foundation for these works.

The original sculpture still exists and can be viewed as originally intended by the artist, appearing as if sleeping. The fascination of most viewers' is that the realism is such that she appears as if she will open her eyes at any moment.

Special thanks to: Martina Jakobs (mask model) and Jenni Tapanila (digital model).

Visit Oliver Wetter's Web site: http://fantasio.info